THE
CRESCENT
SPY

Also by Michael Wallace

Crow Hollow
The Devil's Deep

The Righteous series
The Red Rooster
The Wolves of Paris

THE CRESCENT SPY

MICHAEL WALLACE

LAKE UNION
PUBLISHING

Published by Lake Union Publishing, Seattle
www.apub.com

Amazon, the Amazon logo, and Lake Union Publishing, are trademarks of Amazon.com, Inc., or its affiliates.

ISBN-13: 9781503949454 (hardcover)
ISBN-10: 1503949451 (hardcover)
ISBN-13: 9781503945586 (paperback)
ISBN-10: 1503945588 (paperback)

Cover design by Mumtaz Mustafa

Printed in the United States of America

First edition

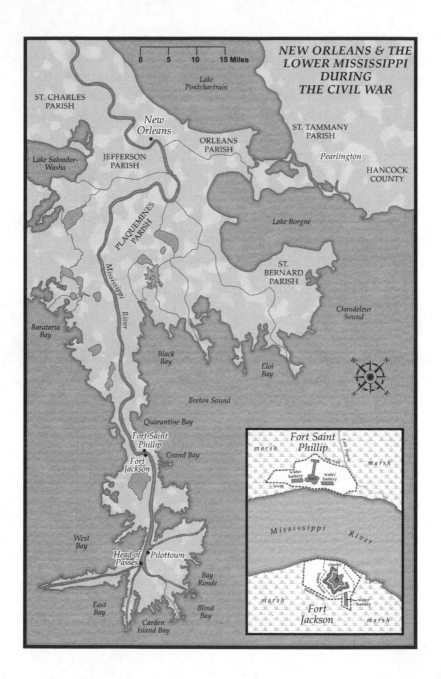

NEW ORLEANS & THE
LOWER MISSISSIPPI
DURING
THE CIVIL WAR

0 5 10 15 Miles

Lake
Pontchartrain

ST. CHARLES
PARISH

New
Orleans

ORLEANS
PARISH

ST. TAMMANY
PARISH

Pearlington

HANCOCK
COUNTY

Lake Salvador-
Washa

JEFFERSON
PARISH

PLAQUEMINES
PARISH

Lake Borgne

ST. BERNARD
PARISH

Chandeleur
Sound

Mississippi River

Barataria
Bay

Black
Bay

Eloi
Bay

Breton Sound

Quarantine Bay

Fort Saint
Phillip

Grand Bay

Fort
Jackson

West
Bay

Head of
Passes

Pilottown

Bay
Ronde

East
Bay

Blind
Bay

Carden
Island Bay

Fort Saint
Phillip

marsh

Bayou Brown

marsh

water
battery

fort

water
battery

levee

Mississippi River

citadel

bastion

levee

parade ground

water
battery

marsh

Fort
Jackson

marsh

CHAPTER 1

Bull Run, July 21, 1861, outside Manassas Rail Junction, Virginia

Josephine Breaux was only one of the many civilians fleeing north with the defeated Union army but was surely the only one who had spoken to both Union and Confederate generals before the battle. She carried a sheaf of papers in her saddlebags that either army would have been very keen to see. Neither side would get them.

Clouds of dust rose off the road, left by hundreds of fleeing horses, carriages, men on foot. The discarded goods of the Union troops lay everywhere: mess kits, tent stakes, bedrolls, broken barrels, even guns and ammunition pouches.

A pale, shaking young man in a bloodied butternut uniform sawed at the harness of a mule still tethered to an overturned cart of flour and cornmeal. He cut the mule loose as Josephine arrived, gave her a quick glance, then leaped onto the mule and rode it bareback up the road, kicking and cursing to get the animal to move faster. Other soldiers cursed him as he muscled them aside with the mule.

As Josephine was riding past the cart, she glanced down and saw a man in a gray uniform trapped beneath it. His shoulder was a bloody mess from a gunshot, and to add to the insult of war, a Union supply cart had tipped over and pinned his legs.

"Water," he said. "Somebody bring me water." He had a soft Southern accent. South Carolina or Georgia, from the coast, near as she could tell.

None of the fleeing soldiers paid him any attention, but his voice was so pleading, his injuries so pitiable, that she couldn't help herself. She dismounted from the horse given to her by a Pennsylvania cavalryman and untied the metal canteen in its wool shoddy from the saddlebag.

She secured her frightened horse to the overturned cart and bent and put her canteen at the man's lips. "Here, drink this."

The man took a long pull of water and looked at her through clear blue eyes. He was eighteen or nineteen, at most. Only a year or two younger than she was. "You're one of us, aren't you?"

"No, I—"

"A patriotic Southern lady. Please. I need a surgeon."

She looked him over. Doubtful he would survive even if he could reach medical care at once. But with both armies badly mauled and suffering varying degrees of panic, that would never happen.

Josephine had thought herself hardened to bloodshed. She'd inspected the makeshift hospitals of Washington after the skirmishes earlier in the summer, noted with horror, but an iron stomach, the baskets of legs and feet, the brutal harvest of the surgeon's saw. And once, as a girl, traveling the Mississippi with her mother, she'd seen the aftermath of a steamboat's boiler explosion. Men, women, and children blown to bits.

This battle had been more horrible still. At first, she'd observed at a distance, watching from a Confederate command post atop a ridge that offered a fine vantage point over rolling green hills, woods, and pastureland. Gunfire filled the air with crackles and puffs of smoke. Artillery pieces boomed and lifted off the ground and rolled violently backward as they fired. Men crumpled and fell. But at a distance.

Then, without warning, a regiment of Union troops broke toward their hill. The Confederate general ordered his reserve company to defend their outpost and sent for reinforcements. For the next half hour, the ridge became the scene of a hellacious firefight. Artillery trained on their position, and soon the entire hillside shook with explosions. Dead and dying men lay everywhere. Josephine hunkered behind a fallen tree, bracing against the rocks and clods of dirt that rained down on her every time a shell landed nearby.

"Please," the trapped Confederate soldier repeated. "Ride back. Tell Colonel Hampton I'm injured."

"I'm sorry. There's nothing I can do."

Josephine couldn't go back to Confederate lines. After escaping the battle on the ridge, she'd spent an hour furiously scribbling notes while hiding in the woods. If the Confederates read what she'd written, they'd take her for a spy.

Through the dust clouds she heard other men crying out, groaning, begging for help. Gunfire sounded from her left—close, but obscured from sight by the dust. She had to get out of here before the battle swept over the road. Reluctantly, she put the canteen in the man's hand and rose to her feet. He begged her not to go. She had no choice but to harden her heart and ride for Washington.

But when she tried to regain the saddle of her horse, she found she could not get herself up with the stiff crinoline underwire holding her skirts at a distance. The Pennsylvania cavalryman had hoisted her into the saddle, and she couldn't manage it alone.

More gunfire sounded to her rear. By now, few Union troops were left on the road, and these ones were wounded, panicked at being left behind. She asked one man for help regaining her horse, but he shoved her aside and kept running. A bullet whizzed across the road. From the hazy woods on the other side came answering fire. She tried again to reach the saddle.

The blasted crinoline was like a coiled spring, pushing her back from getting her foot in the stirrup. Josephine unsheathed the huge bowie knife strapped to the saddle and sliced open her dress and the underwire beneath it. She peeled off the crinoline. In moments, she stood in her bloomers with the expensive dress and its underwire lying eviscerated in the dirt road. She gained the saddle and rode northeast toward Washington.

Within minutes she was pushing through the shattered Union regiments. First the walking injured, then the footsore already exhausted by forced marches before the battle, and finally the reserve units who had broken in fear at the Confederate counterattack instead of holding their position. The stink of battle clung to them: gunpowder, sweat, blood.

Here and there officers were attempting to form a rearguard defense against the Confederates who would surely be sweeping up the road. Josephine was not so sure—the Southerners had seemed as disorganized in victory as the Union was in loss. And she'd seen the rebels' own panic earlier in the battle. Most of them, she guessed, would be reluctant to march one more mile toward Washington. Not today.

A man wearing the bars of a first lieutenant snatched the reins of her horse as she tried to force her way through. A second man, a private, jerked her, kicking, from the saddle. He set her down in the road, while the lieutenant climbed up. Josephine had the presence of mind to snatch out her papers from the saddlebags.

Then she grabbed the lieutenant's leg before he could ride off. "That's my horse."

He kicked at her. "Let go, woman. We don't stop the rebs and they'll be in Washington by morning."

He turned the horse and rode several paces back toward the battle, shouting instructions. The man had a full mustache on an otherwise smooth face and carried himself with the same confidence that rang out in his voice.

At first his commands had no effect whatsoever. Men kept streaming past him, sweaty and sunburned, their lips chapped. Black powder stained their lips and cheeks from tearing open cartridge packets. Many had tossed down their weapons, but several still carried muskets and rifles.

"You!" the lieutenant cried at one of the armed men as he drew his pistol. "Stop there, you coward, or by God I will blow out your brains."

The man's only response was to toss down his rifle and run. The lieutenant cursed him but didn't shoot. Gradually, however, he found men willing to obey. A small but growing knot formed around the horse. They were mostly Massachusetts men in green coats and pants, but two wore the baggy trousers, open jackets, and red caps of the Fire Zouaves, a regiment of volunteers raised from the New York Fire Department.

Meanwhile, the private who'd yanked Josephine from the saddle now gave her a regular inspection, eyes widening as he seemed to notice for the first time that she was in her bloomers.

Once dragged from the saddle, she should have set off at once, but she'd been transfixed by the sight of the lieutenant trying to rally his men against a Confederate attack. She'd been composing a description of the scene in her mind. Belatedly, she realized the danger in lingering.

"What in tarnation happened to you?" the private asked.

A lie came easily to her lips but not a very good one. "My carriage upended fording Bull Run. I had to get out of my dress or drown."

Except she was dry, her bloomers clean. She waited for him to point out this obvious flaw in her story.

The young man stared at the papers in her hand with a slow, dull expression. Nevertheless, she could see the gears turning in his mind. He took off his hat and scratched at his sweat-matted hair.

Her heart leaped into her throat. This was it. He would snatch her notes and see everything she'd written. Then what would happen?

With as much dignity as she could muster, she turned away and continued up the road, wearing her bloomers and her white and brown Balmoral boots, her waist pinched in by a corset. She'd lost the pins in her hair, and her curls spilled out. Bits of leaves and twigs had lodged in her hair during a spill on the hillside above the battle. The only thing that would make her look more ridiculous would be a parasol to shield her from the hot afternoon sun.

The private abandoned his lieutenant for the moment and fell in next to her, gawking. Two more soldiers came in next to him, muttering as they trudged away from the men who were forming a defensive picket at their rear.

Josephine had taken a risk making her notes while still behind Confederate lines, but she was no safer here. Pinkerton agents were busy in Washington, searching for spies, and if they had any value at all, they'd be looking for infiltrators and secessionists trying to sneak their way over the Potomac in the aftermath of the battle. If they saw what she'd written, she might face arrest.

"We'd better take her in, Murdock," one of the other men said at last.

"I suppose you're right," the first man said. Murdock, presumably. He had a wisp of a beard at his chin that made him look younger than if he'd shaved it off. "You seen the captain?"

"Nope, you?"

"Nah."

"You're a fine pair of scoundrels," the third man said with a chuckle. "You just want to stare at a pretty lady in her bloomers. Why don't you let her be?"

"That's right," Josephine said. "I can manage perfectly well on my own. Now leave me alone."

"What are you carrying there?" Murdock asked.

"Have you men no honor?" she asked. "The enemy is about to overrun Washington. Your officer is trying to form a defense. Why don't you go back and help him?"

"Ain't no officer of mine," Murdock said. "I just helped him get a horse. Anyways, I'm a ninety-day recruit, and my time is up in another week. I'm not going to die here. Let the rebs have their slaves and their confounded honor. I'm going back to the farm to help my pa with the harvest."

He spoke with plenty of swagger for a man fleeing the battlefield, carrying a musket and a pouch still bulging with ammunition. She was about to point this out, even mention what she'd heard about General Jackson holding firm on the other side under a withering Union attack, when snipers began shooting from a farmhouse to the left of the road.

There couldn't have been more than five men firing through the broken-out windows, and the house was not more than fifty yards from the road. A dozen determined men could have put the attackers to flight, but instead a fresh wave of panic swept over the beaten Union troops. More guns clattered to the ground, and the men fled on up the road. Josephine ran after them.

When she regained her bearings several minutes later, she found herself in the middle of an entirely new group of soldiers, with a number of civilians in their midst. She turned at the sound of an open carriage clattering up the dusty road, pulled by two horses.

"Ma'am, are you all right?" a slow, deep voice said.

The driver was an elderly black gentleman sitting on the perch. He held the reins in one hand and mopped at his bald, sweating head with a handkerchief in the other.

"Don't you stop, John!" a woman said from inside the open carriage. "Run them off the road if you must."

"But it's a lady, mistress. Caught out in her unawares."

The woman stood and peered over the driver's shoulder. She was an older woman with silver-gray hair pinned into a bun beneath a red velvet bonnet. She carried a parasol as additional protection against the blasting sun. Josephine had seen this woman before but couldn't place where. At a society ball, perhaps.

"Good heavens, child, what happened to you?" the woman asked.

Josephine cast a quick glance around to make sure that Murdock and his companions hadn't found her anew, then told the woman a better lie than she'd told the soldier, explaining that she'd been with a group of sightseers from the city when stray artillery began to land in their midst. Her dress caught on fire and had to be cut off. Later, she'd lost contact with her companions.

"Mercy!" the woman exclaimed. "And to think we were fools enough to treat the battle as a picnic. I'll never make that mistake again," she added wryly.

"May I have a ride back to the city?" Josephine asked.

"Well, of course you may, you poor thing. John, help her up."

Josephine made much better time in the carriage. The woman introduced herself as Mrs. Stanley Lamont, a name Josephine recognized. Her husband was a judge in Baltimore. That was the secessionist part of Maryland, although Josephine couldn't remember the judge's own sympathies—the Union, apparently, as Mrs. Lamont soon let on that her husband was in Washington to meet with the president. And yet John seemed to be a slave, so she was no abolitionist, either.

Mrs. Lamont had foolishly joined a group of congressmen, their wives, and others from society who'd traveled down to watch the battle. Like the people in Josephine's own fabricated story, her group of sightseers had been scattered by the battle, and now the woman was making her way back to Washington without her friends. She seemed relieved to have company.

Mrs. Lamont wrapped her shawl around Josephine's shoulders to preserve her modesty and draped the edges of her dress over the younger woman's lap as well. She said nothing about the papers that Josephine was still clutching.

By the time the sun fell mercifully to the west, they'd come up into Arlington on the south side of the Potomac, opposite Washington. Arlington had been occupied by Union troops since May, who were converting it into a giant fortress to protect the outskirts of Washington. Trenches tore up the fields, connected by palisades. Brick and stone forts lay in various stages of construction. It was a Sunday, and there would have been little work in any event, but the worker camps seemed strangely deserted, as if everyone had fled across the river into Washington once word came of the defeat.

In Arlington itself, the porches filled with laughing, jubilant spectators. No need for official word, the Virginians could see the result of the battle with their own eyes and were evidently delighted at the outcome. There were no waving Confederate flags, however. Nobody was that foolhardy.

A snarl of traffic clogged the road in front of the Long Bridge before it crossed the river to Washington on the opposite bank. Troops guarded the entrance to the bridge, checking soldiers and civilians alike. To Josephine's dismay, two men in plain clothes were giving some of the civilians special attention, pulling them aside and asking questions. Pinkerton agents.

Josephine sat on her papers to hide them. Mrs. Lamont watched her carefully.

"You keep your mouth shut, child. Let me speak to them."

When they drew near the bridge, one of the men in plain clothes approached the carriage. He wore a bowler hat and a jacket buttoned in spite of the heat. Thick black whiskers blanketed his face. After casting a dismissive glance at John, he fixed the two women with a sharp, penetrating gaze and asked Mrs. Lamont her name and business in the city. His accent held a soft Scottish burr.

She told him the same story that she'd given earlier, then added that Josephine was her niece.

"And why is your niece in this state of undress?"

Mrs. Lamont tugged the edge of her own dress higher onto Josephine's lap. "The indignities of war, sir," she said in a cold voice. "Now be a gentleman and let us past."

He shrugged, and they were soon passing onto the Long Bridge. Light slanted in through the slats in the wooden trusses that held up the roadbed.

"Old men make wars," Mrs. Lamont said suddenly, as if something had been bothering her. "Yet it's the boys who suffer and die."

Josephine thought of the Confederate soldier pinned beneath the cart. Probably still alive, still suffering. She said nothing as the horses continued in the sluggish procession across the bridge. At last they reached the other side. For the first time in hours, the knot in Josephine's stomach began to unravel.

"Thank you for helping me," she said. "I'm not a spy. I can see that you're wondering. The papers, and all. They're not for the government, and not for the secessionists."

Mrs. Lamont patted her hand. "There is no need to explain to me, dear. This is a time of divided loyalties. Your secrets are your own."

CHAPTER 2

It was early afternoon the next day before Josephine roused herself and made her way back to the offices of the *Morning Clarion*. She was exhausted from the heat, the flight after the battle, and the work at the paper that had kept her busy late into the night. But she soon found something that lifted her spirits and energy more than the cup of coffee she'd hastily gulped before leaving the boarding house.

A boy was selling copies of the *Clarion* at the head of Marble Alley. She was so pleased to see the result of her hard work that she handed him a silver half dime and told the astonished boy to keep the change.

For a long moment she stared at the headline with a satisfied glow. The city seemed to fade into the background. The marching feet, the whinny of horses, the screech of pump handles, the martial trumpet to the north, the bang of hammers building a new barracks a mile to the east—all faded to a dull buzz as she read the headline over and over.

BITTER DEFEAT!

REBS ROUT UNION TROOPS, VOW TO SEIZE WASHINGTON

That was all true, and yet vowing to seize Washington and accomplishing it were two different things. But the reality—"hungry, battered rebels milling in disorder, unable to move toward the city"—would hardly sell newspapers.

The newspaper offices lay up Ninth Street, which was clogged with soldiers and wagons. Men on horse—some soldiers, some not—rode this way and that. A vast tent encampment spread below the Capitol Building and was packed to overflowing, so chaotic and disorganized it may as well have been a prisoner-of-war camp.

The Capitol Building itself frowned over all of this. It had lost its cap before the war, supposedly to doff a new, iron dome that would more majestically represent American power. But for now it looked merely decapitated, a visible reminder of the sad condition of the United States themselves.

She turned up Ninth and toward the offices of the *Morning Clarion*, which lay beyond Ford's Theatre. A group of men loitered in the street outside the newspaper offices. They had a slouchy, sharp-eyed appearance, and she'd have thought them the kind of disreputable merchants recently filling the city to make their fortunes on bloated government contracts if she hadn't had the sudden hunch they were fellow newspaper reporters. Though from what paper and why they were congregating here, she couldn't tell.

Had Barnhart finally plunked down some silver to hire more men for the *Clarion*? Good, they could use the help. So long as they stayed out of her way.

Josephine pushed her way through them and came inside to find the staff already hard at work for tomorrow's edition. Jones was leaning over Finch to watch the man mark up his copy, the cigarette dangling from Jones's mouth dropping ash on Finch's shoulder. Finch's son, a boy of sixteen named Charles, had spread the papers of the competition across a battered desk and was scanning through them, scribbling notes on a pad of lined paper. Wenkle sat atop two stacked crates, his pipe in the corner of his mouth, dictating a telegraph to Miss Lenox. The air was thick with smoke and the oppressive heat of a room with too little ventilation.

Miss Lenox looked up at Josephine's approach, her eyes owl-like through thick glasses. She nudged Wenkle, who looked at the newcomer and stopped. The other three spotted Josephine, stopped what they were doing, and all five stared at her for a long moment. Then Wenkle cleared his throat, and they disappeared as one into the back room.

Josephine was still puzzling out why they'd given her such an odd reception when the door swung open from the back, and she heard the shouts of newsboys, caught a glimpse of mounds of newspapers. Business must be brisk indeed if the boys were returning this late in the morning to refill their carts. Her publisher appeared in the doorway.

David Barnhart was a slender, smooth-faced man, short enough that when his back was turned, he presented the profile of one of his boys. Angry congressmen would sometimes burst into the offices, take him for a newsboy, and bellow for him to fetch his boss at once. Barnhart would shake his head and say that regrettably the publisher was out, but he would pass along their outrage.

Before the war, one congressman from South Carolina, a real fire-eater secessionist, had come in waving pistols and demanding a duel. He'd been outraged by insinuations (perfectly true) that he'd fathered several mulatto children by the slaves of his plantation.

Barnhart calmly put him off, told him that the man he was look-ing for had fled to New York to hide from the senator's wrath. The South Carolinian was now raising regiments in his home state, and had a hand in the shelling of Fort Sumter that had precipitated the outbreak of hostilities.

Now Barnhart should have been grinning in triumph, but his face was curiously drawn. Newsprint smeared across his cheeks and beneath his eyes, making him look like a petulant raccoon. He clenched a rolled-up newspaper in his blackened fingers. She could only think he was still worried about the threat of General Beauregard's troops now presumed to be marching on Washington. He'd been fretting about it last night as she finished her story.

"Don't worry," Josephine told him, "the rebs are still at Manassas. A lucky shot or two and Jeff Davis would be panick-ing in Richmond instead. The other side was so scattered it would take them a week just to muster their forces. By then, Washington will be ready."

"Yes, I know. So you said last night. You could scarcely stop talking about it."

He sounded so glum, but nothing could penetrate the trium-phant feeling in her breast. She smiled and spread the copy of the *Clarion* she'd bought across the table over the papers Charlie had laid out earlier. Standing proudly on the front page was her eighth lead story in the past month, and her best by far. Every bit of it was true, not a lie or false rumor in the lot.

Josephine had spoken directly to generals on both sides, had witnessed key moments of the battle. She had correctly assessed the aftermath of the war and was equally confident in her predictions of how the battle would be seen in the weeks to come. By then, this article would make her famous. She was certain of it.

The article was not just accurate; it was cleverly written. She reread her favorite part with more than a little satisfaction.

But nobody told Johnny Reb he was licked, and Jackson's men held firm on the hill. Sooner than spit, a fat column of Confederate reinforcements came slithering up the road as eager and venomous as a hungry rattler. Our boys took one look and turned tail like an army of frightened rabbits.

No, it wasn't Shakespeare, or even Walt Whitman, but the words had a certain lurid poetry to them. Wait until the New York press read her story. The offers would come rolling in.

Ah, so that's why Barnhart was glum. He was afraid he'd lose her to New York.

"A shame I couldn't publish this under my real name," she said. "It robs the moment of its glory."

"Yes."

"Move aside, Horace Greeley, Joseph Breaux will be the best known writer in the land. If only they knew his true identity, they'd be astonished."

She gave Barnhart a smile that let him know she was not serious. But surely he wouldn't deny her a moment of triumph and yes, even boastfulness.

"Oh, they'll know soon enough. They'll all know."

"No," she sighed. "I can't have that. It will wreck my ability to move behind the lines. No, Josephine must remain a typesetter, and Joseph the man who gets the good stories. She'll get her due later, yes. But not yet."

Barnhart unclenched the newspaper he'd kept rolled tightly in his hands. He unfolded it and spread it over the top of her own.

It wasn't the *Morning Clarion*; it was the *Washington Standard*, their chief rival. She looked down at the headline. It was also about the battle. The opening lines of the story were vague and filled with more alarm than substance. She skimmed to the end of the column. Error and pointless speculation all jumbled into an unholy mess.

"So what?" she said. "It's rubbish."

"That's not the problem."

"Don't tell me you're unhappy. The *Clarion* is galloping out the door today. The boys are back for more copies to sell, the presses are still running. They may as well be printing banknotes today, so cheer up. And I have half composed a smashing follow-up. Give me two hours to write it up."

"Will you stop being so self-absorbed? Look." Barnhart tapped an ink-stained finger on the second article in the paper.

And there she saw this chilling headline:

"JOSEPH" BREAUX UNMASKED AS WOMAN
SHE CONSORTS WITH TRAITORS AND SLAVES

Heart pounding, she read the story, penned under the nom de plume "George Patriot, a Concerned Citizen." But the writing was too sharp, too cunningly gleeful to be anything but one of the best reporters on the staff of the *Washington Standard*.

In a discovery that beggars the imagination, even as it shocks with its scandal and lack of dignity, this citizen has uncovered a monstrous deception at the heart of the Morning Clarion. As brazen as a strumpet of the night plying her trade, a New Orleans native and Secess sympathizer by the name of Josephine Breaux has been traveling between Union and Rebel lines under false pretenses.

This citizen would not suggest that Miss Breaux is responsible for our debacle, but she was spied in the company of that traitor, a fellow Louisianan, General Beauregard, moments before our inglorious flight from the battlefield. Yesterday afternoon, in the darkest moment of our defeat, she was spotted skulking into Washington hiding amongst our injured boys, wearing nothing but her bloomers.

> Propriety blushes, unable to speculate how she found herself
> in this immodest condition. However, one suggestion, which this
> author hesitates to repeat, has it that . . .

Josephine couldn't read another word. She turned over the paper and stared out the window. Men peered through from the street. The ones she'd spotted earlier, loitering outside. Staring after her, she now knew. Shame rose in her breast, and she turned away and covered her face in her hands. Barnhart hurried to shut the blinds.

How was this possible? Those fools at the *Standard* had so little information they'd placed Johnston's relieving Confederate army riding in on horse from the Shenandoah instead of arriving by rail. Yet somehow they knew that she'd been with Beauregard and had fled to Washington in her bloomers. Who could have been the informant? Private Murdock? Mrs. Lamont in her carriage? No, it was impossible.

"How much is true?" Barnhart asked in a quiet voice.

"The part about the bloomers is true enough," she admitted. "But I'm no spy, you know that. And I would never seduce an enemy general to get better intelligence for a story. That's a vile insinuation."

"Then how did you do it?"

She glared at him. "You were supposed to say, 'Of course you wouldn't, that's a wretched lie.'"

"Never mind, I don't care to know the particulars."

She stared at the back page of the *Standard* and its advertisements for hair tonics and cheap boarding houses. Half of those boarding houses were brothels or gambling dens.

"Josephine, you know what must be done, of course."

"No, I am at a loss."

"You're poison now," he said. "That's the real problem."

"Your loyalty is quite breathtaking," she said sarcastically. "What I need is your support, your angry denunciation of this slander. Why aren't you writing that story right now? An outraged editorial. The attack would collapse faster than a Union picket line."

"The jig is up, the secret out. You can't write for the paper anymore."

"Rubbish. I'm a woman, not a leper." Her shame had vanished, replaced by hot indignation. "Of course this changes everything, I know that. But there's no law that says I can't keep writing. If I need to write about society nonsense because I'm a woman, I'll do it, at least until this blows over. But I have no intention of stopping. You can take that and print it."

Barnhart yanked the *Standard* off the table and opened it to the second page of the article, then began reading aloud. "'I am only a concerned citizen, and would not presume to speculate—'"

"Balderdash," Josephine scoffed. "Speculate is all he's done."

"Will you shut your mouth and listen?" Barnhart gave her a hard look, and she fell silent. He continued, "'But word of this woman's outrageous behavior has been forwarded to the War Department, to Generals Scott and McDowell, and to the desk of President Lincoln himself. I would never give the publisher of the *Morning Clarion* advice, but if I were Mr. Barnhart, I would send this treasonous snake across the river, and a good riddance. Soon enough, she'll resurface at the *Daily Richmond Examiner*, or even in Jeff Davis's cabinet.'"

She put her hands on her hips. "Let me get this straight. Your jealous rival suggests you fire your best writer, and you entertain the notion?"

"I have no choice, don't you see?" To his credit, Barnhart sounded anguished, and she almost forgot that he was playing the part of a weasel in this little drama. "We were a Democrat paper before the war. I urged reconciliation before Fort Sumter, and people remember that. Our enemies already call us disunionists. Copperheads."

"I know that. The beast just called me a treasonous snake. I'm a copperhead, that's what he means. But you'll only embolden our enemies if you send me off."

"Your article is a scathing indictment of the prosecution of the battle. Some might call it defeatist, and expect the next piece you write to call for peaceful separation."

"You know that's a lie."

"Of course, of course," he said. "And I'm as pro-Union as the publisher of that rag attacking you. But it doesn't look that way. Not at all, not with this."

"So that's your decision? I am off the paper?"

Barnhart licked his lips. "For now, yes. Perhaps in a few months . . . but I would never leave you destitute. Heavens! Let me pay you your wages, send you off with a little extra."

"I don't need your charity, Mr. Barnhart. This was never about money."

"Still," he said. "Please, allow me." He turned toward the bookshelf with its copies of *Webster's Dictionary* and *The Old Farmer's Almanac* and pulled out a few books. He had a safe behind them where he kept the working funds of the paper in the form of several hundred dollars of banknotes.

But Josephine wasn't about to give him satisfaction. She grabbed her bonnet and was out the door before he could get the safe open, and into the hot Washington sun. Let him run her off. She'd collect her things from the boarding house and catch the next train to New York. They wouldn't be so fussy at the *Herald* or the *Tribune*.

She'd forgotten about the men slouching at the front door, and now they gathered around her, staring. Yes, that one with the yellow-toothed grin was one of the sleazy fellows at the *National Republican*, specialists in stories about runaway slaves and poxied whores whose bodies turned up dead in the Washington Canal. If he'd been with the *Washington Standard* she'd have punched him in the nose.

"Josephine, wait!" Barnhart called from behind her.

She ignored him and stomped down the street, one eye on horse droppings as she tied on her bonnet. Two of the men fell in beside her.

"Have you no shame?" she asked without looking at them. "Following a lady down the street. The lowest field hand in South Carolina has better manners."

"You're no lady," one of them said in a gravelly voice with a Scottish burr. "You're a strumpet and a traitor."

Josephine turned, fuming. "If I were a man, sir, I would demand satisfaction for that insult." She pointed to the soldiers drilling on the opposite side of the street. "There are a dozen hot-blooded men who will happily put a ball in your head when they hear of your insult to my honor."

She was only warming up, and intended to let loose a scathing barrage to atone for all the things she wished she'd said to Barnhart for his craven failure to defend her against slander. Instead, she stopped with her mouth open as she recognized the speaker.

It was the fellow with the bushy beard who had been questioning people last night as they entered the Virginia side of the Long Bridge. Josephine prided herself on her ability to identify accents and should have recognized him from his voice alone. But she'd been distracted.

The second man had slick, neatly parted hair and a thick mustache. With a strong chin and broad shoulders, he managed to seem both cultured and yet have the look of a man who could crack the skulls of street toughs or clear out an opium den by showing his fists. Both men carried Colt revolvers in holsters.

"Who are you?" she asked in a quiet voice, her heart thumping.

As she spoke, some of the other men who'd been waiting outside the newspaper offices now caught up with them. They whispered back and forth.

"Allan Pinkerton," the bearded man said.

Pinkerton! Head of the famous private-detective force, who had helped smuggle Lincoln through the hostile secessionists in Maryland before the inauguration and was now reputed to be organizing a secret service to root out spies and purge Washington of secessionists.

Under other circumstances, Josephine would have relished the opportunity to meet the man. She could test her charms, see if she could get him to spill information as willingly as she'd managed with the generals of the two armies. So many interesting stories to write if she could loosen his tongue.

But under the present circumstances, the name filled her with terror. She was already rattled and only just managed to keep her composure.

"And how can I help you, Mr. Pinkerton?"

Pinkerton glanced at the gathering crowd of people. The yellow-toothed fellow from the *National Republican* was scribbling furiously in a notebook.

"You can come with us quietly," Pinkerton said. "I would prefer not to have a disturbance."

"As you can imagine, I am disinclined to follow strange men who demand my cooperation without explanation. So I ask you, sir, where would you have me go?"

"If you come quietly, no harm will befall you."

"Listen to me, I—"

"But if you cause trouble," he interrupted, eyes narrowing, "I will arrest you as a traitor and see you hanged."

CHAPTER 3

To Josephine's horror, Pinkerton didn't take her back to his offices near the White House, but instead marched her toward the canal via B Street. This area of low-slung, rickety buildings was sometimes known as Rum Row. It reeked of outhouses and garbage, except when the wind shifted and brought over the stink of the fish market on Fifteenth Street.

A few Cyprians—as the papers delicately called whores—stood on their stoops smoking and watching with interest. One woman with red-dyed hair and an inch of face paint made Josephine a sneering offer of employment. Then the woman spotted the rabble following the detectives and their prisoner and started making offers of a different kind.

Pinkerton gave a disgusted snort, and this offered Josephine an opening.

"Please, Mr. Pinkerton, could we not take another route? Perhaps to your office to discuss your concerns in a reasonable way?"

He shot her a withering look. "I know what you did in Virginia. If you don't care to be treated as a woman plying her trade, you should have chosen a more virtuous path in life."

"None of it is true." She staggered forward as he jabbed her with an elbow to get her to speed up. "Please, could we find a place to talk?"

They passed two gambling houses and Miss Izzy's Hotel—another notorious whorehouse—and then finally emerged into the open air near the canal. The air was even worse here, as the sluggish waters of the canal badly needed rain to flush out the garbage and human waste floating in the green, scummy water. She put a hand over her mouth until they'd crossed the canal and passed the sea of tents and milling soldiers encamped around the stumpy, unfinished Washington Monument. Several hundred yards up toward the Capitol lay the Smithsonian Institution, which loomed like a castle of red Seneca sandstone over another large encampment.

Pinkerton didn't take her to the Long Bridge, as she guessed. She'd expected him to dump her in Alexandria or Arlington on the Virginia side of the river, but that was Union-controlled territory, so perhaps he figured she would simply wait there until things quieted down and slip back into the city. That had been her own hope, once she confirmed his implacable insistence that she be expelled from Washington.

But instead, he kept her marching south for block after block, until they reached the arsenal on the spit of land where the Potomac met the Anacostia River.

Pinkerton stopped before the arsenal gates and said to his fellow agent, "I'll tell the president you're off with her. Send me a courier when it's done."

"When what's done?" Josephine asked.

Pinkerton ignored her and turned around to go back the way they'd come, pushing past the rabble, now grown to a dozen men. That left Josephine with the young, broad-shouldered Pinkerton agent with the thick mustache. She sized him up and decided to try again.

"I am sorry, we haven't met, Mr.——"

"Franklin Gray."

"Gray, that's another Scottish name. But I don't hear an accent. Did your parents come over, then? Or has your family been here since the Revolution?"

She was hoping to draw him out, but he gave her a hard look and turned away. He showed the soldiers at the arsenal gates some sort of pass, and the men let them in. The rabble, however, was turned back with a good deal of grumbling. A couple were scribbling in notepads, and one man shouted a question at her that she didn't quite catch but wouldn't have answered if she had.

Dozens of troops guarded the arsenal, and guard towers bristled along the river. Row after row of newly cast cannons lined up waiting to be finished and then fitted onto gun carriages. They all pointed toward the river, as if already preparing to blast their way into Virginia.

After crossing the arsenal grounds, Gray showed his pass again, this time to one of the sentries who patrolled the shoreline. The man ran off to fetch a boat. Josephine asked if they might wait in the shade instead of under the sun. Gray consented, and they retreated to the shade of a tree filled with buzzing cicadas.

She made another attempt. "I am a newspaper writer, Mr. Gray. Naturally, I used feminine charms to get close to the rebel officers— I can play the coquette when I must. But I did not betray our secrets. I'm a patriot, like you."

Gray lit a cigarette. "You are a spy and a traitor. If I had my way, you'd be hung. Count yourself fortunate that Mr. Pinkerton has a soft spot for women."

"What evidence do you have that I'm a spy?" she persisted. "Because of what you read in the *Standard*? They're our enemies, you know. You can't trust those scoundrels."

"Be quiet, I'm weary of your company."

She fell silent. The air grew hotter and hotter, and trickles of perspiration ran down her back and dampened her armpits. At last the soldier returned, this time with four of his fellows, carrying a rowboat between them.

They heaved the boat halfway into the water, where one of the men held it against the current so it wouldn't drift off.

"Go on, then," Gray told Josephine, who was eying the rowboat doubtfully. "Get in."

"Don't tell me I'm supposed to row across by myself."

"I wish it were so. Indeed, I'd send you halfway out and let the guns of the fort sink you like a Confederate raider." He shook his head. "Mr. Pinkerton's orders are to take you to Manassas under white flag and trade you for one of our colonels taken in the battle."

"Nobody will trade for me for a colonel. I told you, I'm not a spy. The rebs wouldn't give you two cents."

Gray smiled. "Mr. Pinkerton telegraphed Richmond this morning. They agreed at once to the trade."

"They did?"

The only way it could be true would be if the Confederates somehow thought she'd betrayed them as well. In that case, she'd be trading humiliation in Washington for a jail cell in Richmond.

One of the soldiers held out a hand to help Josephine into the boat. She folded her arms and clenched her jaw.

Gray drew his gun. "Get in that boat or by God I'll be trading your dead body to the rebs."

Josephine gave it a moment of thought. She couldn't let him take her to Manassas to face angry accusations from Beauregard's staff. But there might be opportunities to escape along the way. Then she could figure out what to do.

After she'd climbed in, Gray put away his gun and took his place at the oars. The soldiers pushed them into the current. Gray let them drift for several seconds, then fit the oars into the oarlocks and dipped them in the water. He began to row almost casually for the opposite side of the Potomac. His oars creaked in the oarlocks, and eddies swirled around the paddles with each stroke. Sitting near the bow, Gray had his back to Virginia. Josephine faced the agent and looked across to the woods and fields of the other side. A small force of laborers were constructing yet another Union fort on the Virginia side of the river.

Any hope that a river breeze would cool her disappeared. The air was steamy, the sun like a hammer. Sweat was soon running down Gray's face and dripping from his mustache.

"Well?" he said. "Are you going to tell me why you're innocent?"

"I thought you said you had orders."

"I do. You have until the opposite shore to convince me."

"You want me to explain now? You've wasted my entire afternoon, refused to let me speak, but now that we're rowing across the confounded river, you want me to make my case?"

"It's up to you. If you'd rather go back to your Confederate lover, that's your prerogative."

This insinuation disgusted her so much that she at first turned away and refused to look at this man. But she'd be a fool to let him best her through her sheer stubbornness, so she relented.

"I only crossed into rebel lines to get a good story. I was nobody's lover, and I told the Confederates nothing they couldn't have read in the papers."

"The blooming fools of the press are all too happy to report every regiment who marches in and out of the city," Gray agreed. "But when enemy reinforcements arrived all the way from the Shenandoah just in time to turn McDowell's attack, we knew they'd received advance warning. There's a spy in Washington, someone who can speak to our generals."

"I'm aware of that," she said. "There have been hints before."

"And we believe she's a woman."

"I know that, too. I've given the matter much thought."

His eyes narrowed. "You have?"

She glared back at him, unwilling to say more. Information was not free, and in this case, she wanted him to think she had more than she possessed.

Gray stopped and took off his jacket. He rolled up his shirt-sleeves to reveal powerful forearms. They'd drifted a greater distance downstream than the distance he'd rowed toward the far shore, but his slow, powerful strokes had still carried them right into the middle of the river.

"We're halfway across," he said. "I'm not convinced."

"What do you want me to say? I'm a writer, not a spy. How am I supposed to prove that?"

"Why did you enter Washington wearing nothing but your bloomers?"

"I dismounted my horse to give water to a dying Confederate soldier," she said. "But I couldn't regain the saddle because of the crinoline. The Union soldiers were in a panic—nobody would help me. So I cut off the dress and the underwire."

"Why not just take it off?"

She gave him a sharp look. "You've never put on a dress and hoops or you wouldn't ask that. There was gunfire, I was afraid of getting killed. I needed to get back on that horse."

"You weren't mounted when you approached the bridge."

"A Union officer commandeered my horse and left me to be mocked by foot soldiers. Mrs. Stanley Lamont took pity on me and carried me into Washington."

Gray was silent for a few minutes, his brow furrowed in thought as he rowed. "And how did you gain access to General Beauregard's camp? You simply walked in with your pen and paper and started asking questions?"

"Of course not. Two days before the battle I approached the Confederate camp posing as a secessionist Marylander." Josephine changed her accent to someone from the Chesapeake: "'General, I've brought a few things to raise your spirits and help you whip them Yankees and abolitionists. Twenty pounds of coffee, fifty pounds of chewing tobacco. Barrels of flour and salted pork. And these home-baked huckleberry pies for you and your staff.'"

Gray raised his eyebrows. "Impressive accent."

"My mother was an actress and dancer on a Mississippi steamboat. She taught me the tricks of the trade. And I've heard all sorts of accents in my life." Now she turned to Pinkerton's Scottish burr: "And believe me when I say that I can mimic them at will."

"Hmm," Gray said, seemingly less impressed this time. "The suspicious part is that the newspaper would pay for all those goods that you gave to the enemy. Why, to get one story? An important story, yes, but you couldn't know that at the time. Not for sure."

"I didn't ask Mr. Barnhart to buy the supplies. And he wouldn't have paid if I had. I have my own funds. That's all I'll say about that."

Gray let his oars fold in against the boat, dipped his hands into the water, and splashed his face and neck, then eyed the opposite shore and began to row again. They were now so far downstream that it would be a long walk west to reach the road to Manassas. Again, she was confused as to why Mr. Pinkerton and Mr. Gray hadn't simply hired a carriage and taken her out of the city by way of the Long Bridge.

"If you're not a spy," Gray said, as if in answer to her unspoken question, "there are plenty in Washington who are. I needed to make a spectacle of your departure. Word will get back to the enemy."

Josephine allowed herself to hope she would get out of this predicament. "Does that mean you knew all along? Was my arrest at the *Morning Clarion* a charade?"

"You are sharp, you understand most of it. The answer is no, not entirely a charade. Mr. Pinkerton wanted to be sure. And I'm not yet convinced." A smile crossed his lips, and for the first time he didn't look like an unfeeling beast. "But almost."

"After I gave Beauregard's staff the supplies," Josephine said, continuing her story with less reluctance, "they were happy to lead me through their encampment, proudly showing me this regiment and that. Telling how they meant to lick the Yanks and march on Washington. I was in Beauregard's camp for most of the battle, and only slipped away near the end."

"*Will* the enemy march on Washington? We were routed yesterday, scattered. Completely disorganized. If they came now . . ."

"So are they. Almost as disorganized in victory as we are in defeat."

"I am glad to hear it." Gray glanced over his shoulder at the opposite bank, now drawing near. He was breathing heavily but did not appear exhausted. "What drives you, Miss Breaux? What is your personal philosophy?"

"Mr. Gray, I write lurid prose to be consumed by the masses. My philosophy, my motive, is personal glory."

He laughed at this. "Very well. But are you seeking glory under the Union flag or with the secessionists?"

"I am a Union girl, sir. Secession is simply another word for treason. And slavery is a canker and an embarrassment, and must be swept away." Josephine nodded. "So long as it does not get in the way of a good story, of course."

"And you would take the oath of allegiance, truthfully and without guile?"

She lifted her right hand. "I will support the Constitution of the United States."

"Good. I thought you would."

Gray pulled the oars out of the water. They were only twenty yards from the grassy slope on the Virginia side of the river, but he let them drift downstream for another few minutes, the muddy current slowly twisting the boat around as they slid past guard posts and tent encampments. The meadows gave way to woods, and when they were beyond the last guard post, he eased them up to shore. He helped her out of the boat.

"I assume you have given up on your plan to deliver me to the Confederates," she said.

"There was never a plan in the first place. If you failed to convince me, I was going to abandon you here and go back alone, leaving you with the threat of jail should you return."

Josephine put her hands on her hips. "Seems a lot of fuss and bother if that was your intent all along. What now, will you row me across and tell Mr. Barnhart to hire me back at the paper?"

"I'm afraid you're finished with the *Morning Clarion*, Miss Breaux."

"You devil, I am not! You will march at once to my publisher and tell him I am innocent of this slander and demand that he reinstate me. I don't care what that rag the *Washington Standard* says, I'm the best writer in the city."

"My, you're a feisty one," Gray said, in a tone equal parts admiring and condescending. "But no, Mr. Pinkerton has other plans for you."

"My imagination fails me, Mr. Gray."

"Miss Breaux, if you declared the oath of allegiance in all good faith, then you have far more important business than penning stories about the war. You will have a hand in shaping it. And if you do well, I promise you all the personal glory in the world."

She raised her eyebrows, and her eyes widened. She made no attempt to conceal her interest. "Oh?"

"First, we sneak back into the city. And when we arrive, there is someone Mr. Pinkerton wants you to meet."

"Who?"

"President Abraham Lincoln."

CHAPTER 4

Franklin Gray led Josephine down the halls of the White House. As the sun went down, the staff was kicking out the various supplicants, curiosity seekers, and the gaggle of ne'er-do-wells who always seemed to be idling around the grounds and property of the presidential mansion. Gray found an inebriated man on the stairs, spitting tobacco toward a spittoon and missing, and the Pinkerton agent ordered him to vacate the premises at once.

They came into the president's office on the south side of the second floor, but she was disappointed when she looked about expecting to see Abraham Lincoln. Instead, Allan Pinkerton stood by the window, a pipe at his lips. He turned when they entered and gestured that they take a seat at a heavy oak table where Josephine knew the president met with his cabinet. She sat on one side, and the two agents sat next to each other on the other.

Lincoln's office was a massive room, some twenty-five or thirty feet wide and forty feet long, but there was nothing gaudy about the furniture or the furnishings. In addition to the table, a smaller mahogany desk was tucked to one side, with a pigeonhole cabinet stuffed with letters and telegrams. Various military maps decorated the walls, the largest of which was a huge map showing the entire South, this one marked with black dots. As it was growing dark, someone had lit the candelabras around the room, but there was no sign of the servant or any other person in the room.

"That was a clever game you played, Mr. Pinkerton," Josephine said. "You had me convinced."

"It was Mr. Gray's idea."

"Where is the president?"

Pinkerton waved his pipe. "Meeting with the secretary of war. He'll come in when he finishes. Meanwhile, we have a few items of business to attend to."

"Such as?"

He reached beneath the table and removed a carpetbag, which he set on the table next to Gray, who unfastened the clasp but didn't open it. Josephine resisted the urge to stare or ask questions, knowing that it would be easy to lose whatever power over the situation she still possessed.

"Did you meet with Jeff Davis when you were in Richmond?" Pinkerton asked.

She raised her eyebrows. "Again? Aren't we finished yet with the suspicion?"

"Please answer the question," Gray said.

"Of course I did. You read the article—you saw what Davis said. I didn't invent those quotes." She fixed each of the men in turn. "But I'm no spy. If this is what you think, say it, I'll depart at once."

"In the first place, nobody thinks you're a spy," Pinkerton said. "In the second, there's nowhere to go—you're finished in

Washington. We've made sure of that. Now you have a chance to prove your mettle, that you really mean the loyalty oath." He glanced at his companion. "Did she take it?"

Gray nodded. "She did."

Josephine crossed her arms. "I told you, I'm not a spy. Not for the Confederates, and not for you, either. I'll listen to what you have to say, but if that's what you're asking, you can toss those hopes out the window. I won't spy."

Pinkerton smiled. "Not even to return to New Orleans?"

She blinked. This was not what she was expecting, and she didn't know how to answer the question. She wasn't sure she wanted to go back. In the first year she had missed the river and the delta with an aching all the way to her bones. Last spring, a traveling exhibition named *Panorama of the Mighty Mississippi* had come to Washington. The panorama was a three-hundred-foot-long, ten-foot-high canvas that scrolled past with painted scenes of the Mississippi: deer and buffalo at the water's edge, Indians in canoes, the ruins of the failed Mormon city at Nauvoo, Illinois. As the canvas moved, a narrator explained to the enraptured audience what they were viewing. All were scenes she had witnessed, and while the painting quality was as poor as one could expect from such a vast, workmanlike scene, it was still close enough to her childhood that she had to get up and leave the theater because she was so overwhelmed with memories, both happy and painful.

"I'm not exactly from New Orleans," she said.

"That is part of the reason we're interested in you," Pinkerton said. "You know the city, but you don't have all of the relationships that might trip you up. And you know the river, which is our specific concern."

"What makes you say that?" she said warily.

"Didn't you grow up on a Mississippi riverboat?"

Josephine thrust out her chin. "And what of it?"

Pinkerton nodded at Gray, and the younger agent opened the carpetbag. He removed a few papers with handwritten notes, and a stack of telegrams on American Telegraph Company cards. Then he removed a black-lacquered box with a scene of a landscape chiseled into the red-and-green-painted lid. The scene was a grand harbor, lined with jagged mountains and filled with Chinese junks.

She sprang to her feet and reached across the table. "Give me that!"

Gray snatched it up and held it out of reach. "Calm down, Miss Breaux."

"You stole that from my rooms!"

"We didn't steal it," Pinkerton said. "To maintain the fiction, we told your landlady you'd been expelled from the city. We simply collected your belongings so Mrs. Mills wouldn't sell them."

"That's pure fimble-famble. That box was hidden behind the wainscot, which means you tore my rooms apart. Did you steal everything? Where's my money?"

"Everything is here," Gray said, "and you will get it back in due time."

"That time is now."

Nevertheless, she sat, fuming that her possessions had been violated, but she was still under their power, disgraced and evicted.

Gray opened the chest. He removed a stack of banknotes and set them on the table, plus a dozen twenty-dollar gold double eagles. He stacked the coins on top of each other, then ran his thumb across the banknotes.

Gray whistled, as if seeing it for the first time, although she had little doubt that these men had counted every last dollar. "That's quite a tidy sum."

While his fellow agent pawed over Josephine's money, Pinkerton packed more tobacco into his pipe and relit it. "How old are you, Miss Breaux?"

"Twenty-four."

"That is a lot of money for a young woman to possess, especially one with such an interesting background. Three thousand eight hundred dollars. Mr. Gray's salary is six dollars a day, plus expenses. How long would one have to work and save to accumulate so much money? You have been in Washington for how long? Three years?"

"What are you driving at?"

Pinkerton puffed and cast a glance at Gray. These two men were working her over in an interrogation that was growing increasingly invasive, clearly designed to break down her protective barriers.

"We have reason to believe you are younger than you claim," Gray said.

"I am not. Anyway, what does that matter?"

"It is suspicious enough for a woman who arrived in Washington at the age of twenty-one to be in possession of three thousand eight hundred dollars in ready money. It is another thing for a girl of eighteen to arrive with those resources."

"And you have deduced all of this since this afternoon?" she asked. "That I am three years younger than I claim and that I arrived in Washington with this money instead of earning it here? Pretty clever work if you only just came into possession of that box. Or had you already broken into my rooms and rifled through my possessions?"

"We won't insult your intelligence with lies," Pinkerton said. "Of course we have been watching you for some time. Ever since *Joseph* Breaux interviewed Jeff Davis three weeks ago."

"That story didn't earn me as much attention as I had hoped," she admitted. "People thought I was embellishing all those things Davis told me."

"We didn't," Pinkerton said. "Certain details rang all too true. Once we had our eye on you, it didn't take much digging to turn up the truth."

"And even less work to put that weasel from the *Washington Standard* on the story. Which one of you did that?" She turned to Gray. "Was that you? I hope you appreciate the humiliation I suffered."

"That was an unfortunate turn of events," Pinkerton said. "But once it happened, we knew we had to move quickly."

She held out her hand. "Can I have my chest back now? It's from Shanghai and a hundred years old, and I don't want you breaking it."

Gray didn't obey, but reached his hand into Josephine's Oriental chest, and she winced, wondering what he would bring up next. She'd received that box at the age of thirteen and had stored all manner of keepsakes and mementos inside. Some had been valuable, others were merely sentimental, and several were embarrassing.

He took out two photographs and set them on the table. Josephine remembered posing for them each, remaining still for what had seemed an eternity, while the sun sent sweat trickling down her face. Then the photographer retreated to his wagon to work in darkness, emerging later, smelling of chemicals, with the picture lacquered onto tin and protected with glass cemented on top with a transparent balsam resin. That she had not one, but two photographic recollections of her childhood was unusual. That they had survived the upheavals of her life was nearly miraculous. Yet on more than one occasion she had considered smashing the glass and destroying them.

"The girl in each of these photos is you?" Gray asked.

"I was an awkward child."

"I don't see that. But I do see a girl of nine or ten here, and perhaps thirteen in this picture."

"And?"

"Is this woman your mother?"

Josephine looked at the picture. She'd stared at it hundreds of times, could picture it in her mind with little trouble. But she saw it now as if for the first time. A young, gawky girl of eight, standing on the deck of a riverboat steamer next to a woman in a sequined dress, who showed too much leg and wore too much face paint. The girl, jutting her chin forward, a defiant gleam in her eyes. The mother, still beautiful and glamorous and only in her midtwenties, a coquettish look on her face.

"I'm not answering the question."

"The question doesn't need an answer," Pinkerton said. "The eyes are the same, as is the nose. This woman is evidently your mother. She must have been young when she had you—sixteen or seventeen."

"She was a professional riverboat dancer. Not what you're implying."

"Nobody is implying anything."

Josephine fixed her gaze on Pinkerton. "What did you say about insulting my intelligence with lies?"

The older of the two men didn't look ashamed, merely puffed again at his pipe and nodded for his fellow agent to continue.

"And is this one your father?" Gray asked. He showed the second photo.

In this one, Josephine was older, in that awkward stage between childhood and womanhood, when she'd felt all arms and legs, like a bony scarecrow. In spite of how she looked, and what came shortly after, that had been a time that she now regretted passing. Her mind had been older, sharper, and she could understand the world, but she had not yet filled out and started drawing unwanted attention.

"Is he?" Gray pressed. "It is harder to tell if there's a resemblance—the man's face is blurry."

"He's blurry because he didn't want to stand still. Anyway, I don't know the answer to your question. We called him the Colonel."

This admission hung in the air a long moment without comment. What did it say that Josephine didn't know the answer to such a simple question? Was he, or was he not her father?

"You were traveling on a boat by the name of *Cairo Red*," Gray said. "There's plenty of evidence for it in your box—passenger tickets, a letter from your mother that mentions it—"

Josephine's face flushed. "You read that? Have you no honor, Mr. Gray?"

For once, the man looked ashamed, and avoided meeting her gaze, but glanced instead to Pinkerton for guidance.

"Go on," Pinkerton told the younger man.

Gray nodded and turned back to Josephine. "But the boat in the photo isn't *Cairo Red*. This is a boat named *Crescent Queen*. We know this because *Crescent Queen* is currently in Memphis, being outfitted with guns to serve in the Confederate navy, and we were able to identify it."

Josephine forced the emotion from her voice. "I lived on *Crescent Queen* for most of my childhood. There was trouble. The last few years I spent on *Cairo Red*."

"What kind of trouble?" Pinkerton asked.

"Never mind," she said abruptly, as more memories came to the surface, like a Mississippi eddy swirling up a dead body from the muddy depths. "My mother had an opportunity on *Cairo Red*, so we took it."

"I've sent out inquiries about *Cairo Red*," Pinkerton said. "We're collecting information about all shipping on the river. But as of yet I have no information on the boat. Perhaps you could tell us more."

"I'd rather not. You'll get your answer soon enough. Suffice it to say that she is no longer sailing the Mississippi."

"Very well. Go on, Mr. Gray," Pinkerton urged.

Gray pointed to the second picture. "How old are you in this picture? Fourteen, perhaps?"

"More or less."

"According to what we found in your personal effects, you were on *Cairo Red* as of 1854," Gray said. "Seven years ago. So you cannot be older than twenty-one now."

"You would make a good newspaper writer," she said grudgingly. "If you weren't such a scoundrel, I'd suggest you speak with Mr. Barnhart at the *Morning Clarion.* He is short one ace reporter."

"How old are you now?" Pinkerton asked again. "And why are you claiming to be twenty-four?"

"I left New Orleans at seventeen, but told people that I was older so as to secure passage on a clipper without attracting attention. I kept up the fiction when I arrived in Washington City. I am twenty years old as of last month. Now are you satisfied?"

"So where did you get all the money?" Pinkerton asked. "Did you bring it with you, or acquire it in Washington?"

"I didn't steal it, I didn't earn it through disreputable activities, and I haven't been paid by the enemy to serve as a spy or in any other capacity. So I don't see how it is any of your business."

"Miss Breaux," Gray pressed. "If all of that is true, then what harm would it be to explain?"

"No, I'm not talking about it."

The two agents prodded her a few more times, but she stubbornly resisted saying anything more. That would bring matters back to the Colonel and to her mother's semireputable career and sad demise, and that was nobody's business. She certainly wouldn't discuss it with these two men. At last they gave it up, as she knew they would. They'd gone to a good deal of trouble to maneuver her into this position and wouldn't change their minds because she had unexplained money.

A knock came at the door, and the two men rose quickly to their feet. Josephine followed their lead.

The president of the United States entered the room.

CHAPTER 5

Abraham Lincoln stood near the door for a long moment, as if waiting for permission to enter. Josephine had seen the man occasionally walking about the White House grounds or exiting his carriage, but this was the first time she had seen him up close since a brief glimpse at the inauguration earlier in the year.

He seemed even taller and more gaunt than she'd remembered. Bags hung beneath his eyes, and lines crawled across his forehead like the picket lines of a slowly marching army. It was as if he'd aged a decade in a few short months.

"Miss Breaux?" Lincoln said. "Your mouth is hanging open wide enough to swallow a dragonfly."

She snapped it shut, embarrassed by her gaping. She'd met plenty of generals and politicians, and even the president of the Confederacy a few weeks ago, but maybe it was the long, hot day full of reversals and the interrogation Gray and Pinkerton had already subjected her to that left her tongue-tied. She felt she needed to say something and blurted the first stupid thing that came to mind.

"You're much taller close up."

A smile lit up his face, and he chuckled warmly. "And you're as slender as a willow and not much older than the Irish girl they've sent to iron my shirts. But if half of what they tell me is true, you're the young lady who will help me win New Orleans."

"Sir?"

"Mr. President—" Pinkerton said at the same time, his voice warning.

Lincoln waved a long, bony hand and sat at the far end of the table. The others sat down as well.

"If she's as clever as Mr. Gray insisted, then she has figured out most of it already. Haven't you, Miss Breaux?"

"What was I *supposed* to figure out?"

"Ah, well, perhaps they were wrong. You gentlemen did tell her about New Orleans, right?"

"Yes, sir," Pinkerton said.

"And you questioned her about the riverboat business, or haven't you reached that point yet?"

"We started, but she is being obstinate." Pinkerton put away his pipe. "Except what we can pry out of her, she won't give us any information until she has sussed out the situation."

"A woman who bridles her mouth before she sets it agallop is precisely what we are looking for, is it not?" the president asked.

Pinkerton scowled. "I suppose."

"My first question for you," Lincoln said, turning his deep, penetrating gaze in Josephine's direction, "is whether you want to see the slavocracy of the rebellious states win their so-called liberty?"

"Of course not. I am a Union supporter and always have been."

"Mr. Pinkerton and Mr. Gray want you in New Orleans. Please

tell me why. I'd like to find out if you're as clever as you seem from your writing, or if someone else has been penning your stories."

She bristled at this, even as she knew he was saying it to goad her into defending her intellect. She only just avoided blurting her thoughts. But one of the first lessons of journalism was that if you wanted information, you should let the other fellow do all of the talking. And she desperately wanted information.

After a few seconds of silence, Lincoln sighed. "You have either been overestimated or underestimated. I cannot quite decide which."

Her pride was eating at her, so she turned toward something else that might prove her quality. "I can tell you why you lost the battle at Bull Run."

"I beg your pardon?" the president said, blinking.

The president's two agents exchanged glances. "I hardly think you're qualified to give military advice," Pinkerton said.

"The rebels boast that every Southerner is worth ten Yankees," Josephine said. "But that's not what I saw on the battlefield. The Union boys were every bit as brave as the enemy. It was only when Union leadership failed that the common soldier turned tail and fled."

"So the problem was our generals?" Lincoln asked. "Is that your claim? That their officers are more intelligent than ours, better versed in the art of war?"

"I wouldn't even say that. I met Beauregard when I came in to inspect his army. He was easily fooled, and I didn't get the impression he was any more clever than your average congressman."

Lincoln chuckled at this. "Go on."

"What their commanders possessed, and what was lacking in ours, was *energy*. The enemy took the initiative. During the fight, they saw how the battle was flowing, and they made adjustments, while ours proved incapable of changing course."

"We had more men and horses," Lincoln said. "We shouldn't have needed to change course. Sometimes the best way across the river is a straight line."

"Unless there's an alligator in your path," Josephine said, "in which case it's wise to paddle downstream a stretch before you make the crossing." She nodded. "Things went wrong, as they always do in battle. Our generals might have altered their plans in response, but they were ponderous, uncertain. They made the worst sort of mistakes, the kind that come from inaction."

"If you're going to commit an error, best do so with alacrity," Lincoln said.

"And that's why the rebels won the battle. They made adjustments, they kept their nerve, and they pressed the attack when we faltered."

"Tell me, is Washington in danger?" Lincoln asked.

Pinkerton cleared his throat. "Mr. President, I don't think this girl—"

"I want her thoughts. The city is in an uproar, and people are expecting Beauregard to come marching up the road any moment now. Perhaps the young lady has some insight."

"There's no danger," Josephine said, more confidently than she felt. "Not in the short term. The enemy is nearly as stunned as we are."

"Hmm." The president leaned back in his chair. "'Clever as a congressman,' you say. I must remember that." He gave her a long look. "Where did you learn all of this?"

"Sir?"

"Military details, how to execute a campaign, and so on and so forth."

"I read, Mr. President."

"You read. Miss Breaux, excuse my skepticism, but you . . . *read*?"

"I read, yes. And I observe. I ask intelligent questions. And I think, usually in writing—it is how I clarify my thoughts."

Pinkerton cleared his throat. "Mr. President, she's only a girl—I hardly think she's capable of understanding the very complex situation we are facing."

"Does it matter that she is a young lady, so long as she has a good mind for the subject? An ax and a saw can both fell the same tree."

"If you don't need the lumber," Josephine said, "a battery of twenty-four-pounder howitzers can clear an entire forest in short order."

"I should hire you to write my speeches," Lincoln said, chuckling. "Do you have any further observations about the unfortunate events in Virginia?"

"Only one," she said. "You have men who will fight. Now you need generals who can do the same."

"She hasn't told us anything we couldn't have figured out ourselves," Pinkerton said grudgingly. He nodded at his younger companion. "Mr. Gray filed a report that said much the same thing."

"Using twice as many words and with half as much clarity," Lincoln said. "Reading it was like peering through a fog bank and trying to make a map of the far shore. Miss Breaux turned on a limelight and burned away the fog."

The president had been flattering her—she recognized this—but it was working. Josephine found herself wanting to please him. Her sense of adventure was roused, and she found herself chewing over the idea of returning to the Mississippi. The thought both thrilled and worried her.

"You mentioned New Orleans," she said. "Can you tell me more?"

Lincoln looked her over. "It will be dangerous. You might find yourself swinging from the end of a rope."

"I'm not afraid of that."

"So you say now. Yet taking into account what you faced in Virginia these past few days, it's clear you've got steady nerves. New

Orleans will be a grand adventure, a chance for heroism of the highest sort. Are you the woman for the job?"

"Mr. President," she said with a smile that was half-coquettish, half-skeptical—a smile learned from her mother, who was rarely denied by men of any kind—"now you're appealing to my vanity."

"Is it working?"

"Quite frankly, yes, it is. I'm flattered and I'm intrigued, and there's no denying it. But I need to know what I'm getting into."

"I'm sure you've guessed this much," Lincoln said. "The key to this war is control of the Mississippi, from Illinois to the Gulf of Mexico, together with that river's several tributaries. And the key to the Mississippi is New Orleans. It's the biggest city and port in the South, site of manufacturers and possessing a population base from which the enemy can raise tens of thousands of troops. The very sinews of war pass through New Orleans."

He delivered all of this with the same broad frontier accent with which he had been speaking earlier, but something had changed in his tone. She could sense the keen mind that had led a country lawyer on a path to the presidency of the United States. He was holding the map of the South in his mind and probing at her weaknesses, looking for a way to strangle the rebellion.

Pinkerton and Gray listened raptly to the president's thoughts. The younger man rested his hand on Josephine's banknotes and let his thumb run along the edge of the money like a riverboat gambler playing with a deck of cards.

"New Orleans is a snapping turtle buried in the mud," Lincoln continued, "protected by a shell of forts both upstream and down and all the gunboats the enemy can muster. Taking the city is key to shearing off the western states of the rebellion, but right now that is impossible. And that is why we need you in New Orleans.

"Once there, you will be given specific tasks suitable to your impressive range of skills. Your duties will be among the most important of the war. When you have done your work, New Orleans will return to the Union, and enemy hopes will collapse. God willing, this terrible conflict will come to a swift end. You will play a key role in this heroic endeavor."

Throughout this little speech, Josephine felt her ego swelling, and though she recognized that this was the president's intent, that didn't make her immune to its effects. Lincoln had mixed flattery with an appeal to her sense of adventure and glory. Nothing he had given her was useful information—had she been a Confederate spy, Richmond would have reacted to it with a dismissive shrug. Of course New Orleans was critical. Everyone knew that, but she still felt like she was privy to secret war knowledge by hearing it from the mouth of Abraham Lincoln himself.

"Now," Lincoln said, rising to his feet, which spurred the other three to rise as well. "I have a long night of work ahead of me. I feel like a sailor with a leaky boat, running about, slapping pitch on the timbers to keep it from taking on more water. So I will leave the three of you to your planning."

"But I still don't know what you want me to do," Josephine protested.

"I am sowing many seeds, and I hope that with time some of them will bear fruit. That is all I can say at the moment. For now, I leave this matter in the capable hands of Mr. Pinkerton and Mr. Gray. And you, too, exercising what energy and ingenuity you can bring to bear. Best wishes in New Orleans, Miss Breaux. Now you will excuse me, I am hard pressed."

Lincoln made for the door, but Josephine sputtered as he walked past her. "I haven't even said I would go."

"That is true," Lincoln said when he reached the door. "There's nothing we can do to force you. But for the sake of your country, I hope you will."

Josephine looked from the president to the two agents. Pinkerton tucked his pipe into his breast pocket and raised his eyebrows in an implied question.

"Well?" Gray said.

Josephine hesitated. She could almost smell New Orleans, the thick, almost tropical scent, smell the river as it cut its wide, inexorable path through the heart of the continent. Already, she could feel the weight of so many memories, some beautiful, some ugly and terrifying. She might come to regret her naïveté, but at the moment she was less worried about the risk of being caught by the Confederates and hung as a spy, and more frightened of being hoisted in the noose of her own past.

Against those fears was personal glory, a chance to test herself, to prove her value. And yes, she possessed a gambling streak that may or may not run in her blood. She thought about the Colonel before shoving aside those memories.

"You'll have everything you need," Lincoln prodded. "These two gentlemen will arrange transport to New Orleans, and will make sure you have the resources to support yourself in enemy territory."

She made her decision.

"I'll do it." Josephine eyed Gray, who still had her banknotes, coins, photographs, and letters spread on the table in front of him. "But if your men will return what they've stolen, I won't need your resources, because I'll have everything I need."

CHAPTER 6

Given that Josephine had abandoned her plan of searching for employment in New York in order to work for the government, it was ironic that the first thing she did after leaving the White House was take a night coach to Baltimore, followed by a train ride to the heart of Manhattan, where she disembarked at a depot on Twenty-Seventh Street. She hired a hansom cab to carry her downtown, where she checked into the dingy Luxor Hotel, only a few blocks from Newspaper Row.

But instead of marching triumphantly into the *Herald*, the *Times*, or the *Tribune* flourishing clips from her most triumphant articles, she skulked about the hotel for several days, waiting for Pinkerton to send instructions. Pinkerton had seemed worried that she would be recognized in Washington, which was why he'd sent her north from Washington to await transport.

Josephine took one of the horsecars that ran on rails up to Central Park, where she munched on a bratwurst bought from a German with a cart and watched a group of sweating Irish laborers dig a pond with pick and shovel. She bought all the newspapers and read them front to back. When an article seemed particularly well written, she tore it out and tucked it into her satchel to study later. Meanwhile, she caught up on events following the disaster at Bull Run.

Lincoln had demoted McDowell and brought in General George McClellan to lead the Army of the Potomac. A dashing young West Pointer, McClellan was said to be quickly whipping the troops into shape, and had succeeded in stemming the panic that Washington would soon be overrun. It remained to be seen how he would fare against the Confederates.

As for her humiliation, there were a few small articles, mostly in the *Tribune,* about the unmasking of "Joseph" Breaux, and speculation on whether or not she was a secessionist spy. The jaded New York press said no. The *Tribune* slyly suggested it might offer her a job if she were to resurface. Her heart ached at this, but now that she'd committed to President Lincoln and his spies, she wouldn't renege.

On the fourth morning, Josephine got a telegram from the cryptically named E. J. Allen, which instructed her to collect her bags and proceed to Brooklyn, where her passage was booked on a clipper named *The Flying Siam*, destination Havana. She hired a cab, which joined a press of horses, carts, and foot traffic to the East River, then took the ferry across. Once in Brooklyn, she boarded the clipper and took the small stateroom that had been designated for her use.

Josephine had no sooner tossed her bags onto her bunk than the bell clanged, and the whistles blasted on the docks. She hurried out to join the other passengers and crew on the deck. The ship flew a Canadian flag, but she heard German, Irish brogues, Spanish, and broad Canadian French among the crew. The passengers were largely Americans and Europeans, with a handful of Cubans sprinkled into the mix.

The Flying Siam hoisted her sails and came down the East River with the outgoing tide, where she joined the larger harbor. From there, they struggled to maneuver among the smoke-belching tugs, the clippers coming off the ocean, and the heavy traffic of light barges, fishing smacks, and the ferries heaving back and forth between New York and New Jersey. A mighty sloop of war wallowed offshore, its guns bristling. Gulls wheeled overhead, their calls mingling with the sounds of bells and whistles from the various ships, coastal forts, and lighthouses.

This burst of clandestine activity was mysterious and exciting, and it wasn't until they were well offshore that the first worry tickled at her belly. She'd expected to receive more instructions on the ship, but so far, nothing.

The bells rang for supper, and after she'd eaten a dinner of quahogs and beans cooked in salt pork, she returned briefly to her stateroom, a small, dingy space that smelled of its previous occupant. There were tobacco stains on the wall, and the spittoon had been emptied but not cleaned. At least they'd changed the sheet on the cot.

Instead of lingering in the room, Josephine made her way to the deck to watch the sun sinking in the west. A fresh, briny breeze snapped in off the sea and tugged at her black curls, trying to pull them free from her bonnet. All was quiet on deck except for the slap of waves against the hull, the creak of ropes and canvas, and the occasional calling of sailors. A lighthouse blinked several miles off the starboard bow. She pulled her shawl around her shoulders, suddenly chilly.

Was she really going to Havana? And what in heaven's name would she do when she got there? Look for the American legation or settle into a hotel and wait for someone to find her?

"Enjoying the night?" a man said behind her.

She recognized the voice and was relieved when she turned to see Franklin Gray approaching. He wore a dark wool jacket with trousers and a felt bowler, pulled down so it wouldn't blow away in the breeze.

"You weren't at supper," she said.

"I stayed in my room until dark. Seemed prudent. Did you spot any suspicious characters?"

"Several. But nobody who seemed particularly interested in me. Are we being watched?"

"I don't know," he said. "We carry illicit cargo. After Havana, we'll carry still more. If there are Union agents aboard, they haven't been warned of our presence. Mr. Pinkerton wanted as few people as possible to know of our departure."

"So we *are* going to Cuba. I'd wondered if we'd get around Key West and make straight for the delta with a load of contraband for the enemy."

Mr. Gray took out a silver case and offered her a cigarette before he lit his own. She declined.

"*The Flying Siam* will never run the blockade. It's too big, too easily recognized. We'll transfer to something even less luxurious, I'm afraid. I apologize for the room. A lady should have something more accommodating."

"If you knew the kinds of things I saw growing up on the river . . ." She smiled. "I'm not bothered by the conditions."

The tip of his cigarette glowed. "Wait until you see the rats scurry up and down the ropes at Havana."

"If a man—or woman—gets hungry enough, he'll *eat* a rat."

He laughed at this. "I was skeptical about Mr. Pinkerton's plans for you. But now I see that you are the perfect woman for the business at hand."

"A woman is always underestimated. A clever woman doubly so."

"How did you gain General Beauregard's confidence at the battle?" he asked. "It surely wasn't only your huckleberry pie."

"Don't discount my pie, Mr. Gray. It has weakened the knees of many a man."

Josephine may have fought and scrabbled in a world of men, but she was not above using those feminine charms she had learned from her mother, and if Gray wasn't a fool, he would see that she was doing the same thing to him right now that she had done to the rebel general. She decided to test him.

She took the cigarette from his fingers and brought it to her lips. "Do you know what I asked General Beauregard when I gave him the pies?" She changed her voice to mimic the Chesapeake accent she had affected with Beauregard. "'How do you intend to whip the Yanks, General? They seem powerful determined.'" She handed back the cigarette. "That's all it took. He laid out his entire order of battle."

"I'm glad you're on our side, and not the enemy's, Miss Breaux."

"There are women in Washington who are spying on you at this moment. If you think our generals and congressmen are more tight-lipped than theirs, you are deceiving yourself." Josephine leaned in confidentially. "May I call you by your given name, Franklin? Or is it Frank?"

"Please do. And Franklin is fine. There were a million and one Franks where I grew up."

"I am pleased to meet you properly, Franklin." She held out a gloved hand, which he took. "I prefer Josephine to Miss Breaux . . . if you feel comfortable, of course. But not Jo or Josie, or anything like that. They make me sound like a child."

"We wouldn't want to remind anyone that you are only twenty years old."

She forced a laugh and hoped it sounded bright and cheery and not defensive. "That is true."

"Where is your mother? And this man you call the Colonel—where is he?"

The questions caught her off guard. She had been thinking how easily she had broken the stiff exterior Franklin had carried in Washington and wondering whether she could simply ask him how they meant to use her spying in the Confederacy. Only now he had turned the tables.

"That is . . . indelicate."

"It's not puerile curiosity. I have several possibilities of how to bring you into New Orleans, and I want to be sure we won't stumble into any of your relations."

"Neither the Colonel nor my mother will be in New Orleans, I promise. If I do see relations, there will be no problem. I wouldn't recognize them, and they wouldn't recognize me."

A knot of pain formed in Josephine's belly. She wouldn't see her mother, because her mother was dead. The Colonel wasn't, so far as she knew, but he may as well be.

"I am glad to hear it," Franklin said, "but I would still like to hear the details. Whenever you are comfortable, of course."

But Josephine had soured on the conversation, and she was now more keen to return to her quarters than to stay and gnaw at old wounds. She feigned a yawn.

"Perhaps another time, Mr. Gray," she said, dropping the informality so recently established. "I am tired, and I have a book I am reading that will occupy my mind until bedtime. Good evening to you."

The book was a slim volume discussing *Vom Kriege—On War*—by the Prussian General Clausewitz. Josephine had purchased it from an elderly Jewish bookseller in Central Park for a dime, marked down from fifteen cents after she'd greeted him with a Yiddish phrase she'd learned from a traveler on the Mississippi. A West Point officer had once told her about the book, claiming that it was the best discussion of war theory, and she'd been excited to find it. Unfortunately, it wasn't *On War* itself but a treatise discussing certain points of the book. The chapter about what Clausewitz called "the fog of war" was fascinating, but frustratingly incomplete, and the British naval officer who'd penned the treatise wrote with such leaden prose that she had to set it aside.

Josephine turned down the oil lamp and lay on her cot in the darkness, her porthole window opened to air out the stateroom. The smell of the ocean was different than the river, but the gentle motion and the sound of the calm water gliding along the hull only dragged her deeper into her memories. She turned up the lamp again, changed into her long nightgown, brushed out her hair, and washed her face from the metal pitcher with the stopper that hung by its neck from a rope next to the washbasin. Before she climbed into bed, she opened her Oriental box and took out the picture of her mother in the sequined dress. After a few minutes, she put it away and turned down the light for good.

Josephine lay down on the cot, pulled the sheet up to her neck, and stared into the darkness overhead.

She was eight when that picture was taken, and must have known the Colonel for a long time already, but the day of the photograph was one of her earliest, strongest memories of the man. That morning, *Crescent Queen* had come out of the Ohio River where it met the Mississippi, and Josephine was on the deck with her bare, tanned legs hanging over the edge of the promenade, looking down at the two powerful currents sliding by each other, one gray and sleek, the other the color of muddy coffee. Only gradually did they mix.

A flatboat drifted off stern, and men danced on its deck, one man playing a fiddle and the others kicking their heels and waving knit caps. A keelboat heaved alongside the flatboat, and here several more men from the long, slender craft joined their voices. A third boat, this one another keel, heard the singing and rowed over to join the little flotilla. The men were Cajun and Irish and wild-haired Buckeyes and Hoosiers with beards halfway down their chests.

Josephine recognized the tune as "Bucktooth Burro" and began to sing along.

Oh, my burro has buckteeth an' he loves hisself a carrot, an' he eats turnips by the bushel.

For the next twenty minutes, the riverboat, its paddle still as they worked on the boilers, drifted downstream alongside the three smaller boats, and she sang along with the river rats: "Woozy Creek," "Double Chin Sue," and "What Makes Frenchie Love 'Taters." She knew them all. It was a welcome change from the piano music played in the riverboat saloon where her mother danced and sang. Uninhibited, with nothing but pure joy behind the music.

A skinny, freckled young man with a pointed red cap like something out of a Mardi Gras parade spotted Josephine and waved, and soon all the men were dancing for her, waving their caps and lifting their voices. Josephine sprang to her feet, lifted her skirts to her knees like the dancing girls did in the saloon, and did a little two-step, which made them whoop and holler.

Josephine was sorry when *Crescent Queen* vibrated as the boilers started up below. Black wood smoke huffed out the tall stacks. Long trails of sooty smoke trailed out behind the boat as the big side-wheel turned, pushing the river behind it. The steamer began to pull away downstream from the smaller craft. The men gave the girl a final wave of their caps, and soon their voices faded.

As the music died away, an argument caught Josephine's ear.

The first she heard was her mother's voice, high and irritated. "You are a no-good weasel. A scoundrel and no gentleman. If you think I'm going to fall for this sharp practice—"

"But Claire, if you'll only listen to me—"

"No!"

"It's only for a few days. What's the harm?"

Josephine was intrigued by the man's voice. It sounded familiar, but she couldn't place why. The voice didn't belong to the funny little Irishman from the bar whose accent she liked to imitate; he sometimes came up to argue about the dance numbers and singing. And it wasn't the passenger from Boston who had come around a few days ago to pester her mother. Josephine thought he'd disembarked in Cincinnati at the end of the trip.

The girl made her way around the promenade to the room she shared with her mother. It was above the saloon, and late at night when Josephine was supposed to be sleeping, she would listen to the pounding feet of dancers, the pianos and banjos, and the cries of drunk men.

The argument came through the window, and as the girl pushed open the door, neither of them seemed to spot her.

Her mother's stage name, which always appeared in big letters on the bills that they glued to barns and drink houses in the river towns, was Claire de Layerre, and Josephine thought she was the most beautiful woman in the world. The way men looked at her, it was obvious that the rest of the world thought the same thing.

Claire had already dressed in her glittering dance gown but had not yet put on her lipstick, her rouge, or the big sparkly costume jewelry that Josephine liked to try on so she could admire herself in the mirror. Claire faced a man in black trousers, a black broadcloth coat, a white shirt, and black tie. The shirt was frilled, and he wore an outrageous vest fixed with pearl buttons. A big gold watch poked out of a vest pocket, together with a long gold chain. He had dark, curly hair and a mustache with drooping tips. The girl had seen him before but couldn't remember where.

"Two weeks," the man said. "Then I promise I'll meet you in New Orleans and return you double."

Claire snorted. "Two weeks will turn into two years."

"Not this time, I promise."

Josephine was still trying to puzzle out where she'd seen this man before when the two adults took note of her.

"Well, bless my sweet-gum tree!" the man said, his big, handsome eyes lighting up. "Six months gone and you've grown like a willow."

"Eighteen months," Claire said dryly.

"That long? Surely not." He beckoned to Josephine, who remained rooted in place. "Come on, then, Josie, I've got a treat for you." He reached into the pocket of his jacket and fished out a small golden-colored drop wrapped in waxed paper.

This brought her forward, though she couldn't figure out how this man knew her name. She glanced at her scowling mother for permission to take the candy. It didn't come, but that didn't stop Josephine from taking it and popping it in her mouth.

"Eighteen months," Claire repeated. "It was after that riverboat blew up at Vicksburg, so I remember the date just fine. You were marking cards with that one-eyed Yankee from Albany."

Now it was the man's turn to scowl, and he glanced behind him to the open door. "Now, you hush. I wasn't marking cards, you hear. I had a run of good luck."

"And now your luck has run out. So you come sniffing around like a coonhound. How'd you find us, anyhow?"

"Studying the bills. They've got your name all over 'em."

"Who are you?" Josephine said around the honey drop in her cheek that filled her mouth with a delicious sweetness.

"You don't remember?" He blinked. "Why, I'm the Colonel."

"Oh, the Colonel!"

That explained it. Her mother was always talking about the Colonel this and the Colonel that. Sometimes he was a "no-gooder," other times "that fine gentleman." Right now, the way her mother was talking to him, he seemed to be a "confounded thieving coon," which Claire used to describe everyone from bloodthirsty river pirates to the men who sold coffee they'd cut with chicory.

The Colonel sat at Claire's dressing table, and the mirror behind him showed the back of his neck and his starched collar. He used another honey drop to coax Josephine over, then hefted her up onto his knee.

"Your mother knows I've sent her a good sum of money over the years."

"So have a bushelful of other fellows of dubious character," Claire said. "It don't mean nothing."

He ignored her and continued to speak to the girl. "Books for you, and clothes as befitting a young lady." Here he looked over her knee-length skirt and her bare, dirty legs and feet below that. "You don't seem to be wearing them."

"That's 'cause you don't bother sending anything her size," Claire said. "Anyway, she tears 'em up scrambling up and down the rail, jumping in the water fully dressed, and other nonsense."

"All I'm asking is forty dollars until I can get myself to New Orleans."

"But you're rich!" Josephine said. "That's what Miss Francesca told Mama."

The Colonel tousled her hair. "That I am, Josie. But even a rich man may find his pockets empty."

"Forty dollars is a lot of money," Josephine said. While she was listening, she'd forgotten to suck the candies and now realized she was crunching the last of them up. She looked hopefully at the Colonel, wanting another, but he was staring at her mother.

"You're right, Josie," Mother said, pulling her from the man's knee. "A lot of money for someone who says he is rich and throws around fistfuls of gold like it was birdseed."

"I had a couple of bad hands at St. Louis. Bet wrong. But I swear to God I am not flat broke, only temporarily short of funds. I've got to get in on this game." He reached into his pocket and pulled out several banknotes. "See, I've already got fifteen. But we got some stakes here, and it's thirty just to get in. Then I need a few bucks extra in case I suffer some reversals before I bring my pony around the turn for the homestretch."

Claire let out a big sigh. "All right. Get out, you two. I'll find the money."

The Colonel grinned and grabbed Josephine's mother, with the girl squeezed between them. He kissed the woman long and hard, then hoisted Josephine up. "There's my best girls."

Claire pulled away after a few seconds and pointed to the door. "Out!"

The Colonel took Josephine down to the saloon, where the men were already arriving for the show. There, he bought her a sarsaparilla and she amused both him and O'Reilly by imitating the short Irishman's accent. The Colonel challenged O'Reilly to some sort of dice game, winning eighteen cents, which paid for both the sarsaparilla and some gin for himself.

They let Josephine watch the Bouvier Sisters sing the opening act while she ate a lamb pastry at the bar, but by the time Claire de Layerre and Francesca Díaz began to dance, she'd already been sent upstairs to bed.

That night, when her mother came to check on her after the show, Josephine was still awake from all the music and shouting. Mother kissed her on the forehead before slipping back out again, locking the door from the outside. She didn't come home until morning.

Crescent Queen eased up to the docks at Frenchville the next morning after breakfast, and passengers and other traffic came up and down the gangplanks in both directions. Stevedores rolled up hogsheads of tobacco or carried crates of chickens and sacks of flour for the biscuits that were served at every meal aboard. An ugly, cussing man with a scar across his cheek led two barefoot slaves up another gangplank, where they disappeared into the lower deck.

Josephine wondered briefly why slaves always loaded upriver and unloaded downriver in Mississippi or Louisiana, but her attention was drawn by her mother coming out of the stateroom, dressed in her sequined dress as if it were night and she was getting ready to perform. She stood at the rail, while a man set up a big wooden box camera on a tripod on shore. Josephine vaguely remembered something they'd been saying in the bar about a picture for the papers.

The Colonel was standing next to the cameraman during the photograph, and when the man pulled off the black cloth after taking the picture, the Colonel whispered something in his ear. A silver coin glinted in the Colonel's hand as he passed it off, and then the two men were waving in Josephine, who had been gawking to one side. They told her to stand next to her mother. The cameraman changed out the plates for a second photo.

Fortunately, Josephine had been cleaned up to go into town with her mother and the Colonel, but she still felt as glamorous as a plucked chicken standing next to her mother in her dancing gown.

Once Claire had changed from the gown into her crinoline dress and her feathered hat with parasol, mother and daughter joined the Colonel to visit Frenchville, which was having its annual country fair. The three of them spent a few minutes looking at the prize heifers and listening to the bull auction, but the girl was impatient to get to the amusements. Josephine ate iced cream and fried dough balls drizzled with honey before they went to the teeter boat. The girl and her mother tugged as hard as they could on one rope, with the Colonel pulling the rope on the other side. The boat swung higher and higher. After a few minutes, the iced cream and dough balls began churning in the girl's stomach. Fortunately, they took her down before she threw up, and she was feeling better by the time they finished looking through the slit of a phenakistoscope at a flickering scene of a dancing bear.

Late that afternoon, the three of them found a discreet spot in the shade of a sweet-gum grove downriver of *Crescent Queen*, which had already blasted two whistles indicating departure in thirty minutes. Josephine watched two men haul in a line with a catfish the size of a log, while Claire and the Colonel sat kissing beneath the trees. When Josephine turned back from watching the men wrestle the fish onshore, her mother was passing the Colonel a wad of banknotes, a sour expression on her face.

"New Orleans," he said. "Two weeks. I'll pay you back double."

"I don't care about double," she said. "Forty will suffice. And maybe you can stay a little longer than one night and part of a day. We'll be in the city the better part of a month for repairs."

The Colonel kissed her again. "I'd love to spend it with you. And this little scallywag." He grinned at Josephine, and came over to kiss her cheek, which made her blush. "You be good, you hear? And no more diving into the river. It spooks your mama. You know she can't swim a lick. You be good and I'll bring you a whole bag of lemon drops."

After a final tip of the hat, he strolled whistling up the path, not toward the boat but into Frenchville again.

Claire sighed. "I do believe we've seen the last of that no-gooder for a stretch."

"We'll see him in New Orleans," Josephine said, still looking admiringly at the Colonel, who had not yet disappeared around the bend. "That's only two weeks."

Her mother didn't answer this, but tugged Josephine's hand and led her back to *Crescent Queen*, where passengers and crew were boarding. It was almost dusk, and the frogs started up a chorus along the riverbank. When Josephine was up top on the promenade, she looked back toward the town, trying to catch a glimpse of the Colonel, but couldn't spot him.

When *Crescent Queen* arrived in New Orleans later that month, the Colonel had not yet arrived, but there was a package waiting that included both the borrowed money—paid double, as he'd promised—plus the black-and-white photograph of mother and daughter standing on the railing of the riverboat.

"Will you look at that, Josie?" Claire said, handing it over to Josephine, while she hid the money in a compartment beneath her dressing desk. "That fine gentleman is as good as his word. We never should have doubted him." She hummed and sang to herself as she got ready for the show.

Later that night, when the riverboat was sitting outside the levee near Jackson Square, and the saloon was in full, raucous swing below, Josephine turned up the lamp and stared at the photo, remembering everything about that day in Frenchville and enjoying it as if she were eating the fried dough and iced cream all over again.

As for the Colonel himself, he did not show up after two weeks. Rather, it was two *years* later that he appeared. She had long since given up on him as a scoundrel, as her mother insisted.

But when he did finally arrive, he was carrying a treasure that would change Josephine's life forever.

CHAPTER 7

It took several days to sail down around the tip of Florida and into the harbor at Havana. The city was a sweltering tropical port of low-slung Spanish colonial buildings, with the massive fortress of La Cabaña rising on the eastern side of the harbor. When *The Flying Siam* eased into port, her hold, which had presumably been searched in Brooklyn for contraband, nevertheless disgorged all manner of Northern manufactures that disappeared into the swarm of goods and humanity on the docks, wharfs, and warehouses. Ships of every nation and flag jostled side by side in the harbor, and the waterfront swarmed with Confederate agents and profit-seeking blockade-runners.

Franklin told Josephine they would be three days in Havana waiting for a fast steamer to run the blockade, and he wanted to test her observation skills. After booking separate rooms in the sprawling, dilapidated Royal Sevilla, they went out posing as a blockade-runner and his wife.

On the docks, British and French merchants were bidding up the price of smuggled bales of cotton, and in turn there were Confederates everywhere, buying and loading cargoes of guns, percussion caps, rum, salt, coffee, tea, and even hoopskirts and corset stays. From all the gold changing hands, it seemed that Havana was booming.

Franklin tested Josephine after this excursion and seemed satisfied with both her memory and her powers of observation. Their relationship had been cordial rather than warm after that first night leaving Brooklyn, but once they'd started referring to each other by given names, it proved impossible to resume their earlier distance. He seemed a clever, honorable man, but she did not deceive herself that they'd formed a true friendship.

And if she were honest with herself, Josephine wasn't sure if she was capable of any such relationship. As a child, her friendships had been liberal and frequent but always shallow. Having free rein of first *Crescent Queen*, and later *Cairo Red*, she would meet other children for short, intense friendships that ended at the next bend of the river, the next port of call.

Franklin's idea was to come into New Orleans as strangers, and so they boarded the blockade-runner separately. It was a fast, low steamer that carried fifteen passengers and a hold stuffed with six small rifled cannons and whatever else the captain could squeeze in around the main cargo: boots, percussion caps, casks of wine, boxes of square nails, and several barrels of gunpowder. They left at night in case Union warships were patrolling offshore, and cut straight for the Gulf Coast.

When dawn came the next morning, the engines seemed to be straining against the choppy waves, and when Josephine joined the passengers on deck, she found them all watching a column of smoke to their rear at the very edge of what one could see without a spyglass.

"Yankees," a woman told Josephine. "Captain thinks it's a steam frigate. Thirty guns—one volley would blow us to kingdom come. But don't worry, we're not in danger."

"How can you be sure?" Josephine asked, keeping her eye on the column of smoke.

"Trust me. I've done this run three times. We're built for speed—we'll outrun them."

The side-wheel kept churning, and Josephine knew from the high-pitched whine that it was going flat out, the men below shoveling coal into the boiler as fast as they could. The longer they ran, the more they risked overpressuring the boiler. After her experiences on the river, that prospect filled her with a special kind of terror.

The woman was wrong. Over the next hour, a small figure gradually took shape beneath that column of smoke, and it became obvious that the blockade-runner would be overtaken by the blockade enforcer. Josephine risked looking for Franklin, and she spotted the Pinkerton agent near the stern, his hands around the spray-soaked rail, nervously twisting at the wood as he watched the ship approach. That made her more worried than ever.

Shouldn't the navy have been warned of their passage so they could slip by unmolested? What if the Union ship overtook them? Would they fire their cannons and sink the blockade-runner, or just board it?

The first thing to go were the heavy boxes of nails, then the gunpowder, and finally two of the cannons, heaved up to the deck by the crew and pushed over the edge. The low-lying schooner-rigged side-wheel lifted higher in the water, but still the navy frigate stayed within view. The captain and his first mate discussed in agitated tones whether to dump the remaining cannons or to throw over the passenger baggage as well. It was clear that any- and everything would go except for coal for the boilers and the passengers and crew themselves.

Then a man at the stern with a spyglass gave a shout and declared that the frigate was falling behind. Cheers rang across the deck.

"Well," the woman said to Josephine. "That was a narrow shave, as my husband would say."

"Which one is he?" Josephine asked, looking among the passengers.

"Oh, no. He's in Memphis. I'm traveling alone—my husband did business up north before the war and earned some enemies in Louisiana. So I'm his business agent this time around."

Josephine had been standing next to the woman for a good hour, hour and a half, but her attention had fixed on that smokestack and the approaching (now receding) Union warship. Now she turned and sized the other woman up for the first time.

And had a moment of shock as she turned and met the woman's smile. The woman was older now, her red hair color seemingly dyed, as if to cover a graying head, and her corset and stay couldn't conceal a waistline that had expanded since her riverboat days. But it was Francesca Díaz, one of the women who had sung and danced with Josephine's mother. Josephine hadn't seen the woman since they left *Crescent Queen* for *Cairo Red*. If Claire had ever met her old friend again after that, she'd never mentioned it to her daughter.

Francesca was smiling, looking at her, and Josephine's shock turned to relief as she realized that the woman didn't recognize her in turn. But that might change if Josephine stood gaping.

"My name is Miss Breaux." Josephine figured her last name was safe, having been picked up during her final stay in New Orleans. She didn't know her mother's true surname—certainly not de Layerre—and hadn't wanted to take on the unsavory stage name.

Josephine held out her bare hand. Unlike Francesca, she had not put on gloves before coming out to the deck. Francesca shifted her parasol—now catching as much sea spray as sunshine—and returned a dainty shake.

"I am Mrs. Hancock. You shouldn't get the wrong idea—my husband is a great patriot and believer in the Southern cause. But this war makes friends of strangers and strangers of friends. There is trouble in New Orleans and the bayou. That's why I went to Havana instead of him."

"Oh, I thought maybe you had family in Cuba."

Francesca laughed. "Oh, no. My family is pure French. From Provence." She gestured at the parasol. "That's why I must be careful about taking the sun. I don't want to turn as brown as a Marseillaise fisherman."

That wasn't what she'd claimed when she went by Francesca Díaz. She'd claimed to be from Spain, and with much the same reasoning about why she avoided the sun. Perhaps a Spanish origin was better for a dancer, with its connotations of *gitanos* and flamenco, but French was better for snaring a rich husband.

Now Josephine took a closer look at the woman, and with an adult eye, jaded and suspicious, as she'd learned during her newspaper writing. There was something dark and exotic about the woman's appearance. She easily could have passed for one of the hacienda owners of Cuba, or had she been in Washington, the Persian ambassador's wife. And now Josephine had another suspicion that had appeared with Francesca's shifting story.

Perhaps Francesca was an old-fashioned New Orleans creole, that mix of French, Spanish, and African. French coureur de bois and mulattoes coming together to give birth to quadroons, octoroons, and all the other mixed colored people with their own culture and customs. It was one thing to be a free person of mixed race in New Orleans but another thing to go upriver to Mississippi, Missouri, or Illinois and by her very existence inspire prejudice, violence, and even blackmail.

It was obvious now that they had outrun the Union frigate, albeit at a cost of two cannons and what must have been hundreds of dollars of other vital supplies. The warship had vanished, and all they could see now was the long stream of black smoke slowly dissipating in the brilliant blue sky over the Gulf of Mexico.

"And what brought you to Havana, Miss Breaux?" Francesca asked.

Josephine smiled. "I lived for a spell up north, but with the outbreak of the war, I had my own . . . troubles. It was time to come home to the South, and I couldn't do so directly. I sailed out of Brooklyn on the twenty-seventh of July."

"You have family in New Orleans?"

"They're scattered," she said. This much was true. "I hope to get a position with one of the papers. I have some newspaper experience, and I thought I could lend my voice to our struggles. There are a lot of foreigners in town, many English and French, especially, and if persuaded, they might carry our sympathies to their home countries."

Francesca's eyes widened. "Wait a moment. Josephine?" Her voice was loud, and several other people looked over.

Josephine's stomach flipped over. Her eyes flickered to one side, and there she spotted Franklin, his hat pulled low over his brow against the sun. He was staring hard.

"It is, isn't it?" Francesca pressed. "It's Josephine Breaux. I don't believe it."

Still two days from reaching New Orleans and already she'd been discovered. Franklin would be furious. He'd no doubt telegraph Washington, who would have no choice but to pull her from the city, unless they simply disavowed her and left her to her own devices. She cursed silently. Unless she could quiet this woman down in a hurry, put her off the scent . . .

"I'm afraid you're mistaken," she said. "That's not my name."

"Oh, please. None of that false modesty." Francesca's excitement seemed to be mounting. "You're a heroine! It's all they were talking about when I left the city ten days ago. So much ink spilled in the papers. That business at Manassas. And the way those blackguards threw you out of Washington. They were no gentlemen."

As Francesca prattled on, it gradually dawned on Josephine that the woman didn't recognize her at all. They hadn't met for years, since the younger woman was still a waifish girl, and Francesca had apparently not connected that child to the young woman of the same given name standing next to her. But the woman *had* heard of a certain reporter in Washington City, unmasked first as a woman, then as a Confederate spy. It had only been a minor news item in the New York papers but had apparently made big news in New Orleans and the rest of the Southern press. One more thing to crow about in the aftermath of the Confederate victory at Manassas.

Later, when the handful of passengers had departed for their various cabins, a knock came at Josephine's door. It was Franklin, apparently abandoning his commitment to ignore her until they were safely ensconced in New Orleans. He chewed nervously on his lower lip.

Josephine had been at her cramped desk next to the porthole window, scribbling notes about the outrunning of the steamer frigate to go with several pages she'd written about her time on the clipper and their three-day stopover in Havana.

She rose to her feet. "I am so sorry. That was a terrible blunder. I never should have used the name Breaux. Why didn't I think?"

She expected him to be angry, but he only shook his head.

"This is my fault as much as yours. We were being watched in Havana, so I didn't collect or send telegrams. I figured any news could wait until New Orleans."

"Watched? By whom?"

"That's not important. The point is that I didn't check or I might have been warned that you were notorious in Louisiana, and we could have found a more suitable last name."

"So what now?"

For a long moment Franklin stood silently at the doorway. He took out his cigarette case but only turned it over in his hand without taking one out. Josephine grew nervous, worried that he would tell her it was over, that she'd be sent back north. And it surprised her how committed she'd become to this plan, not only for personal glory, but for duty as well. The feeling had been growing since Brooklyn and had spread as she watched Confederate agents and smugglers working with great purpose and energy in Havana.

"Don't send me back," she said. "I can travel upriver to St. Louis or Memphis for a spell. I'll change my appearance, take on a new name, practice a new accent, and come back under another guise."

"That's assuming you can get in and out of New Orleans without out the entire city marching you at the head of a parade. What's more, I'd arranged a position for you at Fort Jackson. They have an infirmary, and the surgeon on site needs an assistant, has asked for a pretty young woman who can raise the cheer of the men as they recover."

This wasn't a surprise to her. That evening at the White House, when the president had departed, the two agents had asked her a few questions about her health. They seemed satisfied when she said that she wasn't squeamish at the sight of blood, and pleased when she told them that she'd suffered yellow fever as a child. That meant she was immune to the epidemics that regularly swept up and down the swampy lands of the lower Mississippi. She'd already guessed that they meant her to work in a charitable hospital, posing as a Confederate Florence Nightingale.

"And you're worried they'll give it to someone else while I'm gone?"

"Dr. Mingus isn't one of us. He's holding your position as a favor for a friend, who *is* our man." Franklin shook his head. "And I'm still worried that you'd be recognized. Then there would be questions, especially if you'd affected an accent and false name."

"Then maybe—" she began.

He lifted a hand to hush her and glanced down the hallway outside her room.

Voices sounded, one of the crew talking to a man with an English accent. Franklin tucked away his silver case and looked briefly like he was going to turn and leave. After a moment, though, he relaxed.

"All right, they're gone," he said. "Go on."

She continued. "Then maybe I don't affect anything. Maybe I arrive in New Orleans and accept whatever attention comes my way. This isn't so far off my original plan."

He looked intrigued. "Explain."

She told him about her initial thoughts after Barnhart had dismissed her from the *Clarion*. Even while fuming as Franklin and Mr. Pinkerton led her on that humiliating march past the brothels on Rum Row, she'd been thinking about the New York press. She would buy a ticket to Manhattan and use every tool at her disposal to secure a position: her writing ability, foremost, but also her determination, her ambition, and even her feminine charm if necessary. Why not? If something as ridiculous as her sex meant that people discounted the skill of her pen, then she was damned if she'd turn down what advantages being a woman offered.

So why not, she now suggested, march into the offices of the *New Orleans Daily Crescent* or the *Picayune* and try the same thing? Secure a position with pure swagger.

"Not *pure* swagger," she corrected. "I can write better, faster, than anyone they've got on staff."

"Oh, you were in the habit of reading the *Crescent* up north?" Franklin asked with a smile.

She thrust out her chin. "I don't have to. The best papers in the country are in New York, and they *still* publish ninety percent rubbish."

He laughed, and she could see the tension easing from his features. "It might work."

"Of course it will work," she said. "If I'm as notorious as Miss—"

She almost said Díaz, then remembered that Franklin didn't know that Josephine had met Francesca before. Admitting that would open her to all sorts of uncomfortable questions that she had no desire to discuss with anyone, let alone a near stranger with whom she intended to remain professional and cordial.

"Excuse me, *Mrs.* Hancock. If I'm as notorious and popular as she claimed, then any secessionist paper would be delighted to have me, woman or no. And not writing gossip about snooty creole society, either. I'll be able to come and go as I please, interviewing generals, writing to boost Southern morale."

"You won't be popular for long. If we succeed, you'll be the most reviled woman south of the Mason–Dixon. And if we don't, if New Orleans stays in rebel hands . . ."

"Say it. I won't flinch."

"Very well. If New Orleans stays rebel, and it's found you played the heroine while really reporting to the enemy . . ." Franklin shook his head. "As you said, woman or no . . . you'll be hung as a traitor and spy."

CHAPTER 8

The Mississippi River delta spread deep into the Gulf of Mexico, and though the US Navy had blockaded the main channels, there was no way to stop up the dozens of minor estuaries and channels that emerged from the swamp. To get up the river, the shallow-draft smuggling boat hired a bayou fisherman to pilot them through.

They followed the man through meandering channels among the mudflats, the waterways surrounded by thick grass and the bony knees of cypress. Turtles sunned on logs, and egret and heron lifted heavily into the air as they approached. The pilot was careful to lead them around sandbars and "sawyers"—uprooted trees that had lodged in the water and swayed back and forth to hook unsuspecting boats.

In spite of the expert navigation, they found themselves up a blocked channel turned into an oxbow lake. It was barely wide enough for the blockade-runner to turn around, but when they tried to turn around they hit a bar. The engine strained, the side-wheel churning in the mud as it tried to free them.

And there they remained, as afternoon turned to night. The weather was sweltering and miserable, and clouds of mosquitoes beset them. Lamps illuminated the eyes of enormous alligators gliding by the side of the boat. Josephine retreated to her room to write by lamplight, until the swarming bugs forced her to turn out the light and pull her blanket over her head.

She rose in the morning to find fishermen in flatboats and canoes surrounding the stuck blockade-runner. Josephine felt almost sorry for the side-wheel captain, a small, nervous creole who spoke a patois French with the lean, hungry-looking men of the delta. First, he'd dumped much of his cargo to outrun the navy steamer, and now he was handing over what must remain of his anticipated profits to the men working to unload the goods and lighten the ship.

It took a full day just to unload the cannons, one after another, onto smaller smuggler boats that appeared from around the bend: flatboats with huge paddles attached to the rear and roof. Next went the rest of the supplies, and the passengers themselves off-loaded into fisherman skiffs to be taken into the swamp. Josephine found herself alone with a hollow-faced, balding man who watched her with a sharp expression as he rowed her up one of the main channels to God knew where. As they traveled, he stopped to check lines tied to the branches of cypress trees. From one of these, he hauled in a large catfish, which he tossed, flopping at Josephine's feet, where it lay gulping for air.

The fisherman soon pulled up to a one-room swamp house on stilts, surrounded by towering cypress that dripped with Spanish moss. He held his boat steady while she climbed out. Her feet squished and filled with muddy water as she picked her way through the cypress knees that thrust from the muck. She hadn't reached the relatively dry ground by the house before the fisherman was paddling away without explanation. He came back a couple of hours later with another woman from the ship. She was a rough-looking sort, like a Kentuckian's wife. The two women sat awkwardly on the porch until the man returned yet again, this time with Francesca Díaz, or Mrs. Hancock, as she styled herself now. The woman used her parasol as a cane as she came off the boat wincing. She appeared to have twisted her ankle or suffered some other injury and seemed none too pleased as she took in their surroundings and then hobbled over to the fisherman's shack.

The Cajun fed them beans and crawdads for supper. By now it was dark, and after supper the three women lay on one side of the room, while their host lay down on the other side. He was asleep at once, snoring.

Francesca edged over to Josephine. "I know you're concerned, but I won't let that swamp man touch us. I have a pepperbox pistol. You know what that is?"

"Like a riverboat gambler carries for when he's caught with marked cards."

"Exactly. You're the youngest and prettiest—he'll go for you first. If you wake up to find that ruffian handling you, give a cry and I'll put a ball in him."

"Thank you." Josephine didn't know what else to say. The swamp man had seemed a rough sort, all right, but the only thing he seemed keen about getting his hands on was the ship owner's silver.

Francesca patted her hand in the dark. "Good. Now don't you worry."

"I was never worried. Anyone touches me and he'll regret it."

"You don't say."

The Kentucky wife groaned and muttered an unladylike oath. "Will you two shut your traps? I'm trying to sleep."

"Sorry," Josephine said. "We'll be quiet."

Josephine was glad to be quiet. There had been something in Francesca's tone that sounded like she'd been winding up to ask more personal questions.

Sleep seemed out of the question. The snoring, the mosquitoes, the hard wood floor, the heat, the smell of sweaty bodies—it was all too much. Add to that the cacophony of animal voices: frogs, buzzing insects, little lizards chirping on the walls around them. Nevertheless, she drifted off a couple of hours later, and woke at dawn when some swamp bird flew overhead with a cry like a strangled cat's.

It had taken five days to cross six hundred miles of open ocean from Havana to the mouth of the delta, but it was a full four days more before they were out of the swamps and steaming north on the river again. Josephine paid special attention to the two forts that guarded a defensible bend in the river. She glanced across the deck of the ship to see Franklin watching keenly.

Francesca came up beside her. "You have your eye on that one. He certainly seems an eligible young bachelor." There was an implied question in the statement.

Josephine looked away, as if bashful. She hadn't spoken to the Pinkerton agent since the mishap in the bayou. "Now you sound like my mother."

"And where does your mother live? Here in New Orleans?"

Josephine glanced back, suddenly sure Francesca was toying with her, that she had figured out who she was—knew perfectly well that Claire de Layerre had died on the Mississippi and this was her daughter.

"My family lives in South Carolina," Josephine said. She chose her words carefully, knowing that she'd be stuck with whatever lie she concocted. "My brother is a volunteer with the First South Carolina Rifles, and my father is a colonel in the militia. Defensive coastal work only, they say. He's not a young man anymore."

"Ah, a colonel. I knew you had the look of a cultured young lady. I'll only be a night and a day in New Orleans, but I'd be honored if you'd join me for supper. Where are you staying?"

"The Paris Hotel. In the Quarter. Do you know it?"

"That's where I'm staying! They have a fine restaurant. You really must."

"Thank you, Mrs. Hancock," Josephine said with a sinking feeling. "That would be lovely."

Once in New Orleans, the two women collected their belongings and took a hansom cab up the muddy streets, past the Cabildo onto Chartres Street, to the fading elegance of the Paris Hotel, where its four stories rose over the French Quarter.

Franklin had telegraphed from New York to reserve Josephine a room, but the hotel claimed they had no room under Mrs. Hancock. What's more, all available rooms had been taken by a group of gentlemen militia called down from plantations upstream, who had been marching back and forth between Jackson and Lafayette Squares for the past two days.

Francesca argued with the man at the desk, alternately blaming the hotel and her husband's slipshod memory. The whole situation seemed contrived, and Josephine started to worry that the next step would be for the older woman to turn with affected embarrassment and ask if she could share a bed. *Oh, and confound it all, I seem to have lost my money. I promise I'll repay you.* It was a card the Colonel might have played against Josephine's mother.

The hotel manager arrived. He didn't seem overly pleased at

the two women in their dirty clothes and hair, bedraggled after their crossing and their misadventure in the swamp. Francesca kept pleading.

"Do you know who this is? This is Josephine Breaux. From the papers! Heroine of our great cause."

Josephine cringed. The manager's eyes widened. The obvious rejoinder was that the so-called heroine had a room already, but the man now checked the books with greater motivation. Almost at once he discovered that a guest had left early, supposedly annoyed by the hard-drinking, gambling planter militia. There was a room, after all. And to Josephine's surprise, it turned out that Francesca had the money to pay for it. She'd begun to worry that her mother's old friend would attach herself to Josephine, barnacle-like, attempting to extract money.

The two rooms were on opposite sides of the hotel, thankfully. Josephine paid the extra money to have a bath drawn up and sent her soiled clothes off for cleaning. She dressed in an evening gown with a hoopskirt. She was fighting exhaustion (the bed seemed comfortable, and the sheets clean) and might have skipped dinner if not for her earlier promise. She found Francesca already downstairs at a table beneath the hiss and warm glow of a gas lamp. She'd also cleaned up. With her rouge and powder fresh and her hair in place, she retained much of the charm of her singing and dancing days. Francesca reminded Josephine of her mother, and the young woman felt a pang of loss.

Francesca pressed for more personal information as they ate. Her behavior straddled the line between the quick, easy intimacy typical of riverboat denizens, and suspicious prying. Josephine refined the story about her supposed family in South Carolina, while trying not to embellish details to the extent she would struggle to remember them were she to encounter Mrs. Hancock again. Hopefully, this was their last encounter.

It turned out that Francesca's riverboat wasn't leaving the city for several days. If Josephine didn't know the city, she could accompany Mrs. Hancock in seeing some of the fine houses and gardens of uptown New Orleans, maybe even visit Congo Square if she weren't too afraid of blacks. Unfortunately, Josephine said, she had determined to stop in at the *Crescent* her first moment in New Orleans. She was anxious to turn her energy to the war effort. That started a new round of questioning, this time about spy work in Washington. This time Josephine played coy. She'd love to discuss details, she said, but loose lips could endanger the cause.

At last, she was able to escape to her rooms. She was supposed to be the newspaper reporter turned spy, in Confederate territory to glean information about troops and river defenses, yet so far she had given up more than she'd gained. Fabricated information, admittedly. Instead, she should have been pumping her mother's old friend for anything useful. The woman must know all sorts of things: the state of fortifications up and down the river, the effectiveness of the blockade, the morale and attitude of the people who lived and worked between St. Louis and the mouth of the river. Instead, Josephine had come away with nothing.

From now on, she vowed, she would be in charge of such encounters, and not reactive. But not with Francesca Díaz Hancock. It didn't matter how tired she felt, Josephine was determined to leave the hotel the next morning before the other woman awoke.

CHAPTER 9

Josephine used the trip to the *Crescent* to regain her confidence. She picked up a copy of the paper, plus one of its rivals, the *Picayune*, before leaving the Paris Hotel. A cab carried her away from the hotel, driven by a striking man wearing a long black coat with tails and a top hat that made him look like a young mulatto Abraham Lincoln.

It had rained during the night, which had cleared some of the filth from the gutters, and the air was fresh enough that she was able to lower her kerchief from her mouth and nose as they clopped up the street, so she could concentrate on reading the news.

The date was August 20, 1861—yesterday's papers. The rebels had apparently won a significant battle in Missouri on the tenth, which had reversed Union gains in the border state. The *Crescent* crowed that Missouri was about to join the Confederacy, but this sounded fanciful. In the east, the nearest she could parse through the sneers and false rumors, General McClellan had organized and strengthened the Union Army of the Potomac and was preparing another push south toward Richmond. The US Navy had captured two forts in the Outer Banks of North Carolina, tightening the blockade.

In short, the stalemate continued. Four months since Fort Sumter and the men on both sides of the Mason–Dixon who had boasted of a short war now looked like fools. It was hard to imagine the conflict ending any time soon. Maybe it would last all the way through 1862 and take several more bloody battles before the South came to its senses.

Twenty minutes later her hands were dirty with newsprint, and as she entered the big open room of the *New Orleans Daily Crescent*, she felt immediately at home. The clip-clip-clip sound of the presses hummed through the building. Men hunched over tables, scribbling furiously with ink-stained fingers. Others gave dictation to women with notepads. A man with round glasses thumbed through line drawings with an artist chewing on his pencil. Others were writing ad copy or hauling bundles of paper tied with twine.

Josephine decided that the man with the round glasses was in charge, and walked over to wait until he was done with the artist.

"He looks dead," he told the artist, slapping down one drawing, which showed a man lying in the street, with bystanders surrounding him. "I want him drunk. Put an empty bottle of whiskey in his hand; make these people more amused than shocked. Put a few whores in the crowd."

"The alderman was found on the levee," the artist complained, "not the Irish Channel."

"I know that. It says so in the confounded article. But that doesn't matter. Make it *look* like the Irish Channel. It's more lurid, will get the outrage flowing."

Josephine had apparently found David Barnhart's New Orleans counterpart. Scandal sold papers everywhere.

The artist hurried off, and she cleared her throat.

The man pushed back his glasses. He had dark, curly hair, a face smudged with ink and newsprint, and a sharp gaze that ranged over her with a skeptical look.

"Are you the new stenographer? Jenkins's girl? So help me God, you had better be faster than that Irish woman. That was an insult."

"I've come for a writing job."

"Oh, you have, have you? And what makes you think you're qualified?"

"My name is Josephine Breaux," she said. "Perhaps you've heard of me."

The man's mouth dropped open. Conversation stopped in the tables nearby, and from there, whispers rippled across the newsroom. Soon, everyone was staring.

The sudden attention made her nervous, but at the same time her heart was pumping with excitement. This was the reception she'd hoped to earn up north, an entire newsroom dropping their work to swoon when she entered. If only it were for her writing and not this other thing. This false reputation she'd earned.

The man adjusted his glasses again. "*The* Josephine Breaux?"

"The same," she said, and raised an eyebrow and glanced around the room at the gaping men, mostly young, who rose from their seats and edged over. "I seem to have lost my employment up north and am wondering if you have a reporter position available on staff."

"Well, I'll be a whiskered catfish. Josephine Breaux." He wiped his hand and held it out. "I'm Solomon Fein, publisher of this rag. And of course you've got a spot. Hell, if I need to, I'll fire one of these hacks."

She took his hand for a vigorous shake and found herself grinning back at his smile and enthusiasm.

There was a bit of New York in his accent, mingled with a trace of old Europe. German, maybe? New Orleans was a mélange of immigrants, creoles, free blacks, and Northerners, in addition to the usual fire-breather secessionists, but if there was any hesitation about the war, it wasn't coming from this publisher. The partisanship in the *Crescent* had made her old paper, the *Morning Clarion*, seem like a paragon of impartial reporting.

"In fact," Fein said, "I've got work for you right now, if you're up to a boat ride downriver. There's business at Fort Jackson I need to cover. How fast can you grab your personal effects?"

At the fort? This was almost too perfect. Franklin had wanted her at the fort posing as a nurse. This would be even better.

"Fast enough."

"Very good. Very good." Fein looked across the newsroom. "Delaney, you're off the hanging. You'll be on the murdered Spaniard who turned up in the Algiers Canal. His landlady owns that boarding house above the gin mill on Gallatin."

"Ah, come on, boss," a young man protested. "Last time I went to Gallatin I almost got knifed."

"What, you think I'd send a lady into that filth hole? It's her first day! Go now, when all the drunks are sleeping it off, and you'll be fine. Now get to it. Quick as a cat. The rest of you monkeys, back to work. We've got a deadline."

Fein took Josephine's arm and led her back toward the pressroom. The humming presses shuddered to a stop, and the last paper came off the press for the folders, who were busy supplying a crowd of dirty, print-stained newsboys for their last haul of the day. They came and went through the back doors into the alley behind, hauling wheelbarrows filled with paper bundles tied in twine. Confederate dollars changed hands between the men running the press and the newsboys. Nobody paid Fein and Josephine any attention.

"Your salary is four bucks a week. You cover a murder or enter the Irish Alley, the swamp, or have to run the gauntlet at Girod or Gallatin Street, you get a bonus of two bits."

"Make it eight dollars. Plus bonuses and expenses."

Fein's eyes widened behind his round glasses. "Is that what they paid you in Washington?"

"No. They paid four fifty. But that was in silver. I figure you'll be paying in greybacks. Four Confederate dollars is about two bucks up north. Anyway, I'm worth more than I was three weeks ago. You get something smuggled past the blockade, you've got to pay a premium."

"So much for Josephine Breaux, patriot and heroine of the Southern cause."

"Says the New York Jew who has doubled the price of his paper since I was last in New Orleans."

"Touché." Far from looking irritated, Fein seemed delighted by her banter. He dodged a moving cart of newspapers. "Eight dollars? It's piracy. Wartime profiteering."

"I could check the other papers, see who's hiring."

"Hah. I'd sell my business to Abe Lincoln himself before I'd see your byline pop up on the *Picayune*. Very well, Miss Breaux. Eight dollars a week, all expenses approved in advance."

"Good." She shook his hand.

"Now I'd better get back there and knock heads, make sure not a word of this is breathed on the street until your first story comes off the press. Then I'm going to personally deliver a copy to those lying, illiterate fools at the *Picayune*. I can't wait to see the look on Ludd's face when he sees who I've snagged. You've got what you need? Deadline is midnight tomorrow. I had a steamer arranged to drop off Delaney and another to pick him up tomorrow—you can take his place."

"What kind of writing do you want? Straight facts or something more embellished?"

"Gimme real rabble-rousing, the kind of press that makes old ladies trade their silver for worthless bonds, and sends Quaker ministers running to the nearest recruiter. You weren't just a spy, you can actually write?"

"What kind of question is that?"

"The most important question of all."

"When your friend Ludd reads my piece, he'll fold up his rag and surrender his press to his creditors."

Fein grinned. "I like you, Breaux. You'll go far on this paper." He pumped her hand again. "Now get downriver and cover that hanging. I want to see every drop of sweat on the scoundrel's forehead when he swings."

She traveled on an outgoing side-wheel blockade-runner carrying bales of cotton. They huffed downriver seventy miles, reaching the forts by afternoon. Fort St. Philip appeared first, on the east bank. It stretched along the waterfront, made of stone and brick, the walls covered in sod. She'd spotted it when passing with the runner but now paid it closer attention. It bristled with at least three dozen guns that she could count. Men watched from the walls beneath a Confederate battle flag, which hung limp in the still, humid air.

The half mile of river between St. Philip and the larger fort downriver was filled with dozens of boats: flatboats drifting in the current, keelboats closer to the bank, poling their way laboriously upriver, and a pair of steamboats whose side-wheels left a distinctive hatched wake trailing behind them. But there were no gunboats of any kind. No fire rafts to come roaring with the current to burn enemy ships to the waterline. And no chain barricade to block the river. A strong Union fleet could have steamed right up from the delta and passed them on its way toward New Orleans.

The boatmen put her to shore at the docks upriver from the second of the two forts. This was Fort Jackson, set roughly a hundred yards back from the levee. It had stone bastions radiating outward to provide the widest possible angles for its cannons, which jutted like dark snouts from the casemates.

Josephine took in the defensive posture of the fort as she approached on foot, and was unimpressed. Even from a distance she could see that the cannons were small and old, which meant they were likely smoothbore and not rifled. They'd be no match for Union gunboats. The earthworks were partially eroded by time and the elements, and the embrasures and parapets had extensive unrepaired damage. Josephine had personally toured the fortifications being built in northern Virginia and in and around Washington, and what she saw here was inferior. It brought to mind the unprepared state of national defense in the days before the war began.

She followed an oxcart through the marshy land surrounding the fort and, as the road passed through a thicket of swamp grass, came upon a team of slaves digging a defensive moat beneath the watchful eye of an overseer on horseback. Other than that, she saw few efforts to reinforce the fortifications. Even more shamefully, there were only a handful of men at the lookout points, and nobody challenged her as she strolled across the drawbridge and into the center of the fort. A crude gallows stood in the middle of the yard. It had no platform and was little more than a single wooden hook with a dangling noose.

Josephine hadn't known what she'd find at the fort—Solomon Fein hadn't given her many instructions—but she'd assumed that the military command would be expecting someone from the *Crescent*. Apparently not.

A pair of sweating young guards finally appeared and demanded to see a pass. Further questioning revealed that the pair had never heard of Josephine Breaux, had never read or even heard of the *Crescent*, and knew little about the hanging. One of them said there were two men, a white and a black. The other insisted it was just a black man. Was he slave or free? Nobody knew.

She was getting frustrated when a handsome young officer appeared, dressed in a cadet gray frock coat that draped to his knees. He gave his name as Major Dunbar. She pegged his accent from upriver, probably Illinois, but loyalties had become fluid. He was polite when she said she was from the *Crescent*, and allowed that she could witness the hanging in the morning. When she pressed for details, he grew reticent.

"It is purely a military manner, Miss—"

"Breaux."

"Miss Breaux. I didn't want a spectacle. My only duty is to execute justice so that others may be dissuaded from similar treasonous acts."

"Surely you can answer some simple questions. Is there one man or two?"

"Two traitors were located. One will be hanged. The other will be given six months' imprisonment and hard labor, then be expelled north."

"That sounds . . . lenient. Was the condemned man the ringleader?"

"They were both found guilty before a military tribunal, that is all I can tell you."

"Yet one is hanging and the other will go free after a few months?"

"Miss Breaux," Dunbar said, his tone exasperated. "I have agreed you shall stay and witness the hanging. You may collect whatever details from that you may. But if you wish more information, you'll have to wait for Colonel Morgan. He will return at the beginning of the month."

"Hullo!" a voice cried from the gatehouse.

Two men entered the yard, one older, with a steel-gray beard and a cane, and the other a tall, slender fellow with big ears and a prominent Adam's apple, his hair thick and wavy. It was he who had called.

The younger man proved to be James Hines from the *New Orleans Bee*, and the older Hyrum Potterman from the *True Delta*. A few minutes later, a heavyset, red-faced man came huffing into the yard and introduced himself as Stanley Ludd from the *Picayune*. This was Solomon Fein's rival.

When she introduced herself, all three reporters gaped at her, none more so than Ludd. She imagined him rushing to the fort's telegraph station the instant he was alone to send a message back to his paper. So much for Solomon Fein's hopes to stun the man with a personally delivered copy of the *Crescent* bearing Josephine's byline.

"I don't know what Fein is paying you, but I'll beat it," Ludd said.

"Don't trust this fellow," Potterman said in a deep baritone that made him sound like a real Southern gentleman. He pointed his cane as Ludd. "The *Picayune* is filled with Republicans. Its subscription base is illiterate Irishmen, who buy it for the announcements about bordellos and grog houses. What, that's three advertisements the *Picayune* has run for Lady Nell's just this week?"

Ludd used a handkerchief to wipe at his face and the back of his neck. "You seem quite the expert on bordellos. Are you sure it's wise for a man of your age to be visiting Lady Nell's?"

"These men are both inveterate liars," Hines said, his Adam's apple bobbing. "When you leave the *Crescent*, remember you'll always have a job at the *Bee*. What is Fein paying you? I'll give you two dollars more."

"Not even one column inch, and y'all are already offering me a job?" Josephine asked. "Let's wait until you've read a few of my pieces before we talk."

Potterman tapped his cane tip on the ground. "What, no confidence in your writing?"

She smiled. "On the contrary. I don't want to negotiate before you've seen what I can offer."

The men went several more rounds of banter and bickering. Nevertheless, there seemed to be no real animosity between the three, and they had even come downriver together. The true rivalry seemed to be between the *Bee*, the *True Delta*, and the *Picayune* on one side, and the *Crescent* on the other. In the competition to be the most rabid secessionist, Solomon Fein seemed to have won, and his circulation was on the rise at the expense of the other three.

As for the reporters, Josephine pegged them by type: Ludd was the aggressive striver, the publisher who was also a writer and editorialist, Potterman was the aging reporter who turned in stories that were as thrilling as a log floating downriver, and Hines, the tall, gangly one, was the true writer. He'd already jotted a few words in a notebook and was paying closer attention to their surroundings than the others.

"Well, sir," Potterman said to Major Dunbar, who had been standing with an exasperated expression as the reporters went back and forth. "We understand you have two Yankee spies. One for hanging, one for hard labor. Let's see these villains and pay our respects."

Major Dunbar may have stood as firm as General Jackson at Bull Run when it was only Josephine but, faced with a united front from the New Orleans press, seemed to recognize that discretion was the better part of valor and retreated from the battlefield. He called over the two privates armed with muskets and sent them off for the prisoners.

"Very worrying, Major, very worrying," Potterman said with a look around. "I'm an old military man myself, and I don't like what I see here."

"How many men do you have in the fort?" Josephine said.

Dunbar stared hard in the direction of the departed privates. "That's a military secret. These aren't the only spies on the river. Some spies no doubt read the newspapers."

"We're all patriots," Ludd said indignantly. "We wouldn't publish anything that would harm Southern interests."

That was a ridiculous assertion. Unless the New Orleans press was more disciplined than either its Richmond or Washington counterparts, she expected these men would happily blab the deepest secrets of the Confederacy if it meant selling a few more papers.

"I'm sure you wouldn't," Dunbar said, and his tone made it clear that he was thinking the same thing. "But never you mind. We're well prepared with men and arms to repel any attempt by the enemy to pass the forts, and growing more prepared by the day."

The privates led out the two prisoners, who stood blinking at the sun before they were pushed forward. The men had no shoes and wore ragged trousers and torn, filthy shirts. The chains at their ankles clanked as they dragged along iron cannonballs.

"So these are the spies," Potterman said. He raised his bushy gray eyebrows, and his mustache twitched. "Which one did you say would be hung?"

The other men chuckled at the question. One prisoner was white, the other black. It went without saying which of the men had been sentenced to hard labor and which would swing by the neck.

CHAPTER 10

The four reporters ate an early supper in the officers' mess. The cook apologized for the lack of beef or pork due to the blockade, but he was able to serve a passable gumbo with shrimp and fish. It could have used more seasoning, but there was plenty of it.

Seven other officers sat with Dunbar at the table, and from bits of conversation pieced together during the meal, Josephine guessed there were no more than eighty other troops in the fort. James Hines, the one she'd pegged as the real writer, asked a number of pointed questions, which saved Josephine the risk of sounding too keen for details. Dunbar maintained his discipline in deflecting questions and cut off his officers whenever one grew helpful.

After supper, the reporters drew straws to determine who got first crack at interviewing the prisoners, and Josephine drew the shortest. Not without some sleight of hand on Potterman's part, as she'd spotted the older man shuffling the straws as she drew. She didn't see any great disadvantage to going last, so she let him get away with it.

While she waited her turn, she paced the wall behind the parapet, watching boats slip by on the river below them. A former passenger ferry fitted with welded steel plate puffed downriver, flying the Confederate naval jack of a circle of stars on a blue field. She drew her notebook from her satchel, glanced to make sure no soldiers were watching, and drew a quick sketch, with as many identifying details as she could. She wondered if it were a commerce raider trying to slip into the Gulf or a ship from the fledgling Confederate navy. Either way, it was useful information to pass to the Union.

She heard shouts in what sounded like German from down below inside the fort. Then came Potterman's deep baritone. If the older man from the *True Delta* was already with the prisoner, then it was almost her turn. She'd expected her wait to be longer.

Josephine slapped at mosquitoes as she turned her attention to the interior of the fort. Out came Potterman, shaking his head. He lit a pipe, leaned on his cane, and chatted in a low voice with Ludd.

When she came down, the two men were smoking and laughing. Ludd made some joke about why it took longer to hang a free black man than a slave.

"Well, here is our Southern beauty," Potterman said. "Fine night, Miss Breaux, fine night."

"Your turn," Ludd told her. The heavy man was still sweating profusely in the thick, swampy air. "Though I dare say you won't get anything for your troubles."

"You mean neither of you got anything useful?" she asked.

The two men passed a look and a knowing smile. "I wouldn't say that," Ludd said. "I only said *you* wouldn't get anything. We're old hands at this business. Do this long enough and you can get a good interview from an alligator."

Potterman must have see the irritation flash across her face, because he tucked his pipe into the corner of his mouth and patted her shoulder like she was a child. "There now, child. I reckon you got yourself some scoops up north, but this here business is different. Why, the runaway slave is a simpleton, and the white fellow refuses to speak anything but German."

"I saw you trying to charm the major at supper," Ludd said. "That may work with the Yankees, but Major Dunbar is a true Southerner, a professional. He won't fall for that sort of nonsense." He spread his hands. "Once you take away feminine wiles, there's not much left for you, Miss Breaux. I'm afraid you're in over your head."

The other man chuckled at this as he puffed on his pipe.

"A true Southerner?" Josephine said. "Dunbar was raised in Illinois, as any fool could hear from his accent. As for you," she added, turning to Potterman, who was still chuckling from Ludd's barb, "I saw what you did when we drew straws. You must think I'm blind. You're clumsy, as well as a fool. It's safe to say you'd never make it as a riverboat gambler."

She picked up her skirts and turned away, still fuming, even as she knew she shouldn't have let the patronizing old men get her dander up. For one, she'd soon have the same reputation as a young hothead that she'd earned in Washington. More importantly, she couldn't get in the habit of blurting out information. She was in the information *collecting* business, not sharing.

The ground was so damp here behind the levee, with swamp all around, that the jail was built above grade like the rest of the fort. There were three cells with heavy wooden doors, the first two of which held a prisoner. The third was empty.

The damp had rotted the wood around the bars on the doors, and she supposed that a determined prisoner might dig his way out if he had a spoon or shard of rock to scoop at the rot so as to loosen the bars, and presuming he were slender enough to fit through the window. These two men, however, were chained to the stone wall opposite, out of reach of the doors.

A soldier in a gray uniform stood by the doorway. Josephine suggested he go outside so the prisoners would loosen their tongues, but he would have none of it. Dunbar had warned him not to leave the prisoners alone with any of the reporters.

"Don't reckon you'll try to bust them out," the soldier said, "but the major keeps discipline. I dare say it's been a nice change around here. We're short of men, and morale is low—there's no pretending otherwise."

"Why don't they send reinforcements? Everyone knows how important these forts are."

"The governor raised some men, but as soon as they was properly drilled, Jeff Davis called them to Richmond. Reckon that makes sense. Got to stop them Yanks in Virginia."

"None of that matters if we lose the Mississippi."

"Nope. That it don't."

Losing, or rather gaining the Mississippi was exactly what she was trying to accomplish on behalf of the Union, but she couldn't help but feel sorry for this earnest young man from upriver, maybe Tennessee from the sound of it.

"How long have you been here?" she asked.

"You go on, then, miss. Major says I'm to let you see the prisoners, but I'm not to answer questions myself. I don't want to be out with the slaves digging the canal 'cause I couldn't keep my mouth shut."

"There's that discipline you were talking about. Well, I wouldn't want to get you in trouble when you're only doing your duty. You keep on doing it, Private."

Josephine peered through the bars at the white prisoner, who did, indeed, have a German look about him, now that it had been pointed out.

"Do you speak English?" she asked him.

The man glanced at her and scowled. It was now almost dark outside, with only a little bit of light streaming through a barred window high up. He said something to her. Now that she was closer, it didn't sound like German, but maybe Swedish or Norwegian. She tried again, and again he answered in his foreign tongue. After a few more attempts she gave up, thinking that maybe the two scoffers outside were right.

Josephine turned to the second cell. The black man sitting in the corner looked up as she cleared her throat at the barred window.

"Hello, I'm Miss Breaux. What's your name?"

"Caleb, ma'am."

"May I ask you a few questions?"

"Yes, ma'am. Are you with the newspaper like them other men?"

"Yes, I am. Did they talk to you?"

"A little. Mostly, they tried to talk to Hans, but you can see that didn't help."

"Is he German, or something else?"

"Don't know. He's simple in the head." Caleb shifted, clinking his chains.

"They told me you were the simple one."

"I can't read or write, ma'am, but I ain't simple. I'll show you." He held up his hands. "Want to see how I can do sums with just my fingers?"

He had a pleasant voice and sounded so reasonable that she found herself doubting this whole hanging business.

"No need, I believe you, Caleb." She hesitated. "Are you a spy?"

He hung his head. "'Fraid so. I shouldn't have done it. I know that now."

Any thoughts she might have harbored of uncovering the real truth of the matter, and thus freeing an innocent man, now vanished. It was a typical reporter fantasy, invariably disabused.

"What did you do, Caleb?"

"Well, Miss Breaux, a white man been paying me to watch the militias. I go up to Lafayette Square and watch them Zouaves in their blue pantaloons and tasseled caps. Marching. And I count 'em. Every time I do that, a man gives me a dollar. My sister got the consumption, and I buy her patent medicine for the cough, you see. When the soldiers catch me, they beat me and twist my thumbs, but I couldn't tell 'em who paid me. A Yankee from up north, that's all I figured."

As he spoke, Josephine took notes, trying to catch the flavor of his words and not just the substance. She made a quick sketch to help guide the illustrator, but no doubt Fein would want the artist to show the hanging itself in the most grisly way imaginable and not a forlorn prisoner in the corner with his knees drawn up against his chest. Sell more papers.

"But how did you end up here, at the fort?"

"I got to thinking, if he gives me a dollar for reporting on the troops in N'awlins, maybe news from the forts be good for two dollars. They was asking at Lafayette for free blacks and Irishmen to dig the earthworks, an' I figure I get paid for that, and get paid more when I tell the Yankee how many men and guns there are at the fort."

This was all making Josephine squirm. It was almost exactly what she was doing here herself, spying on the defenses of the river fortifications. But with critical differences. She hadn't suffered back-breaking work in the sun but had sat down with a major to be fed the best food Fort Jackson could offer. She was getting paid by the newspaper, paid a salary by the Pinkertons, and had her own resources as well. This man had risked his life, and what had she done?

In spite of that, she had one thing in common with Caleb. Both of them had thrown in their lot with the United States and not with the supposedly glorious cause of their Southern homeland.

"How'd you get caught?"

"We was working in the sun, digging earthworks, when this Irishman starts saying 'bout how the Government gonna come downriver in their gunboats, and we'll be working for the Yankees 'fore long. That gets me talking, and once I start, I can't scarcely stop. Turn out that Irishman been reporting to the soldiers, an' he tells the major that I'm spying for the Yankees." Caleb looked down at his thick, calloused fingers. "Reckon I *am* the simple one, after all."

Josephine's heart sank as she imagined how it had happened. Maybe the Irishman hated free blacks, competing for low-wage labor, or maybe the soldiers paid him to stir up gossip in the laborers to see what turned out. Either way, Caleb had shown enough initiative to come spying at the forts but hadn't been sophisticated enough to keep his mouth shut at a critical time.

"But I still don't understand about Hans," she said. From the cell next door, the other man babbled something, perhaps hearing his name. "Why did they throw him in chains if you weren't working for him, and if he's simple?"

"Reckon they figure a black man ain't smart enough to do spying hisself. They was beating my feet, asking who I was working for, and I said the first name I think of. Poor Hans, he gonna get six months' hard labor. That's my fault; I shouldn't have said it."

"But Caleb, you know what they're doing to you tomorrow, right?"

"I knows it."

Again, he hung his head.

Josephine was thinking furiously about how she would save Caleb's life, but first she wondered if she should try to extract any more information, especially about the Northerner who had paid the man to count the troops marching at Lafayette Square. But the private in the hall was still standing close enough to hear every word, and she didn't want the condemned man to suddenly remember something useful that would help the Confederates track down the real spy and arrest him.

So she asked Caleb about his family, thinking a bit of background would flesh out her article. He'd been born a house slave to a fine New Orleans family, who had freed Caleb and his younger sister when they came of age. The sister had kept working for the family for a number of years longer, while Caleb had taken up work on the docks as a stevedore. With the blockade, there wasn't enough work there to go around, so he'd taken such jobs as he could find. He'd married a few years ago, had a daughter, but both wife and daughter had died in the yellow-fever plague of 1853. Caleb never remarried, and now he lived with his sister, who'd been badly burned when a gas lamp exploded.

"I fear for her, Miss Breaux. I fear for her good. She can't get work on account of a burned face, and now she need medicine for the consumption."

Josephine left the cells a few minutes later and walked thoughtfully through the yard. Ludd and Potterman were still puffing away and joking. No sign of the younger man, Hines from the *New Orleans Bee*, and she supposed he, at least, was in his chamber doing actual writing.

Ludd and Potterman asked if she'd learned anything from the black man and the simpleton, and she shrugged and said she hadn't, even though her column was already half-composed in her mind, save for the part about the actual hanging. Or a non-hanging, if she could manage it. Ludd and Potterman could read her story in the *Crescent* like anyone else.

It took some time to find Major Dunbar. He was up top on the wall, almost exactly where Josephine had been waiting earlier. He watched boats go by, their lights blinking. A lantern glowed through a cloud of bugs from atop a flatboat, where a banjo twanged and men sang.

Dunbar glanced at her as she came up, but it was too dark to read his expression.

"The hanging is precisely at nine o'clock," he said. "I won't be moving it up so you can file your story earlier."

"Is that what the others are asking?" she asked.

He grunted.

"That wasn't what I wanted to say," she said. "I'm worried there has been a mistake."

"How do you mean?"

"For a start, the white man is simple—he isn't any sort of Machiavellian spy who put that other poor fellow up for it."

"Yes, I know," Dunbar said. "But he's the one Caleb Freedman fingered."

"Under torture."

"Under hard questioning, it's true. But that doesn't matter. A dozen men heard Caleb Freedman's confession, and it was widely reported up and down the river. We'll ship the German north, lock him up a few more weeks, and let him loose in Memphis or Vicksburg."

"But what about Caleb's true master? The one who was paying him to count troops in the city? You know about him, right?"

"Yes, I do. What about him?"

"Have you caught him?"

"Well, no," Dunbar admitted. "But we're searching for the man. We'll get him."

"How will you manage that if you hang the black man? He'll lay low and escape. If I were you, I'd declare leniency—or whatever term you want to use—and let Caleb go back to New Orleans. Then you can watch him, wait for the true spy to show himself, and arrest him."

"You are hopelessly naïve, Miss Breaux. What would your friends from the *Picayune* and the *True Delta* say if I took a confessed spy, some dumb n—"

"But he didn't do anything!" she interrupted. "He was counting men and guns."

"That's more than enough. And in the morning, he will hang. It will serve as an example. Look around you. We're undermanned and undergunned. We can't afford the dregs of New Orleans rising up because they think we're soft. Our liberty is at stake here."

"Our liberty," she repeated. "What a strange term, when half the state lives in bondage."

His face hardened. "The laws of the land are not mine to change. My duty is to fight to make sure we are the ones to set them, not Washington and certainly not the Black Republican who occupies the Executive Mansion."

Josephine tried a different tack. "Be that as it may, it wouldn't hurt to keep Caleb Freedman imprisoned for a stretch until we see what turns up. Killing is awfully permanent. And I've seen a hanging before, Major. It's an ugly thing."

"So have I. Several hangings, in fact. But let me ask you this. Were the deaths you saw at Manassas any less ugly?"

She thought about the men crying for water, begging to be shot and put out of their misery, the young soldiers—boys, really—with missing legs. The scraping rasp of the bone saw in field hospitals. The screams.

"They were ugly," she said in a quiet voice.

"And if we aren't careful," Dunbar said firmly, "the Yankees will see our soft underbelly. There will be death and bloodshed here, too. Is that what you want?"

"No."

"Good. Then we're agreed. The prisoner will hang in the morning, and you will have your story."

CHAPTER 11

Josephine was smiling in the picture taken with the Colonel when she was thirteen. Her expression was cheery, her smile broad. When she looked at it, she could scarcely believe that it had been taken before one of the ugliest moments of her life. First, there was the business with the runaway slaves, followed by the trouble on the riverboat later that night, their last on the *Crescent Queen*.

The Colonel had been traveling with Josephine and Claire for three months as they made a pair of lazy tours up and down the river. Because both Claire and the Colonel were up late into the night, the former dancing and singing and the latter gambling until dawn, Josephine was in the habit of getting out of her blankets on the floor and leaving the others in bed while she climbed up to the promenade to read. Sometimes, when she came back too early, she could hear them making love, and would slink away again without opening the stateroom door.

After the Colonel had disappeared for two years when she was eight, the day of the fair, she'd refused to talk to him the next time he came, and the time after that, a few months later. He finally won her over with a treasure that had changed her life: a wooden crate full of books. By then, she knew how to read and had read whatever she could get her hands on, but these were so much more. In the box she found so many wonderful stories: *Ivanhoe, Frankenstein, The Hunchback of Notre-Dame, The Three Musketeers*. She preferred the stories of war and adventure.

One small book with the dry title of *The Recollections of a Scots Grey Under Wellington at the Battle of Waterloo* sat unread for nearly two years before she picked it up. But when she did, it inspired a curiosity about all matters military that never faded. After that, she took note of every river fort they passed, and pestered Indian fighters and Mexican War veterans who came on board to give her exhaustive accounts of their battles and campaigns.

One morning, she was engrossed in *The Deerslayer*, another well-worn favorite, as *Crescent Queen* slipped between two treacherous bars near the Missouri side of the river. The pilot had eased them around the lower bar while a spotter up front warned about a tree lodged below the surface that pointed upstream, like a reverse sawyer. These were called "preachers," and, because they dipped in the current, could be difficult to spot. This time, they came around safely.

The momentary excitement passed, and Josephine was dipping her nose into her book again when the sound of baying hounds caught her ear, followed by a gunshot. She dropped the book and sprang to her feet, searching the shoreline ahead of them, where movement caught her eye in the brush and trees lining the bank. Three black men grabbed a rowboat that had been hidden in the weeds and pushed it into the current. They were no more than two hundred yards upstream of the slowly advancing *Crescent Queen*, her stacks smoking as she built speed.

The men got the boat away from shore and rowed furiously for the opposite shore, each with an oar. The dogs, the gunshot, the black men—Josephine knew exactly what was happening. This shore was Missouri, a slave state. The opposite bank was Illinois, and free.

Slavers had legal right to cross from Missouri to recover their property, but the folk on the free side were just as likely to grab the tar and feathers as they were to help bounty hunters recover human contraband. Depended on the town.

The baying dogs reached the Missouri shore and with them five white men with guns. They aimed, and there were flashes of light and puffs of smoke, followed an instant later by the crack of rifles. The escaping slaves hadn't made it more than sixty yards offshore, and though they'd hunched down at the sight of their enemy, she was sure the shooters would hit their marks. Miraculously, every shot missed, and the men got up and kept rowing, even as the men on shore hurried to reload. Josephine didn't know a thing about the drama playing out before her but what her eyes and imagination could supply, but she found herself leaning over the railing, straining anxiously, wanting the men to escape.

The fastest two men onshore finished reloading and brought their rifles up almost simultaneously. They fired. This time, the man at the rear of the boat slumped forward without a cry, and his oar slipped from his grasp and went drifting downstream. The other two kept rowing without a pause. They were only yards in front of the steamboat by now, which was bearing down on them at increasing speed. She held her breath.

The other three shooters had reloaded by now, but before they could bring their weapons to bear, the rowboat slipped in front of the bow of *Crescent Queen* with only inches to spare. The steamboat temporarily shielded them from fire.

Josephine raced around the promenade to the other side, her heart pounding. It was early in the morning, and only a handful of passengers were out on the decks and promenade, but those who were up crowded the railing to watch the black men row past in their tiny boat. They struggled to get clear of the ship's wake. By the time the men were downstream from *Crescent Queen*, the steamboat had protected them long enough to get them out of range of the riflemen on shore. And the bounty hunters did not appear to have a boat to give chase. It would seem that the men would escape to the other side.

Some of the passengers on the deck directly below her were making disgusted comments, but a few were shaking hands and slapping each other on the back. Abolitionists, perhaps, or maybe like Josephine, they simply were rooting for the underdog. It was a hard person who could watch men fleeing for their lives from men with guns and dogs and not feel sympathy.

A shout sounded from the front deck, and she looked up to see a skiff shoving off from *Crescent Queen*. It was the rowboat the captain sent ashore for supplies when they were in the bayou and couldn't find a mooring. Now it was rowed by several firemen from the boiler room, burly fellows with powerful forearms and shoulders earned from throwing cord after cord of wood into the furnaces. They rowed after the two runaways. The passengers who'd been pleased by the escape now fell silent, while others cheered.

The side-wheel on *Crescent Queen* stopped churning, and they began to drift back downstream, which shortly brought them close to the drama playing out in the middle of the river. The pursuers kept up with the two fleeing men and their slumped-over companion but drew no closer. Josephine's knuckles turned white from clenching the rail. People on the deck of the riverboat shouted encouragement to one side or the other. This brought arguments and jeers among the two sides. One man threw a punch. Another man went down from the blow. A woman screamed. Soon, it was a brawl.

The rowboat from *Crescent Queen* began to gain as the runaways tired. When the pursuing boat pulled alongside, two of the firemen jumped into the other boat, where they beat at the two men to subdue them. The runaways fought back. One of the black men went over the side and into the water. He came up flailing, drifting downstream, seemingly unable to swim, and struggling to keep his head above water.

The final man gave up, and the remaining men in the rowboat now went after the drowning man in the river. He came up one last time, then went under. By the time the rowboat reached him, there was nothing left but swirling eddies, with the men from *Crescent Queen* poking around helplessly with their paddles. The brawling on the steamboat stopped, and people stared out, subdued.

"Some men are dealt the ace in life," the Colonel said from over Josephine's shoulder. "And others draw nothing but the deuce."

He had pulled on his trousers, but his frilled shirt was unbuttoned at the collar and the wrists, as if he'd tossed it on to hurry out and see what the commotion was about. He had picked up her copy of *The Deerslayer* where she'd dropped it, and now handed it to her.

"Have you ever seen a hanging?" he asked as men from the deck of *Crescent Queen* threw out ropes to bring in the two rowboats.

Josephine shook her head. Her guts felt loose and sloshy. "Is that what's going to happen?"

The Colonel gave a grim nod toward the near bank, where the initial pursuers still waited with their baying hounds. They'd tossed a rope over a tree branch, and one of the men was fashioning a noose. The steamboat nudged toward shore.

Claire and the Colonel wanted Josephine to stay in her room, but they didn't forbid her from going ashore with the bulk of the passengers from *Crescent Queen*. She had a morbid, sickly fascination with the thought of a hanging, something she'd read about many times but never witnessed. Lately she'd taken to writing down the bizarre and curious things she observed in a leather-bound notebook the Colonel had won in a game of faro. Without knowing how, she thought this experience might be important to record.

Hundreds of passengers came to shore in skiffs and milled around in the marshy woods on the natural levee thrown up by the Mississippi. The bounty hunters hung the wounded man first, throwing him groaning across the saddle of a horse and fitting the noose around his neck. When they drove off the horse, Josephine looked away. The crowd fell silent, and there was no sound but the creak of rope and the smooth sighing of the river itself at their rear.

They tossed the dead, bloody slave to one side and wrestled the final man onto the horse. He struggled, pleading, cursing, jabbering something about there having been a mistake. He tried to throw himself off the horse. The others held him up and tried to get the noose over his head.

Josephine was determined to look this time, deciding that she'd been cowardly the first time. The musketeers from her Dumas novel would never look away. She had already picked up enough conversation from the men with the hounds to know that the black men had struck and perhaps killed a white man while escaping their master. It was not the sort of crime that required a judge or jury, but there was still something . . . unjust about the situation that she couldn't pinpoint.

Suddenly, the Colonel stiffened and let out a hiss.

"What is it?" Claire asked.

He gave Josephine's mother a pinched, worried look. "I know that man. He was Leroy de Camp's cook."

"De Camp?"

"A planter from Baton Rouge. More money than skill with cards. Had to sell his land to pay his debts."

"Keep quiet," Claire said. "This is not the time."

Somehow, the condemned man had squirmed out of the noose again, bobbing and dipping his head. The bounty hunters cursed and struck him with rifle butts.

"But de Camp told me he'd freed his house slaves when he sold out. This fellow must be a freedman. He can't be a runaway."

"Say something," Josephine urged.

"Should I?" the Colonel asked Claire, not the girl.

"I-I don't know," Claire said nervously. "Maybe de Camp lied to you. Or maybe he sold this one first to help settle the debts. Why were they fleeing if they're not runaways?"

"Nobody has asked the black man," Josephine pointed out. "Maybe he can explain."

"They say he killed a man," Claire said.

None of the passengers were looking at them. Instead, they were watching the drama play out as the black man got free of the noose again. People laughed. Others jeered at the red-faced, cursing bounty hunters.

"Of course they'd say that," the Colonel told Claire. He was wringing his hands. "If only we were in a free state. Where is that fellow from Boston? As good as admitted he's an abolitionist. I'd like him with me if things get ugly."

"You're going to do it, aren't you?" Claire said. She shot a glance at her daughter. "Josie, go back to the rowboat and wait. Hurry, now. It's a mob, and we're about to do something foolhardy, heaven help us."

Josephine didn't obey.

The Colonel cleared his throat, took off his hat, and waved it to draw attention to himself. "Here, now," he began tentatively. "I have something important to say."

A few faces turned toward them, and he cleared his throat again. But then a shout came from the men with the horse and the runaway, and all attention turned back to them.

The bounty hunters had got the noose over the man's head at last, and the instant it was fit in place and tightened against his throat, someone slapped the horse on the rump and it shied off. The black man fell from the saddle, and the rope caught around his neck. This time, after the long struggle, the crowd from the riverboat let out a big holler. The Colonel tried to push forward but couldn't get through the crowd.

In spite of her earlier promise to herself, Josephine looked away again. She didn't look back until it was over.

That night, the Colonel did something stupid. It was an elementary blunder for a professional riverboat gambler. He played cards while he was drunk.

Josephine was upstairs in her room when it happened, first writing about the hanging, and then in bed, trying unsuccessfully to fall asleep. A few days later, when the Colonel had disappeared again, her mother told her what had happened.

After tossing back a quantity of gin, the Colonel had joined a game of poker in the saloon with three men he'd identified as plantation-owning slavers, determined to take them for everything they had. For a time, he'd had some success, but then, being drunk, made a sloppy mistake. The Colonel, who had always declared himself a square player, was caught palming cards and dealing from the bottom—what they called "laying the bottom stock." The outraged planters, already down several hundred dollars, had searched him at gunpoint. They found him in possession of all manner of cheats: a shiner for reading opponent hands, a poker ring with a needle for making indentations in the back of cards, and several other so-called advantage tools.

Guns were drawn. Demands came for a second lynching.

That's when Josephine's mother came down from the stage, where she'd been dancing. Wielding the pepperbox pistol she kept strapped to her inner thigh for fending off overeager suitors, she fired off three shots, hitting one man in the shoulder, while the Colonel wrestled free a pistol from one of his accusers.

Josephine was still awake in bed when her mother and the Colonel came flying in. They locked the stateroom and dragged the bureau in front of the door. Claire reloaded her pepperbox while the Colonel threw open his trunk and recovered a bowie knife, which he set on his lap as he took a seat opposite the door. Neither of them would tell Josephine what was going on.

The next morning, the captain of *Crescent Queen* eased up to the shore a few miles south of Hog Shoals, Missouri, where Claire, the Colonel, and Josephine were unceremoniously dumped with their possessions. A muddy farm road led through the woods and north along the bank toward Hog Shoals. Josephine sadly watched the boat huff upriver and around the bend with a blast of the steam whistle.

"Well, then," Claire said, gathering up her skirts and sitting on her trunk. "A sad end to that chapter of life."

"What do we do now, Mama?" Josephine asked nervously. "Can you get another position, or are you too old now?"

Josephine was thirteen, with an overheated imagination that came from reading too many novels, and she had already imagined scenarios in which she was taught to dance for groping old men.

"Heavens, Josie, I'm barely thirty years old, and I only fess to twenty-seven. Just last month, the owner of *Cairo Red* offered me a position and a bigger stateroom. I suppose that's our next step, assuming we can find the confounded thing. It might be in Ohio, for all we know."

The Colonel ignored Claire and Josephine while he rummaged through his trunk. He filled his pockets with gold watches, coins, and silver snuffboxes. Then he took out a small wooden box with a black-lacquered surface and a curious, red-and-green-painted scene on the lid. He tucked it experimentally inside his jacket with a frown before glancing over to Josephine.

"Here, why don't you keep this until I get back."

The girl took the box and traced a finger over the painting, which was a mountain-lined harbor with Oriental boats. The box was empty.

"Whatever you do, don't lose it," he said.

"How would I lose it? I'm not going anywhere. Anyway, what's so special about it?"

"Just keep it safe. Promise me that. No matter what."

"All right," she said, confused.

"So that's it?" Claire demanded. "After I saved your life, got thrown out of house and home, this is how you repay me? And what about my girl? You're going to leave her here in the woods? And with these heavy trunks, too. They have all of my clothing, Josephine's books—everything we own in the world. What kind of man are you?"

"Of course I'm coming back." The Colonel came over and tried to kiss Claire, but she pushed him away. "But for all I know those men sent word to shore and I'll find a half-dozen ruffians waiting to rob us and toss our bleeding, unconscious bodies into the river. I'll make sure it's safe and then send for you."

"You are a liar and no gentleman," Claire said. "I saw you stuffing your pockets with gold. You wouldn't have done that if you thought you'd be robbed."

"Don't go away," Josephine said sadly. She knew her mother was right, not just because of the gold, but also because of how he'd spoken about the box.

Now he came to give the girl a kiss, this one on the forehead. "I'm not going anywhere. I'm being cautious. Two hours, that's all you have to wait, then I'll have a carriage back here to carry you into town. We'll figure out what to do then."

He set off at a brisk pace up the road. Claire and Josephine stared after him.

Two hours later the carriage came back, but not with the Colonel. When they got to Hog Shoals, they discovered that he'd jumped on another steamer and set off back down the river.

Josephine wouldn't see him again until the night her mother died.

CHAPTER 12

Josephine filed her first story about the hanging at Fort Jackson via the fort's own telegraph office. It was a hastily sketched piece, with placeholders for details that some other staff writer at the *Crescent* would have to fill in.

After that, she caught a ride upriver on one of the Confederate navy's ships of the mosquito fleet, the converted revenue cutter *Pickens*. To her eye, a single shot to the flimsy deck would send the boat down to the mud, and it was weakly armed with a pair of twenty-four-pounder carronades and single eight-inch columbiad. Nevertheless, other boats in the river saluted *Pickens* with flags and waving hats as if she were the *USS Richmond*, a massive sloop of war with twenty-two guns lurking in the Gulf that could have outgunned the entire mosquito fleet on her own.

Josephine took note of river defenses as *Pickens* struggled against the current, but the bulk of her effort was spent writing a longer story about the hanging. Unlike the incident in her childhood, this time she had forced herself to watch as the rope choked the life out of a man. She figured she owed it to Caleb Freedman. He was being hung as a Union spy, the same crime of which she was guilty. It was only by the grace of Providence that their positions weren't reversed.

Caleb had asked quietly for mercy as they led him into the yard, but he hadn't cried or begged, and had barely trembled when they fit the hood over his head and slipped the noose into place.

The entire eighty-two men of the fort had come to watch, as well as a few dozen from St. Philip on the opposite bank. Not a very impressive garrison. Some of the soldiers jeered, but Major Dunbar ordered them into silence and delivered a biting remark about how the man in the noose was showing more dignity than the lot of them.

They hoisted Caleb up, where he struggled for two long minutes before falling still. After that, Dunbar, looking troubled, ordered the man lowered and buried in an unmarked grave in the swamp. When Josephine boarded *Pickens*, she cast a glance up at the fort to see Dunbar at the parapet, staring downstream. To her eyes he seemed to be wrapped in a dark mood.

Fighting against the current, *Pickens* made it barely halfway to the city before nightfall. It wasn't until noon the following day that she unloaded on the levee outside Jackson Square. She took a cab to the newspaper to file her stories.

Fein was in a sour temper—seemed Ludd had indeed telegraphed a story letting out that Josephine Breaux was in the city—but he cheered up when he looked over the ten pages of handwritten work she threw down on the table. There were four articles. The biggest was about the hanging itself, and full of speculation about spying in the city. The second and third were information about happenings in the Gulf that she'd picked up from soldiers, smugglers, and fishermen she'd interviewed at the fort and in the river. The final one was about the efforts to improve the defenses at Jackson and St. Philip. She'd left out her biting observations; those were in a final piece that she hadn't written for the paper, but for other eyes.

"Very good, very good," he said, reading through. He dipped a pen in red ink and slashed through two lines, scrawling something in the margins. "Colorful. You have a way with words."

She peered over his shoulder. "What are you scratching?"

"This part about the spy's sister and her consumption."

"Don't scratch that. It paints a picture."

"A *sympathetic* picture. We don't want that, not for a condemned spy they tossed in an unmarked grave. Anyway, you've got plenty of human detail. This part about Dunbar's irritation in not getting those rifled cannons is good. Stirs up the blood of any true patriot."

She grumbled as he made more marks. He left in the part about bayou fishermen selling their wares to the Union ships but made red slashes through the paragraphs explaining that the fishermen had suffered the loss of their secondary trade because of the blockade. With that taken out, the fishermen became nothing more than greedy profiteers.

Finally, he looked over her sketches. "Remedial. A shame. Otherwise, you'd be the perfect reporter."

"I never claimed to be an artist."

"No, but a fellow can hope. No matter. I'll get Schmidt to draw them up fresh and pretty."

"What do you want from me now?"

Fein polished his eyeglasses with his handkerchief. "You've earned a few hours' rest. I'll send a message boy to the hotel with your next assignment. Maybe more about the mosquito fleet. You've got a good eye for military details. And as a woman and true patriot, you'll no doubt get access to all sorts of interesting people."

"That didn't help me at the fort. If anything, my questions made Dunbar more suspicious."

"Oh, really? Ludd's piece claimed you were flirting shamelessly with the major. That you used all the advantages of your sex to get what you wanted."

"That's a lie!"

Fein grinned. "What, I shouldn't have believed the publisher of a rival newspaper, the man who calls me 'the Rabbi' in print and accuses me of spying for the Yankees? The man who no doubt tried to hire you away the instant you met him?"

As quickly as it had flared, her anger now fizzled. "He calls you that? Ludd is lucky you don't challenge him to a duel."

"A duel! The only dueling I do is with the pen. But that reminds me of our most important newspaper policy. The name Stanley Ludd will never appear in the pages of the *Crescent*. Should you ever need to refer to the man in print, we always call him Stinky Lard."

She couldn't help but laugh. "That is the most childish thing I've ever heard."

"I know! That's why we do it."

Josephine went back to the hotel and finished writing her observations for Franklin. She expected to have a note waiting at the desk or to see the Pinkerton agent at supper, but he didn't appear. A message came in the morning, but it was from the paper.

After Fein's comment about the mosquito fleet, she'd hoped the paper would send her to the shipyards to see the progress on *Manassas*. It was a powerful tugboat being reinforced with railroad iron, meant to break the blockade, and rumor of its construction had reached the eastern papers way back in July, a few days before the battle after which it had been named. But instead of covering

Manassas, Fein wanted her wandering through St. Thomas Street and Corduroy Alley to watch for hungover officers and enlisted men. Under no circumstances was she to approach the district after dark.

She soon found out why. The cab driver refused to carry her into the area known as the Irish Channel, so she had to walk the last two blocks over broken cobbled streets. Shacks with low gable roofs lined the streets, built of torn-apart flatboats and broken cypress planks and looking like they would collapse if not held up by their neighbors. It was still morning, and this was a place that would only come to life in the evening, but the few people she saw let her imagination fill in the rest. She found an empty crate to sit on, took out her pad, refilled her fountain pen with a dropper, and began to write furiously.

The buildings of the Channel are as disreputable as the thieves, footpads, drunks, and other unsavory characters who gather within. Presenting a slouching, slovenly appearance, they lean against each other for support like drunkards, each one more dilapidated than the last. Every building is either a grog house or a bordello. Men lie in the alleys, drunk to stupefaction and as often as not robbed and beaten while they lay senseless in their inebriation.

She stopped as a man in a butternut uniform staggered onto the porch of a building whose gas lamp flickered behind panes of red glass. He squinted against the morning light and clutched his temples as if they threatened to burst. When he had recovered, he cast furtive glances up and down the street, and there he spotted Josephine. He straightened his jacket and tried to look nonchalant as he strolled away. Josephine scooped up her belongings and sprang after him.

"Good sir," she cried, hurrying to catch up. She lifted her skirts to dance over and around something that looked like a combination of dog filth and the contents of a drunk man's stomach. "My husband has gone missing. Please help."

This bit of deception caught his attention, and the poor fool tried to be helpful as she asked about where she might find the supposed husband.

The uniformed man was a captain in a rifle militia. He claimed to have entered the Irish Channel to look for one of his men who had failed to report for duty. Even as he made the claim, it was obvious he didn't expect Josephine to believe the fiction. Indeed, he looked downright ashamed, and she determined not to publish his name or regiment in the paper. Soon, she sent him on his way.

By the time the Irish Alley began to rouse itself a few hours later, she had enough material for several stories—filled in with the type of in-article editorializing that Fein seemed to like. It appeared that much of the clientele of the brothels and grog houses were military men who were supposed to be in the city to protect it from attack. Instead, they were drinking, gambling, and whoring in the Channel.

She retreated from the district to find a cab, figuring that if she hurried back to the hotel to finish her work, she could file a story in time for tomorrow morning's edition. Fein would be surprised to see more work so soon. But when she was halfway back, she belatedly remembered her true purpose in the city. She ordered the driver to take her up to Lafayette Square instead. There, she watched a company of militia marching back and forth across the square. The energy was torpid. More so when compared to the feverish environment in Washington in the days leading up to and following the battle at Manassas. Even the drummer struggled to keep a sufficient pace, his sticks seemingly as heavy as lead.

A woman who stood among the watchers told Josephine that the army had ordered the best units to Virginia already. The ones left were mostly immigrants, backwoodsmen, and others with suspect motives.

Over the next week, Josephine reacquainted herself with every corner of the city. She was feted for her supposed spy work up north by a widow named Mrs. Dubreuil in the Garden District, who lived in a fine house and served food and drink in such quality and quantity that it was as if the blockade did not exist. That gave Josephine an article questioning whether the wealthy of the city were prepared to sacrifice to win the war. And what were their motives, anyway? Should Union troops suddenly appear, no doubt the rich would cheer their appearance, because it would reopen the river to the flow of luxuries.

Of the dozen stories written since leaving Fort Jackson, this was the only one Fein killed. Well, he published it in the end, but only after he'd handed it to another writer to abuse and torment. The young man could barely string two sentences together. And when he finished, the story was full of glowing praise for the great and wise leadership of New Orleans. Josephine knew why Fein had killed her article, but she didn't like it and insisted he strip her name from the byline.

Apart from that, Fein praised her work and gave her prominent placement day in and day out.

By mid-September it would have been impossible to write a story like the one in the Irish Channel, because the captain in the bordello would have known her. The people of the street rarely recognized her, but New Orleans society came to know her by sight. She would be walking along the street when a carriage would pull up and some gentleman or lady would insist on driving her to her destination, no matter if that were on the other side of the city.

But people also told her things, and her fame opened doors to interview military officials, blockade-runners, railroad officials, and telegraph operators. Even Governor Moore invited her to see him after news came that the Confederates had been pushed out of the western counties of Virginia. Moore delivered a twenty-minute diatribe about Union aggression and expected her to print the whole of it. She gave him two sentences, buried in an article about the Union blockade.

In her hotel room, Josephine pried off the wainscoting and chipped away the plaster behind until she'd created a hollow for her notes meant for Washington. And then she waited impatiently for Franklin Gray. She'd been in New Orleans almost a month and had seen nothing of the man. If he didn't make an appearance by the first of October, she decided, she would find an excuse to travel to the delta and attempt to make contact with one of the Union ships lurking offshore.

Then, on September 18, a tip from Fein sent her to the St. Charles Hotel, where she came upon a meeting by two brothers by the name of Tifts with Commodore Hollins of the river fleet. Something about the construction of a new warship. They were close-lipped about the project, but within a few days she had uncovered more details. There was not one, but two big new ironclads being built in the city, named *Mississippi* and *Louisiana*. This raised even more questions. Where would they find all of the machine shops? Who would build the boilers and the propellers? Where would they get so many tons of iron plating? Word had it that the boats would be in the water by mid-December and breaking the blockade within days of that. Josephine had her doubts.

She went upriver a few miles to Jefferson City to where the two boats were being built on adjacent yards. The site was already a hive of activity, but closer inspection revealed chaos: plenty of lumber and unskilled labor, but few tools and little supervision. She was looking for someone named Murray, the man in charge of building the hull of *Louisiana*, when she spotted Franklin Gray standing on the levee.

He was arguing with a man delivering lumber from a barge, something about a mismatch between what had been ordered and what had arrived. A score of workers stood listening to the argument instead of unloading the lumber. Franklin glanced her way as she approached, before continuing his argument. In the end, he accepted only a small portion of the shipment.

"Excuse me, sir," she said to Franklin when the barge owner stomped off, cursing. "I'm from the *Crescent*. Can you tell me what seems to be the problem with the lumber?"

The workers were staring at her.

"Get back to work!" Franklin snapped at them, then looked at her with a frown. "I'll tell you, all right." He showed her a paper with a confusing mishmash of figures and numbers. "This is what I ordered." He laid the paper flat on a stack of nearby lumber and scratched something with his pencil. "And this is what they delivered." He pushed the paper in front of her. "Go ahead, see for yourself."

She glanced at what he'd written.

Congo Square.

There was no day or time written, but she guessed it could only be Sunday afternoon, when the slaves were allowed to gather and dance and the square was a chaotic scene that would make it safe to meet.

Josephine avoided showing surprise or confusion. "As bad as that?"

"As bad as that," he confirmed with a grim nod. "Now, if you'll excuse me, we have a boat to build."

CHAPTER 13

The slaves began dancing in Congo Square at four every Sunday afternoon, and Josephine made sure she arrived well ahead of time. The sun was hot overhead, so she took refuge in the shade of the sycamore trees that lined the square, to watch and wait.

At first there were more white spectators than slaves, as well as a number of officers from the Third and Fifth Wards armed with billy clubs to break up disturbances, but by three, more and more slaves and freed blacks came streaming into the square. Women in calico dresses wore red and yellow kerchiefs around their heads in the form of a creole *tignon*, while the men wore fine pants and jackets, albeit a little worn at the knees and elbows, the discarded garments of their masters. Their children wore dyed feathers in their hair and ribbons around their necks and pinned to their clothing.

Enterprising folk, white, black, and every shade between, set up tables beneath cotton awnings or carried trays hung about their necks. They sold pies, beignets, lemonade, ginger beer, and small ginger cakes that people called "mulatto bellies" for their color. Josephine bought one of these cakes, and, when it was gone, bought another.

At four, the police blew whistles, and the dancing and music started. A man banged on the head of a cask with two big beef bones, and three others started up with tambourines.

"Dansez Bamboula!" a tall, slender black man yelled. "Badoum! Badoum!"

He leaped into the air with a jingle of bells tied around his bare ankles. Other men joined with shouts of their own. They wore bells, ribbons, and shiny, clanking bits of tin around their ankles. Women swayed and joined their voices to the chant. Children came leaping in with shouts or stood swaying and chanting. Soon, the center of the square was a single mass of black, dancing bodies. Of the observers, who seemed equally divided between whites and blacks, a handful of the white men lingered around the edges, almost but not quite swaying, as if they wanted to join in but couldn't quite bring themselves to do so.

Josephine spotted Franklin on the opposite side of the square, trying to fight his way around the edges to her side. It took some time before he arrived, and then he led her to one of the quieter parts of the square, where they took refuge between a tall, over-hanging tree at the mouth of a narrow alley filled with garbage.

"Have you been in trouble?" she asked, curious but also a little annoyed that he'd abandoned her for the last month with no direction.

He rolled up his sleeve to show a pink, freshly formed scar on his forearm. "Knifed and beaten by two men on my first week in the city. If two strong fellows hadn't surprised my assailants and chased them off, I'd have been done for."

"Heavens! I'm glad you're all right."

"I wasn't on Girod Street, or in the Swamp, either, but a respectable district. And the men didn't rob me—I was carrying forty dollars of gold to pay off an informer. An informer who disappeared just before we reached New Orleans, by the way. Something bad seems to have befallen him."

Her mouth felt suddenly dry. "It wasn't the man they hung at the fort, was it?"

"I read about that. No, this was an old Spanish gentleman. The fellow they found floating in the Algiers Canal."

"That's right," she said. "Delaney wrote something about it in the *Crescent*. They said he was drunk."

"Could be. He liked his whiskey, from what I was told." Franklin glanced up as a handsome and well-dressed mulatto couple walked past on their way toward the dancing. "Or it could be he was killed by the same men who attacked me. I might have been fingered as a suspected spy. There are some suspicious types at the shipyard—I couldn't take a chance the other day. If I'm caught, I don't want you associated with me."

"I'll keep working alone," she said, "but I need a way to send and receive information."

"What do you have so far?"

Josephine had brought her leather satchel filled with papers, mostly observations and sketches, but also a fair bit of analysis and speculation. She pulled out a sheaf of papers a half inch thick, and Franklin's eyes widened. She kept watch while he studied the papers.

"Cocky," he said at last.

"Cocky?" It wasn't the response she'd been expecting. "All that work, and that's your response? Cocky?"

"Don't get me wrong—your eye is keen, your specificity of detail is remarkable. But"—and here he looked over the sheets before beginning to read back one of her lines—"'The Confederacy has put inferior minds in charge of the work. Any fool could see that the water battery, for example—'"

"Am I wrong?" she interrupted, remembering full well the line in question without having it thrown back in her face. "After all, *you* can see it, can't you?"

"Josephine, for heaven's sake. Are you always this touchy about your work? Don't you work with editors at the paper? How do you possibly manage?"

"I put the sweat of my brow into that, and your first comment is that I'm cocky. You don't see how that raises my hackles?"

He winced. "All right, maybe you have a point. It's excellent—you know that. But I wish you could soften your prose. There's too much of the lurid newspaper writing in it. It overwhelms the rest."

"Very well," she said, a bit grudgingly.

He looked back and read in silence for a few minutes. "This really is quite good. You have a knack for this work."

She liked his new tone better. "The best information came that very first assignment."

"Getting inside the fort? That was a stroke of luck."

"That's what I thought at the time," she said bitterly, "but I've been sitting on it for a month. Word has it they've got General Lovell in charge now, and as soon as he arrives he's going to beef up the defenses."

"I'm sure you can make a return trip under some pretext."

"You're missing the point. We've got to get this to Washington so they can do something with it."

"That's why you're touchy, isn't it? You're upset that you've had this analysis for so long and nobody has seen it."

"Perhaps," she admitted. "I have ideas. I want to see them implemented."

"Our job is to report, not to decide." Franklin had reached the part where she described the defenses of Fort Jackson, and was studying it with a thoughtful expression. "We're not military experts, after all."

"I'm expert enough. No chain barrier across the river. Old guns sitting on rotting carriages. Ten minutes of firing and they'd be out of powder. Get a few boats over the bar and into the river and they could capture the forts with two hundred men."

And now Franklin came to the part where she'd sketched out a battle plan to do just that. Yes, it was highly presumptuous, but it was also obvious once she'd put her mind to figuring out how to seize New Orleans for the Union. Capture the downriver forts while they were weak, then bring the entire fleet outside the city and force its capitulation.

"We can't send this."

Josephine put her hands on her hips. "Why not?"

"Because you're . . ."

"A woman?"

He grimaced. "Yes, to be blunt. Not that I personally think that matters," he added hastily. "And even if you were a man, you have no military experience. A woman and a civilian—they'll dismiss it at once."

"Is there something wrong with my analysis?" she demanded.

"Not at all. I'm surprised, of course. Not one civilian in ten would know what a water battery was or would have so clearly identified where the secessionists should place their chains. I'm only glad this is in our hands and not the enemy's."

"You see. I *do* know my military details."

"That was never in doubt. It was your analysis of Bull Run that brought you into our service. But imagine putting this in front of the men of the Union War Department. Here's a plan for capturing New Orleans, as envisioned by a twenty-year-old girl. I suppose I could put my name to it."

"No, you will not. Nobody steals my byline."

"All right, I won't take your idea and call it my own, but surely you see my point."

"Maybe a little," she admitted grudgingly. "Listen, I have plenty of experience rewriting to specification. I'll soften my language. Instead of saying 'Do this, do that,' I can equivocate. Something like this: 'One might observe the desultory preparations and suppose that the rebels have denied the possibility of a naval assault from below the city. They appear unwilling to entertain the notion that a well-armed fleet of steamers, accompanied by troop transports sufficient to hold the city . . .' And so on and so forth."

He chewed on his lip. "Fine. But if we send this through and it earns me an angry retort from Washington, then no more extemporizing." He handed back the papers, which she put into her satchel. "You'll deliver these yourself."

"How will I do that?"

"First, rewrite that bit, like you said. After that, wrap them in paper, seal them in wax, and deliver them personally. Try not to be conspicuous." He gave a name and an address, which she recognized.

"Mrs. Dubreuil! I met her at a party raising funds for the war. I thought she was the perfect Southern patriot."

"And she no doubt thought the same of you. Well, that will complicate things. You'd best go at night, come around into her gardens, and stay out of the gaslights when you pass off the papers." He glanced around. "And now, I'd better leave you."

"So, what? Keep doing what I'm doing? Don't you have any more instructions?"

He rubbed at his chin, brow furrowed. "Have you seen *Manassas*?"

"The ram? Yes, it's in my reports. It went steaming downstream about a week ago."

She had stifled a laugh at her first glimpse of the converted tugboat. A crowd had gathered on the levee to watch the strange contraption, which people said looked like a turtle, but to her eye it was more like an enormous, half-submerged metal cucumber with a huffing smokestack. At first glance, it was more amusing than threatening in appearance. It only had a single forward-facing gun, was poorly maneuverable, and was barely strong enough to breast the current. But on second thought she was able to imagine how it might be used in battle. Sent downstream against a fleet, shells would bounce harmlessly off its plating while it maneuvered to drive its point through a wooden hull.

Complicating matters, *Manassas* was owned by private investors who had a prize-money agreement with Richmond that allowed them to raid Union shipping across the world, from the seas of China to the Greenland whaling fleet. If *Manassas* could only reach the Gulf. Which it couldn't, thanks to the federal fleet.

"We need to find it," Franklin said. "Most importantly, is it still in private hands? Or has the Confederate navy seized it? There was some talk of that."

"Is there a naval action planned?"

"I don't know," he admitted. "I've been ordered to locate the ram, that's all. It's giving Washington fits—they don't know how it will fare in battle against our wooden sloops. But if I'm being watched and I suddenly start leaving the shipyard to go looking for it . . ."

"I'll find *Manassas*."

"Good. We'll meet here every Sunday afternoon to share intelligence. With any luck, I'll figure out if I'm being followed." He gave a wry smile. "And whether or not I've been cashiered for allowing you to draw up military campaigns in your leisure time."

"Stop worrying. At worst, the War Department will prove themselves fools and ignore it. But if they don't, you'll end up looking mighty clever for encouraging me."

"Be careful on the river," he said. "The time will come when they'll hang female spies the same as any man."

And with that, Franklin fought upstream against the crowd and was shortly out of sight, leaving Josephine with her leather satchel filled with papers. She left the shade of the sycamore trees, bought another ginger cake, this time with some lemonade to wash it down, and watched the dancing in the center of the square. A creeping sense of loneliness came over her, in spite of the fact that she was mobbed by people. The crowds only emphasized her isolation, as if she were a single grain of sand cast on a wide beach.

The dancing, singing slaves kept up their celebration without break, the beef bones marking an endless rhythm on the cask head. The leaping, the prancing, the shouting and song, all combined with the drowsy heat to lull her into something akin to a trance, and she found herself on the edge of the mass of slaves, swaying, humming with the tune. At last, the sun dropped behind the buildings, and when it did, the police whistled the end of the dancing. The beef bones stopped their banging. A long, disappointed groan went through the crowd, and it began to dissolve away.

As the mass of people thinned, Josephine spotted a white woman in a taffeta gown with hoopskirts. She held the arm of a dignified gentleman with one hand and leaned against an ivory-topped cane with the other. Josephine was studying the pair, thinking there was something familiar about them, when the woman turned and their gazes met.

It was Francesca Díaz, or Mrs. Hancock, as she styled herself now. Josephine should have recognized her by the red-dyed hair, if nothing else. The man must be her husband, the trader from Memphis, although Francesca had claimed he was unwelcome in New Orleans. Before Josephine could turn away, Francesca whispered something in her partner's ear. He turned to look.

Josephine's heart froze. Her legs wobbled.

It was the Colonel. Their eyes met, and though he was fifty feet away, his expression wouldn't have been more readable if they'd been standing face-to-face. Not only did he recognize her, but he had been expecting her, too.

Josephine picked up her skirts and fled.

CHAPTER 14

Josephine took a cab to the hotel. When she arrived, she ordered the driver to wait, rushed to her room, stuffed all of her possessions in her trunk and carpetbag, and hurried downstairs to find a bellhop to load up her trunk while she settled accounts. An hour later the cab was clattering away from the hotel. She watched the streets for any sign that Francesca and the Colonel were on their way to the hotel to look for her.

About an hour later, she found new lodging near the elegant French Opera House at Bourbon and Toulouse Streets, in a place called the Jefferson. The hotel had lovely, well-shaded gardens with fountains and flowering wisteria vines. Her room was twice as large. And twice as expensive. But she liked the privacy of the walled gardens and a back entrance of the hotel that didn't open onto a square or busy street. The hotel manager recognized her and let her stay under an assumed name.

When she was safely in her room that night, she tried to write about what she'd seen at Congo Square, but her mind kept wandering. She took out the Oriental box and opened it, first to look at the photograph taken with the Colonel and then to flip the catch and run her finger along the secret compartment. She wrestled with her memories of that horrible night when her mother died, but couldn't put them out of her mind.

There had been a rough stretch of several weeks on the river after losing their position on *Crescent Queen*, when money ran dry and Claire was unable to find work. There were plenty of offers, but only on disreputable vessels that were little more than floating brothels. One slummocky Yankee fellow had even suggested in his oily way that Josephine could also find employment with his boat. Mother and daughter could make a team. Claire had drawn her pepperbox and threatened to blow his brains out.

Later, shaking, Claire suggested they go to St. Louis and look for work. This was another risk. Both mother and daughter loved the traveling life, and there was no guarantee she could find anything reputable in the city, either.

But when they got to St. Louis, *Cairo Red* was at the docks, and the boat owner, a man named Mr. Clifton, was as smitten with Claire de Layerre as when he'd first seen her sing and dance. She gained a job and a double stateroom that seemed at first to be an upgrade from their previous quarters. But it was clear that the room, like *Cairo Red* itself, had seen better days. The carpets were stained, the paint faded. In the saloon, a mahogany railing had broken and never been repaired, and knife marks scored in the wood spoke of past brawls. The boilers made an ominous groaning sound when the boat was at full steam.

There was also an issue with pay that Josephine couldn't quite figure out. Claire and Mr. Clifton argued for the first two weeks, and at one point it grew so heated that Claire demanded that the pilot stop at the next town and let mother and daughter off. Somehow, that blew over. After that, things were calmer. Claire was vague about why Mr. Clifton had been so difficult about money.

With as much as Josephine read, and as closely as she watched and observed, always writing her thoughts in notebooks and journals, it showed how blind she was that she didn't realize the truth until she was fifteen. A man in the saloon made a comment to another dancer, which spurred Josephine's memory of something Mr. Clifton had said, which reminded Josephine of a comment her mother had made in Memphis when buying a new gown.

Her mother, to put it bluntly, was a prostitute.

No, Claire de Layerre wasn't like the strumpets in the French Quarter who would do it pressed up against a wall and who augmented their wages by knocking drunk clients over the head with paving stones and robbing them. Claire didn't sleep with strangers, and she never offered her services openly. But there were three or four regular travelers—old, wealthy gentlemen—who would spend a few nights or weeks with her and leave gifts of money, jewelry, and clothing.

Not that Josephine had been under any delusions about the wholesomeness of her mother's earlier lifestyle. Claire had never married the Colonel, couldn't say for sure even if the man was Josephine's father or not, and had no doubt enjoyed other lovers over the years, some of whom were generous gift givers. But since arriving on *Cairo Red*, financial necessity had turned her behavior pecuniary. Josephine longed for the days when they traveled with the Colonel. Sometimes it had felt like a real family.

When she was sixteen, she determined to leave the river for good. The situation on the boat had become intolerable. Her figure had filled out, and she could have passed for a young woman of nineteen or twenty. Not that her true age would have mattered to the sleazy clientele of *Cairo Red*. She endured so many drunk, groping hands, so many lewd propositions, that she shortly took to staying in her room except for a few hours in the morning, when the worst offenders were too hungover to make trouble. For a girl who had once enjoyed the run of the riverboats, able to meet with and chat with boatmen, slaves, stevedores, gamblers, pilots, fine ladies and gentlemen, and every other type of person, this was intolerable.

Josephine prepared a plan and, when given the opportunity, showed her writing to a newspaperman from way upriver in St. Paul. She told him she was twenty-one, and bluntly asked for a job. He seemed impressed by the writing and offered a position under the tutelage of a veteran of the society pages. Writing society gossip sounded awful, but it was a place to start.

Josephine broached the subject when her mother was getting ready for a show, expecting resistance. But to her surprise, Claire seemed pensive.

"I knew you were fixing to do something like that."

"You did?"

"The way you fancied up your talk, like the books you're always going on about. Your accent, too."

"I don't want to sound like a river rat, Mama. I want to sound respectable."

"If only you weren't so young. Couldn't you wait until you're seventeen? That's only six months. And it's so far upriver—we almost never make it to St. Paul. Why not Memphis or Baton Rouge? If there's war, you don't want to be on the wrong side of the border."

"If there's war, I don't want to be trapped down south, that's for damn sure."

"Josephine!"

Maybe it was the colder, more vigorous climate, or maybe it was the free labor up north, as opposed to the slavery that grew more and more oppressive the farther south on the river one traveled, but the Northern states felt vigorous, alive. That was the future of the country. If the fire-eaters had their way and tore the country in two, she knew which side would command her loyalties. It wouldn't be the side that sent men with guns and dogs to hunt down men running for their freedom.

"I want to go north, Mama."

"But I'll be so worried about you alone up there. What if something happens? It isn't safe."

"If you think it's safer on the boat, you haven't been paying attention."

Claire put in a turtle-shell comb to pin back her long, curly locks. She turned from the mirror, and her expression was sad. "I have been paying attention, and I know. Oh, I can't bear the thought of you leaving. But I can't bear the thought of you following my footsteps, either. This is no life for my daughter. It never has been."

Her mother seemed on the verge of tears, and Josephine felt so sad for her that she wanted to cry herself. All of a sudden it seemed like the most selfish thing she could do, leaving her mother to fend for herself.

Josephine came over to the table, and her mother rose. They embraced, with Claire's head resting on her daughter's shoulder.

"It won't be forever," Josephine promised. "I'll send for you as soon as I get established."

"What would I do?"

"Laundry, perhaps. Or mending. Something respectable."

"Oh, Josie, you know I could never leave the river."

Claire was only thirty-three, and still beautiful, but that would all change within a few years. Women who earned a living showing flesh on Mississippi riverboats had little future once they approached forty. It wasn't just the aging appearance; it was the hours spent every night dancing. Already, Claire had picked up a host of nagging injuries, a weak, oft-sprained ankle the worst of the lot.

What did her mother possibly think she could do when she

could no longer dance? Manage the younger, livelier girls? They were bursting with their own talent and ambition and would only scoff. No, Josephine was worried that her mother would find her way to a river port and be forced to earn her living in the ugliest way possible until at last her body gave out and she died filthy, drunk, and diseased in some alley.

"Mama," Josephine began, wondering what she could possibly say to change her mother's mind.

Someone knocked on the door.

"Oh, that's probably Herr Maier," Claire said. "He likes a quick visit before the show. Something about seeing me in all of this finery. Could you go read in your room for a few minutes, dear?"

Josephine sighed as she entered her room and locked the door. She knew exactly what this "visit" would entail. Normally, she'd throw herself into one of her well-worn books to distract herself from any unpleasant noises emanating from the next room, but she was too agitated by the conversation.

Mother opened the door in the next room, and there was an exclamation of surprise that quickly turned to an argument. Alarmed, Josephine sprang to her feet, prepared to defend her mother against some scoundrel who'd burst into the room.

But when she opened the door to her room, she was shocked to see the Colonel. It had only been three years, but to judge from his appearance, she would have thought it had been ten. Bags surrounded his bleary eyes. Heavy stubble covered his face and rendered his once elegant mustache ridiculous. His frilled shirt was yellowed and threadbare, and his vest was missing its pearl buttons, replaced by white-painted wooden ones. His gold watch and chain were gone. His trousers had a poorly stitched tear at the knee.

"There's my girl," he said as Josephine entered. His eyes twinkled, but his tone sounded strained. "Good heavens, look at you. You're all grown up. What a beauty our Josie has become."

"There's no *our* Josie," Claire snapped. "There is only *my* Josie. You made your decision. You made it long ago. Now get out."

"Mama, don't," Josephine said. "I want to know why he's come."

"You got us thrown off *Crescent Queen*," Claire said, ignoring her daughter. "And now we're stuck on this leaky, unsafe . . . Do you know what Josie is forced to endure these days?"

The Colonel looked down at his scuffed shoes. "I can imagine," he said in a soft voice. "And I'm truly sorry for that."

Josephine also hadn't forgotten how the Colonel had tried, weakly, it was true, to raise his voice against the lynching of a free man on the riverbank. Yes, his drunk attempt to cheat at cards had precipitated their ejection, and there was no good explanation for why he'd subsequently abandoned them, but she had wondered for the past three years what had become of the man. She needed answers before he disappeared again.

"Why did you leave us?" she asked.

"I didn't mean to. I only went up the river to apologize to the owner of the boat and beg him to take you back."

"Liar," Claire scoffed.

"We know that isn't true," Josephine said. "You were filling your pockets with gold. You never left a message for us, either with the coach or in Hog Shoals. We searched for you up and down the river, sent a telegraph to your friends in Memphis, did everything to help you find us. You knew *Cairo Red* wanted Mama, and you could have found us at any time. But you couldn't be bothered."

He spread his hands. "But here I am. I'm late, I know it. But I came. This time I promise I'll keep watch over my girls."

Claire made another disgusted sound before returning to her table and mirror to prepare for the show. The Colonel met Josephine's gaze and gave a sheepish shrug. She returned a furious scowl.

Josephine didn't know what made her more upset, that he would up the ante on his lying, or that she knew that he would again weasel his way into their affections, only to vanish once more. It might be three days or three months, but he would disappear. He always did. In fact, she thought, running a gimlet eye over his bedraggled appearance, she suspected that other motives had brought him.

"You've had a run of bad luck," she observed.

"The worst of my life. I lost my nerve, and that cost me."

"Did you lose your nerve, or your advantage tools?"

"No, no, I learned my lesson after that night. I threw the shaved decks in the river, got rid of the shiner, filed off the pin from my ring so I wouldn't be tempted to mark the cards. I never needed them in the first place. I was a square player who made a mistake."

"So you want money," Josephine said. It wasn't a question.

"What kind of man do you take me for?"

Claire turned from dabbing rouge. "You know perfectly well what kind of man we take you for. Now why don't you leave us alone?"

Yet there was no longer any heat in her words, and Josephine could tell she'd already softened. Soon, Claire would send a message of regret to Herr Maier so she could spend the night with the Colonel. And would that be such a bad thing? The Colonel may have been a scoundrel, but he did care, in his way. Maybe Josephine could explain the situation with the St. Paul newspaper, and together she and the Colonel could figure a way to get her mother off *Cairo Red* and onto a better class of boat.

"Then you don't need money?" Josephine asked.

"Not at all." He reached into his pocket and jingled some coins, although it was notable that he didn't remove them. No gold. Most likely a few pennies and half dimes. "But I was wondering . . ." He licked his lips.

"Let me guess," Josephine said, "you don't need us to give you money, you just need to *borrow* it for a few hours."

"I was wondering if you still have the lacquer box."

Her eyebrows lifted in surprise. "You want it back? To sell?"

"It's yours. It was a gift. But do you have it?"

"Of course she does," Claire said. She examined herself one last time in the mirror, then rose. "Josie isn't like you, she holds on to her valuable possessions."

"May I see it?" he asked Josephine.

"No. I don't trust you." Josephine pushed him toward the door. "Now get out. If they haven't thrown you overboard for cheating, we'll talk after Mama's show."

When he was gone, mother and daughter looked at each other and sighed.

"Can you imagine?" Claire said. "We haven't seen him for a month of Sundays, and he shows up now."

"But what do we do about it?" Josephine asked.

"I suppose it wouldn't hurt to let him stay for a night or two," Claire said. "But you probably guessed I'd say that."

"I did."

"Do you think it's a mistake?"

"Who can tell? He won't stay, that's for dead certain, but does that matter? He's no worse than Herr Maier."

"I'm not so sure about that. Herr Maier isn't flat broke." Claire winced. "I'll have to put Maier off somehow. It's fortunate he didn't come up while the Colonel was here. There might have been a duel."

"Oh, come now," Josephine said. "Do you really think the Colonel is brave enough for dueling?"

"No, probably not." Again, Claire sighed.

They went downstairs. They'd come up the Ohio, having picked up a number of Kentuckians on their way, and the saloon was packed with smoking, gambling, hard-drinking men. It was a mean, cussing crowd, and Josephine endured pinches and lewd offers before she got herself seated at the bar, where the bartender threatened to bash in the head of anyone who bothered her.

When she got settled, she saw that the Colonel had already insinuated himself into a game of faro. Off to ride the tiger again, as they called it. Tonight looked particularly dangerous. If he started to lose, he'd be broke in a hurry. If he started to win, his opponents seemed like the sort who would carve him up with bowie knives. He started off strong, and expressions darkened around the table.

She was so intent on the game that she didn't immediately notice that the bar was vibrating strangely. It was only when a metallic screech penetrated the wooden wall to her side over the shouting, laughing men in the saloon that she realized that something had gone wrong.

That noise was coming from the boilers.

CHAPTER 15

Josephine shot to her feet at the sound of the screeching boilers.

Shouts reached her ear, and she glanced out the doors, which had been opened on either side of the saloon to allow a breeze to pass through. Men came running out of the boiler room, eyes white and bulging through faces darkened with soot. They hurled themselves over the railing and into the river.

If there had been any doubt, that eliminated it. The aging, poorly tended boilers of *Cairo Red* were about to blow. The groaning must be a bulging boilerplate, and attempts to let off steam had failed, perhaps due to a stuck or broken valve. The engineer and the firemen who fed wood into the boilers were fleeing for their lives.

Terror clarified her mind. Across the saloon, men argued, shouted across at each other, called for more drinks, laid down cards. Some form of recognition was dawning on a few faces, and these men had already turned to tug on the sleeves of their companions, or reach for the hands of the surprisingly large number of wives and mistresses in the room. There were even several children. Josephine only had moments before general panic set in, and then she'd be trapped inside as the mob rushed the doors to escape.

Josephine spotted her mother near the back doorway of the saloon. Claire and another of the dancers were sharing drinks with an older gentleman, laughing at some witticism. The Colonel sat at a table nearby, deep in his faro game, marking the casekeep that kept track of the cards that had been played.

She shoved her way through the crowd. When it didn't part fast enough, she used her elbows. A shout sounded from her right, where others seemed to have recognized that disaster was imminent.

Josephine grabbed the surprised Colonel by the back of his collar and tried to haul him to his feet. His gambling mates guffawed, as if thinking she was a scorned lover, coming to take her revenge.

She shouted in his ear. "The boiler is going to blow! Get out!"

Others heard, and by now fear was spreading across the crowded floor. Dozens of people started jostling their way to the exits. Many were going out the sides, but this would place them near the boilers on the gunwale. She had to get out the back.

Without waiting to see if the Colonel would follow, she forced her way through the crowd, reaching her mother moments before the rear exit became clogged with screaming, brawling passengers and crew. Josephine grabbed her mother's arm and dragged her outside to the aft deck.

"What is happening?" her mother cried.

"Get back! As far from the boilers as possible."

Claire's eyes went wide. "The boilers? My God!"

Smoke and cinders were roaring out the top of the stacks. The heat was so intense up there that it had caught the stacks on fire, burning all the partially combusted ash that had accumulated over the years. Josephine glanced down at the river, where more people were throwing themselves overboard. It was almost dark, and hard to spot the opposite shore, but it had to be at least two hundred feet away. Josephine could swim that distance, but her mother couldn't.

"We have to get off the boat," Josephine said. She eyed her mother's dress, which had layers and layers of petticoats, most of which she would remove as she danced, until she was practically down to her stockings. Rhinestones and sequins weighed down the outer layer. "Get undressed. Hurry."

The Colonel came out as the women started working each other's clasps and loops. He glanced at the stacks, then turned a skeptical eye to Josephine. "Seems a lot of fuss for nothing. I really don't think a stack fire is going to make the entire—"

He never finished his sentence.

A tremendous flash of light lit up the night sky. A boom and a concussion of air threw Josephine off her feet. She landed on her back, ears ringing, head cloudy. Barely conscious. A column of fire and debris shot skyward from the center of the boat. As she lay stunned, the debris began to rain down. The heavier pieces landed first: twisted pieces of steaming metal, giant, flaming beams of wood. This was followed by burning furniture, spears of broken wood, barrels, chunks of wood, and people. Many, many people. They fell broken and torn in pieces all around, on the boat and in the water. A bloody leg slapped wetly onto the deck near Josephine's head, followed by the entire torso of a man. Then something—dear God!—that looked like a bloody doll but that she knew was not.

Josephine struggled to rise. She couldn't stand and fell again. Her head was swimming. Her limbs were lead and wouldn't do what she told them to do. The eerie silence in the wake of the explosion was replaced by the roar of fire and the screaming of those still living.

At last, she began to recover her wits and regained her feet. All around lay the dead and dying. They were burned, broken, scalded by boiling water, mangled and twisted. Dozens and dozens. The deck was on fire all around, and the entire center of the boat had turned into a mass of flames.

She found the Colonel, rising slowly to his feet with a stunned expression on his gaping face and blood streaming from both nostrils. And she found her mother, groaning, clutching her head. Her hair lay spread across a flaming piece of the paddle-wheel guard and was burning up on the end. Josephine struggled to pull her mother clear of the fire.

Cairo Red was an inferno, with flames already shooting skyward even as the smaller bits of debris continued to rain down. The boat was listing. Water would be gushing into the hull. It would soon go down.

The Colonel grabbed Josephine and spun her around. His eyes were wide, his shirt wet from his bloody nose. "Where is the box?"

"Box?"

"The lacquer box? Where the devil did you put it?"

"We're going down. Help me get Mama out of her dress."

"Where is it?"

"Damn the box. We're going down."

He shook her like a terrier with a rat. "Tell me!"

"Behind my cot."

He turned and ran off toward the stairs that led up to the promenade. The fire was spreading rapidly along the upper levels, and as she looked after him in dumbfounded amazement, she figured she had seen the last of him. The fool had survived the explosion only to be burned to death.

She turned and struggled to get her mother out of the dress. The clasps, hooks, and loops that had been so easy to unfasten moments earlier were now wet from the water sloshing over the deck as the boat listed onto its side. Josephine's fingers were numb, as if they'd been struck by a hammer. All around, people screamed and struggled. Many were dead, others horrifically wounded and suffering. Some threw themselves into the water, or were flailing and drowning in the river, their stricken faces illuminated by the burning barrels, furniture, and chunks of decking that floated downstream with the general conflagration.

Josephine got the outer dress off her mother. After that, the rest of the layers came off quickly until the woman was down to her undergarments. Josephine started on her own clothes. Her mother was still woozy but seemed to be recovering. She looked up.

"Josie. What—"

"Mama, we have to swim for shore." Josephine couldn't get the clasp off at her neck. The dress was torn and the metal hook twisted. She kept struggling.

The deck heaved beneath them. The water was swirling all around now, and as she looked up and into the raging fire of the upper decks, she saw with horror that the remnants of the side-wheel, the heavy walking beam, and the saloon were already submerged. The remaining stack tilted toward them, still leaking smoke. It crashed onto the aft deck with a shudder. And then *Cairo Red* sank beneath them.

Josephine grabbed her mother by the hair as the rail snagged them and threatened to drag them to the bottom. Water sucked at her, tugging downward. She fought against it, got her mother to the surface, sputtering. Josephine hooked a hand under her mother's chin and kicked her way toward shore.

Josephine had grown up a river rat, with no fear of the water. She'd learned to swim so young that she couldn't ever remember not knowing. She'd long since stopped diving overboard in her underclothes as she'd done as a child, but she hadn't forgotten how to swim.

But her confidence quickly faded. Her mother was thrashing in terror; Josephine's own clothes were waterlogged and tugging her down. She struggled to keep both of their heads above water. There was no way she'd make it all the way to shore. A big chunk of decking floated by, and she grabbed for it. But there was a man fighting for it, too, one of his arms twisted and mangled. He couldn't reach the planking, but he did get his free arm hooked around Josephine's neck. He tried to climb on her back.

She went under, struggling and kicking to get away from his desperate lunges. When she'd come up and fought herself free, she'd lost her mother. Crying out, still fending off the wounded man, she looked about. A large chunk of the burning upper deck of *Cairo Red* was still floating to one side, and it cast the river in light, illuminating the dead and dying. Josephine spotted her mother, bobbing along, still flailing.

"Mama!"

Josephine swam after her. She fought clear of another bit of flaming debris, two more injured, screaming people who tried to grab her, and then was logjammed behind several floating barrels. By the time she got around them, her mother had disappeared.

"Mama!" Panic was spreading in Josephine's breast. "Mama!"

Her voice drowned in the screams of other survivors. She swam around, calling, begging for help from any who seemed to be swimming uninjured toward the shore. Twice more she fought off screaming, frightened survivors. She was too exhausted from her own struggles to help and still desperate to find her mother. When she could swim no more, she clawed her way to shore and hauled herself through the mud to throw herself feebly onto the bank. The last burning wreckage drifted downriver and out of sight. From up and down the riverbank came the cries of the wounded, people hollering for help or shouting out for loved ones.

Josephine fought off her exhaustion and climbed to her feet. She waded into the shallow water near the bank and splashed downriver, calling for her mother. There were dozens of survivors all along the bank. None of them were her mother. Josephine continued, ignoring pleas for help in her desperation. About an hour later, the Colonel must have heard her voice, because he was calling to her from a dry, grassy bank. She pushed through the darkness until she found him. He did not have Claire. He hadn't seen her.

But of course he *had* rescued his precious Oriental box. He'd even managed to haul it to shore in a rapidly emptied cask of tobacco, so it wasn't even wet. He tried to take Josephine in his arms and comfort her, but she beat on his chest, uttering every riverboat oath she'd ever heard, until he relented and let her go.

"Maybe she . . . ," he began. "She might have . . . somewhere on the riverbank. We'll keep looking."

"She didn't make it! You let her die!"

"It was an accident. Nobody could have known it." He sounded shaken. "Claire!" he shouted into the darkness, as if that would help. Then, to Josephine. "We can keep looking."

"I'll keep looking. You stay here. I want nothing to do with you. Do you understand? I never want to see you again."

"I'm so sorry." He reached out for her.

"Leave me alone."

"Here, take this at least. Please." He had reached for her to shove the Oriental box into her hands.

"I don't want your confounded box, I want my Mama back."

"Please, keep it. Take it with you. It's very valuable."

He turned and started shouting for Claire again. This only made her more upset, so she set off again downstream and left him alone in the dark. Somehow, she kept the lacquer box, instead of hurling it into the river, as was her first inclination. She kept searching throughout the night.

When daylight came, Josephine was exhausted, hungry, and broken in spirit. In her heart, she knew that her mother had drowned in the river, but she couldn't stop looking. She came across a man who had taken in two children who'd lost their parents, and when a woman came staggering out of the brush, Josephine and the other two adults decided to round up survivors instead of waiting helplessly. They trudged through the swamps and muddy flats along the riverbank, fighting clouds of mosquitoes as they gradually worked their way upriver.

By the time the first boats began taking in survivors, Josephine and her companions had gathered over ninety souls. Reading later about *Cairo Red*, she would learn that only 147 people had been rescued after the disaster. The number of dead and missing was unknown, but estimated at four hundred. Among those taken that day were the captain, the owner of the boat, and nearly all of the musicians and dancers.

Also among the missing was Claire de Layerre. Her body was never found.

A few weeks later, Josephine was in New Orleans and desperate. She'd spent most of the eight dollars she'd kept in the Oriental box and had nothing to sell but the box itself. She took it to a curio shop in Exchange Alley in search of a good price. The owner was out, but his wife offered seventy-five cents and stood firm at that price.

"If it's all the same to you, I'll wait until your husband is back," Josephine said stubbornly. "The box is worth far more than that. Feel it. It's heavy, it has good workmanship."

The woman snorted. "Believe me, it's not. It's the sort of thing sailors pick up in Hong Kong to give to their sweethearts back home. Seventy-five cents is generous. But if you want to wait, suit yourself."

Josephine did, only to get a similar answer from the woman's husband. She tried two more stores, but neither offered her more than four bits. Discouraged, she returned to her dingy hotel, which was barely a step up from a brothel. She was down to her last thirty-two cents. Either she figured something out in a hurry or she'd be spreading her legs to keep herself fed and scrape together enough for a passage to St. Paul. God willing, the newspaper position would still be open. If not, the leg spreading may become her permanent occupation.

Upon the realization that she was actually contemplating whoring herself out, she dug her fingernails into her palm and stifled a scream. She looked at the box, wanting to smash it to pieces. Of all of her possessions—books, journals, clothing—it was the blasted box that had been saved. She hated the damn thing. It only reminded her of her mother, of the Colonel. She determined to go back to the curio shop and sell it for seventy-five cents.

Why did the Colonel think it was so valuable? That made no sense. The man had won and lost all manner of treasures over the years. Yet he had taken the biggest gamble of all to run into the middle of the burning heart of *Cairo Red* to rescue this box. And then given it to her in what seemed like a fit of guilt and despondency. Even a rat could suffer a guilty conscience, she supposed, but the box? Why would he risk his life for it?

Josephine opened the box and searched for a catch or false compartment. The most likely place seemed to be the lid, which was about an inch thick, and fairly heavy. But though she held it up to the oil lamp and ran her finger along the underside, there didn't seem to be any place to open it. She thought about smashing it open to be sure, but she couldn't afford to. She needed that seventy-five cents.

So she shut the lid and set it on her lap, where she ran her fingertips across the red-and-green-painted harbor scene. One of the carved Chinese junks moved beneath her thumb. Josephine caught her breath. Working carefully at the boat, she got it slid open and then eased her little finger into the tiny space revealed below. There was a click, and the lid popped open.

The lid of the box held its own separate compartment, a box within a box. With an invisible seam and an ingenious hooking mechanism of fine metal wire and hinge, the space was large enough to hold a few folded-over bills or a handful of gold coins. The perfect hiding space for a gambler needing to transport wealth. During a flush period, this particular gambler had given the box to his mistress's daughter for safekeeping. Like a bank, for if he ever needed emergency funds.

It was stuffed with wads of cotton, to keep whatever was inside from rattling around. She removed this carefully, then tipped the lid and gave a gentle shake to ease the items within first to the corner, and then into her hand. Several cool, hard objects dropped into her palm, like tiny stones. They glittered green and red when she lifted them to her eye.

There were ten rubies, each the color and size of a pomegranate seed, and two large, glittering emeralds, the size of wine grapes. For a long time she admired them in the palm of her hand, where they glittered with reflected lamplight. So beautiful. And obviously so valuable.

She would have to be clever and very, very careful. Men would see a girl in possession of such a treasure and immediately set about stealing it by fraud or violence. But if she could change the gemstones for money, it would provide the answer to all of her problems.

Josephine carefully put each of the stones back into the secret compartment, shut the box, and hid it. Then she began to scheme.

CHAPTER 16

Josephine made it known at the newspaper that she was looking for the turtle-like *Manassas*, and Solomon Fein, with his instincts for sniffing out a good story, soon gave her a critical hint. He'd heard that Stanley Ludd from the *Picayune* was in the river off New Orleans on Commodore Hollins's flagship, CSS *Calhoun*. Three other ships from the mosquito fleet, *Jackson*, *Pickens*, and *Tuscarora*, had pulled in to join *Calhoun*.

"Something is brewing if Stinky is on board," Fein said. "Might be this business with *Manassas*."

Four Union vessels had crossed the sandbars and come up the river as far as Head of Passes in late September, where the river broke into the numerous swampy channels of the delta. A few days ago, on October 5, the lightly armed Confederate steamer *Ivy* floated down to reconnoiter Head of Passes, where she briefly engaged the powerful lead ship, the twenty-two-gun *Richmond*, before fleeing for her life. Josephine knew there was talk of an attempt to drive the Union out of the river, but that was an expedition that could easily result in disaster. With the two big ironclads still under construction in the yards, having the ram would be critical to success.

Ludd looked irritated when Josephine came aboard *Calhoun* later that afternoon. "What are you doing here? Don't you have society gossip to cover or some such rubbish?"

She smiled and set her carpetbag significantly at her feet. He had been dismissive every time they'd met, but with each story she filed, his attitude became less amused and more defensive. In this case, she could hardly blame him for being annoyed. Had the situation been reversed, she'd have been equally irritated. Smaller boats were bustling back and forth from the four small warships to shore, and the general activity of the crew made it obvious that they were about to draw anchor and set off downstream. Yet there were no other newspaper writers aboard; Ludd had been expecting to scoop whatever story was developing.

Ludd had a notebook out and had been interviewing Commodore Hollins, a sharp-eyed old sea dog with a black-and-gray-streaked beard; a round, bald head; and a penetrating gaze. She had met him briefly at one of Mrs. Dubreuil's fetes, and he had been polite, but reticent.

Now it seemed that the government had ordered him to cooperate with the local press, so he endured a joint interview from the two reporters from the *Picayune* and the *Crescent*. When they asked difficult questions, he gave vague answers, his expression not unlike that of a man having a tooth extracted.

"He wasn't very forthcoming," Josephine observed, watching Hollins's proud, erect carriage as he made his escape.

"He was before you showed up," Ludd said. "Thank you for that," he added sarcastically.

The mosquito fleet steamed downriver with the five-knot current, and they arrived at the forts on the evening of October 11. There they found the turtle-like *Manassas* sitting at anchor off Fort St. Philip, a few of its civilian crew lounging in the cool air on its ironclad back, smoking, playing cards, and swatting at mosquitoes. Nearby lurked *McRae* and *Ivy* from the mosquito fleet, keeping an eye on the privately held commerce raider as if to ensure it wouldn't try to escape.

Shortly after their arrival, Hollins sent across a boarding party to seize *Manassas*. The longshoremen on the deck of the raider watched passively until Hollins's men drew near, when panic set in. They dove down the hatch like rats scurrying into holes, which made the men watching from *Calhoun* laugh and slap their knees, and the boarding party shout and cuss. When Hollins's men reached the boat, there was a brief scuffle, then the rats started jumping into the river and swimming for shore. Those who remained surrendered.

"Damn fools," Ludd muttered. "Bet half of them are Yankees. They'd just as soon turn her over to the enemy."

Doubtful. They weren't Yankees *or* Confederates, Josephine thought. They were vermin drawn from all points on the river, and from no point in particular, on the commerce raider to make a fortune engaging in legal piracy. When it looked like they might be pressed into the actual Confederate navy, forced to do some real fighting, they wanted nothing to do with it.

"Hope they string them up," Ludd said. "Make a good example of them."

None of the crew of *Calhoun* paid the reporter any attention, so he turned his beady eyes to Josephine, who wished he would shut up so she could take in every detail of the drama still playing out in front of them.

"It won't be long now," Ludd continued. "We'll set off down-river at once."

"Do you know something?" Josephine asked.

"Only that we're going to drive those cowards out of the river. I have no idea how they'll do it, but I'm sure Hollins has a good plan."

Josephine had no idea how they'd do it, either, and it seemed quite unlikely from where she stood. Six small boats, plus an untested ram, against four of the Union's massive sloops of war. Any one of the federal ships should be able to whip the Confederates single-handed. In fact, if she'd known how to send a message down-river to warn them, they could set out a trap and bag the whole of the mosquito fleet. Maybe a fisherman could take Josephine down.

No, she decided. That would end any chance she had to spy in Confederate territory, and surely the Union ships would have no difficulty, warning or no.

They didn't set off at once. Instead, when morning came, Hollins had the new crew of *Manassas* steam up and down the river try-ing to get a feel for the ram. It was sluggish and poorly maneuver-able. After about an hour of watching this, Josephine was given the opportunity to go to shore at Fort Jackson to meet with the defenses. Figuring the commodore wouldn't set off for Head of Passes until dark, she took the opportunity to do some additional scouting.

To her dismay, the fort had been transformed since her visit in August. Slaves were at work reinforcing the earthwork, while engi-neers had already put in a new water battery and bombproofs—rooms, powder stores, and storehouses covered with thick sod roofs. The thickest beams and dirt berms reinforced the new magazine, which made it less likely that a single shell would blow the whole thing to kingdom come. Older quarters had been renovated and new ones constructed. The garrison had increased to nearly three hundred men and growing. Several dozen flat, barge-like fire rafts loaded with pitch-soaked wood sat moored upstream of the forts, ready to be lit and towed into service should enemy craft approach.

Major Dunbar also seemed transformed. Gone was the dour, thin-lipped man of August, replaced by a man in a better uniform with a better attitude, and now confident of his own defenses. He praised General Lovell's new leadership and happily showed Josephine that many of the old cannons had been sent out, replaced by heavy-caliber rifled guns. He told her about the new entrenchments being planned, the earthen breastworks that would be thrown up to protect the water battery, and showed her the dilapidated hulks of old ships being towed to form an unbreakable barrier chained across the river.

Josephine was worried. What would have been easily run by a Union armada a few short weeks ago was now a strong, dangerous gauntlet of fortifications and guns, and growing stronger by the day. She hid her dismay and took furious notes. When Dunbar warned her not to publish specifics in the paper, she nodded her agreement and kept writing. The only thing enemy spies would take from her article, she assured him, was that the forts were now impregnable.

"You are a true patriot and a fine lady, Miss Breaux," the major told her. "May I have the honor of your company in the officer's hall for supper?"

She looked him over. Dunbar was a handsome man in his early thirties and, with his position and manners, would be considered a fine catch for any young lady. Assuming Union troops didn't storm the fort and shoot him dead, of course. But she remembered the hanging of Caleb Freedman. It was an unnecessary death, and this man had let it happen. She hardened her heart.

"You are too kind, Major, but I need to be on *Calhoun* by dark," she said. "The commodore hasn't told me when he's leaving, and I can't risk missing what is sure to be a glorious victory. My publisher would never forgive me."

Major Dunbar looked momentarily disappointed, then inclined his head slightly. "Perhaps another time. Best wishes, and stay safe."

Josephine felt momentarily sorry for turning down his invitation, but by the time Hollins's men were rowing her back to *Calhoun*, the excitement of the pending battle swept aside all other thoughts.

Commodore Hollins waited until after midnight, when the moon went down, and then he ordered the mosquito fleet to pull anchor and make for Head of Passes, towing a number of fire rafts.

A lieutenant made a halfhearted attempt to talk Josephine into going to shore for her own safety, but when she pointed out that nobody was sending away her rival from the *Picayune*, he let her stay. The man had seemed more motivated by chivalry than any real fear for her life. The crew of *Calhoun* was in good spirits, and nobody expected anything but success.

These men were still naïve, untested by battle. Josephine remembered too well the hell of the battle at Manassas, the dead and groaning wounded. Put together with her memory of the explosion on *Cairo Red*, it was easy for her imagination to construct a number of terrifying scenarios.

Head of Passes was only ten miles downstream from the forts, and all too soon Hollins ordered lights extinguished as they came drawing around the last bend. To Josephine's surprise, there had been no Union pickets to send up signal rockets, but it was unclear whether the dark and cool mist over the river had shielded them, or if the Union had simply neglected to send out men to watch.

Ludd also seemed nervous and had been pacing back and forth across the deck, stopping periodically to ask Josephine if she'd heard or seen anything. She had pieced together the commodore's battle plan by asking pointed questions of the crew, but she wasn't going to explain it to her rival, so she shrugged and claimed ignorance. At last, the tension seemed too much for Ludd, and he fled belowdecks where he supposed he'd be safer.

Near as she could tell, the plan was simple. Hollins would send *Manassas* in first, to seek out the biggest Union warship and ram it. The instant the ram made contact, its captain was to send up three signal rockets to notify the rest of the mosquito fleet, after which the men on *Ivy*, *McRae*, and *Tuscarora* would light their fire rafts and send them downstream. There, the chains that held the rafts together would hopefully close them against the prow of one of the other Union ships and set it on fire. When that happened, and with *Manassas* continuing to sow fear and confusion, the rest of the mosquito fleet would steam into battle, firing with everything they had.

Calhoun pulled in behind the ram, which could no longer be seen in the darkness. Here Hollins ordered the crew to maintain position, the paddle wheels holding them steady in the current, while he waited for *Manassas* to do its work.

From ahead came a burst of sparks from the single stack of *Manassas*. They'd kept her fires damped, but now, Josephine knew, they were throwing in pitch, sulfur, and tallow to stoke the engines as they gained speed. All stealth was gone. Now was the time to play out the battle.

From the Union forces ahead came a red signal light, followed by another. Dark, menacing shapes formed a V across the river downstream. Suddenly, the night exploded with the flash and roar of cannon fire. Illuminated was a big Union warship, and the dark, low-slung shape of *Manassas* thrusting toward it, seemingly unharmed by all the shells blasting in its direction. A second Union warship let loose with a roar of cannon.

There was a terrific grinding, splitting sound. Metal tearing through wood. Three signal rockets went up, and a cheer went up from the deck of *Calhoun*. The ram had struck true.

Hollins shouted orders. Men went running everywhere. Someone tried to drag Josephine below, but she resisted, and he soon gave up. One by one the fire rafts of the Confederate force were lit, and they drifted downstream, their flames illuminating the night in garish orange and yellow light.

Now all four of the powerful Union warships were blasting away, shooting at *Manassas*, at the fire rafts, and into the darkness, as if they could sense the Confederates lurking upstream. One of the Union sloops came steaming upriver. It dwarfed *Manassas* below and would soon overtake it. But then the Union crew seemed to see the fire rafts drifting toward it, and the sloop reversed course and fled back downstream. Now it was *Manassas* that seemed likely to be caught by the burning rafts. Josephine had a vision of the rafts entangling the iron ram and cooking all the men inside like frogs boiling in an iron kettle, but at the last moment the ram steered toward the shore, as if attempting to ground itself among the knees of bald cypress trees.

The Union ships continued to launch broadsides, and shells came raining down all around. The smaller boats from the mosquito fleet returned fire, but it was obvious that if the Union could get around the fire rafts, their superior size, guns, and speed would make short work of the Confederates. For the first time, the men of *Calhoun* seemed close to panic.

But as the fire rafts of the Confederates drifted into the Union anchorage, the big sloops raised sail, fired up their boilers, and headed downstream to escape the conflagration. Only a couple of smaller, auxiliary ships kept up the fight.

Unfortunately for the Confederates, both *Manassas* and *Tuscarora* had run themselves aground in the chaos of battle and the small Union vessels remaining were enough to fight the mosquito fleet to a standstill. Once again, Josephine was shocked that the more powerful Union warships had not stayed to fight. If they had, the Confederates would have been in trouble.

The next few hours were a chaos of short, running battles. The mosquito fleet, trying to organize itself, eventually pulled upriver to regroup. When dawn came, word came that only a couple of small Union boats remained at Head of Passes, and Hollins ordered the mosquito fleet to regroup and charge back downriver. They came around a bend in the southwest passage and discovered that one of the federal sloops and a small side-wheel steamer had come upriver again. In the Confederate fleet, *Ivy* had the biggest gun and seemed to be scoring direct hits against the main Union warship, but it was shortly driven off again by the Union ship's big guns.

Finally, the Union fleet seemed to be retreating for good, and Hollins ordered his forces to pull back upriver to lick their own wounds. They'd taken too much damage and expended too many shells to keep up the fight. Several of the Confederate guns had been knocked off their carriages, two boilers had taken damage, and the ram *Manassas* was crippled, its stack knocked off, and it needed to be towed upriver. Still, Hollins's men were celebrating on the decks. Rumors were flying that they'd sunk one of the big Union warships and crippled two others that would be lucky to make it into the Gulf without going down. The blockade was as good as broken.

Josephine hadn't seen that. She'd seen a battle won only through the incompetence and lack of command from the Union side, and through sheer luck by the only slightly less disorganized Confederate mosquito fleet. None of the Union ships had been lost. She was sure of that.

But later, as she filed a jubilant report, she reported the misinformation that would also soon be appearing in the *Picayune* as well. She filed two more, longer stories, sent upstream by courier, while she stayed behind at the forts to do reconnaissance and to meet with the crew of *Manassas*.

On October 23, the crippled ram finally arrived in New Orleans under tow, a full week and a half after the battle. Josephine traveled with the towing boat, writing and writing and writing during the entire trip. Far from discouraged by the Union loss, she was energized by what she'd seen and learned.

From the docks, she made her way straight to the house of Mrs. Dubreuil in the Garden District, armed with a fully realized plan for the Union capture of New Orleans.

CHAPTER 17

Mrs. Henry J. Dubreuil, neé Margaret O'Reilly, was a statuesque beauty, her hair still black and lustrous even though she appeared to be over fifty. She had one of those interesting faces that made Josephine wish she had studied portraiture so she could paint it, with a strong chin, high cheekbones, and hazel eyes flecked with green.

The woman seemed momentarily surprised when the doorman admitted Josephine, but quickly recovered. She said she had another guest in the back parlor, but if Josephine could wait in the music room, she would return shortly. Meanwhile, she would send in tea for Josephine while she waited.

Mrs. Dubreuil lived in a handsome two-story brownstone with wrought-iron fencing protecting its sumptuous gardens. The fireplace was marble, the furniture of black walnut, upholstered in damask. Thick burgundy carpets covered the floors. A beautiful green-lacquered grand piano sat in one corner. The tea arrived served in fine china, with silver teaspoons imported from England. Josephine ate the cucumber sandwiches, wishing she'd taken the time to return to the hotel to change and clean up before rushing over.

She was hungry, however, and after two weeks living with sailors and soldiers, seemed to have lost her manners. She'd devoured the entire plate of sandwiches before she caught herself. What was keeping that woman? It must have been forty minutes.

Unbidden, Josephine's thoughts turned to that night in Congo Square at the end of September, when she'd spied the Colonel and Francesca arm in arm. They'd spotted her, too. Josephine had studiously avoided thinking about them, but now she couldn't help it as she considered who Mrs. Dubreuil might be meeting with.

The first shock had been seeing the Colonel with her mother's former dancing companion. Josephine couldn't remember anything more than friendly, cordial behavior between the two women during the time on *Crescent Queen*, but of course Josephine had been thirteen years old at the time. Maybe the Colonel and Francesca had been lovers all along. They must have found some way to connect after the Colonel was caught cheating at cards. He'd been persona non grata on *Crescent Queen*.

Never mind that. How and when they'd ended up together wasn't as important as figuring out why they were in New Orleans. Francesca must have recognized Josephine during the crossing on the blockade-runner. Probably not at first, or she wouldn't have changed her story to claim she was French, and not Spanish. But eventually she had recognized her, maybe during that dinner at the Paris Hotel. Francesca then traveled upriver to Memphis to tell her husband, the so-called "great patriot."

After that, the two of them must have come to New Orleans with the express purpose of searching for Josephine. But why? To look for the gemstones the Colonel had hidden in the lacquered box? Or did he mean to worm his way into her affections again? Hah. Josephine could not, would not forgive him for what he'd done. And if Francesca was his wife or mistress, that made her an enemy, too.

Josephine was starting to think about that horrible night of her mother's death. With the memory of the river battle at Head of Passes so fresh, it was easy enough to recall the way the fire reflected off the river. The heat, the noise. And that brought the memory of screams, the scent of burned flesh. The panic when the drowning man threw his arm around her neck and pulled her under.

To distract herself, she picked up her leather satchel and took out the thick sheaf of papers—the work of two weeks, and, she was convinced, information and analysis vital to the war effort. She was engrossed in rereading it when the door to the music room opened. It wasn't Mrs. Dubreuil, but it wasn't the Colonel, either, thank God.

Instead, she found herself facing Franklin Gray. The young Pinkerton agent looked trim and in good health, and pleased to see her. She rose to her feet, her relief giving way to embarrassment at her bedraggled appearance.

"What are you doing here?" she asked. "Oh, was it you Mrs. Dubreuil was meeting with on the other side of the house?"

"She wasn't meeting with anyone. That was to keep you still while she sent for me. When I heard, I came as fast as I could." Franklin shook his head, looking disappointed. "We have a system for sending information. Why didn't you follow it?"

"That system led to the ridiculous lost opportunity at Head of Passes. I had advance notice of rebel intent, but no way to warn the fleet. If I'd had a way to send a telegraph—"

"You could have sent a telegraph straight to Washington and it wouldn't have done any good. The fleet had no way to receive it. Anyway, what's the rush now? You weren't supposed to make direct contact with Mrs. Dubreuil." Franklin held out his hand for the papers, but she was reticent. "Come on, hand them over," he said.

"This has to get through. And to be honest, I don't trust you to do the job."

"I would never censor your observations."

"It's not my observations that will make you balk, it's my analysis."

"Oh, right." He looked irritated. "More from the petticoat general."

Her face flushed with heat. "Why, you devil! How dare you?"

"It's your own fault." Franklin held up his hands to head off her huffy reply. "We agreed that you would equivocate last time around. Instead, you sent the same 'do this, do that' report that you showed me in the first place."

Some of her anger deflated. "I tried to rewrite it, but I couldn't manage. All that equivocating larded up the prose. If there's one thing I can't stand, it's flabby writing."

"It wasn't a question of writing, good or bad—"

"It's always about the writing," she interrupted.

"It's a question of politics. You can't tell these generals what to do. You have to let them believe they came up with the idea themselves. That goes doubly if you're a woman."

Josephine grunted. "So what happened? They dismissed it out of hand?"

"Worse than that. I was ordered to send you back to Washington so they could find someone more tractable."

"I'm not going back. I don't care what they say."

"Now, hold on. It didn't end there. I protested—there was some argument. Somehow the whole business found itself on the president's desk. He threw sand on the fire, and that was the end of it. You'll stay in New Orleans."

Josephine sat down with a sigh. She thought about all the hours she'd spent writing her military suggestions. No doubt it would be tossed in the rubbish bin as soon as it arrived in Washington, if the couriers even risked carrying it via the network of trains and riders necessary to travel the breadth of enemy territory. And this was not the sort of information that could be sent by telegraph.

She thumbed through the papers until she found what she'd written about the current condition of Fort Jackson and Fort St. Philip. "Look at this."

Franklin sat next to her and looked it over. "Hmm."

"So you see that we missed an opportunity. A few hundred men could have taken the fort in August. Not anymore."

"Just because it could have been taken, didn't mean that we had the means to do so. You saw it yourself—Commodore Hollins routed us from the river."

"I've considered that, too." She pulled out a few more papers. "Forget the nonsense I wrote in the *Crescent*. This is my true analysis. We should have won easily. The Confederates had initiative and energy, but nothing more. The rebels didn't break the blockade, we raised it for them by fleeing in terror. And after all that, I'll bet we've closed the passes again already."

Franklin didn't answer that, but shrugged without looking up from her papers.

"There's no need to keep secrets from me," she said. "Right now I know more than the War Department."

"You're right. Nothing was sunk on the Union side. The blockade is back in place. Captain Pope is being replaced by someone with more intestinal fortitude."

"Pope?" she asked. "He was the one on *Richmond*? Very poor showing. If he'd taken two ships upstream, he would have found the ram lodged in the mud and destroyed or captured her. Likely would have trapped Hollins's entire fleet before they reached the safety of Fort Jackson's guns."

Her confidence was growing, and now she took out her battle plan and put it on his lap.

He thumbed through the thick, handwritten document, complete with sketches. "What is this?"

"This is how we capture New Orleans."

His eyebrows raised. "Oh?"

"Read it," she urged.

"No, you tell me."

"New Orleans is on a swamp. Fewer than five thousand poorly trained militia defend it, and it can only be reinforced by water, either from the river or from Lake Pontchartrain. And any reinforcement would take weeks. Even with sufficient men, New Orleans wouldn't be easy to defend. Few fortifications, and half the city lies below river level. A ship like *Richmond* could blast holes in the levee and flood it."

"If the rebels can't defend it, then how do you propose that the Union do so once it's taken?"

"It can't be defended from the land. But we have a navy. The Confederacy has merely a mosquito fleet. It can sting and bite. It can't sustain a campaign."

"Until the ironclads are finished. That will change the rules of the game."

"And when will that happen?" she asked.

"They say the first of the year. I'm not so sure. Maybe February?"

"All the more reason to move now." Josephine took back one of the papers and turned it over to show her calculations. "I figure we need ten thousand men to take the city by force and garrison it, and ten or fifteen warships to patrol the water between the Gulf and Baton Rouge."

"You make it sound so easy. There are a dozen enemy forts and fortified cities between here and Union territory. It might be a year before we can control the Ohio, let alone come down the Mississippi to seize Vicksburg and Baton Rouge. Until they fall, New Orleans is safe."

"I'm not talking about sailing down the river. I'm talking about coming up. Bringing wooden ocean vessels over the bar from the Gulf."

"After what just happened? Now is hardly the time—"

"Especially now. Trust me when I say it would work. The key is to get past Fort Jackson and Fort St. Philip. That's the only difficulty."

"Oh, is that all? And I suppose you have a scheme for that?"

She chewed her lip. "That's admittedly a weak point in my plan. But not insurmountable." She pointed to a diagram of the land below Fort Jackson. "Look down here. The Confederates haven't cleared the woods. Troops could land here, protected from the enemy guns, and march overland to take the lower fort. After that, we cut the chain barrier and bring the boats to make a fast run past St. Philip to New Orleans. Once the city falls, St. Philip will be forced to surrender or starve."

Franklin studied her diagrams and analysis in silence for several minutes. At last, he shook his head. "I simply don't know enough about either naval or land operations. This is either brilliant or harebrained. Maybe both." He looked at her, admiration and wonder in his eyes. "How do you know so much about these things?"

"I am a quick study," she said with a hint of false modesty.

"Yes, but where? How do you even know these military terms?"

"I've always been fascinated by military matters."

"You said as much in the White House. I didn't understand the full extent of your interest or knowledge. Why? And how?"

"Why, who can say? I had a book about Waterloo that I read as a girl and learned everything I could about Napoleon. I talked to old soldiers and looked at forts on the river. But my interest was casual, undisciplined. Then, as soon as the war broke out, I realized that with a more thorough knowledge I could be a war writer without equal. That sounds boastful, I know, but you've read the rubbish that passes muster with the papers."

"Most of it is rot," he agreed. "Go on."

"I started reading everything I could get my hands on about the subject. An officer from the military-strategy department at West Point kindly loaned me a trunk full of books. Then I interviewed officers and enlisted men as the fighting started in Virginia and along the coast. I toured forts, inspected encampments."

"But you're a woman."

"Exactly. How do you think I kept my cover as Joseph Breaux for so long? Nobody expected a woman to be covering military affairs."

Franklin looked back at her pages. "I may not know much, but one thing I do know is that generals don't like advice from civilians. Even the president has a hard time getting through to them." He hesitated. "If I send this, there's a good chance that I end my career."

"But if it works, if the War Department adopts the plan and takes New Orleans, you'll be a hero."

"That's where you're wrong," he said. "I'll get all the credit if it fails. But if it works, generals and politicians will take the glory."

"But you'll always know the truth. That's what matters."

He gave her a look. "Oh, so now you're disavowing personal glory?"

Josephine grinned back at him. "Of course not. When the war is over, I plan to write a tell-all. Once the truth is out, they'll put my bust on a pedestal beneath the Capitol rotunda."

"While they burn you in effigy in Charleston and New Orleans."

"Only if we lose." She gave him a sharp look. "Does this mean you'll send it?"

He hesitated, then nodded. "I'll send it. So help me, God, I will."

Josephine walked back to the Jefferson Hotel instead of hiring a cab. A late October breeze drove away the heat and the damp air, leaving the day clear and pleasant. Birds chirped and squabbled in the branches of trees. Along Gasquet Street, Spanish moss draped from the live oak trees that framed tidy, brightly colored cottages.

She passed an elderly gentleman smoking a corncob pipe from one corner of his mouth, while his hands busied themselves trimming dead roses with a pair of shears. A white-haired woman knelt on a twisted rag a few feet away, tugging weeds from a bed of begonia.

The man looked up as Josephine passed, and tipped his hat. "Good afternoon, miss. Right fine weather for a stroll."

"That it is." She looked over his work. "What a lovely garden. Did y'all do all this yourself?"

The man beamed. "That we did." He cut a long-stemmed pink rose and handed it over the wrought-iron fence. "It's the prettiest rose in the garden, but I dare say it's not half so pretty as your fresh face."

"Oh, Charlie, will you let the young lady go?" the woman said, her voice holding only mild exasperation. "She doesn't need an old codger like you goin' on with all them sweet words."

Josephine leaned over the fence and kissed the old man on the cheek, then winked at his wife. He blushed, and his wife cackled in glee.

As Josephine rounded the corner, she heard the old woman tell her husband, "Well, look at you, gapin' like a fool. Now you'll be cutting blooms every time a pretty young girl says a kind word, until I have nary a rose left."

Josephine was still smiling when she came in the garden entrance of the hotel. She took the creaking wooden steps up to the second floor and walked down the carpeted hallways to her room, but when she put in the key, the door wasn't latched, and it swung open at her touch.

A man was inside, his back turned to her, bending at the foot of her bed, rifling through the contents of her trunk.

CHAPTER 18

Josephine stared at the thief bent over her trunk. She was trembling with anger.

"Stop what you are doing," she said, "or so help me God, I will kill you."

He stiffened and turned slowly. "Hello, Josie."

It was the Colonel. His mustache was still black, but gray streaked the dark, curly hair on his head. He was more slender than she remembered, and also not as tall. For some reason, she always thought of herself as coming up to his shoulder, but no, he wasn't more than an inch or two taller than she was. It had only been four years, but there were fresh wrinkles on his forehead and around his eyes. Or was that another thing she'd failed to notice?

What's more, his suit was tired and worn. He still hadn't reclaimed his pearl buttons and gold watch. His shoes were scuffed and in need of a visit to a cobbler. There were no rings on his fingers. Only the hands themselves looked unchanged, the nails neatly trimmed, the palms he was rubbing nervously together soft and uncalloused. They were the hands of a man who eschewed labor. Who craved soft living.

She cast her eyes over the bed, where he'd tossed her books and clothing. "A simple robbery, is that what you've come to?"

"Where is the box? I told you to keep it."

"I was poor, so I sold it."

He closed his eyes and took in a deep, labored breath. "You . . . you sold it? When?"

"Years ago. A little place on Exchange Alley offered me seventy-five cents."

"Oh, sweet angel of mercy. Why would you do such a thing?"

"What was I supposed to do? I was sixteen, I had nothing. You let my mama die."

"I didn't."

"Damn you, Colonel, you did so. You ran off for your precious box, and she drowned in the river. Because of you. Because of that confounded box."

He sat on the bed and buried his face in his hands. A shudder worked its way through his body. Josephine set the leather satchel to one side and closed the door. Then she stood with her hands on her hips, looking at him coldly.

"Please," he said at last, looking up. "You know it was an accident. The boiler . . . I had nothing to do with that. Many people died, not just Claire. It was a great tragedy."

Josephine had no intention of letting him ease his conscience with bromides. "Tell that to God at the judgment bar. You as good as killed her yourself, you know it. And for what, a curio worth all of six bits. Yes, I sold it for seventy-five cents. And I'm not sorry, either. It was either sell the box or hawk my body on Gallatin."

"I never wanted that. You know it's true. I wanted you to be a writer, like you dreamed."

"Of course you did, and that's why I never saw you again after that night. Because you wanted so badly to help me."

"I searched for you. I tried."

"Liar."

"Look at my girl," he said after a long moment. "So grown up and pretty. And a heroine of the cause. Once Francesca told me she'd met you, I finally put two and two together. Josephine Breaux. Should have realized earlier. Breaux was your mama's surname."

Josephine shook her head, frowning. "It was? It was just a name I grabbed in New Orleans before I left."

"You must have known."

Had she? There was no specific memory of when she'd decided on the name Breaux, only that she'd known she couldn't go by de Layerre, her mother's stage name.

"She must have told you," the Colonel said. "You tucked that away and you remembered."

"That was her surname name, you swear?"

"On my honor. Claire Breaux. She changed it so her brother wouldn't come looking for her."

Mama had a brother? This was thrilling new information. Josephine had wondered many times about relations, had concocted fanciful stories of her mother's origins. Claire had had a family somewhere who disapproved when she ran off to become a riverboat dancer. A religious family, Josephine told herself, by the name of Breaux, who always attended Mass and prayed to St. Anthony for the return of the missing girl. One brother, she imagined, would continue the search after the others had abandoned hope, traveling up and down the Mississippi, searching brothels and poorhouses.

"What more do you know of her family?" she asked. "Tell me."

The Colonel looked uncomfortable. "There isn't much to tell. Claire didn't like to talk about it. Her mother was a disreputable sort."

Josephine began to deflate. "More disreputable than riverboat dancing?"

"She was the madam of a bordello and grog house in the Irish Channel. An opium eater. Claire's father was a drunk wanted for murder in Mexico."

"My grandfather was Mexican?"

"I have no idea. Maybe just an adventurer. I've told you everything I know."

The news came like a blow, and her illusions broke apart. Josephine's own father was unknown—possibly this scoundrel in front of her—and her mother a riverboat dancer. Her known grandmother had been even more disreputable, her grandfather a drunk and a murderer.

"But what about Mama's brother?" she asked, seizing desperately on this detail. "He was looking for her?" Maybe there had been another in the family, one who'd got himself out, made something respectable of himself. Josephine's uncle. What had become of him?

The Colonel winced. "Claire ran away from home at twelve. Seems her half brother took a fancy to her. He was eighteen, and already a troublemaker."

"Dear God."

"I wouldn't worry about Claire's brother," he said. "Your mama thinks he was hung for killing a negro woman after she refused him."

"That's my kin?" she cried, despairing. "What chance does that give me?"

The Colonel came over and reached for her hand. "You have plenty of chance. You're a fighter."

Josephine jerked away from his touch and glared at him until he backed off. She hadn't meant to say that last part aloud and was ashamed that she had.

She corrected herself now. "I've made my own chances. And not you, nor anybody else will take that away from me."

"I would never try. I'm proud of you, and what you've done, so young, yet already so accomplished."

"You've come, you've had your say. You see I don't have anything to give you. Now go away."

"Where did you sell the box? Do you remember exactly?"

"No, I don't. Anyway, it was years ago—you'll never find it now. If you want another seventy-five-cent box, you'll have to send for it from China."

"It wasn't just a box, don't you understand that? There was a hidden compartment. I kept emergency reserves in there. For if things went badly for me. I'd have a way to get back on my feet."

"And I was supposed to know this? I looked inside. I saw nothing."

"You could have smashed it open."

"I needed the money. I was starving."

He grimaced at this. "Did you have to . . . ? You know . . . ?"

"To what? Say it."

"Sometimes we do terrible things to survive. I could never forgive myself if I thought you'd sank that low."

For a moment she wanted to say yes, she'd done all of that and more. Stick the knife in and twist it. But she didn't truly believe this man had a conscience, and such a lie would get in the way of her pride.

"No, I never whored myself. I never danced, and I was never the mistress of any devil of a slave trader, either. I survived on my own wits, no thanks to you."

Your own wits, and several thousand dollars of gemstones.

And what of it, she thought stubbornly. Her mother had drowned. Josephine had lost everything: her writing, her books, her clothing, the money Claire had set aside for mother and daughter, should they ever find themselves in trouble. All she had was the box and a few dollars that had run out too quickly.

When she'd found the gemstones, she had immediately set

about in turning them into ready money. She sold one small ruby in Exchange Alley and bought passage up the river with the proceeds to sell the rest. She traveled all the way to the Ohio River, and on to Pittsburgh, which she believed would be less corrupt, more transparent than New Orleans. In total, she collected almost $7,000 by selling the gems. Of this, she donated the proceeds of one of the large emeralds to the Sanitarium for the Burned and Indigent in New Orleans and kept the rest for herself. If she had any remorse whatsoever, it was for the poor fools the Colonel had suckered at cards with use of his advantage tools.

The Colonel looked relieved when she told him she hadn't prostituted her body to survive. "You look well. I'm pleased to see it. You might have heard that I have remarried." He rose and began to put away the books he'd taken out of her chest.

"Don't touch that. Just—just step away. I don't need you pawing through it." Josephine narrowed her eyes. "How do you mean, remarried?"

"True, true. I never actually married your mother. I wasn't the marrying type then. I should have, though. Should have made us a proper family. Then you could have taken my name, respectable-like."

"Josephine the Colonel? Lovely name."

He winced. "It's Hancock. I didn't share that because . . . well, there were men who wanted me dead. Still are, but seems they've gone north for the duration of the war."

"So, Colonel Hancock. What regiment did you serve in?"

"Well, I—"

"You are how old—forty-five, maybe? And you seem in fine health to me. A genuine officer would have no trouble getting a commission. When do you ship off to join the Army of Northern Virginia to fight the Yankees? No? A Union fellow, then? I've heard they need men, too."

"I will seek a commission. Shortly."

"You're no military man. I knew that a long time ago, and I can see it even more now."

"Josie, please. Be reasonable. There's no need for us to be enemies."

"You killed my mama. And after four years with no word—not the first time you'd vanished, mind you—I come home to find you trying to rob me."

"I wasn't going to rob you. I only wanted to find the box. Then I was going to share my emergency stash with you, I swear it."

"Go into the hallway. Wait there while I think it out."

He looked like he was going to protest, but after a nod, he complied. She shut the door and flipped the latch, in case he was tempted to pick the lock again.

When Josephine was alone, she opened her carpetbag and removed the Oriental box, which she always took with her when she would be gone for more than a day or two. She sat on the bed with the box in her lap, and she slid the carved boat to reveal the catch. A thick wad of banknotes was stuffed into the lid. She removed two twenty-dollar Confederate bills. After a moment of thought, she peeled off two more bills.

Shortly, she had the box closed and hidden. She opened the door and handed the Colonel the greybacks. "This is all you'll get."

"I didn't ask for charity," he said, but nevertheless took the money and pocketed it.

"I'm not doing it for you. I'm doing it for Mama. That's what she would have done, even as she cursed your no-good hide. Use the money to get back on your feet, or throw it away gambling and drinking. It makes no difference to me."

"Thank you, Josie."

"Either way, it's the last money you'll see from me. Go back to Memphis and never trouble me again."

CHAPTER 19

Josephine changed domiciles again after the visit from the Colonel. This time she took care in finding the right place, deciding to dispense with hotels entirely. They were expensive and drew attention to someone supposedly living on the salary of a newspaper reporter.

Instead, she found a woman on Villere with a room for let. Nellie Gill's husband was a lieutenant currently stationed with the garrison at Fort Henry, Tennessee, and she needed a lodger to get by.

Nellie was a true Southern patriot, born in South Carolina and married into a family of cotton exporters whose fortunes had crashed with the onset of war. The woman organized dances, raffles, and bazaars to raise money for the cause, and was so excited to have the famous Josephine Breaux as a lodger that she wanted to set off at once to tell all of her neighbors. But when Josephine expressed worry that the Union would send an assassin to punish her for spying in Washington, Nellie listened, wide-eyed, and swore she wouldn't breathe a word.

Josephine continued to meet with Franklin throughout November, joining him every Sunday afternoon at Congo Square. There was no word, either positive or negative, about her proposal to take New Orleans. It didn't seem that the government was paying attention. Instead, word came of an armored fleet that the Union was constructing upriver. These were nicknamed "Pook's turtles," after Samuel Pook, the builder, though they weren't rams like *Manassas*, but shallow-draft gunboats. Everybody, both North and South, seemed to be bracing for the river fight to begin up on the Ohio and Tennessee Rivers.

Nevertheless, General Lovell stayed busy fortifying New Orleans and its approaches. Thousands of slaves and poor Irish worked with pick and shovel to extend the entrenchments from New Orleans to Lake Pontchartrain. Downriver, the work on Forts Jackson and St. Philip continued apace. Lovell finished his barrier across the river, comprised of several hulks—old ships, no longer seaworthy but still able to float—held together with strong chain and fifteen massive anchors. Any Union ships trying to break the chain would find themselves under withering attack from St. Philip ahead, and enfilading fire from Jackson. Josephine still thought her plan could work with a strong enough force, but seeing the strengthened defenses in early December eroded her confidence.

In mid-December, Josephine showed up at Congo Square to meet Franklin, but she searched the crowd in vain. It was chilly, and she wrapped herself in her shawl, eating ginger cakes and sipping hot cider while she watched the dancers and waited. It was lonely without Franklin's company. She'd come to depend on his conversation to break the pressure of the daily subterfuge that had become her life.

At home, Nellie Gill was decent company, albeit stuck on her husband in Tennessee and how he would whip the enemy single-handed.

Josephine hadn't grown tired of war talk—the subject endlessly fascinated her—but she was exhausted by the constant need to denounce Lincoln as a Black Republican, to talk up the bravery of Southern boys and the cowardice of perfidious Yankees.

It was much the same at the newspaper. Solomon Fein had a delightful, irreverent humor, and her fellow reporters were cynical and idealistic in turn, characteristics she recognized in her own temperament. But there was never any question about the politics of the *New Orleans Daily Crescent*. They were Southern, Louisiana, and Democrat partisans, in that order.

Only with Franklin could she be open. Admit her loyalty to the Union, share the depth of her observations. Almost every meeting was accompanied by verbal sparring, but in their conversation she sensed a probing, intelligent mind equal to her own.

And so, when the sun began to dip and the dancing and singing grew frenzied in anticipation of the closing of Congo Square, she was excited to see Franklin pushing his way through the crowds to where she waited beneath the sycamore trees next to her favorite beignet stand.

Josephine looked him over. "You're flushed. Are you ill?"

"I feel fine."

He looked around, taking in their surroundings in a way that had become familiar. Searching for anyone who seemed to be watching the two of them instead of fixed on the spectacle. Yet this time he was jumpy, nervous.

"Something is happening," she said. "Did Washington send news about my plan?"

Franklin didn't answer. Instead, he reached into his pocket and pulled out a box small enough to fit in the palm of his hand. "I have something for you."

Josephine started. She began to reframe his nervousness. What the devil was this—a repeat of the Major Dunbar incident? Except

Dunbar, with his supper invitation and obvious intentions, had been a handsome stranger. Franklin Gray was her associate, with a long-cultivated familiarity that had passed to friendship.

"I really don't think—" she began.

"Go ahead, open it."

"Mr. Gray, please. Let's think about this for a moment."

"'Mr. Gray,' is it? Aren't we—" Then his eyes lit up with amusement. "Ah, I see. That's funny. No, it's nothing like that, as if I would ever. Hah."

That quickly, her worry flashed to anger. "I'll have you know that plenty of men have been, and continue to be, interested. So don't consider yourself such a fine specimen of manhood as to be above the likes of me."

"Josephine, no. That's not what I mean. You caught me off guard, that's all. But I merely brought something to assist you in your duties. It wasn't a declaration of amorous intent. Of course, as a woman we both know you are . . ." He waved his hand vaguely.

"No, please. You don't need to say it."

As fast as Josephine's anger had flared to life, now it deflated just as quickly. In its place was burning embarrassment. Not only had she leaped to erroneous conclusions upon sight of the small box, but then, when thinking he was dismissing her, she'd bristled like a scorned lover.

Why was she so touchy of late? It was that conversation with the Colonel, still eating at her. Learning the truth about her family origins. It was a hidden blemish, a terrible, leprous patch of skin that would show if she didn't keep her collar buttoned high and her face veiled.

She reached for the box, but he pulled it back with a frown. "A moment. Are you all right?"

"Please, I'd rather not discuss it."

"There's something wrong. I saw it pass over your face."

"Embarrassment. I reacted badly." She reached again for the box, but when he hesitated, she added, "Be a gentleman, Mr. Gray. Don't press me, I beg you."

He handed over the box.

Inside was a man's pocket watch. It wasn't an expensive thing, with a gilt cover, not gold. The design on the cover was unusual: a crescent with a star. Ottoman, she thought. Or maybe Persian. She looked up at Franklin with a questioning expression.

"You wanted a way to contact Washington independent of me," he said. "This is your means."

"Explain."

"There's a man who works at the Cabildo who's in the sworn service of the Union. If you need a telegraph sent, go in late on a weekday, sit on one of the benches for seeing the magistrate, and take out the watch to consult it on a regular basis. Make sure it can be seen by anyone who is watching. When you've done that for a good bit, go outside. There is a brass message box on the corner of the building with slots for each of the clerks and other officials. The brackets are rusting, so the box hangs loose from the wall. Stick your telegram in an envelope and wedge it behind the box where it can't be seen. Wait until evening to make sure our man has retrieved it. Sign your telegram C.S."

"C.S.?"

"'Crescent Spy.' That's how you're known in Washington."

She smiled at this. "Cloak and dagger—like a French novel. Why can't you simply tell the man to expect me? I'll go in as a reporter and announce my presence. He can find me in the square after dark and I'll hand it to him directly."

Franklin shook his head. "Our friend is too cautious for that."

"That makes no sense. Is he trustworthy, or not? Does he think *we're* the untrustworthy ones? That we'd give up his name under hard questioning?"

"He is a slave," Franklin said.

"Oh. I see."

She thought of the condemned man at Fort Jackson. Caleb had been hanged for the simple crime of counting men. At the same time, his supposed white coconspirator had been sentenced to a few months of hard labor. This man at the Cabildo had assessed his risk, figuring that if his white counterparts fell under suspicion, they might turn over a black slave to save their own necks. Josephine would never do that, and she didn't believe Franklin would, either. But could they blame the man for doubting?

"Yes, now I understand," she added. She took the watch and tucked it back into the box.

"Don't test the system. It's only for emergency use. I have my own, similar watch. This one I had made on Exchange Alley to match the design. But it would be unfortunate if someone besides our man had noticed my watch, and then saw yours. He might think how curious it was that two different people had watches with the same Mohammedan crescent and star."

She nodded. "Emergency use only."

It was now dark, and the police blew their whistles to call order to Congo Square. The men with the beef bones continued banging for several more seconds in a small show of defiance, and then the music and dancing ground to a halt. Awnings dropped on the food carts, and vendors shouted suddenly reduced rates for their wares. A mass of bodies, both black and white, streamed toward the side alleys.

Franklin glanced around the square, eyes picking through the crowd. "I have something else important to discuss, but it's not safe here anymore."

He hailed a cab on the edge of the square, which led them clomping in a serpentine path through the city, south toward the river. Franklin asked why she'd found new lodging, which she explained away as the need to leave the hotel and find something more homelike. He should probably know about this business with the Colonel and Francesca, but she didn't know how to broach the subject without prying open the entire stinking barrel of fish.

They came into the uppermost section of the Garden District, where Franklin ordered the driver to halt his horse two streets up from the waterfront. After climbing the little dirt path to the levee, they took a stroll along the river.

The weather had turned cool and windy, which drove away both the mosquitoes and the thick smell of the river. One of Commodore Hollins's gunboats puffed upriver past the levee. It was a side-wheel steamer, either *Ivy* or *Tuscarora*, but she couldn't tell which from the thin light cast from deck lanterns.

"Not that I don't enjoy an evening constitutional," she began, "but you said you had something important. Now I'm worked up wondering what that could be."

"Now that I've got you here, I'm having second thoughts about asking your help. It will be dangerous."

"I'm not afraid of danger."

"A little fear is healthy. You don't do us any good dead, Josephine. That business at Head of Passes had me worried."

"Is there another battle brewing? I haven't heard anything."

"When the battle comes, you'll know it. The whole country will see it developing."

"Now you're toying with me."

"Have you been to the new Marine Hospital?"

"I saw it from the street. Large place, many buildings. A sure sign that the Confederacy is settling in for a long, hard road if they're expecting that many wounded."

"But it's not filled yet, only two or three wards occupied from fighting up Tennessee way."

"And?"

"So General Lovell has occupied near half of the hospital and turned it into his arsenal," Franklin said. "He is shipping in powder by the ton, and building a factory to make cartridges and shells. It won't only be the army that benefits—Commodore Hollins is counting on that arsenal, too. The Navy Department won't give him what he needs, so he needs it manufactured locally."

Josephine had heard some of this already. Lovell had been at work in the hospital since before its completion. But if powder was arriving in quantities measured in tons, the pace must have accelerated.

"Seems sensible given the neglect of the city's defenses," she said. "Lovell thinks New Orleans is under threat. Jeff Davis doesn't agree. So if Lovell wants to defend the city, he'll have to take matters into his own hands."

They fell silent as a couple strolled toward them on the levee in the opposite direction.

"Without that armory," Franklin continued after waiting for the couple to pass out of earshot, "the rebs will have a devil of a time keeping their forces in the fight."

Josephine stopped abruptly and grabbed Franklin's elbow to pull him around. "Hold on. So there *is* a battle brewing."

"Naturally," he said, his voice teasing. "We're in a war."

"Right here? In New Orleans?"

"That was the plan all along, remember? That was *your* plan."

"Thank heavens. Five months since I left Washington—seemed like it would never happen."

"It might be another five months still," Franklin said. "I don't know. I don't even know from which direction it will come—upriver, or down. Either way, we'll have a dogfight. Meanwhile, I've got orders, and that is to blow General Lovell's arsenal straight to Hades."

CHAPTER 20

A few days later, Josephine arrived at the Marine Hospital to find reporters from the *Bee*, the *Picayune*, and the *True Delta* already on site and harassing the several patients who had just arrived from Vicksburg by way of a hospital boat.

Rumor had spread among the newspapers that a famous patient was on site. Perhaps the poet Henry Timrod, who was reportedly serving at one of the forts upriver. There was no famous patient; that was a rumor spread by Josephine herself. In reality, she needed cover so she could poke around the hospital without falling under suspicion. She couldn't have people remembering how she'd shown up a week or two before the sabotage. Her fellow reporters provided cover.

Naturally, one of the other reporters was Stanley Ludd. When Josephine stepped out to take a stroll through the yard, he was already outside having a smoke. He watched her with a beady, pig-like expression.

"A curious waste of time, Miss Breaux. Curious indeed. We all rushed out to chase this phantom story, only to find that the most celebrated patient is a fellow who once won a ribbon at the county fair for the virility of his prize bull."

"I don't intend to waste my time, Mr. Ludd," she said, only catching herself at the last moment from using his nickname at the *Crescent*: Mr. Stinky Lard. "Good stories are everywhere you look."

And ahead of her, she spotted a very good story indeed. The brick buildings of the factory and arsenal lay at the far end of the hospital lot, where men came and went through a back gate, itself guarded by several armed soldiers. Along that side of the compound lay the stables as well, a ramshackle construction of boards and lumber odds and ends, nailed together in a slipshod manner. The picket fence that encircled the hospital lot followed the back wall of the stables for a stretch. Beyond the fence lay a marshy, poorly drained field.

Ludd puffed his cigarette as he fell in behind her. "You've been a machine, Miss Breaux. A veritable one-woman printing press. If the quality of your writing weren't so uniformly strong, I'd wager that Fein had been throwing your byline onto stories written by his typical stable of hacks."

"All those stories are mine, Mr. Ludd."

"So I believe, so I believe. I don't know how you manage."

"I am young. I have energy to spare."

She felt herself puffing. That was only the writing he could see. Ludd knew nothing of her prodigious output on behalf of the Union.

But she couldn't get carried away. He had to stop following so she could chat with the soldiers at the gate unmolested. She had to get at them from an angle. It would be suspicious to come right out and ask what she needed—when is the change of the guards? how do you secure the powder from theft or sabotage?—but with a few friendly words from a young woman maybe they'd volunteer something useful. But not with Ludd slithering after her.

"Amazing energy," he said. "I only lament that Mr. Fein enjoys your services, not I. Perhaps my initial offer was insufficiently generous."

Josephine stopped and put her hands on her hips. She returned his dismissive words from that night on *Calhoun*: "'What are you doing here? Don't you have society gossip to cover or some such rubbish?'"

"Touché. I behaved badly."

"Yes, you did."

"I thought I had a scoop. I was irritated that I hadn't. Then, when I read the broadside of stories you fired off after the battle, I saw how you'd outmaneuvered me. I reported that *Preble* had been sunk. You claimed *Richmond* had been the one damaged, but not sunk. I claimed that the river would henceforth be open to Confederate shipping. You said *Manassas* wasn't strong enough to break the blockade on its own. I called you a naïve child in print, a defeatist, and you cut me to pieces. When the true facts of the case became known, I saw that you possessed all of the qualities I need.

"I have men who are prolific," he added, "and men who can put poetry into print. I have never met anyone who could do both."

She knew it was flattery, but his words filled her with a warm glow, like she had a bellyful of fine whiskey. It was dangerous, this need for praise. Too much, and she'd be drunk on it, and unable to do her duties.

"What is Fein paying you?" Ludd asked.

"Fifteen dollars a week."

"I'll give you twenty. That's a thousand dollars *a year*."

Josephine's eyes widened. In reality, Fein was only paying her eight. She'd said fifteen only to put Ludd off.

Her silence seemed to encourage him, and he pressed on. "You have many qualities, Miss Breaux. I need you at the *Picayune.*"

"I do have many qualities, Mr. Ludd," she said. "And among them is loyalty."

The following Sunday, Josephine and Franklin met near the cathedral instead of at Congo Square. As Christmas approached, the city seemed to forget the war and threw itself into the parades and other celebrations of the season. Josephine and Franklin watched the carolers with their candles and bells, and bought beignets and hot eggnog while strolling past the bonfires lit along the levee to welcome Père Noël.

The alcohol loosened Franklin's tongue, and he told Josephine stories about his childhood in Massachusetts: the swimming hole where he'd go with his brothers, his kind and tender sister, Ruth, who died of scarlet fever, his dog, Bandit, who once made off with the entire Christmas goose. One of Franklin's great-grandfathers was still alive. The old man had planted apple trees two years ago at the age of eighty-eight and optimistically thought he would live long enough to get a good harvest.

Only as Josephine and Franklin walked back along the levee did she realize that his chatter was due as much to nerves as to the eggnog. He told her that he wanted to move against the arsenal at Christmas, while the city was distracted.

"The soldiers are local militia," he said. "They'll be spending time with family, drinking brandy and eating too much goose and turkey. The city itself will be relaxed. It won't be hard to do what we need to do."

Josephine's pulse quickened. "What is our plan? Sabotage?"

He nodded. "On a grand scale."

"What do we do? What do you need *me* to do?"

His brow furrowed. "I only meant 'we' in that the information you already collected will help me infiltrate the Marine Hospital."

Josephine waited anxiously for news of some disaster at the arsenal, but nothing came. On Christmas Day, her landlady, Nellie, knocked on her bedroom door and said with a knowing smile that a handsome gentleman caller wished to see her. Nellie would give them privacy in the parlor.

Franklin told her what had gone wrong. Late that very night after the walk along the levee, he had approached the hospital compound through the swampy fields abutting the back side. Armed with a crowbar, he intended to pry off the boards on the rear of the stables to gain entrance to the interior. But before he could move, two guards with muskets and lamps came patrolling around the exterior of the compound, peering into the darkness from beneath forage caps. Franklin was fortunate not to be spotted.

Far from relaxing security, it seemed that General Lovell had increased scrutiny on the exterior approaches.

"Work is accelerating," Franklin told Josephine in a low voice, with a glance at the parlor door, as if worried that Nellie would be eavesdropping. "Another shipment of powder came in from upriver three days ago. And Lovell is casting shells in the city foundries, bringing them in for storage. I've got to find a way inside."

"What's wrong with the front door? It's a hospital, not a prison. You enter the hospital, leave through the back, and cut across to the arsenal."

"The front has guards, too. I'll be challenged."

"Not if you enter as a patient. A gentleman soldier, so you can get to the back ward, where the officers stay. Frank Beaudoin, creole planter, lately commissioned as an officer in glorious service of the cause."

He looked intrigued, but cautious. "They'll hear my accent the moment I open my mouth."

"So change your story. There are plenty of Yankees in New Orleans."

"Maybe at the yards, but not among the officers."

"Then don't talk. There was a mishap with a firearm, and you have a wounded jaw. But being a gentleman, you have your own private nurse." She loosened her mouth and let a full New Orleans accent pass through. "And she can do all of the talking."

A cab pulled up in front of the Marine Hospital later that week, and Josephine helped Franklin out, who gave a dramatic groan, as if the very movement caused him pain. Cotton bandages wrapped around his head and jaw. She'd dabbed them with pig blood, which had now dried, leaving a caked mess. He wore a uniform with a captain's bars that she'd procured on Exchange Alley.

While Franklin stood swaying, Josephine took out a carpetbag, so full that it couldn't be latched. The edge of a pair of trousers peeked out. She paid the cab driver, who drove his horse on with a flick of the whip and disappeared, jouncing, into the night mist.

Josephine eyed the two soldiers in butternut jackets and forage caps who stood on the porch of the two-story brick building. Gaslights flickered on either side of the door, reflecting on their young faces as they peered down at the newcomers.

"Please, sirs," Josephine said, "could you help me with the captain?"

They came trotting down the stairs and took Franklin's arms. He took a few shaky steps toward the front door. She'd had him swish his mouth with whiskey before they left the cab so he'd have the smell of a man trying to drink away his pain.

"What happened to him?" one of the soldiers asked. "Yanks?"

"Not hardly," she said. "He did this all by his lonesome."

The other one whistled. "You don't say. At home, or were it with his men?"

Franklin groaned, and held up a hand, as if trying to keep Josephine from telling the story.

"Now you hush," she told him. "It's the foolhardiest thing I ever heard, and it'll serve you right to hear it a few times. Live fire drilling," she told the men. "Shot himself straight through the cheeks. Fortunate he only lost two of his teeth, not his tongue."

"Or his brains," the first one said.

"Sound like he don't have none to spare," the other said with a grin.

She chuckled at this. "I was wondering. Anyhow, I 'spect he'll recover, if the doctor is any good."

"Doc Gibbons is the best, they say. 'Course, he won't be in 'til morning."

Franklin groaned.

"I figured as much," Josephine said with a glance at her patient. "But the captain'll be needing something stronger than whiskey for the pain. There now," she said as they got him up the stairs and in the front door. "I don't suppose one of you boys could help me find a bed for Captain Beaudoin?"

"Be happy to, miss."

"I'll come, too," the other said.

She'd meant the query as a way of discerning their general discipline. Could they be coaxed away from their posts? But she realized an added benefit as they picked their way through the first building and into the rear ward where the officers kept beds. They passed two orderlies, but because she was being escorted, nobody questioned Josephine and Franklin.

The officer ward only had three other patients. One lay in bed on the far end of a long, open hall, a book on his chest, an oil lamp at a little desk next to his bed. Even from a distance, she could see the mass of blisters and scabs on his face and neck. A second man, this one nearer, was also reading a book by lamplight.

As soon as Josephine had Franklin's boots off and got him in bed, she sent the young soldiers back to their post. She found a chair and pulled it up next to the bed.

"Now we wait?" she asked in a low voice. He nodded without speaking.

The nurse appeared a few minutes later. She was heading toward the poxied man in the corner, but veered in their direction as soon as she spotted them. Josephine rose to her feet.

"Who is the patient?" the woman asked.

"Captain Beaudoin. I'm his private nurse, but I won't get in your way." Josephine sketched out the same story she'd told the soldier, then added, "I promised to stay with the captain until Dr. Gibbons arrives in the morning. I don't mean to be any trouble— I'll only sit here waiting."

"Of course. Do you need anything else?"

"I don't suppose you have laudanum? I gave him whiskey, but he's still in pain."

On cue, Franklin let out a groan.

"I'm afraid not. If we did, it would be shipped to Virginia for our boys on the front line."

The woman looked familiar to Josephine from her visit to the hospital a couple of weeks earlier, but it was dark in the hall, and with Josephine's accent disguised, she hoped she wouldn't be recognized.

The woman looked like she was going to say something else, so

Josephine spoke first to put off any potentially difficult questions. "They don't have a quarantine room for smallpox?"

The woman glanced toward the patient in the corner. "It's not smallpox. It's something . . . more delicate." She reached into the pocket of her apron and pulled out a little vial. "A night with Venus, a lifetime with Mercury."

Ah. The man was suffering from syphilis, the treatment of which was mercury salts. One more soldier who had succumbed to the fleeting pleasures offered by the bordellos of the Irish Channel. Better the smallpox. If it didn't kill you, it left you scarred, but you'd never suffer it twice. Syphilis was a lifelong companion.

"Well, thank you," Josephine said. "Please don't trouble yourself with us. The captain only needs some rest and a visit from the doc."

As soon as the nurse left, the third patient in the room got out of his bed and hobbled over using a pair of crutches. He had a bandaged leg, but there was nothing wrong with his tongue. He wanted to know what unit the captain served with. Josephine stammered something about the Eleventh Louisiana Rifles, to which Franklin shook his head and muttered something incomprehensible. It seemed really important for the second man, a fellow captain, to figure out, and he kept at it for several rounds before he gave up.

Josephine took it only as excessive inquisitiveness, because the man then went on to proudly explain how he was the head of the Wilson Rangers, a group of "gentlemen who would defend the honor of the city against Yankee scoundrels."

She almost laughed. She'd written a story about the rangers, who called themselves the Blackleg Cavalry—former river gamblers and other sorts who'd gained large sums of money through sharp practice. Her article in the *Crescent* had been glowing, speaking of their fine spirit, the handsome figures they cut in the saddle. Her private report for Northern eyes had painted a different picture. She told how they spent more time lounging in the shade reading and swilling beer from jugs than they did drilling. How they seemed to be in it for the adventure and the opportunity to romance grateful Southern girls. If trouble came, the company would melt away like sugar snipped into hot coffee.

"Finally," Franklin muttered when the man had returned to his bed. "I thought I'd need to knock him over the head."

An hour passed before the syphilis patient turned down his oil lamp, followed by the other reader. The Blackleg fellow turned his light down last, and then the nurse made a final pass through the ward, her footsteps quiet as she walked up and down the mostly empty aisle between the beds. When she was gone, they were plunged into darkness, with only a tiny bit of moonlight filtering through a high window to form a luminous square on the middle of the plank floor. And still Josephine and Franklin remained quiet.

It must have been nigh on midnight before Franklin sat up on his cot and grabbed for his boots. He stripped away the bandages and stuffed them into his pockets. Josephine waited until his dark shadow rose in front of her; then she grabbed the carpetbag and led him quietly toward the far door.

CHAPTER 21

Josephine's heart was pounding as she held the back door cracked for Franklin to slip outside. It was a dark night, the barest sliver of moon in the sky. They waited in the shadows of the hospital building, looking across the yard.

The two-story brick arsenal sat next to the cartridge factory and its now-quiet smokestack but otherwise was apart from any other buildings in the hospital compound. Even the stables lay some seventy or eighty yards east of the arsenal. This was good. Somehow she'd misremembered the arsenal on the other side, nearer the stables, and worried about the need to throw open the stable doors before the attack. A good horse was also valuable war material, but she didn't have it in her to burn all those animals alive, never mind the strategic expediency. Fortunately, she now saw that the stables were on the far side of the cartridge factory, which would shield the horses from the blast.

Frogs croaked and trilled from the marshy fields beyond the fence, joining their chorus to the hum, buzz, and chirp of insects. After about ten minutes, a solitary figure trudged through the yard, a musket over one shoulder, and a lamp held in his free hand, swarming with moths. The watchman gave a casual inspection to the shadowy places near the arsenal before disappearing around the corner of the building.

Franklin looked up and down the yard. "Now!" he whispered.

They ran across the open space until they reached the safety of the other building. Franklin fished out a set of keys that clinked noisily. He spent precious moments testing one key after another in the lock.

While he did this, Josephine prepared the rest of the material. First, she checked the fuses to make sure that they were still held together and hadn't been knocked apart. The fuses were of Confederate design, and likely unreliable, but the general idea was simple. A tapered cylinder of paper was filled with mealed powder soaked in whiskey and marked in tenths of inches. The fuse would be cut to length and stuffed into a shell, enabling it to detonate after five, seven, or ten seconds. In this case, they'd gummed three fuses together, which, after testing on other fuses, seemed to give about twenty-five to thirty seconds. In case of failure, there was a second set of fuses so they could return and try again. Half a minute wasn't much time to run away, and neither of them could guess at the size of the explosion.

When Josephine was satisfied with the fuses, she verified that the white phosphorus matches were dry, and then wadded up bits of cotton and stuffed them in her ears. She balled two more pieces for Franklin.

It took him several attempts to find the right key, but at last the latch clicked and the door creaked open. He put away the keys, and twisted the cotton and stuffed it into his ears.

"Should I wait here with the spare fuses, or go in with you?" she asked, her voice sounding muffled through the cotton stopping up her ears.

He took the fuses and the matches. "Go back to the ward and wait. I'll come running and we can join the general evacuation."

"I'll stay here. You might need help."

"I won't need help, and I worry if you go running around in the dark you'll trip over your skirts."

"Don't worry about me. I won't trip."

"Once I get inside I have to light some of these matches just to see where I'm going. If there's loose powder in the air . . . *boom*."

"I've got good night eyes. I'll help."

"No time to argue. Go."

He slipped inside and pulled the door shut behind him. She thought about following anyway but swallowed her pride and hurried back across the yard instead. Once there, however, she couldn't bring herself to go inside and wait by his empty hospital bed. Any of a dozen things might go wrong, and there was no way she'd be waiting helplessly inside if that happened.

Long seconds passed. Her heart was pounding in her temples, and it felt like a swarm of crickets had been turned loose in her belly. She stared at a spot in the black wall opposite her where she supposed the door must be, willing it to open. It had been too long. Something had gone wrong. The guard would be returning shortly. She set down the carpetbag and descended the porch, ready to cross over and go inside.

The door swung open on the factory. A figure came running across the flat, muddy ground. There wasn't enough moonlight to pick out his features, but his wildly churning legs and flailing arms bespoke panic. He seemed to spot her, and waved wildly.

"Go! Get inside. Too close!"

There was a low thump, like an artillery shell burying itself in the ground and detonating, together with a flash of light in the windows of the factory. Josephine threw herself to the ground.

A split second later, the building exploded. She was still in mid-air, halfway between standing and falling to the ground, when there was a blinding flash of light and a shuddering, terrific, bone-crushing detonation. The shock wave threw her away, and she found herself on her back, stunned, a column of fire boiling into the sky. In its light she caught sight of chunks of mortared brick the size of large carriages lifting skyward, enormous beams hurling outward.

Suddenly, she was in the water next to the exploding *Cairo Red*, and she saw in her mind's eye the killing debris of that explosion raining down and knew she had only an instant before it happened here, too. Franklin was a few yards away, also down, but trying to regain his feet.

"No!" she cried. She could barely hear her own voice over the roar of the fire, the thump of secondary explosions, and the deafness from the original detonation.

The heavier debris landed first, huge beams and flaming chunks of roof. They were followed by brick and metal shards falling like lethal rain. There was nothing she could do but curl in a ball, hands over her head, trying to survive the bombardment. Something struck her shoulder with the force of a hammer blow, and she cried out.

At last it stopped, and she struggled to her feet. Her right shoulder ached, and she could barely lift her arm. The factory was a raging fire, with a dozen smaller fires across the yard. Franklin lay groaning in the middle of a heap of broken bricks. He bled from a nasty gash on his forehead, and clutched at his ribs. But he was alive, thank God. They were both alive.

She clawed away the bricks, grabbed him with her left hand, and tried to pull him up. "Move! We'll be caught."

The guard came running, shouting for help. But his attention was on the fire, not the two figures struggling in the middle of the open yard.

Franklin seemed to be recovering his wits. He grimaced in pain as he struggled to his feet, but he didn't make a sound. Josephine got the door open, grabbed the carpetbag—all with her left hand—and they slipped into the hospital ward. She told Franklin to hand over the bandages, grabbed them out of his pockets when he was slow to respond, and gritted her teeth against her own pain as she quickly wrapped them around his bloody forehead. Then she led him limping toward the front door of the officers' ward.

Chaos enveloped the Marine Hospital as they picked their way toward the front gates. The small garrison of a dozen or so men seemed equally divided between those rushing to fight the conflagration at the arsenal and those racing in the direction of town to fetch help. Those patients who could move streamed out the gates, risking cuts on their bare feet from all the blown-out glass from the windows.

Josephine dragged Franklin along with this group of men. His head was bleeding right through the bandages, and if anyone was paying attention they might wonder why he seemed to have fresh wounds, not to mention that both of them were filthy from falling in the muddy yard and then having a cascade of brick dust and wood chips come raining down on them.

Lamps and gaslights were on all along the edge of the city to their north, and men on foot and horse soon came hurrying up the road even as the patients evacuated in the opposite direction.

Josephine didn't dare hail a cab, not with dozens of people streaming toward the hospital. The fewer people who saw Franklin with his bloody head, the better. Rumors would be flying as people searched for the saboteur. So the two of them kept to darkened streets, which took them down several disreputable alleys. In one of them, two men came out of a grog house, apparently decided that Franklin was drunk and should be robbed, and threatened them with knives. Franklin drew his pistol, and the men slunk off like a pair of river rats. It's a good thing they were so cowardly; Franklin could barely hold the gun steady.

"I'll never make it," Franklin said a couple of blocks later.

"Where do you live?"

"Canal and Rampart."

That was still nearly two miles away. "Let me get a cab."

"We can't risk it. Find a dark alley and leave me. I'll take my chances. In the morning I'll feel better." He pointed. "Right there, behind that rubbish."

"You won't feel better, and I'm not leaving you. Keep going."

"I tell you, I can't make it home."

"My place is only a mile away. We'll come in the side door. Nellie will either be asleep or on the corner, gossiping with the neighbor ladies about the explosion."

"A mile?" He groaned. Then he seemed to straighten, gather his reserves. "I'll try."

He grew weaker as they continued, and she worried that he was carrying some secret wound. She threw his arm around her shoulder again during the last two blocks. Finally, they reached Nellie Gill's cottage.

Josephine only just got Franklin up the back stairs and onto the bed before Nellie came up looking for her. Nellie said she'd been awake in the parlor, unable to sleep after the blast, when she heard her lodger come in. Josephine claimed that she'd thrown on clothes and rushed toward the fire after hearing the explosion, hoping to cover the story. Soldiers had turned her away at the hospital gates. All this was said from behind a cracked door so Nellie wouldn't see what a mess she was.

Nellie prodded her to come out, anxious for more gossip.

"I've already begun to undress," Josephine said.

"Undress? There are Yankees in the city! We're under attack!"

"We're not under attack," Josephine said calmly. "It was a lone saboteur—that's what they're saying. Anyway, it's late, and if I don't write what I saw, there will be the devil to pay tomorrow at the paper."

At last Nellie gave up and went back downstairs.

Josephine latched the door and hurried to Franklin's side, where she lit the lamp on the bedside table. He had a pale, sickly appearance, but when she peeled away the bandage from his head, the wound had mostly clotted. She wet a cloth at the basin and dabbed at his forehead until she could get a better look. The wound was superficial, and the skull didn't appear fractured. But he didn't look well at all.

"Where do you hurt?"

"All over. Like I was jumped in an alley and beaten up with bricks and chains."

He had his gun on his lap, and she set this aside. She tugged off his boots and began to unbutton his shirt. He put his hands up.

"What are you doing?" he asked.

"I'm worried you've got another injury. I need to look."

"Do you have training as a nurse?"

"Only what I learned from observation at military hospitals in Washington. But I should be clever enough to notice if something is amiss. Once I know, I'll call a doctor if necessary. The bricks-and-chains story will hold well enough. You almost *were* jumped."

"If you do that, your landlady will know I've been here."

"Let me worry about that."

She pulled away his hands and finished unbuttoning his shirt, which she peeled off and set to one side. Franklin had strong shoulders and arms, and curly black hair that trailed down from his chest to his navel and his strong abdominal muscles. A curious flutter entered her belly as she looked up to his handsome face. His eyes were closed.

Not now, you fool. Stay focused.

Josephine felt at his chest, running her fingers down his sternum. She hesitated at his belly but, given that her primary concern was some injury to his internal organs, felt along his stomach for anything that seemed amiss. She watched his face as she did so, as she'd seen a surgeon at a military hospital do. There was no grimace of pain.

Since nothing seemed amiss on his front torso, she urged him to roll onto his side. If she couldn't find anything on his back, she'd have to take off his trousers, a thought that made her blush. Franklin sucked in his breath as he obeyed.

"What hurt just now?"

"Ribs."

She got him all the way onto his stomach and lifted the lamp for a better look. Ugly purple bruises splotched his back where bricks had rained down, leaving marks from his shoulders to the small of his back. Her own shoulder was still aching, and no doubt if she took off her dress and held up a mirror she'd see her own bruising there. It would be sore for days, she guessed. But Franklin's injuries seemed much worse than her own.

Franklin drew in his breath as she prodded the bruises. When she got to his left side, he made a sound far back in his throat. She touched again, poking at the ribs where they curved along the spine.

"Ow, easy."

"Broken ribs," she said. She touched again, eliciting another groan. "Likely several of them."

"Ouch. Careful, there."

"Moving you in that condition was a shock to the system. You've already got better color now, though. I suspect you need a couple of weeks of rest is all."

"I can't be down two weeks," he said. "What about my leg?"

"But you were walking. Does that hurt, too?"

"Like the devil." He pointed at his left leg. "Just below the knee."

"Unbutton your trousers, please."

"Is that necessary?"

"It's either that or call for a doctor."

He unbuttoned his pants, and Josephine tugged them off. He was wearing only his underclothes, and she was careful to look down at his legs and not . . . *elsewhere.*

There was a nasty, swollen lump on his left leg roughly two inches below his knee. To her relief, the bone wasn't deformed—that level of break would mean the surgeon's saw—but when she poked at it, he bit down on his knuckles.

"Broken?" he asked, voice strained.

"I don't know," she admitted. "But if it is, all that walking didn't help. I should have risked a cab."

"You did the right thing."

"You're not getting up, that's for sure. If the bone separates, you'll lose your leg. I'll splint it tomorrow."

"I can't stay here."

"You can and you will. Right in that bed, not moving a muscle except to sit up with the bedpan. I'll sleep on the floor and bring you food."

"But what about your landlady? Doesn't she clean?"

Josephine thought about Nellie's habits. She entered once a week to scour the bedpans, sweep, beat the rug over the balcony railing, and wipe the windows with water and a rag. And Josephine didn't think she could be easily put off from it, either.

"She comes every Friday. That gives us almost a week." Josephine bit her lip, worried that she wouldn't be able to move him that soon.

Franklin needed help. *She* needed help. Josephine glanced to the Oriental box on the dresser. Inside was the pocket watch with the curious gilt cover. Surely if anything counted as an emergency, this was it.

CHAPTER 22

At dawn, someone came banging impatiently on Nellie Gill's front door. Josephine had been dozing fitfully in the rocking chair by the window, and sprang to her feet, alarmed. Her pulse slowed when she looked out and saw one of Solomon Fein's delivery boys below her on the porch, panting and out of breath, an envelope in hand. Nellie poked her head out and took the message. The boy waited while Nellie came back inside.

Josephine had washed up last night and put on her nightgown, and now she threw her shawl over her shoulders and made for the bedroom door so she could get in the hallway before Nellie came up with the note.

Franklin lay on his belly, with his bare back uncovered. The bruising looked even worse by the light of day, now a deep purple, one injury spreading into the next. He was snoring softly, and she shook his shoulder to wake him from his well-needed rest. He turned his head, blinking, a groan emerging. She slapped a hand over his mouth and put her finger on her own lips. Then she hurried to the bedroom door as Nellie came creaking up the stairs.

She came into the hall with the shawl around her shoulder as Nellie reached the top. The woman handed over the note. "From the newspaper. Is it about the fire at the hospital?"

Josephine unfolded the papers. Solomon Fein's spiderlike script crawled across the page.

Dear Miss Breaux,

You've no doubt heard about the fiendish attack on the hospital arsenal. If you have written anything, send it post haste. No need to go to the hospital. Keller will be covering the story. He is General Lovell's cousin.

Josephine scowled. Cousin? And because of that, Keller had an inside track to a good story? Was that what Fein was claiming? What did that matter when Keller couldn't write? In past articles that she'd reworked on his behalf, a German had been confused with an Englishman, a murderer swapped for his judge, and Florida had migrated north until it was somehow located between Georgia and South Carolina. If Keller wrote about a mule, you could be sure he meant a horse.

Nellie studied her face. "What does it say?"

"They've given the story to some dolt."

"Oh, I thought maybe people had been killed. You looked so upset."

Nellie's naïve comment reminded Josephine how foolish her

professional jealousy was, given the situation. She looked back at Fein's letter to read on.

> *But don't fret, I've got a better story for you. A chance to play the heroine again. A woman came in this morning looking for you. She lives on Duggan Street, near the Marine Hospital. Saw two figures flee the hospital not five minutes after the blast: an injured man and a woman supporting him. Overheard them talking about sabotage. Said she has a good description of them both.*
>
> *She's a German, name of Otz. Wants to give the story to you, because she thinks there's spies in the army and the government. I figure she wants to see her name in the paper under your byline. This is a chance to get the story first. Maybe we can find these fiends and get them talking before Lovell and Hollins string them up.*

She looked up to see that Nellie was still studying her. Josephine kept the alarm from her face. Who was this Otz woman? Had Josephine been so careless as to mention sabotage during their flight from the hospital? She couldn't remember doing so, only remembered urging Franklin on, but her head had been ringing, her ears stuffy from the blast. Events were hazy. It might be true.

What was clear enough was that Otz had accurate information. How close was her description? It had been dark, but she must have noticed the bandages around Franklin's head. That wound on his forehead was too low to conceal with a hat; if the woman gave an accurate description, he'd have to flee the city. How could he do that with several broken ribs and a fractured leg bone?

She turned to the second page.

> *Mrs. Otz will be at the Paris Hotel for lunch.*
> *We will pay, so collect a receipt for the cost of the*
> *meal. Look for a handsome woman, about thirty-*
> *five or so. She'll be alone, watching for you through*
> *a lorgnette. 12:30.*
>
> *Yours,*
> *S. Fein*
>
> *P.S. Suggest something cheap off the menu. Don't let*
> *her order the lobster and filet. The haddock is good.*

"Go downstairs and hold the messenger boy," she told Nellie. "I have a return note."

Back in her room, she grabbed her notebook, her fountain pen, ink, and blotter, and sat at the desk, where she scribbled a quick reply.

> *Mr. Fein,*
>
> *Couldn't get to the hospital, so have no story. Was*
> *stopped at the gates by soldiers. Meant to return this*
> *A.M. but will meet Mrs. Otz at P.H. instead. If she*
> *has good inf. I'll find these villains and get a story*
> *before they hang.*
>
> *Yours,*
> *J. Breaux*
>
> *P.S. The haddock at the P.H. isn't fit for a starving cat.*

By the time the cab carried Josephine toward the French Quarter a few hours later, she was bathed, her hair brushed and pinned, wearing crinoline and petticoats over a velvet bodice, with mother-of-pearl combs holding her dark curls under her hat. If she'd carried a small French handbag instead of the leather satchel with her writing implements, she could have passed for a fine lady on her way to a benefit luncheon to raise funds for the Confederacy.

When the cab rounded the corner at Royal and Hospital Streets, she looked south and saw a cloud of smoke still hanging gray and sluggish in the air toward the hospital. If she hadn't been so worried about what this Otz woman did or didn't know, she'd have leaned forward and ordered the driver to carry her there. She had a good idea of the devastation they'd wrought to General Lovell's efforts, but wanted to make a visual confirmation. And, she admitted to herself, she couldn't bear the thought of that idiot Keller botching the story.

The cab clattered down the uneven cobbles into the Quarter and shortly pulled up in front of the Paris Hotel. She paid the driver and went inside, studying every single person coming and going, from hotel guests to bellhops. A sharp-eyed young officer in a gray coat was smoking near the restaurant entrance and studied her as she approached. Her heart rate kicked into a brisk trot.

Miss Breaux, is it? We have some questions for you. Yes, some very hard questions.

But when she stepped past him, he only nodded. "Afternoon, miss."

"Good afternoon to you, sir."

Once inside, she looked across the restaurant. It wasn't busy on a Sunday afternoon, and there were only seven or eight tables with patrons. Of these, only one person was alone, a woman in a green silk dress with a lorgnette held up to her eyes, who was looking toward the entrance. She spotted Josephine and waved her over.

Josephine sidestepped a waiter as she crossed the restaurant. She kept her face relaxed, and had mostly tamed her emotions by the time she reached the table. Then the woman dropped the lorgnette.

It was Francesca Díaz.

Josephine froze. "What are you doing here?"

"We have an appointment, do we not?" Francesca said with a smile.

"There must be some mistake."

"Is there, now? Miss Breaux, the so-called heroine of the Confederacy, and Mrs. Otz, a German lady who witnessed something most peculiar near the Marine Hospital last night." She said this last part with a German accent. "You see, dear, you are not the only one who can play a part. Are you going to stand there drawing attention to yourself? Or will you join me for lunch?"

Josephine glanced up to see the waiter approaching and pulled up a chair at the table. She took the menu and waited until the waiter was gone before fixing on Francesca again. "What do you want?"

"At the moment? Lunch. I'm hungry."

"And I'm busy. I have stories to write, and I don't need this nonsense. Did the Colonel send you?"

"No. In fact, the Colonel begged me not to come." Francesca shrugged. "'Begged' might be a strong word. He was uncomfortable with my purpose. And he doesn't relish the thought of his precious Josie falling into trouble. But we have suffered setbacks of late, which calls for difficult decisions. Once I convinced him that any trouble was of your own making . . ."

Josephine couldn't stomp out of the restaurant until she knew what cards this woman held in her hand, but first she had to take control of the conversation. She'd been caught off balance when Francesca lowered the lorgnette, but she was regaining her wits.

"When did you know it was me?" Josephine asked. "From the moment we met on the ship out of Havana, or not until that night at Congo Square?"

"Neither. You looked terribly familiar when I first met you, but I was too excited to be meeting the famous Josephine Breaux. I still couldn't place you until we were lying in the dark after the swamp man rescued us from the sand bar. Then you said that bit of bravado about not being afraid of the man groping you in the dark. It reminded me of someone I once knew—a girl with the swagger of a riverboat gambler. Someone also named Josephine. Hah. Pretty clever. Not you—me, for figuring it out."

"You sound quite self-satisfied," Josephine said. "Anyway, it doesn't matter. I already told the Colonel I don't want to see him again. If you're here on your own behalf, fine. If you're here on his, you can forget it."

"I didn't call you here for either of those reasons. You have something that belongs to us."

"No, I don't. If you're talking about the box, it was given to me. Anyway, I sold it on Exchange Alley, like I told the Colonel."

"I don't believe it. The Colonel told me what was hidden in the box, how valuable it was. So tell me, if you didn't sell it, how did you end up with all of this?" Francesca waved her hand at Josephine's dress and gestured at the mother-of-pearl combs in her hair.

"I work hard. I earn money for my efforts."

"I'll bet you do. Money for *all* of your efforts. Be that as it may, you're twenty years old. I was once twenty, and willing to do all manner of things to survive. But a young woman like you—mother dead, no money to her name, no family to search out and beg for help? She's destined for the brothels or the dance halls. You've apparently done none of this."

Josephine bristled, in part because she knew it was true. She had no doubt that if left destitute *now*, she'd pick herself up and start over using her wits and confidence. But four years ago had been another matter. Without those gemstones, where would she be now? For that matter, if she interviewed the painted women in the Irish Channel, how many would she find who had once been full of hopes, every bit as clever and ambitious as Josephine?

The waiter came, which saved her from having to respond, at least for the moment. Francesca ordered the lobster and filet. Fein would be delighted at that. Josephine asked about the haddock. Thankfully, it was not in stock, or Josephine would have felt obligated. Instead, she picked something chicken with a fussy French name.

"We knew you had money," Francesca said when the waiter had left. "But we couldn't figure out where you kept it. That time you caught the Colonel was the second time we'd searched your rooms."

"How dare you? I should summon the police right now."

"Save me your sanctimony. So we've been following you. That's why we were at Congo Square that night. It wasn't a coincidence. Two other times we saw you there, meeting with that handsome man with the mustache. That same fellow was on the blockade-runner. Strange coincidence."

"And?" Josephine affected nonchalance. In reality, her palms were sweating. "I am allowed to have gentlemen suitors, am I not?"

"Again, with the act. When will you drop it? You know the rest. I told it to your newspaper friend. Mrs. Otz spotted two people fleeing the conflagration at the Marine Hospital. One was a wounded man with a mustache. The other was you. Mrs. Otz, of course, was me. I couldn't figure out why you'd gone to the hospital. So many questions I have."

"You can't expect me to explain everything," Josephine said. "There are enemies in New Orleans. Union agents who wish to punish me for the spying in Virginia I did for the cause."

"Oh, you're a spy, all right," Francesca said. "But not for 'the cause,' as you put it."

Josephine started to push away. "I won't sit and listen to this slander."

"Sit down or I will go at once to General Lovell and tell him who destroyed the arsenal."

Josephine stopped and pulled herself in to the table again. "You're more wrong than you can imagine."

It wasn't a very effective lie, and they both knew it. Nevertheless, she was forced to commit to her position, like a gambler on a bad run of luck who throws down all his money on a single hand.

"But my work is important enough that I'm willing to listen," Josephine continued. "I can't risk the Yankees learning what I'm doing. What do you want? Money?"

"The Colonel wants to see you. That's the first thing. He wants to meet you at Jackson Square in front of the Cabildo and talk."

"That's all?"

"He'd also be mighty grateful if you'd loan him a hundred dollars so he can get back in the game. But frankly, he has lost his touch. We earned a thousand dollars blockade-running, and he lost it in two nights of faro. A bit of silver falls into his hand and he'll be off to ride the tiger again."

"Done. A hundred dollars. One meeting with the Colonel."

"You misheard me," Francesca said. "I said that would satisfy the Colonel, but I'm not so forgiving. Those gems didn't belong to you—"

"If there *were* gems, they wouldn't have belonged to you, either."

"But I am his wife now. So yes, they did." The woman waved her hand. "But never mind the gems, or the ill-gotten money you received from selling them. You are a spy and a traitor. A woman like that should pay for her crimes."

"And by 'pay' you mean money in your palm. How much?"

"Six thousand dollars."

Josephine drew her breath. So much. She'd been thinking a few hundred, maybe a thousand. "I don't have it."

This much was true. She had a little less than four thousand remaining. But it was true that she'd received nearly six from the sale of the gemstones, after her donation to the Sanitarium for the Burned and Indigent. She had spent a fair bit of it getting established in Washington: taking courses in etiquette, buying books on grammar and rhetoric to perfect her writing skills, and a wardrobe befitting her assumed station. And then there was the money she'd spent to move back and forth between Union and Confederate lines, and the supplies she'd donated to General Beauregard's camp to convince him she was a secessionist from Maryland. Since arriving in New Orleans, her expenses and her income had more closely matched.

"Then get it," Francesca said. "I'll give you three days."

"That's impossible. How do you propose I do that?"

"You'll find a way," Francesca said firmly. "We'll meet again on Wednesday. Same time, same restaurant. When you've paid me, you can go to the square, where the Colonel will be waiting."

"This is preposterous. I most certainly cannot do what you suggest."

"No? Then I'll go to General Lovell and tell him the truth. Miss Josephine Breaux was seen fleeing the arsenal after the fire in the company of a wounded man recently arrived from the North. Here is the description of the wound to his head. If you look, you will no doubt find him hiding in or near the home of Mrs. Nellie Gill, whose husband serves with the army in Tennessee."

"Don't do this," Josephine begged.

"Six thousand dollars. You have three days."

The waiter appeared with their food. He put down Francesca's lobster and filet first, then slid in Josephine's plate with a flourish.

"Good news, mademoiselle. The chef found a final piece of haddock in the icebox."

CHAPTER 23

On Monday morning, Josephine returned to her room with two hardboiled eggs taken from Nellie's kitchen, some hard cheese, part of a bun, and a jar of fig preserves she'd swiped from the pantry. She served them to Franklin on a copy of yesterday's *Crescent*, while she retreated to her desk to compose a telegram.

> *Urgent.*
> *F.G. injured in blast.*
> *Enemy knows where hiding.*
> *Must evacuate by Wednesday.*
> *C.S.*

It gave her a small thrill to sign it thus. *C.S.*—the Crescent Spy.

When Josephine finished, she folded it in an envelope, retrieved the curious pocket watch from the Oriental box, and stuck both envelope and watch into her satchel. When she looked up, Franklin was watching with a scowl. He'd taken a bite from one of the eggs, but set the rest of it aside.

"I don't want you sending that," he said. "It's an unnecessary risk."

"You don't even know what it says."

"Something about bringing me a doctor, am I right? I'll be fine. By Friday when your landlady comes, I'll be able to get out of here on my own."

"That's not what it says, and you won't be up and about by then anyway."

He swung out of bed, wincing when he tried to put weight on his injured leg. "Let me see that."

"Get back in bed," she said. "That's an order."

He raised an eyebrow. "Excuse me?"

"I have new information—don't give me that look, I'm not telling you what—and you need to trust me. You're injured, so for now, I'm in charge, and I'll make the decisions."

She set the satchel by the door and returned to push him back into bed. He didn't resist, but called to her again as she opened the door, still sounding uncertain. She ignored him and went downstairs and into the street to hail a cab.

Franklin's instructions had been to enter the Cabildo in the afternoon, so she couldn't send the telegram for several hours. Instead, she went to the offices of the *Crescent*. There, she found the newsroom racing ahead under full steam. Editors and writers hunched over desks, scribbling, while typesetters assembled copy, their hands flying across the mold, arranging letters.

Solomon Fein was berating Harold Keller in loud terms and slapping him with a rolled up sheaf of papers. "You know how many more copies the *Picayune* sells because of this? The *Bee*, the *True Delta*—they'll all make us look like fools.

"Thank God you're here," Fein said, spotting Josephine. He shoved Keller's pages at her. "Please tell me you can make something of this."

"Keller's story of the arsenal explosion?"

"Presumably. You tell me. Might be a story of Caesar's invasion of Gaul from all I can make of it."

She skim-read the story. Keller had buried the most important information at the bottom of the story, had placed the hospital on the wrong side of town, and claimed that it had been guarded by fifty men of the Tenth Louisiana Infantry, a company that had shipped to Virginia last summer. Apart from that, the writing was dull, uninspired. He didn't have a single description of the explosion or the fire. The story's only redeeming value was a quote from Keller's cousin, General Lovell. Assuming that was accurate. The rest he'd apparently invented whole cloth.

"It's a mess," she said.

"That's what he said," Keller burst out. "But nobody has explained to me *what* is wrong with it."

"You!" Fein said, pointing to the door with a scowl, as if Keller were a naughty puppy that had piddled on the rug. "Out!"

When Keller had slunk away, Fein turned back to Josephine. "Please tell me you can fix this mess."

"How long do I have?"

Fein consulted a pocket watch. "Seventy-two minutes."

"It won't be pretty. Workmanlike, at best."

He gave a sigh of relief. "That will do. I'll run your Otz story on the front page and push this piece of garbage to the back."

"About that," she began. She'd felt a little smug to see Fein's poor decision about the arsenal play out as expected, but now her satisfaction faded. "I don't have a story."

Fein's eyes widened. "You don't? Oh, God." He slapped a hand to his forehead. For all his theatrics, she'd have thought he'd entered the offices to discover an angry mob smashing the presses.

"This Otz woman is a glory-seeking liar," Josephine said. "She didn't see anything. She doesn't know anything. Trust me, I'm good at sniffing out such sorts."

"What does that matter?" he said desperately. "Take what you have and wrap it in equivocating language. Throw in your own speculation. We're trying to move papers, not testifying in court."

"I don't have anything. Not a word."

"Josephine, why? You didn't write me anything at all?"

She reached into her satchel. "I have this."

She handed him one of the spare articles that she'd stockpiled in the past week, written during one of her feverish writing sessions. It was about the sale of Confederate war bonds in the grog houses and brothels, full of amusing anecdotes, like a redheaded whore nicknamed Molly Bricktop, who had been freely offering her company to any man who purchased a hundred-dollar bond. Molly Bricktop proudly claimed that more than forty patriotic gentleman had already purchased the requisite bonds.

Fein skim-read it. He grunted. "Hmm. Not bad. But not front page, either. Maybe I could move Upton's piece to the lead and put this in its place. You can hack something out of Keller's dreck, and we'll put that below. When did you write this?"

"As soon as I had endured Mrs. Otz's fanciful tales, I spent a couple of hours trying to make something of it before I gave up. There was just enough time left in the day to go around to the Irish Channel, where I was sure I could dredge up something. I got up early this morning and wrote the story."

He grabbed her right hand and turned it over. A skeptical look passed over his face. "You have barely any ink on your fingers and none on the edge of your palm. You haven't been writing this morning."

"All right, I admit. I never even tried. I knew Otz was nuttier than a Vermont squirrel, and I threw out everything she said. I was sitting on this bond story already." That was somewhat closer to the truth.

"Never sit on a story. Whatever you have, whenever you have it, I want it. I'll never have too much. I could fill the whole blasted paper with your work." He pointed to Keller's article, still in her left hand. "Now sit down and make something of these chicken scratches. Then go out to the hospital and see if you can get anything more."

"Should have sent me in the first place."

Fein only grumbled at this and hurried off.

Keller's story really was a mess, and it was closer to ninety minutes before she came up with something satisfactory. By the end, Fein was pacing back and forth behind her, looking over her shoulder and asking if she was finished if she so much as stopped to compose a sentence in her head. She finally told him that if he didn't leave her alone she was liable to smash a bottle of ink over his head. Her final version was still weak, and she refused to let her name appear next to the story, but Fein seemed satisfied.

He ordered her off to the hospital to get the eyewitness accounts that Keller had failed to deliver, but she didn't go. For one thing, she didn't want to risk running into the nurse who'd given her and Franklin a bed in the officers' ward. Not now, less than two days from the blast, when the woman's memory would be sharpest. For another, it was already early afternoon, and she didn't know if she could make it to the hospital and then back down to Jackson Square before it would be too late to send the telegram. Today was Monday, and she only had two more days to get Franklin out of Nellie's house before Francesca made good on her threat.

Instead, Josephine traveled to the Quarter, where she sat in the square, writing her article about the destruction of General Lovell's arsenal. No need to go back out; she'd witnessed it. She'd *caused* it. She described the boom, the column of fire. She told about the mad flight from the hospital, explained how windows had shattered blocks away and how the explosion had shaken buildings all the way to the levee. She also inserted misdirections fabricated from her own imagination. A nurse claimed she'd spotted two soldiers sitting on a barrel of powder, smoking. Someone else thought it was boys from the Alley who'd broken in to steal supplies and somehow set off the detonation. But of course one couldn't discount Union spies. Two men with Boston accents had been sniffing around the hospital two days earlier.

When she finished, she took out the pocket watch with its curious design of crescent and star. It was after three. She crossed the square to the Cabildo, the mansard-roofed building constructed by the Spanish as their government offices and still used by the city. Inside, she sat on a bench next to an overly talkative old woman who was knitting socks. The woman claimed that she'd already delivered sixteen pairs, the wool purchased with her own pin money, and the socks knitted with her own hands. Josephine kept up a pleasant conversation, while checking her watch every time a black man passed.

The old woman left. A young soldier took her place, and confound it if he wasn't also talkative. Josephine gave him a false name when he got too friendly. She'd brought a copy of *Ivanhoe* in her satchel and tried to read the book to show she was disinterested in conversation, but he was persistent. She was relieved when the clerk finally called him in to see the magistrate.

A mulatto girl of eleven or twelve in a calico dress and with a bright-yellow *tignon* tied about her hair took the soldier's place. To Josephine's relief, the girl sat quietly, her hands folded in her lap. Josephine read in peace for some time, but when she looked up, the girl was peering over her shoulder to steal a read. When Josephine met her gaze, the girl looked away with a guilty expression.

Josephine smiled encouragement. "It's a good book—I don't blame you."

The girl wouldn't meet Josephine's gaze. She needed prodding. "Can you read?"

"Yes, miss," the girl said in a shy voice. She looked like she wanted to say something else, but closed her mouth and looked away again.

"What is your name?"

"Diana, but Ma and Pa call me Di."

"I like Diana better," Josephine said. "It's like the goddess of the hunt from the old Greek stories. Where did you learn to read, Diana?"

"My mama taught me. Is that book . . . ?"

"Is it what?"

"What's it about?"

Josephine smiled and showed the title. "It's a silly story of knights and fair ladies, but it's good fun. Would you like it?"

"Oh, no, miss! I couldn't."

"I've read *Ivanhoe* at least ten times. I've been meaning to buy some new novels, and this will give me an excuse. Please, you'll be doing me a favor."

Diana took the book and clutched it in her hands, eyes wide. That shining look in her eyes reminded Josephine so much of her own eagerness at getting a new book that she couldn't help but smile. That smile was infectious, and soon the two were grinning at each other as if they were sharing some delicious secret.

A black man came in from the square, carrying a wood crate over his shoulder. He spotted the girl and the woman smiling at each other and veered over.

"Hey there, Di," he said. "You ain't botherin' this fine lady none, you hear. Apologies miss, this child—"

The man stopped, his eyes dropping to the pocket watch that Josephine had set on her lap upon spotting him. His gaze flickered to her eyes, and his tongue darted to his lips.

"No trouble at all," Josephine said coolly. "We were only talking about books. It so happens I have a spare copy of this one." She put the watch in her satchel and stood up. "I hope you enjoy *Ivanhoe*, Diana."

The girl glanced back and forth between the man and Josephine, seeming to recognize that something had passed between them, but confused as to what.

Josephine wanted to ask more, curious about the child, who was evidently of mixed parentage. Yet unlike most such situations, her father appeared to be the black one, which meant her mother must be white. Spanish or French, perhaps? They were less fussy about such things than Americans. Yet even in New Orleans it was an unusual situation.

And one that would remain a mystery. She remembered Franklin's warning and had no intention of putting either father or child at risk.

Josephine went outside and took a pass through Jackson Square, looking for suspicious sorts who might be watching. A dozen old men near the cathedral played martial music with trumpets and drums. Children bought roasted nuts and lemon cakes from men with carts. Up near the levee, men unloaded barrels of molasses and crates of coffee from a flatboat.

Josephine saw nothing amiss but no longer trusted her ability to see if she were being spied on. She and Franklin had taken reasonable precautions the other night when approaching the hospital, yet Francesca had spied on them anyway. And so Josephine lingered near the brass message box, trying to figure out how to wedge her envelope behind it without being spotted.

Her chance came a few minutes later, when the small band started up again, this time with more vigor. Several dozen horses trotted into the square in formation, ridden by the Wilson Rangers, the dandied-up former riverboat gamblers. This brought half the square over to cheer them on.

Josephine took advantage of the commotion and walked straight to the message box attached to the exterior of the Cabildo. She turned as if to lean against the wall and slid her envelope into the gap between the brick and the back of the box. After that, she returned to one of the benches and waited. Around about dark, she saw the broad-shouldered figure she'd met inside earlier come outside, lean against the building near the box to have a smoke, and then stroll off a few minutes later.

On Josephine's way out of the square, a boy handed her a printed bill.

UNION SPY—REWARD!
$100 GOLD FOR THE CAPTURE OF THE DIABOLICAL FIEND
WHO ATTACKED THE MARINE HOSPITAL
$50 GOLD FOR THE CAPTURE OF ANY ACCOMPLICE

Below the announcement was a sketch of a man with dark hair and a mustache, his head wrapped in bandages.

CHAPTER 24

Josephine wrapped Franklin's head in fresh bandages. The wound below was clean, thankfully, but it was still a nasty, easily visible gash and would leave a scar. His forehead felt cool. No fever, thank heavens.

Franklin was sitting in bed, nibbling at the edge of the savory pastry she'd brought and drinking from a mug of beer that she'd poured. It was the first time he'd eaten more than a few bites since the accident, and this cheered her. Two days without food had only made him weaker and was keeping his body from mending properly.

After disposing of the old bandages, Josephine sat on the edge of the bed and lifted up the blanket to look at his leg. It was swollen, a bruise the size of her palm turning green and black. He drew in his breath sharply at her touch, but the bone seemed whole.

"How long does it take to get an answer from a telegram?" she asked, pulling the blanket down again.

"You won't get an answer. The system is for sending information out, not getting it in."

"Then how does the information come back through Mrs.
Dubreuil? Like when they sent an answer to my plans for taking
the city?"

"Sometimes instructions come, and Mrs. Dubreuil summons
me. There's no way of knowing if or when—they don't send those
trivially. There's too much risk."

"This is hardly trivial. I said you needed urgent help. I need to
know when it will come."

"There's no help to send."

"I don't believe that. Where else do we have agents?"

"St. Louis?" he said with a shrug. "South of that . . . ? Anyway,
it's not urgent. I'll stay here until Friday. By then I should be well
enough to hobble out of here. I walked here. I can walk far enough
to hail a cab to carry me home."

Josephine showed him the wanted poster given her at Jackson
Square earlier that evening. He studied it in silence for a few seconds. At last he gave a forced smile. "What a handsome man. Too
bad he's a diabolical fiend."

"This is no joke," she protested. "Look at the bandage. You'll
be recognized."

"I'll pull a hat low."

"That scar isn't going away anytime soon. Every time someone
looks at you, they'll wonder what happened. Then their thoughts
will turn to the bills they saw posted around town."

"It's a risk I have to take. Let's give it a few weeks. The uproar
will blow over."

"We'll let the government decide about that," Josephine said.
"They'll get my telegram and send someone. I told them we had
until Wednesday."

"You did? Why would you say that? You'll put lives at risk."

"That's how long we have. On Thursday, you'll be found and arrested. The enemy will be told where you're hiding."

"You're not making any sense. Who would possibly tell them?"

Josephine walked to the window, rubbing her hands together. Francesca's threat ran through her head. She could hear the cunning tone.

Six thousand dollars. I'll give you three days.

"Josephine?"

"I'm being blackmailed."

"What? How? By whom?"

"I either pay six thousand dollars by the day after tomorrow or the enemy will be told where you are hiding. I don't even have six thousand. I have four."

"You're not making any sense. Who is this?"

"It doesn't matter who. I made mistakes. They've come back to stare me in the face."

"Josephine . . ."

"That's all I'm going to say," she said stubbornly.

He was silent for a long moment. "I could get some money. Maybe. Could try at least."

"You know we can't pay. This week it's six thousand. Next week it's ten. Sooner or later, we'd be arrested anyway."

"It might buy time."

"I can't do it."

"Josephine, please. You have to trust me. Who is this? How does he know?"

You have to tell him. It's his life you put at risk.

She took a deep breath and returned to sit on the edge of the bed. "Do you remember the money you found in the box?" she said. "Its origins are . . . not entirely honorable."

When Josephine finished sharing the ugly history of her childhood, Franklin looked toward the far wall, his gaze fixing on a piece of flaking plaster high up near the crown molding.

She hadn't told him everything, of course. Some memories were too painful, and she already did enough picking at them, as if they were partially healed scabs, without voicing them as well. But she told him how she'd grown up on the river, a child of an unknown father, her mother a dancer of an indecent sort who sometimes offered her company to men in return for profit. She told about the explosion, the rescued box, and the jewels. She explained about Francesca and the Colonel.

"I know what you must think of me," she said when the silence became too much to bear.

He turned and held her gaze. "I don't judge you, Josephine."

"You say that, but I don't believe it. Everyone judges."

"You were a child. None of it was your fault."

"I know what you're thinking. You must think I've done all sorts of things. That a woman of my bloodline and experience would no doubt continue to do such things, should circumstances warrant."

"I am not." His tone was firm, and she almost believed him. "My father is a mill foreman in Massachusetts, and just now I was thinking about some of the girls who work for him, the circumstance that make them work such long, backbreaking hours."

It seemed like a forced comparison. As in, *I know what it's like to be a child in a difficult circumstance. I once met some girls who worked the looms.*

But then he continued. "A few weeks before I met you, I was cutting through Rum Row on my way to the Executive Mansion when one of the Cyprians hailed me from her stoop. I'm not in the habit of paying attention to lewd summons, but I chanced to glance over. It was a girl I'd seen before, one who had worked in my father's mill. She had been thirteen, fourteen. Now she was perhaps seventeen. The work in the mill was grueling, the hours long. But honorable. Yet she had apparently abandoned the mill to prostitute herself in the lowest alley of the lowest cesspool of Washington."

"What does that say about the mill?" Josephine asked.

"That was my very thought, yes. I knew the mill work was difficult, but how desperate must she have been to leave that work to sell her body? And who was I to judge her? Only God knows." Then, to Josephine's surprise, he took her hand. "And I would never judge you, either."

"Yes, well." She swallowed, felt awkward, and slowly withdrew her hand. His touch was not unpleasant, and her heart had beat a little faster. But, no. Not now.

"Let me assure you," she said, "I would never betray you under any circumstances. And I meant the oath I took in Washington, too. I made my decision; I chose my side. I will stay true, should that oath lead to humiliation and even death."

"I know it," Franklin said. "So how do we extract ourselves from this predicament? There will be no help from Washington, none that will arrive in time. You must believe me."

"I need to get you out of the city."

"You're wrong. You need to get *yourself* out of the city. If you can find a place to hide me while I recover and escape yourself to Memphis where you won't be recognized, then nothing this woman says will matter. There will be an uproar, you will be cursed as a traitor, but nobody will be able to touch you."

"I already told you, I'm not abandoning you, and I'm not abandoning my duties, either. That's the part that *you* must believe." Josephine paused to let this sink in. "And if it comes out that I'm a traitor to the Southern cause, other people will get the blame, starting with the New York Jew who published me. He'll be wrecked, the *Crescent* destroyed. I can't do that to him."

"So we're back to needing six thousand dollars."

"Never."

"Then what?"

"I covered a murder in Washington once," she said, thinking. "Or a supposed murder. The police suffered a distinct lack of enthusiasm for the case, and soon let it drop. Part of their disinterest was that the victim was an immigrant, a drunk who started fights and welched on his bets. The landlord heard shouts one night, someone screaming in German, another voice in English. The next morning, there was blood in the room, but no body. They never found one."

"Maybe he fought an attacker and fled for his life."

"That was what the police said. But there was a lot of blood. No man could lose that much blood and survive. Maybe it was a pig, the police countered, slaughtered to make it look like murder. The German staged the whole business, ran off to avoid his debts. No body, no murder."

"I don't follow," Franklin said. "How does that apply here?"

"In our case, no injured spy, no sabotage at the arsenal. At least not by me, the heroine of the Southern cause. I am skilled with words—I can frame this as a jealous accusation from a woman of a dubious background."

"This woman has other information about you. Information that could be verified. Your childhood, your mother's life."

"That's a scandal I can face. If I must." Her words were bold, but her stomach flopped over at the thought.

"It might work."

"It *will* work. But we have to get you out of the city, and quickly." She pointed to the reward bill. "This seals the matter. Between that and Francesca's accusation, you have to leave."

"But how do we manage? There's a thousand miles of rebel-held river above us, and two forts downriver."

"Upriver is too far. I'll have to get you to the Gulf, to the Union blockade."

"So, past the forts," he said. "Past the barricade and chain."

"Yes, exactly that. The alternative is to hide you while the city searches for you. Sooner or later, you'll be caught and hung."

"Too dangerous. I can't let you do it."

Josephine bristled. "I'm not a child, so don't treat me like one. You're injured and bedridden, and that means that I'm the one to make the decisions."

"What I worry is that you're behaving in an overly sentimental manner, and that will put you at unnecessary risk."

"Overly sentimental? Why, because I'm a woman? Because I'm young?"

"Because of personal considerations. You know what I mean."

Now her eyes widened. "Are you suggesting that we have formed some sort of understanding? That I have *romantic* designs upon you? We have not, and I most certainly do not have such designs. If you believe that, you're deluding yourself."

"Oh, for God's sake. That's not what I meant at all."

"Then what are you suggesting?"

"Because of your mother. What you told me about the Colonel. He left her behind and she drowned, and you would never do such a thing. You feel responsible for my safety. That's all I mean. And I'm telling you I can swim on my own, I don't need you protecting me at your own risk."

"I only told you that story so you'd understand why I was being blackmailed, not so you could explain why a riverboat girl would show some basic human decency. Do you think I'm incapable of loyalty? Of doing my duty?"

"That's not what I mean, and you know it."

"Don't bring up my mother again, or anything that happened to me on the river. I don't want to talk about it; I don't even like to think about it. And I don't want it thrown in my face. Are we clear?"

He hesitated, looking for the briefest moment, as if he wanted to protest again. Then the look went away and he stared back. "Understood."

"Good. Now go to sleep. You need to mend, and I need to think."

She turned out the lamp and retreated to the darkest corner of the room to change into her nightgown. When she was done, she wrapped herself in a blanket and sat in the rocking chair for another long, restless night. Franklin said nothing. A few minutes later his breathing grew steady and slow. Josephine's anger deflated.

What's wrong with you?

She'd misunderstood him not once, but twice. Snapped angrily at him for the crime of phrasing his words in a vague enough way that she could leap to the worst possible conclusion. He wasn't in the wrong; he was only trying to do his own duty. Embarrassed at having disclosed the tawdry details of her childhood, she'd lashed out.

Josephine pulled the blanket up about her head as if to smother the thoughts and memories that kept churning through her mind. She forced herself to calm down and to bend her thoughts to getting Franklin out of New Orleans. She'd wasted Monday trying to send a telegram to summon help. Tomorrow was Tuesday, New Year's Eve. On Wednesday, Francesca would arrive at the Paris Hotel, expecting $6,000 and prepared to betray Josephine if she didn't get it.

CHAPTER 25

The next morning, Josephine handed Solomon Fein her story about the arsenal fire and waited nervously while he sat at his desk and read it. A frown creased his brow, and he ran his fingers through his curly black hair. The noise and turmoil of the newsroom swirled around them. When he'd finished, he took off his glasses and polished them on his shirt.

"Something wrong with my story?"

"It's fine, I suppose."

"There wasn't much to work with. Eyewitnesses in the city heard an explosion at the hospital and saw a column of fire. Windows blew out. Buildings shook. Some large quantity of powder, cartridges, and shell were destroyed. The army won't say how much."

"Nor should they, with the saboteur still at large."

"Everything else is conjecture."

"It's not the conjecture that's a problem. The prose is workman-like, adequate. But it doesn't shine. I was hoping for more."

"I know," she admitted. "I wrote it quickly."

"You always write quickly. This time you seem distracted. Are you burned out? I've been riding you for months, throwing everything your way. Maybe it's too much. Wait, you're not still sore because I put Keller on the story first, and this is your way of punishing me?"

"I'm not punishing you, I swear."

"Then what is it? Why is this story . . . mediocre?"

"I don't know. Maybe my enthusiasm waned coming to it so late and already having to flog Keller's dead dog."

He set down the pages on his desk. "I'll run it, of course. It's not front-page material, though, not two days after the blast. What else have you got?"

This was the opening she needed. She glanced around to make sure nobody was close enough to overhear, and pulled up a chair. "That's the other thing. There's a big story I'm working on, and it's distracting me."

He perked up. "I like the sound of that. How big?"

"I've got to travel downriver for a few days."

"It's not Major Dunbar, is it? I hear he's sweet on you. If you're going to the forts so he can woo you . . ."

"Don't be ridiculous."

"Then he's *not* sweet on you?"

"I don't care if he is or isn't—that has nothing to do with me or my work. It's not the forts that are drawing my attention, or their officers, for that matter."

"Then what is it?"

She pushed past his question. "I'll need your help. Can you get me a blockade-runner? Someone clever, someone who isn't overly attached to the cause. Someone who won't ask questions, who will deal with Confederates and Yankees alike."

"Why?"

"Because I need to be smuggled to the Gulf. I have a contact in the fleet, a Union officer who really was, as you put it, sweet on me. Back when I was in Washington. He has information. Something big is happening."

"Good Lord. It's an attack on New Orleans, isn't it?"

"I believe so."

"From the Gulf?"

"I can't see how they'd get past the forts," Josephine said. "They couldn't in October, and General Lovell has been hard at work strengthening our defenses. It might be the enemy ironclads upriver. Rumor has it they're on the move."

"How sure are you of this information?"

"I'm not sure of anything. That's why I need to get downriver. Can you get me someone?"

"It won't be cheap."

"Of course not," she said. "But it will be worth it."

"I don't know. Seems risky. I can't have you arrested by the Yanks."

"I won't be. Trust me." This was the truest thing Josephine had said during the whole conversation. "I have plenty of tricks, and my gentleman friend and I have a rendezvous planned."

"Have you thought he might be playing you? That he might have nothing, has told you whatever he thinks you want to hear so he can seduce you?"

"Oh, come now," Josephine scoffed. "Who do you think I am? Nobody will play me, and I won't be seduced. Can I have the transport or not?"

"I don't know. It's dangerous business you're about."

"Listen to me," she said. "I swear this to you. Even if I don't return with the entire battle plan of the Union army, I will bring back all manner of useful information about the enemy's intent for naval actions on the Gulf and in the Mississippi."

Fein ran his fingers through his hair again. "Very well. I'll find a runner. When do you need it?"

"This evening," she said without hesitation. "Your man can't know it's me. He can't know it's a reporter, or anything at all about the passenger, for that matter, not even whether he's waiting for a woman or a man."

"That shouldn't be a problem. I never speak directly to this man, and he never speaks directly to me. Safer that way."

Even better. That made it unlikely that word would get back to Fein that she had deceived him about traveling to the Gulf.

"And I can't be challenged or seen in any way at the forts," she added. "Can he manage?"

"I'm sure he can, but it will be expensive."

"You already said that. Pay whatever he asks. If I don't deliver, you can deduct it from my pay."

Josephine reached into the satchel at her feet and retrieved the pocket watch with the gilt cover and the Persian-looking crescent and star. She set it on the desk next to her and made a quick sketch of it on a pad.

"This is all I want your man to know," she said. "A passenger will arrive at the levee outside Jackson Square at eight o'clock. This passenger will be carrying this watch and will be beneath one of the gas lamps, continually checking the time." She put away the watch and folded the sketch and put it in Fein's hand. "With nothing more than that, can your man be relied on to get me downriver?"

Fein nodded.

"You won't regret this," she said. "This is information that will change the course of the war."

"If you're right, Richmond will need to know about this."

"And they'll get it," she said. "Just as soon as it appears in the *New Orleans Daily Crescent* under my byline."

At this, his uncertainty faded, replaced by a grin. "Now that's my girl. You had me worried there for a minute."

Josephine planned the evening like a military expedition. First, she hired a cab to be waiting on the next street over from Nellie's house at seven. Then she went home to get Franklin out of bed and dressed, with a bag holding a change of clothing, a pistol, and other personal effects. After dinner, she went downstairs, prepared to lead Nellie outside with some nonsense about a strange animal she'd spotted snuffling through the flower bed. It proved unnecessary, as the woman was already on the porch with the rest of the neighborhood, watching the militia march down the street on its way to the parade ground.

Josephine hurried upstairs. It was a struggle getting Franklin down the back stairs and into the garden by the side gate. She'd stashed a pair of crutches in the garden shed, and once he had them, they were able to make better time down the side street. With a hat pulled low over his head and the daylight already gone, only the crutches would draw attention on the darkened side street, but none of the handful of passersby challenged them.

There were a few tense moments waiting for the cab, which arrived ten minutes late, but then they were inside, Franklin's bag at their feet, and the driver up front leading the horse down the cobbled street.

Franklin wheezed and clutched his ribs. She took out a vial of laudanum, but he waved it away, saying he needed to keep his wits about him.

"Why does it hurt more now than three days ago?" he asked.

"I'm not sure. Maybe it's your body telling you to go back to bed and let it mend."

"Doesn't seem such a bad idea, if you ask me."

"Everything is arranged. You'll be safely in the Gulf in two days."

She wasn't confident about this assertion. Fein's man must be a scoundrel or he wouldn't have agreed to smuggle a passenger past the forts, a request that would arouse suspicion in any smuggler sharp enough to thrive in the present circumstances. If the smuggler saw the injured man, spotted the wound on his forehead, he might figure out the game. A quick glance at the cards in his hand would reveal more profit to be made handing over a spy for a hundred dollars in gold than whatever Fein was paying him.

Traffic was light, and the cab driver's horse young, not like some of the nags that dragged their tired, bony bodies up and down the streets, and they arrived at the levee barely twenty minutes later. They stood in the shadows on the edge of a brick warehouse, Franklin leaning on his crutches.

"What now?" he asked.

She pointed in the direction they needed to travel. "Can you manage?"

He nodded.

She had dressed him in the butternut jacket with captain's bars at the house, and now she removed a forage cap purchased in the city and placed it on his head.

"There. Now you look like a proper soldier. You took a wound and came downriver to recover under your wife's tender care, who is staying with her sister in New Orleans. That story should be easy enough for both of us to remember."

"I hope you're the wife, and not the sister."

"Hah!"

"I beg your pardon, it was a poor jest. After the stupid things I said last night, I should be more careful."

"I know how you meant it," she reassured him. "And I know you had no ill intentions last night, either. My pride got the better of me, and my behavior was wretched. I'm the one who should be begging forgiveness."

"We'll make a pact," he said. "I'll forgive your pride if you will forgive my clumsy tongue."

"Done."

Fifteen minutes later, they were sitting on a downed sycamore log that had been half buried in the levee with its top skimmed off to serve as a crude bench. They'd tucked the crutches into the shadows behind the log, and Franklin put the watch in his breast pocket, prepared to pull it out and check anytime someone walked by close enough to see. A gaslight flickered above them, lighting the docks. The sound of cornets and saxophones drifted from Jackson Square to their rear. It was New Year's Eve, and the celebrations were beginning in front of the cathedral. In a couple of hours they would spread throughout the Quarter and move up to the levee as well. But at the moment, the levee was nearly empty.

In past years, the riverfront had been swarming with stevedores, both free and slave, day and night. New Year's Eve would have been no exception. They would be unloading flour, vegetables, and beef from upriver, and molasses, sugar, salt, and manufactures from the Gulf. But river traffic had choked to a near standstill. Tonight, the Mississippi in front of the levee was nearly empty, except for a single barge preparing to depart downstream with a pair of long, dark cannons lashed on its deck, surrounded by crates of guns and foodstuff for the forts. A good twenty soldiers milled about smoking and talking. The main group stood forty or fifty feet away from Josephine and Franklin, and one would glance in their direction every minute or two. She worried that the blockade-runner would take one look at the military traffic and renege on his promise to Solomon Fein.

Franklin took Josephine's hands and leaned in as if he were her husband and they'd come up to the levee to get away from the crowds at Jackson Square. Her hands felt small and frail in his big ones, a sensation that gave her a peculiar feeling in her belly.

"Come with me," he said. "Not to be *with* me, you understand. But to be out of harm's way with the fleet."

"I won't lose my nerve now," she said. "Let Francesca accuse me. Remember what I said. It doesn't matter if there's blood. No body, no murder."

"I don't believe that, and neither do you. It's no longer safe for you here."

"Mr. Lincoln didn't ask me to be safe. He asked me to do my duty."

"Yes, but what was it you told him? If there's an alligator in your path, you should go downstream a stretch. This is your metaphor made true. You should paddle downstream."

"I'll paddle downstream when New Orleans falls. Not a moment before."

Franklin put a hand to her cheek. "My dear," he whispered.

She caught her breath. Out of the corner of her eye she spotted movement, which proved to be a pair of soldiers strolling along the levee, muskets held sloppily in hand. Before she could decide if this is what had drawn Franklin's touch, he withdrew his hand and pulled out the pocket watch. It wasn't for the benefit of the soldiers, but for an elderly gentleman with a cane who followed a few paces behind the two men. The man with the cane didn't take notice of the watch, or look in their direction at all.

"What time is it?" she asked while he still had the watch open.

"Ten past eight. Your man is late."

"Studying the surroundings, perhaps. Seeing if we look like a threat."

"Or scared off by the soldiers," he said. "Anyone who would smuggle a fugitive wouldn't put his neck out if he thought he might be caught."

Another soldier came toward them, this one from the group of men milling near the gangplank that led to the barge. He took out a cigarette, while Josephine and Franklin pretended not to notice, speaking to each other in the low tones of reunited lovers. At last he came over and stood a few feet away, watching.

"I'm fixing to have a smoke," the soldier interrupted at last. "But I'll be durned if'n I don't have a match. I don't suppose—"

Josephine didn't believe this. Whether or not he had matches, his companions back at the river surely did, as they were puffing away. The soldier had come to give them a once-over, for whatever reason. Suspicion maybe, or perhaps curiosity about Franklin's uniform.

But Franklin obligingly fetched a vial of matches from his pocket and lit the man's cigarette, who then turned to go. Suddenly, something occurred to Josephine.

"What time is it, dear?" she asked Franklin.

Franklin's eyes widened slightly, and he hurriedly fished out his watch, which he flipped open so the lip with the crescent and star faced the soldier, caught with the reflection of the gaslight. The soldier turned and took a puff. No emotion registered on his face, and her hopes sputtered.

But then the man spoke. "Two downriver? That's a change. It will cost you."

"How much?" Franklin asked.

"No," Josephine said firmly. "One person, not two. Just my husband, not me."

"Listen carefully," the man said to Franklin. His folksy accent was gone, replaced by something both cultured and calculating. "Don't turn, but there's a warehouse to your right about fifty feet away. Did you see it?"

"Yes," Franklin said.

"Go inside. There's a box about the size and shape of a coffin standing in the back left corner. The lid is loose—you can pry it open with your hands and step inside. In about ten minutes, we'll be loading up the rest of the crates."

"You can't drop him at the forts with the rest," Josephine told him.

"Don't tell me my business," the soldier said. "The forts are only the first stop. The rest of the shipment goes to an outpost near Head of Passes." He turned back to Franklin. "Understand? Good."

He gave a curt nod and turned away to rejoin his companions.

Josephine cast a lazy glance over toward the warehouse the soldier had mentioned. It was little more than an oversize, ramshackle shed, the kind built from flatboats floated down the Mississippi and broken apart for building material rather than hauled painstakingly back upstream.

"It looks clear," she said. "As soon as the soldier is back with the others, you should go."

"Be careful."

"You, too."

"When the attack comes, find a safe place and wait until the fighting is over."

"You know me better than that," she said. "I'll be where the story is. Now go."

He placed the watch on her lap as he rose. Only when he was up and hobbling toward the shed did she remember the ugly bruise on his leg. She hadn't felt a break, but the way he was walking she wondered if maybe there had been a small fracture. Yet she couldn't give him the crutches; that would surely draw more attention still.

So she sprang to her feet, pocketing the watch as she caught up with him. She put her arm around his waist, grabbed his belt, and lifted with all her strength every time he put his left leg down. This caused him to groan as she pressed into his broken ribs, but it kept him from limping quite so markedly.

"Thank you," he whispered as he left her and entered the shed.

Josephine turned around, worried that the eyes of the soldiers near the barge would be fixed on them. Instead, they all circled around a man gesturing wildly as he related some anecdote. Moments later, the group of men guffawed and slapped each other on the backs. She had no doubt it was the smuggler telling the story to draw their attention. The man did know his business.

She returned to the log bench to wait. A few minutes later, an officer came down from the barge and shouted at the soldiers to get to work. Those with weapons set theirs down, and the lot of them went to the warehouse and hauled out the boxes. This took a good hour. Toward the end, she spotted a long, coffin-like box being hauled roughly along by four men. They grunted as they passed her, complaining about the weight.

It was ten thirty before a tug came huffing up to pull the cannon-laden barge into the current, together with its soldiers and crates of goods. By then the celebration was in full swing along the levee, and a boat with fireworks had been towed into place. A few minutes later, the tug and barge disappeared down the inky channel of the Mississippi River and into the night.

Josephine stayed on the levee with the revelers as midnight approached. Bands played martial music, while black, white, immigrant, and native-born joined in singing and dancing and drinking. Fireworks launched from the barge anchored in the river, illuminating the night. In spite of the cheers and lusty voices raising in song, there was an edge to the festivities, worry and anger perhaps making people drink harder than usual, celebrating as if it was their last time before war and the blockade wrecked things forever.

The bells on the cathedral chimed midnight, and a great cheer roared from the crowd. Josephine opened the pocket watch. She thought about Franklin and wondered whether she'd ever see him again. She still held the memory of his hand on her face, her arm around his waist, and her body pressing into his.

The cheers died down within a few minutes, but the party raged on. Josephine closed the watch and made her way down from the levee to go home.

CHAPTER 26

Wednesday, January 1, Josephine rose early to chase down the morning papers. The city came awake around her with all of the enthusiasm of a team of surly mules. The newsboys were late and irritable, the cabdrivers made as if to run her down when she crossed the street, and two men scooping horse droppings into a cart were snarling at each other until she thought they would come to blows.

Back in her room, Josephine spent the rest of the morning cleaning up stories she'd been working on, then wrote a note for Francesca, using her left hand. It was a trick she'd used in Washington when she wanted to disguise her handwriting. In this case it wasn't to fool Francesca, but because the very existence of a note would be incriminating. She needed a way to deny it.

Note composed, she set off for the Paris Hotel, arriving at a quarter to noon, where she arranged for a waiter to deliver the note at precisely twelve thirty. Then she climbed the stairs to the mezzanine to discreetly look down at the restaurant. Francesca entered a few minutes before the arranged time and was led to her table. She ordered wine and waited. Above, Josephine checked Franklin's watch. At precisely twelve thirty, the waiter approached Francesca's table and slipped her Josephine's note.

Francesca opened it. She stared at the note for a long time. From Josephine's vantage, she saw no reaction, but knew her mother's old friend must be boiling as she read Josephine's response, blunt in its delivery, occluded in its message so that it would not be an additional tool for blackmailing.

> *There is no body, so you have no crime to report.*
> *You will get nothing from me now or ever.*
> *Go home to Memphis or you will find your*
> *own past exposed, and your husband's enemies will*
> *be told he is in the city.*

Without waiting to see what Francesca would do, Josephine descended from the mezzanine and left through the hotel's front door. She didn't hail a cab, but walked swiftly down the first side street she reached. The streets and boardwalks were nearly empty, and she relaxed as she came upon Jackson Square. A handful of drunks slept in corners of the square, surrounded by broken bottles, horse droppings, torn papers, confetti, and other refuse from the previous night.

She was passing in front of the cathedral before she remembered the second of Francesca's conditions. Josephine was to hand over $6,000 and then go to the square to meet the Colonel outside the Cabildo.

She stopped short and darted her gaze toward the Cabildo. There he was, waiting beneath the very sycamore tree where she'd lingered before leaving her telegram. He had his hat off, and twisted the brim in his hands. He was staring up a side street, where the carts and cabs entered the square, or he would have spotted her already.

Josephine expected anger at seeing him again, but as she studied his tired, worried expression, she could only feel pity. She was suddenly sure that he knew nothing of this blackmail business; that must be Francesca's doing. If not, why would he be waiting for her, as if expecting a reconciliation? She made a sudden decision.

He looked up as she approached. The worry dissolved on his face, replaced by a hopeful smile.

"You came. I thought you'd changed your mind."

"Do you know why I'm here?"

"I'm sorry, I couldn't think of any other way. I knew you wouldn't listen to me, but I thought you might listen to Francesca. I hope she didn't press too hard. She can be powerful determined."

"You have no idea what she asked me, do you?"

"I don't follow. How do you mean?"

She glanced across the square. At any moment, Francesca might be arriving from the hotel, furious and set upon revenge. Josephine gave the Colonel a gesture to follow and started up toward the levee. He followed.

"Your wife is trying to blackmail me," she said when they'd crossed the street and left the square behind.

"Over what?" he asked, sounding bewildered. "Over the contents of the box? How would that be? Anyway, I told her that wasn't your fault. Of course you didn't realize the value of those gemstones, as young as you were. Francesca seems to think that you did, that you sold them for thousands of dollars. That you still have most of that money and should give it back. That's not true, is it?"

Josephine sighed. When she got to the levee, she came to a stop. "What do you want, Colonel? Money?"

"No."

"Then what?"

"I want to be what I should have been all along. I want to be . . ." His voice trailed off, and he looked out to the river, where another barge with a cannon lay anchored, waiting to be hauled down to the forts.

"A what?"

"You know what I mean."

"You can't even say the word. You want to be my *father*?"

He rubbed his hands together and nodded.

"As if you even understand what that word means," Josephine said. "What's more, did you even have a claim in the first place? I look like my mother, not like you or any other man my mama knew."

"You're right." He tried to take her hands, but she pulled away. "But I used to watch you while you were reading your books, your face all puckered up in concentration, and thought that I could have been. I wanted to be."

"Then why didn't you?" she cried. Her throat was tight, and she struggled to get the words out. "All you had to do was stay. That's the only thing we ever asked of you."

"I don't know. Something restless in my feet, that's all I can say. They wanted to keep moving, wanted to take me to new places. Always new places."

"We were on a blasted riverboat, you idiot. That's all it did, go place to place."

"You don't understand."

"Then explain it to me, for God's sake."

"It's not too late. We can start over. I'll be your father if you let me." He tried to take her hands again, but she pushed him away.

"Don't touch me. It *is* too late. My mother is dead, and I have no father. I never did. And I won't pretend otherwise, not now, not ever."

"Josie."

"Don't call me that!"

He stared at her for a long time. "So that's it?"

"Yes. Go away. Don't bother me again."

"Then why did you come?"

"I already told you, your wife is trying to blackmail me. And yes, she does have something over me. Not the box, something dangerous. If you care at all, if you ever did, you will convince her to leave me alone."

"I'll try. She is a strong-willed woman."

"So was my mother, remember? And I am more strong-willed than either of them. If you push me, I will fight back until I have destroyed you and your wife both. Do you understand me?"

He didn't answer, but looked at her with that sad expression, full of pain and longing.

Josephine turned and left. It was all she could do to keep herself upright. She'd thought herself beyond his ability to hurt her, but hearing from his own mouth that he wanted to be her father left her shattered. She knew he was incapable, that if she let him into her life again, he would only disappear again. A week, a month, a year. Soon enough, he'd be gone. He'd left Mama to drown, for God's sake.

Yet even though she knew that she had given up nothing, lost nothing, she ached to her bones as if she had.

Josephine didn't return to the offices of the *Crescent* until January 9, a week and a half after Fein had supposedly sent her down to the Gulf. All eyes in the newsroom turned her way, and a number of them came over to pump her for information. Rumors had been flying as to her whereabouts. Some thought she'd gone up to Baton Rouge or even St. Louis, while Keller said he'd heard President Davis had summoned her to Richmond and sent her along to Washington to spy.

She scoffed at this. "All the way to Washington and back in nine days?"

As Keller sputtered an answer, Fein came rushing from the back room. Ink smudged his glasses, and he was carrying a roll of paper, which he handed off the instant he saw her.

"You!" Fein said. "Where the devil have you been?"

Josephine reached into her satchel and pulled out a fat sheaf of papers, which she waved in his face. Heads craned trying to get a look.

"Give me that," Fein said.

"Not here."

He dragged her into his office and shut the door, where he demanded to see the result of all of his money and her time. She had written six stories, some even legitimate, but first she handed over the big one. The big lie. He sat down to read at his desk while she stood above him.

UNION PLOT EXPOSED!

POOK'S TURTLES TO ATTACK NEW ORLEANS!

FIENDISH ATTACK ON THE LEVEE!

Fein looked initially excited, but his expression turned grim as he read. The article described a massive Union force forming in southern Illinois, led by eleven ironclad gunboats to clear the Mississippi, and eighty thousand federal troops to occupy forts seized during their sweep downriver. They would begin at Fort Henry on the Tennessee River in February, control the river to the state of Mississippi by March, and finally take Vicksburg before dropping into Louisiana to control the river all the way to the Gulf by late spring. If New Orleans resisted, the enemy would blast holes in the levee, which would flood the city just as the river was cresting with spring runoff. To divert Confederate naval forces, the Union navy would shortly attack coastal fortifications from the Carolinas to the state of Mississippi.

She thought it was a good outline of a legitimate campaign, as sketched by a layperson with an excellent understanding of the river and its navigable tributaries, and a solid, but less thorough knowledge of military matters. She guessed that the Confederate land and river forces would have something to say about how casually she had the Union seizing all those forts, but she thought her story sounded plausible enough that it would make Richmond sweat and turn its attention from the river below New Orleans.

The niggling worry was that she had outlined an actual Union campaign through sheer luck. In which case she might be endangering Northern forces. Not if they'd listened to her obviously superior idea about coming up the river from the Gulf to rush Fort St. Philip and Fort Jackson before attacking New Orleans from the south. But could she count on that? She had only Franklin's word on the matter.

"This is . . ." Fein stopped, and let out a low whistle. "Yes, this was worth it. You have more?"

In Josephine's second story, even more fanciful than the first, she described a clandestine meeting with a loose-lipped Union officer. He told of flagging Northern morale, of worries that Britain would shortly recognize the Confederacy due to the still simmering Union diplomatic blunder of the so-called Trent Affair. The Union officer was not optimistic about the planned assault from the north. He thought that fifty thousand Confederate troops on the upper river and reinforced fortifications would turn back any attack. And after the debacle at Head of Passes, the Union had ruled out any attack from the Gulf.

When he'd finished reading, Fein took off his glasses and polished them with a far-off expression. When he put them back on and looked up at her, he'd only succeeded in further smearing the lenses with ink.

"You know what Ludd will say in the *Picayune*, don't you?" he asked.

"He'll make nasty insinuations about how I got the enemy officer to talk."

"And that doesn't bother you?"

"Of course it bothers me. But it's hardly the worst thing I've faced. I'd suffer that and more for the cause."

"Ah yes, the cause." He pointed to the other chair in the room and told her to sit down. "Let's talk about that."

She obeyed. "Yes?"

"Did you read the story in the *True Delta* last week about protecting the city? No, I don't suppose you could have, being in the Gulf. Maginnis suggested making New Orleans a free city, separate from both the Union and the Confederacy. We could trade with both sides, avoid fighting either."

"Sounds like treason."

"And ridiculous, on the face of it. Though at least half the city was against secession in the first place, the half that was in favor of it would have tarred and feathered anyone who defended the Union. That said, both sides remain in the city to this day."

"I don't follow. Where are you going with this?"

"My point is, there's a large seditious population in New Orleans. If the Union ever captures the city, these people will trip over themselves collaborating with the enemy."

"Who are these traitors?" Josephine huffed. "I've never met any."

"You wouldn't have, would you? Not with war fever raging. But it's a safe bet that the blockade-runners and smugglers like the man who took you downstream would be the first to cross over."

Fein apparently didn't know that the runner was a Confederate soldier. That man wouldn't do any crossing over. Unless he proved completely craven and deserted, he would end up fighting for the cause, whether he wanted to or not.

"That's one man," she said. "Who else?"

"I'm not looking, mind you, but if I were, I'd turn my attention to Irish, Italians. Other foreigners. Men born in the North who came to New Orleans to make their fortune. Free blacks, runaway slaves. Old white creole families who still speak French at home and keep no slaves. Few of these people have any great affinity for Richmond."

"How about a German-born Jew from New York?" she asked.

"I'm a patriot," he said quickly. "But I'm also a realist."

She took a small risk and let out some of her true thoughts on the subject. "They say it's not about slavery, but over rights, but sometimes I wonder if it's either of those things. People are proud. Maybe that's the only reason men go to war. Pride and honor. The South goes to war because the North marches into their territory."

"And that's why you fight?" he asks. "With your pen, I mean? In defense of your native soil against invaders? That's why you take such risks?"

It was a valid question, although not in the way he supposed.

Since she was a child, Josephine had traveled up and down the river dozens of times, passing from slave state to free and back again. She was under no illusion that Northerners were saints, but neither were the Southerners. One vision of the future would hold, either an empire of land and slaves in the South, with growth and energy and free labor always pressing forward in her northern neighbor, or the North would triumph utterly. In which case, it was evident to one and all that the United States would grow into a vast, continental power of unprecedented strength, while the South became a weak, broken colony of the former.

Neither vision appealed to her, but when she remembered the slaves fleeing across the river by boat, thought about Caleb at Fort Jackson as they led him to the gallows, she could feel no soft place in her heart for Southern honor, for any great and glorious cause that would tear the country in two.

"I don't mean to bend you to cynicism," Fein said after she had not answered for several seconds.

"I'm in the news business. I'm already bent."

"My comment about the cause was not to make you doubt. And it was certainly not to make you question my own commitment. But should the worst come to pass, and the Union gunboats fight their way downriver as you say, don't be a heroine. There will still be need for our services in New Orleans. To raise spirits during a dark time, to shine a light on the doings of the corrupt and powerful. And I'll need you. You're notorious in the North, but I'll protect you if I can. For your part, you'll need to be practical."

"I understand."

He took the other stories she'd written and skimmed through them while Josephine waited for his assessment.

She was beginning to suspect that Fein was every bit as cynical as the man who'd smuggled Franklin to safety in the Gulf. But then he said something that made her reassess.

"You've given me plenty of material," he said. "I want you to take a few days off. Unless I tell you otherwise, you're not to do any writing for the paper. Instead, I want you to write a story for the War Department. I want you to write your assessment of our dire military situation for the benefit of the government. Use your most persuasive language. Assure them that what you wrote for the *Crescent* wasn't mere scaremongering to sell more papers.

I'll send copies to President Davis, the War Department, and to Commodore Hollins, General Lovell, and General Lee."

"Will they listen to me?" she asked.

"They had better. If not, we'll lose the whole blasted river. Then our hopes will be very black indeed."

Josephine eyed Fein with new understanding. Any hope that she had found someone to whom she could confess her true purpose drained away. Solomon Fein may have been preparing for the worst, but this man wanted the South to win the war.

CHAPTER 27

Josephine's misinformation reaped great dividends. In the first few weeks of January, only General Lovell seemed to pay attention to threats from the Gulf. Hollins steamed upriver with the mosquito fleet, where there did seem to be movement on the part of the Union. A powerful flotilla, backed by some twenty thousand or more troops under Ulysses Grant, was moving on the Tennessee River. Lovell raised new regiments for the defense of New Orleans, but Richmond ordered them upriver as quickly as they formed.

Then, at the end of the month, curious news filtered into New Orleans. It came first via the Washington papers, who claimed that Flag Officer David Farragut had assembled a "great expedition" composed of *Pensacola*, *Richmond*, and several other massive steam frigates, together with thirty other vessels containing mortars and powerful rifled cannons. They were going to attack the Gulf fortifications of the Confederacy. The story reached the Richmond press first, then was reprinted by the *Picayune* on January 29.

Irritated that Ludd had beat him to the story, Fein ordered Josephine to crow in print about how her captured battle plan was playing out exactly as foretold—these were merely preparations for the Union coastal attack designed to divert Confederate naval attention from the real assault to come from the north, down the river. This she did, while wondering with twisting excitement in her belly if this were the invasion force meant to cross the bar and attack Fort Jackson and Fort St. Philip.

Meanwhile, the delays continued on the powerful Confederate ironclads being built in the city. *Mississippi* was supposed to be delivered by mid-December, and *Louisiana* on January 25, but by the end of the month, both boats remained unfinished at their respective yards.

Louisiana finally skidded down the blocks into the river on February 6, sending water sloshing high up the levee, where Josephine watched with a throng of cheering spectators. She wondered what Franklin would have thought could he see the gunboat in the water. She constructed sly, cynical observations, and imagined whispering them in his ear in an attempt to raise a smile. But it had been more than five weeks since she'd seen him.

As for the crowd, their enthusiasm was explosive as they cheered *Louisiana* floating proud and mighty in the river. No enemy ship could stand against her might. Josephine watched quietly, taking notes, and when she returned to the city reported what she'd seen with credulity, while noting privately that the ship had weeks, if not months ahead of her to be worthy of battle. *Louisiana* needed to be clad with iron, fit with her boiler and other machinery, and mounted with guns.

Her sister ship, *Mississippi*, waited in the lot next door, also partially constructed. She had her boiler installed but was still lacking iron or guns and was missing the massive shaft to propel her through the water. The shaft was reportedly under manufacture at the Tredegar Iron Works in Richmond, being refurbished after it had been salvaged from a shipwreck. When Josephine heard that, she knew without a doubt that any shipbuilding competition with the vast, smoking factories of the North was doomed to failure.

The same day *Louisiana* slipped into the water, word came of a ferocious new struggle on the upper rivers. Supported by Flag Officer Andrew Foote's gunboats, the so-called Pook's Turtles, General Grant had transported thousands of troops below Fort Henry on the Tennessee River. Union guns pummeled the fort until the Confederates withdrew to Fort Donelson, a dozen miles away on the Cumberland. At first it seemed as though the South would hold the line and possibly push federal troops out of Tennessee and off these two vital tributaries of the Mississippi, but after a series of bloody attacks and counterattacks, superior Union reinforcements carried the day. Fort Donelson surrendered on February 16.

The Richmond newspapers had been preoccupied with the struggle in northern Virginia between McClellan and Lee, but now turned to the reverses in the West with a good deal of alarm that was noted bitterly in New Orleans, who felt that the entire western theater had been neglected. In the city itself, the mood was first somber, then alarmed as the implications trickled in. The remaining Confederates in Tennessee and Kentucky had been divided between Columbus and Nashville, two hundred miles apart, with a powerful and confident Union army between them that controlled both the rivers and the railroads.

If there was any comfort to be had in New Orleans, it was that, while the way seemed open to the Union all the way into Alabama if they continued down the Tennessee, powerful forts continued to hold the Mississippi itself, together with Hollins's mosquito fleet, which still roamed undefeated. That might buy time to raise more militia and strengthen forts upstream from New Orleans.

Rumors continued to trickle in about Farragut's ocean fleet, which increased the general anxiety in the city. Confederate currency collapsed, and people hoarded silver coins. Coffee hit a dollar a pound and continued to climb. Flour was twenty-two dollars a barrel. Many household items were only available on the black market, and then for outrageous sums. The warehouses and docks remained silent except for military traffic, but Exchange Alley was booming, as was the usual market in liquor and women.

At the end of February, a runner somehow made his way past the blockade. He came to the office of the *Crescent* and insisted on speaking with Josephine. He then demanded five dollars to give her exclusive information about what he'd seen. She paid it.

A massive Union fleet was gathering off the delta. There were so many support boats and transports that the runner simply ran up the Stars and Stripes and steamed through. The ships were from Farragut's fleet, and they were evidently looking for a way to get their sloops of war over the bar and into the river.

There was no disguising the information, so she wrote it as favorably as she could. The largest Union sloops, with their deep drafts, would founder getting over the bar, she insisted. Even if they did cross, Fort St. Philip and Fort Jackson would easily repel any attack by wooden warships. General Lovell's masterful defenses rendered these Gibraltars of the Mississippi impenetrable. What's more, the mosquito fleet and its brave Southern fighting men had proven they could put superior Union forces to flight.

That night she went to the Cabildo and looked at her pocket watch until her contact appeared. She went outside and tucked a message behind the box.

Fleet Spotted Trying to Cross the Bar

Rebels Alarmed But Unprepared
Advise Continue As Planned

It was hubris of the first order, thinking she could affect the course of the battle at all, much less at this late moment. Farragut was either in the Gulf trying to cross the bar, or he was not. He either had sufficient force to reduce the forts and steam past safely, or he did not. The army following on troop transports either had sufficient forces to occupy New Orleans, or they did not. At this point they were fully committed, and would not alter their course one iota based on a stray telegram from their agent in the city. But maybe the confident message from the heart of the rebel city would be enough to encourage men for the hard fighting sure to come.

The battle would bring more bloodshed. She knew this, and it diminished the excitement she felt knowing that her strategy was soon to be tested. Less than a year had passed since the first shots at Fort Sumter, and any hopes that it would be a short, blood-less war had long since vanished, but perhaps the battle for New Orleans would break the back of the rebellion. God willing, the end of 1862 would see the end of the war. But first, many men would die. Some of them would be on the Union ships now trying to cross the bar.

Was Franklin on one of those ships? She thought yes. Two months had passed since the attack on the arsenal, and he would be recovered from his injuries, his ribs and fractured leg mended. Pinkerton would want him back in New Orleans when it fell. The city would be surly, even hostile under occupying forces. The Confederates would be scheming to retake it. There would be more need for spies than ever.

The next day, she went to Mrs. Dubreuil to leave another report on the military situation. This one, she suspected, might not make it to Washington and then down to the fleet before the battle commenced.

On March 11, Josephine went downriver to Fort Jackson to interview Major Dunbar about the preparations and find out if Union ships had been spotted in the river. The river was at flood stage, and uprooted trees and other debris had piled up behind the chain and its hulks, and part of the barricade had already given way. Hundreds of men were in the river on boats and the barricade itself working to clear the debris.

Dunbar showed her a new shipment of ten-inch columbiads that were beefing up the fort's defenses, but her attention was on the drama playing out in the river. Some fifty men were at work trying to lever out one of the largest oak trees she'd ever seen, which had punched straight up through the deck of one of the main hulks. The hulk was now half-submerged and sinking. Other hulks had broken loose and were drifting away in the current.

Two side-wheelers came downriver, waved flags at the spotters atop the ramparts of Fort Jackson, and picked their way through the gap in the barrier. Moving with the current and under full steam, they quickly disappeared downstream.

"Where are they going?" she asked.

Dunbar lifted a hand to shield his eyes as he stared downriver. "Hollins sends a pair of boats once a week to make sure the enemy hasn't reached Head of Passes."

"Why don't we have forces there permanently?"

"There's nothing to fortify. It's a mosquito-infested swamp. Pilottown is a dozen shacks on poles in the mud. Besides, last time the Yankees came, we drove them off easily enough."

Yet it was obvious from the frenetic pace of work at the forts that expectations were that a major attack was soon coming.

She was still at the fort the next day when the rumble of heavy guns sent soldiers and civilians scrambling to the parapets. Hollins's two side-wheelers came steaming into view from their downriver reconnaissance mission. Just as they reached the protection of Fort Jackson's guns, three light-draft steamers came into view, stopping to lurk some two miles downriver. There was a flash of light, then another, followed several seconds later by rocking booms. A jet of water spouted into the air a few hundred yards short of the lowermost Confederate boat. The other shell slammed into the mud of the riverbank.

"Twenty-pounders," Dunbar said. "Good thing our boats pulled back when they did."

Josephine had no way of telling if his assessment of the guns was accurate, but her heart was pounding. She expected to see the entire Union fleet round the bend, Farragut's sloops followed by mortar boats. By night, the forts would be aflame, the powder stores exploding, and she would be trapped within.

The two lead Union ships each fired another shot. These also fell short. They followed the third boat in drifting slowly back downriver. And that was the end of the engagement.

But alarming news soon reached Fort Jackson from Hollins's boats. Farragut had seized Head of Passes and run up the Stars and Stripes at Pilottown. He'd sent fast picket boats upriver, and when Hollins's steamers came down with the hope of sinking an unwary enemy vessel, they'd found the Union navy well organized and with an aggressive posture.

More information came from a pair of fishermen Hollins's men had picked up in the river. Much of Farragut's fleet had crossed, although the larger, deeper-draft ships remained in the Gulf. Some of these ships drew as many as twenty feet and needed to be lightened before they could be forced over the bar. Meanwhile, General Benjamin Butler was waiting on Ship Island off the coast of Mississippi with an invasion force of twenty thousand men. An argument broke out among the officers at dinner as to whether it would be possible to get the heavier Union ships upriver, and whether they'd be effective even if they could cross the bar.

Not if *Louisiana* and *Mississippi* could be brought to the fight, it was decided. The huge ironclads would blast the wooden Yankee vessels straight to hell. Why the devil were they still upriver, unable to move under their own power, unable to fight?

The next morning, Josephine returned to New Orleans with the first steamer, composing articles about the breaking river barrier, the brief battle downriver from the fort, and her speculation about how the Confederates would win the struggle.

She returned to her lodging at Nellie Gill's house to discover a messy stack of correspondence, most of it relating to her work with the *Crescent*, but also a short, cryptic letter.

> *You are a cold, cruel person, harder than any man and more cunning than any woman. You have abandoned us to poverty and ruin. I would remind you of your mother's prior affections, but your heart is as cold and unfeeling as iron. May you gain the reward you so richly deserve.*
>
> *F. D.*

Josephine didn't know what to make of it. The writing was neat, a woman's hand. And the initials—F. D.—could only mean Francesca Díaz again. The woman's attempts at blackmail having failed, she had apparently been reduced to begging. Yet there was no specific plea for money, no address to send such a sum should the note prick Josephine's conscience.

And what of the accusation? Josephine didn't know the predicament to which the woman alluded, and wouldn't have been responsible for it if she had. No doubt it had something to do with the Colonel and his spendthrift ways, backed by some reference to the friendship that had existed between Francesca and Josephine's mother while the two women traveled and performed on *Crescent Queen*. Beyond that, Josephine was baffled.

"I owe you nothing," she said aloud. "You approached *me*. You threatened *me*."

The note troubled Josephine for several days, but her work and the rapidly changing situation in the city soon put it out of her mind. General Lovell had placed the city under martial law. Men over the age of sixteen were required to take a loyalty oath or vacate the city at once. Travel between parishes was restricted to those with passports. Josephine had no trouble securing one.

By the end of March, New Orleans began to resemble Washington City after the Battle of Manassas the previous summer. Lovell had raised thousands of new recruits, and they were drilling endlessly on the parade ground and in the public squares. Every day barges carried heavy guns downstream to the forts, together with all of the other matériel of war. The boats of the mosquito fleet, clad in iron and bales of cotton, steamed south, carrying more men and supplies.

Josephine despaired that Farragut and Butler would arrive in New Orleans to find it filled with twenty thousand Confederates, hollering mad and ready to repel any invasion.

But on the sixth of April, word began trickling into New Orleans of a battle raging at a Tennessee church by the name of Shiloh. At first, the news brought jubilation. General Grant was routed, falling back under the assault of Johnston and Beauregard. By the seventh, it seemed that the battle had become a bloody stalemate between a hundred thousand men, with tens of thousands dead and wounded.

But within a few days, it became clear that while both sides had taken and delivered terrible blows, only one army remained standing when the battlefield cleared: the North. Meanwhile, Union gunboats had seized another large fortress on the Mississippi. Memphis was threatened.

A desperate President Davis telegraphed General Lovell to send his new troops north to defend Corinth and Memphis. Lovell had no choice but to comply. Men began streaming out of the city on their way to points north.

In New Orleans, the people knew. Only Fort Jackson and Fort Philip guarded the downriver approach to New Orleans. If they fell, so would the city.

CHAPTER 28

On the evening of April 15, Josephine had retired to her room at Nellie Gill's house to write her story for the next day, as well as put together more notes about the preparations, rumors, and attitude in the city, when a frantic knocking at the front door brought her to the window. Solomon Fein stood at the door, pounding. A carriage and driver waited in the street.

"Thank God you're here," he said when Josephine had thrown on a shawl and rushed downstairs. "It has started."

"You mean the surveying?"

Word had been trickling into the city for the past two days that Farragut had sent crews of surveyors up near the forts under protection of gunboats. While the gunboats drove off Confederate sharpshooters, the Yankees planted flags in the brush and weeds along shore. The Confederates returned at night to seek out and pull up as many markers as they could find. The fear was that the

Union intended to pull their mortar boats just beyond range of Fort Jackson's guns, from which point they could bomb the fort to rubble.

"The surveying is done," Fein said. "The enemy towed some bomb boats into position downriver and is testing his mortars."

"What do you think, another feint?"

Fein shook his head. "Lovell is at the fort. He telegraphed New Orleans and said in no uncertain terms that the attack has begun. This is it—the big story. I'm going down to cover it myself. My boat leaves in thirty minutes. I want you to come with me, but I won't force you. It will be risky. People will die."

"I'm coming."

Josephine's heart was thumping along at a good pace now as she raced upstairs to pack a carpetbag. When she came outside, Fein was already in the cab, and he leaned out the door, beckoning urgently. All the way to the levee, he drummed his fingers on his knee, cracked his knuckles, double-checked his own writing supplies, took off his glasses to polish them, then repeated the drill.

They raced down the dock and reached the boat just as one man was untying the rope and another was preparing to haul up the gangplank. The river was calm and the air cool as they slipped downriver. The sounds of a brass band reached her ears from Jackson Square, but was shortly replaced by the throb of the boiler, the churn of the wheel, and the smooth, liquid sound of the river itself, sliding past the hull.

Within a few hours, Josephine heard a rumble as of distant thunder. The soldiers on deck leaned over the rail, listening quietly. Boats from the mosquito fleet eased by off port, and signal lights flashed between them.

The rumble grew louder as the night continued, and she remembered the battle of the previous summer, the pounding of artillery, the shaking ground. It would get worse. Her hands tightened around the railing. Soon, she could see flashes on the horizon.

Fein found her on deck and lit a cigarette. "I tried to sleep, but it's no use." He held up his hand, to show how it trembled. "I'm all nerves. I don't know how you managed in Virginia."

"They call it 'seeing the elephant,'" she said. "The first time you're in battle. You don't know how you'll fare—if you'll fight, or if you'll cower and be trampled."

He gave a nervous laugh. "I'm thinking trampled."

"Want me to ask the captain if he'll put you to shore?"

"No. I won't cower in New Orleans while good men give their lives. So I'll have to go forward, coward or no. I only wish I were as brave as you."

"I'm not brave," she assured him. "I'm terrified."

But when they reached the forts in the morning, the attack had ceased. The Union had crept up to a loose raft in the barrier in the night and set off a submarine charge, which destroyed the raft and opened a gap in the barrier. Confederate steamers had assembled to repair the breach. Other than that, there was little evidence of an attack, only a few gaps in the earthworks where mortars had exploded.

Major Dunbar was talking to Ludd from the *Picayune* on the parapet when Josephine found him cheerfully pointing out the Union sloops downriver, out of range of Jackson's guns.

When the major spotted Josephine, he excused himself from Ludd, who appeared visibly annoyed at her arrival, and led her along the parapet.

"There will be more trouble to come," Dunbar said. "But we've weathered the first attack."

She glanced to the center of the fort, where Ludd had descended to greet Fein in front of barracks newly bombproofed with sod. The conversation between the two men seemed cordial enough.

"We heard the enemy fire," she said. "It sounded like mortars, but I only see cannons, and they're out of range."

Dunbar pointed downstream around the bend, opposite the Union sloops. "There's a mortar flotilla behind the trees. If you look, you can spot one of the masts poking up. About four thousand yards. We could hit them with our rifled guns if not for the woods."

It was exactly the stretch of woods she'd identified earlier, and she thrilled at the thought that her reconnaissance might have made it into Farragut's plans. He was using the trees perfectly, lobbing mortars over the top while using them to shield his boats.

"Is the mortar fire accurate?" she asked.

"Cursedly so," Dunbar said cheerfully. "But he has fired at least—"

His voice cut out as a thump sounded from downstream. The shell was moving slowly enough that she could see it rise above the woods, form a large arc, then begin to descend. All of a sudden she remembered reading about a Union soldier who'd watched a cannonball bouncing lazily toward him, thinking he'd had time to move, only to have his legs torn off.

Dunbar must have thought the same thing, because he threw his arms around her and dragged her to the ground, where he shielded her with his body until the shell hit and detonated somewhere on the opposite side of the fort.

Josephine rose and dusted herself off. "Was that necessary, sir?"

"My apologies, but it is better to be safe than . . . Good heavens!"

She followed his gaze. The mortar had landed on the drawbridge on the far side of the fort and had not only blown a hole in it and made it impassible to horse or cart, but had also snapped off a pole that strung the telegraph line in and out of the fort.

He raced off to see to repairs. No sooner had he departed than the Union "bummer" crews began launching a barrage of mortars that were soon falling every twenty to thirty seconds. Josephine retreated to one of the sod-covered bombproofs to wait out the attack.

When the barrage ended, soldiers came into the yard to put out fires.

That night, she spoke with General Lovell, two colonels, and a captain from the mosquito fleet who came ashore expressly to meet with her.

"You've just come from New Orleans?" the captain asked. "Any news on the ironclads?"

"Neither can move under her own power. It will be weeks before they can leave the levee."

He cursed, then hurried off, muttering something about towing them into place as floating batteries. The next morning, she met two other naval officers, and it was clear that they, too, were more pessimistic about the looming battle than the sanguine men of the forts.

The mortar fire continued on and off through the night of the sixteenth and into the following day. Commodore Hollins sent a few gunboats beyond the barrier to attack a group of Union surveyors, but two Union ships soon chased them back into the protection of Jackson's guns.

The Confederates had by now assembled a large collection of fire rafts above Fort St. Philip of the same kind that had thrown chaos into the Union during the skirmish at Head of Passes last October. Each was the size of a Mississippi flatboat, and stacked high with hundreds of cords of fast-burning pine, together with cotton, tar oil, and other combustibles.

Not long after the incident with the gunboats and the surveyors, the Confederates lit four fire rafts, opened the barrier, and towed them through. They flamed so high as they passed the fort that Josephine could feel the heat from where she watched on the parapets. Once through the barrier, the rafts drifted lazily downstream toward the Union ships. Three floated harmlessly to one side, but a fourth came straight toward one of the big sloops. *Hartford*, she thought. Before it got too close, a Union gunboat took it in tow and hauled it away. Shells from the fort splashed short.

In the early afternoon, Hollins tried again, this time sending three steamers downriver. They took position in the middle of the river and shelled the mortar boats for several minutes before two of the bigger Union warships came upstream. Staying out of range of Jackson's probing attacks, the Union ships traded blows with the undersized guns of the mosquito fleet. When one shot knocked over a mast of a Confederate steamer, Hollins's remaining two boats were forced to take it in tow and retreat upriver.

Josephine watched and noted all of these events from the parapet, her paper on her satchel, where she wrote furiously during lulls in the action. She stuffed cotton into her ears for when shells exploded nearby, or when one of the fort's big guns let off an exploratory shot, and she flattened on the ground every time a mortar came flying in. Otherwise, she didn't let the fighting drive her inside. Every hour or so Fein came up to ask how she was faring, then light a cigarette with a shaky hand and let it smolder without smoking before he went below again.

Mortar fire continued into the night, but it was quiet enough in the small room they'd given her in one of the bombproofs, with only a dull rumble above, that she could almost believe those defenders who were still convinced that the Union action was a feint to draw attention away from the real action upriver.

So far, both attacks and defensive sallies had seemed probing, almost playful. She'd heard of no deaths, either in the fort or in Hollins's mosquito fleet, and only a few reports of injuries. The Union could no doubt say the same thing, given the ineffectual Confederate fire.

Josephine was so tired that she slept soundly. Only direct hits woke her, and then only briefly, as the building shook, and dirt fell through the rafters from the sod above. But as she woke the next morning, she immediately sensed a change in the intensity of Union fire. She climbed the parapet to find Dunbar up top with a spyglass.

He glanced in her direction. "They're closer, look."

She took the spyglass. The Union bummers had towed their mortar schooners upriver to the places surveyed earlier, where they were still concealed by the trees. Only the forward-most boats lay within range of Jackson's fire from the casemates, but even then, only partially exposed.

Thump, thump, thump, thump.

It sounded like a distant drum, the drumhead in need of tightening. Dunbar grabbed her and dragged her down behind the parapet just as the bombs began to fall. They exploded overhead, and the walls shook. Smoke hung in the air when she lifted her head, and men were running, ducking across the yard below them. The nearest mortar had hit no more than thirty feet away, leaving a blackened crater on the parapet. She climbed back up, shaken, her head ringing.

Soon enough, she was forced to abandon the wall walk, as the mortar fire intensified, then intensified again. Josephine found relative safety with the men operating one of the eleven-inch cannons firing shells in response. A division of Union gunboats had come within range and now began to shell the fort, and this attracted the fire from the well-protected cannons inside.

Josephine stuffed more cotton in her ears and put her hands over them as she looked out through the slits at the action on the river. The fort shuddered with another barrage of mortars, sending dust sifting from the rafters. Moments later, the Union fired another broadside from its sloops. Shells slammed into the wall and threw Josephine and the gunners to the ground. A young soldier lay crying next to her, his wrist badly twisted, probably broken. She volunteered to take him down to the infirmary. The gunnery sergeant nodded, pale-faced, before turning back to order return fire.

The injured boy was still crying when she got him to the yard, tears cutting streaks in the powder that blackened his face. "Don't let them do it."

"Do what, cut off your hand? Surely it's not as bad as all that?"

He bent his wrist. "It's not broken at all, only sprained. That's what I mean. They'll send me back."

A shell fell whistling into the yard. It struck the ground a few yards away and sent mud flying. The boy staggered and they grabbed each other for mutual support.

"Please, help me get out of here," he said. "I can't take it anymore."

She stared at him. "You mean desert?"

"No, I would never . . . *yes*."

The boy had seen the elephant. She could see it in the wide-eyed, stunned expression, as if a shell had exploded too near his head and addled his brains. He was shaking so hard that she thought his knees would buckle and he would collapse.

"If you want to leave," she said, "there's a crew outside repairing the telegraph lines. If anyone asks, that's where you're going. Then slip into the swamp beyond the water battery. Union pickets lie two miles to the south. Give them information, and they'll guarantee your safety."

CHAPTER 29

Shells fell all day and into the night. The bombardment never ceased. Sometime after midnight, men came pounding on her door and she emerged into the hallway to find it filled with smoke. A shell had penetrated the bombproof and set the wooden support beams on fire.

She stumbled outside to find half the fort aflame and the night lit up with orange, smoky firelight. Shells came screaming into the yard, where they buried themselves in the wet ground and detonated. Mud spumes spouted into the air. The ground shook so hard it felt as though the fort would soon collapse into rubble.

In spite of all of this, the fort was still standing. Several men had been killed, and another dozen injured, but casualties were still light. The biggest injury seemed to be morale, and Dunbar reported with disgust that several dozen men had failed to report for duty, presumably deserting. Josephine thought guiltily about the boy she'd encouraged to flee toward Union pickets.

"I've set guards," he told Josephine and Fein. Ludd had fled upriver the previous night with a signal boat, leaving the two reporters from the *Crescent* alone to report the battle. "We've caught a few deserters, but too many have slipped through. An example must be set. From this point, anyone caught deserting will be shot."

"Isn't that a little harsh?" Fein asked.

"Every man who leaves his post makes it that much more likely that his fellow soldiers will be killed."

When he left, the two reporters stood in the doorway of one of the few bombproofs not on fire, staring up at the sky. The mortars were targeting the water battery outside the walls at the moment, but soon enough the barrage would return, and they wanted to be ready to flee inside.

Josephine had been thinking about the reporter from the *Picayune*. "Can you believe that Ludd left already? Did he expect to find a picnic and a fireworks display?"

Fein cleared his throat nervously. "We should go, too. They say *Louisiana* left the levee under tow. We could meet them midway up and get a good story there."

"You can go, I'm staying."

"Then let's cross to Fort St. Philip at least," Fein said. "We'll still see the battle, but away from this confounded bombardment."

More bombs came into the yard. One buried itself in the ground some twenty feet away, and soldiers in the fire brigade threw aside their water buckets and leaped to the side. The two reporters ducked inside and cringed, waiting for it to go off. This one failed to detonate.

"Josephine, for God's sake," Fein said. Another shell shook the roof. "We can't stay here."

She hesitated. In spite of her bold words, that last bombardment had left her rattled. But she couldn't leave. It wasn't simply a question of watching the battle; she was collecting information for the Union fleet downstream. They must have used hundreds of tons of powder and launched thousands of bombs, shells, and shot, yet so far had not diminished the ability of Fort Jackson to keep fighting back. Few men inside had been killed. If federal troops marched on Jackson, they would be slaughtered. Would she be able to collect this information from the safer side of the river? And could she get this information downriver from either location?

"All right," she said. "We'll move to Fort St. Philip."

But this proved easier to plan than to execute. They found Dunbar only to learn that even military traffic across the river had been cut. The Yankees had fired up the docks, he said bitterly, and what's more, the Confederate fleet was too afraid to venture beyond the barrier except to push down fire rafts when darkness fell.

The guns from the fort had won at least one hard-earned concession from the enemy. Some of the most accurate mortar boats on the east bank had taken damage, and Farragut had moved them to the opposite side of the river. Here, they were more protected, but more of their shells began to fall astray.

Even so, Dunbar shared the grim result of two days of full-scale bombardment. The casemates, parapets, and the parade plain had been pounded. Shells had knocked out two thirty-two-pounders in the water battery, and several heavy guns in the fort were either destroyed or disabled.

"What about *Louisiana*?" Josephine asked.

"They brought her in tow. She's anchored above Fort St. Philip."

Fein made encouraging noises at this.

"But she can't move under her own power," Dunbar continued, "and the mechanics are still trying to get her guns properly mounted. I want her towed below the barricade. It would be something at least."

"Like a floating battery," Josephine said. "That makes sense."

"Yes, and damn near impregnable." The major shook his head. "The navy won't do it. They say they need three days to get her ready for combat."

"Three days!" Fein said.

"Yes, I know," Dunbar said glumly. "In three days we'll all be dead."

The next night, someone came to shake Josephine from her sleep. She lay wrapped in a blanket, still dressed in the filthy clothes she'd been wearing for days. Soldiers slumbered all around her. They tossed and turned on the hard ground, some moaning in their sleep, others muttering to themselves.

At first she thought the person trying to wake her was only the ground shaking, the endless rumble and buckle of the bombardment that seemed never to end.

"Josephine, wake up!"

She blinked at a lamp held in front of her face. "What is it? Are they here?" There was a dream still lingering on the edge of her memory, something about soldiers storming the gates of the fortress.

"The boat is ready. We have to go now." It was Fein peering down at her. One of the lenses in his glasses had cracked.

Josephine threw off her blanket and grabbed the satchel she'd kept held between her knees while she slept. She stuffed the rest of her few belongings into her carpetbag.

Outside, there was enough light to see by the remnants of the citadel still burning in the center of the yard. Fein ducked his head and raced across, with Josephine following. Another bomb hit, followed by the roar of two cannons from the casemates. The two reporters left the fort through the open gates, ignored by the soldiers on watch.

They found a rowboat waiting at a newly reconstructed dock on the upriver side of the fort. Four sailors sat at the oars, and the passengers included a gray-bearded engineer who said he'd come across from St. Philip to check the magazines, as well as two of General Lovell's staff officers. The final passenger was a young soldier with his hands tied in front of him and wearing a blindfold. Some miscreant, she supposed, being hauled across to the other side to face a whipping, or worse. He was trembling so violently that she couldn't help feeling sorry for him.

The river was a glossy black, reflecting the flashes of light from the Union warships downstream. Behind them, the fort answered fire with fire, while atop the ramparts, the Confederate flag still flapped in the breeze, defiant in the face of all the might the Yankees could throw at them. In spite of the crippled morale inside the forts, it seemed as though the Union was no closer to their objective than when they'd begun.

"Please," the young soldier said, flinching at the sound of cannon fire as the rowboat entered the current. "Could you please let me see? I don't want to die blindfolded."

This only brought jeers from the sailors rowing the boat and further disgusted comments from the officers.

Josephine's pity only grew. "I don't see the harm. His hands are tied."

"He's a damned coward," one of the sailors said. "He don't deserve nothing from us."

"Save your tender feelings," one of the officers added, a lieutenant. "This man is going to hang for desertion."

"All the more reason to show compassion."

Josephine made her way to the bench holding the prisoner and pulled off his blindfold. It was the young soldier with the sprained wrist that she'd encouraged to desert. He fixed her with a haunted, desperate look. She stared back in shock and horror.

"It is true," he whispered. "There's no saving me now."

"I'll talk to them. I'll tell them—"

"No," he interrupted. "Please, don't." The young man lifted his bound hands and took a folded sheet of paper from his breast pocket, which he handed to Josephine. "For my mama. I wrote down her name. She lives in the Third Ward."

"This man is a coward and a traitor," the officer said. His voice was as unforgiving as the shells screaming over their heads to slam into the casemates of the fort. "That's all his mother needs to know. That he was running to enemy lines, prepared to kiss those Yankees' boots and thank them kindly for their savagery."

Fein had been watching with a concerned expression, and now he spoke up. "This man is going to die tonight. So might we all. What harm is there in showing a little mercy?"

Josephine took the young man's note, cast a defiant stare at anyone who seemed likely to offer further contradiction, and tucked it into her satchel with her own writing.

The rowboat was roughly a third the way across the Mississippi when fire caught Josephine's eye from upstream. What was at first a flickering light became a billowing bonfire drifting toward them. The navy had set loose one of their fire rafts to float down at the federal fleet.

This put down any further talk about the prisoner. The rowing sailors cried out at the unexpected inferno roaring toward them and redoubled their efforts. The officers snarled profanities, both at the sailors for not rowing fast enough and at the navy itself for not bothering to find out whether anyone was attempting to cross before sending down a raft. Viewed from the parapets, the fire rafts had seemed so slow and lazy as they drifted downstream, that it was never a surprise to Josephine that the Union invariably snared them and dragged them harmlessly away from the big ships. But viewed from a rowboat in the river, the raft seemed to be barreling down at them. It was still a hundred yards away when Josephine could feel the heat.

It looked as though they would just squeak past before it hit them. But then one of the sailors leaped overboard and swam toward the near shore. One of his fellows cursed him. A lieutenant pulled out a revolver and calmly plugged shots into the water, but none hit the coward, who escaped into the darkness. The man had jettisoned the oar as he went, and it now slipped out of the oarlock and fell into the river. A second sailor leaped overboard while the others were grabbing at it.

Josephine had been holding it together until the second man hit the water. Then suddenly she was back on *Cairo Red* the night the boiler exploded. Firemen and engineers had leaped overboard and left the passengers to die. Burned, scalded, blown to pieces. And drowned, like her mother.

The fire raft now towered above them. Heat roiled over the water. Both raft and rowboat were now drifting downstream toward the barrier.

She ignored her carpetbag but clutched her satchel. If she went over, she would lose all of her writing of the past few days, now amounting to at least forty pages.

Another splash. It was the engineer, who bobbed up and began paddling to safety. He was followed moments later by the two remaining sailors and one of the lieutenants. One remained, plus the young prisoner, who stared at the fire with a wide, slack-jawed expression, as if stunned. Plus the two reporters from the *Crescent*.

Josephine moved to untie the young prisoner.

"What are you doing?" the remaining officer demanded. He wasn't the one who'd been speaking so angrily moments earlier about the prisoner's cowardice—that one had fled in terror—but this officer still looked uncertain, and made as if to draw his firearm.

Her hands struggled with the knot. "He's a man, not an animal. Will you see him burned alive?"

The lieutenant dropped his hand from his weapon and came over. "Move."

While he untied the young man, Josephine wedged her satchel under the seat where it would be safest from the flames. Even if she died, the Union might find the rowboat only partly scorched and rescue her papers. Meanwhile, she had to save herself. They were approaching the barricade, which had been partially separated so the fire raft could pass. Men stood on the deck of one of the hulks, shouting and waving their arms in warning, as if the people on the rowboat had somehow missed the inferno bearing down on them.

The moment he was untied, the prisoner dove overboard and disappeared beneath the water, resurfacing a few feet away. He flailed inexpertly at the water in an attempt to swim clear. Josephine rose to follow him into the river.

Fein grabbed Josephine's arm. His face glowed red in the light of the fire now only yards away. "Don't leave me! I can't swim!"

Fort Jackson loomed above them. Flashes of light emerged from the guns. More lights from incoming fire splashed against the walls and parapets. The rumbling, booming sound of battle continued unabated, but above it all came the crackle and roar of pitch and pine from the fire raft. It was approaching swiftly on their right side and threatened to catch them on the bow and drag them up against the barrier where they would all burn to death. Unless . . .

"The oars!" Josephine shouted. She shoved at the lieutenant to get his attention. "Go!"

Fein grabbed one of the remaining oars, but now that he'd freed the prisoner, the lieutenant seemed stunned, staring rigid and petrified at the roaring inferno bearing down on them, even while the others shouted to get his attention. At last Josephine got him out of the way, and then she joined Fein in rowing furiously away from the fire raft.

It drifted by on Josephine's right, so close it felt as though her clothes would catch fire. Josephine didn't stop. Then the raft was past. But it didn't slip safely through the barrier. Instead, the current carried it up against the nearest hulk anchored to the river bottom. The fire illuminated two figures in the water, clinging to the hulk. Two of the men who had leaped overboard to safety. The fire raft nudged up against the hulk. Men on the deck used long, iron-tipped poles to shove it back into the current, while others came running with buckets to douse the flames that leaped from the raft to the barrier ship.

The men in the river screamed as they were caught between the fire raft and the hull of the ship. Their voices joined into a single high, terrified screech, and Josephine slapped her hands over her ears. She let go of the oar and it strained against the oarlock, trying to tug free in the current.

Once again she was back at *Cairo Red*, this time standing on the deck as the boiler blew into the sky. People burning, screaming, the heat . . .

They were through the barrier and floating downstream. The fire raft came through as well, but by now it was far to their right and no longer a threat.

"Help me!" a voice cried from the water. It was the young soldier. He floated a dozen yards or more off starboard, still in the path of the fire raft.

His cries jolted Josephine from her terrified inaction. She urged him toward the boat until he came within range of an outstretched oar. He grabbed on, and they reeled him in and hauled him up, wet and coughing up water.

Moments later, they came across one of the sailors and managed to pull him in as well. Two other men had burned, and one had presumably swum safely to shore. That left only one man unaccounted for. They couldn't see him anywhere.

A row of Union sloops lay downstream in an arc across the river. Their cannons flashed, one after the other, until the air filled with such a roar that it became like a never-ending clap of thunder. The federal ships weren't shooting at the rowboat, but at the fire raft, trying to sink it before it became a threat. But the cannons were close enough that it felt as though the rowboat had come under fire all the same.

Shells splashed into the water and whistled overhead. Timed shots exploded above them. Answer fire came from the fort, and while it was trying to *protect* the raft, not sink it, some of these shots also splashed into the river when they fell short of their targets.

There was no question of stemming the current and making for the bank, so they kept their heads down and rowed only to keep clear of the fire raft that kept pace with them. The guns were so loud and continuous that they shook Josephine's bones and made the rowboat vibrate as if it would be torn apart.

Josephine never saw the shot that hit them. Never heard it above the general din. But it was as if a giant fish had come swimming from the muddy depths of the Mississippi and given the underside of the boat a shove with its mighty snout. Her stomach lurched out from underneath her.

The boat lifted above the water—or at least half of it did. The other half was still below her. She was looking *down* on it. For a moment she caught Fein's surprised, terrified expression in the flash of light. He looked up at her, even as the nose of the rowboat on which he sat buried itself in the water. Then the light was gone, and Josephine came crashing down.

Her head slammed into an oarlock, and she went black as she pitched into the river.

CHAPTER 30

When Josephine came to, she was sputtering water and flailing. For a moment, she didn't know where she was, only that she was in the river, fire lighting up the night, and for an instant she thought it was *Cairo Red,* burning on the river, a thousand miles to the north.

But as her head cleared, she realized that the explosions were coming from the Union fleet downstream and from Fort Jackson above. One hit the water nearby, sending a spout skyward. Water crashed on her head and pushed her under again.

When she came up, something nudged into her back. It was the back half of the rowboat, overturned and still floating. Two figures were clinging to it.

"Help us!" one of the men called.

It was Fein. He'd lost his glasses and squinted at her through the light of the fire raft still burning a few yards away. He gripped the side of the broken boat with one hand and the back of a slumping man with the other.

"My writing!" Josephine said, remembering her satchel.

She flailed about, desperate to find the leather case floating by so she could haul it out of the water before the pages were destroyed.

"Josephine! Help me, please."

"Where's my satchel? It has all my papers."

"The devil take your story. You can rewrite it. I can't—" He grabbed again at the man he was holding on to, who threatened to pull loose and drift away. "I can't hold on."

And Fein couldn't swim, either, she remembered. Josephine gave a final, desperate search for her satchel in the inky water before giving up to paddle over to the overturned boat. She grabbed on with one hand and dug the fingers of her other into the unconscious man's shirt to help Fein hold him in place.

A shell exploded, and she saw the unconscious man's face in the flash of light. It was the young soldier. Josephine tightened her grip with a new urgency. She couldn't let him go, couldn't let him drown. Not now. God help her, she had to hold him up.

A shell hit nearby and drenched them anew. Lights flashed from Fort Jackson, a whole row of them, and they ducked down as more shells screamed overhead.

"I'm losing my grip," Josephine cried. She gave the soldier a shake. "Wake up!" she pleaded. Then, to Fein, "He's slipping. Help me!"

With Josephine and Fein each using one arm to hold the boat and the other to lift, they dragged the young man onto the keel of the overturned, partially destroyed boat. He was surprisingly light and easy to move higher.

"Dear God!" Fein said, his voice strangled.

Such horror filled his voice that Josephine turned to look downstream, wondering what fresh terror they were floating toward. The river below was filled with warships, many of them blasting toward the fort, but they were close enough now to Farragut's fleet that the Union shells were soaring overhead. It was only the Confederate guns that threatened them now.

It wasn't until she looked back to the unconscious soldier that she saw what had horrified Fein. The young man's arms and torso were completely out of the water now, sprawled across the keel. As for his waist and legs, they were somewhere else. All that was left of his lower half was a mess of uncoiled intestines and other internal organs. The shell that tore the rowboat apart had cut him in two.

Fein turned away as if he would be sick into the water. Or maybe he *was* sick, but she didn't see it. She could only stare at the young man—a boy, really. Remember his trembling voice, his fear, the way he'd begged her to help him escape the bombardment. The letter he'd given her to take to his mama.

Movement on the river dragged her attention to the Union fleet. One of the ships had thrown over a grapnel to snag the fire raft and tug it out of the way, but either they missed or the line snapped. The raft drifted toward one of the large sloops, where men scrambled around on the decks with what looked like buckets of sand and water at the ready. Fire roared to the height of the masts, but in the end, the raft drifted by harmlessly.

Even so, the ships had scrambled to get out of the way, and many of them were jumbled together trying to regain their former position. One of the big ships narrowly avoided running down the broken rowboat and the people clinging to its side. Some of the larger sloops had put out launches to try to haul the fire raft away, and now one of these veered and came rowing toward Josephine and Fein. They had been spotted. A man on the boat drew a pistol and held it at the ready. Josephine waved a hand to show they were no threat.

"Well, that's it," Fein said in a grim voice as the boat drew near, the men on board shouting a challenge. "We're prisoners, now."

A man knocked on the door of the cabin where Josephine sat, wrapped in a blanket with a mug of hot soup in hand. The lieutenant who had been interrogating her about the forts hadn't heard of Josephine Breaux, was only vaguely aware of the Pinkerton detectives, and had refused to take her to Flag Officer Farragut or even to the ship's captain. He now rose to answer the door.

A flood of relief passed through when she saw the strong jaw, the dark mustache, and broad shoulders of Franklin Gray. A pink scar traced across his forehead, the healed wound from the sabotage at the hospital arsenal.

"I hoped it was you," he said. "Once I saw your newspaper friend and heard he'd been brought in with a young woman. And once I looked over the remains of your rowboat, I knew for sure."

"Am I glad to see you."

"And who are you?" the lieutenant demanded of Franklin after doing a once-over of his civilian trousers and blue frock coat stripped of insignia.

Franklin handed the man a piece of paper. "Government agent, authorized by the secretary of war. Flag Officer Farragut has given me permission to interrogate any prisoners, deserters, or secessionists who fall into our hands."

"Very well, sir," said the lieutenant with what sounded like relief. He had been growing increasingly frustrated with Josephine after she'd refused to cooperate. Now he took his leave. Once he was gone, Josephine threw her arms around Franklin and the two friends embraced.

After exchanging more pleasantries, Josephine's first worry was that Fein not be mistreated. He wasn't, Franklin assured her, but neither was he cooperating.

She set her mug of soup onto the little desk at which she sat. "He'll be disappointed in me."

Franklin pulled up a chair. "Is he a fire-eater?"

"Not at all. He's a newspaperman. Practical, chases good stories. I figure he'll settle into his work if we take the city, complaining about the Union when he can get away with it. But he's a decent man. He shouldn't be abused."

"I'll pass the word."

The cabin shook from a fresh barrage of outgoing cannon fire. The fighting had settled down in the two hours since she'd been taken aboard, with occasional flare-ups. They waited until the firing stopped.

Franklin sketched in his activities of the past few months. After the sailors carried him off the levee for the cannon barge, he'd banged around from boat to boat inside the coffin-like box until finally a Cajun fisherman on a keelboat pried open the lid two days later. He'd arrived at Pilottown at Head of Passes. From there, it was a simple matter of promising a bribe to get him to the Gulf, where he'd then spent a lazy winter in Farragut's fleet as it assembled offshore.

Josephine's intelligence had streamed in with regularity and was one of the key reasons that President Lincoln, the secretary of the navy, and Flag Officer Farragut had pushed through with the plan to come over the bar and into the river with wooden warships.

"So this isn't a feint?" she asked, still not entirely convinced that the entire battle wasn't indeed a diversion to allow Flag Officer Foote's gunboats to steam unopposed down the river, as her phony battle plan had claimed it would be. "What about Foote and General Grant?"

"Not a feint. They have their hands full. No way Foote comes down past all those forts. Vicksburg alone could hold him off for months."

"What now?"

"My orders are to bring you to Farragut. He wants to hear your intelligence for himself."

Josephine considered her bedraggled appearance. Her hair was a wet, tangled mess. Her dress was torn, wet, and muddy. She'd lost her shoes, and they'd given her men's socks and a man's boots. She didn't suppose there was a single change of clothing for a woman anywhere in the entire fleet.

Franklin must have seen her looking herself over. "Don't worry about that. You look like someone who has survived a battle—they'll understand."

"It's not just that. I'm also missing my papers. All gone into the river."

A self-satisfied smile crossed Franklin's face, the kind a man wore when he had a clever secret. "Wait here. I'll be back."

Josephine hardly dared to hope. When he reappeared moments later, she was so overjoyed to see her satchel in his hand, barely wet, that she once again threw her arms around his neck. She only just stopped herself from kissing him full on the mouth and aimed for his cheek instead.

He laughed at her reaction but was clearly delighted. This time, he held her a moment longer than necessary before releasing her. Josephine snatched out her papers and set them on the desk, turning up the lamp so she could see better. Only the top few were damp at all, and the ink had barely run. The young soldier's letter was there, too.

And there, beneath the paper, was the Colonel's Oriental box. Why she'd even brought it downriver was hard to say. It carried nothing but a turtle hair comb and the gilt watch with the curious markings; the money itself she'd hidden back at Miss Nellie's. The box seemed to live a charmed existence. It was not wet or damaged in any way.

Josephine set the box next to her pages and the soldier's letter and used her sleeve to dry out the moisture at the bottom of the satchel. "How did you get this?"

"They almost let the rowboat drift downstream with the rest of the debris coming down from the barrier," Franklin said, "but an alert sailor hauled it in. They discovered the satchel wedged beneath the seat. Did you have any other possessions? We couldn't find anything."

"I don't care about them, only the satchel. I was going to jump overboard when we got too close to the fire raft. I thought if the boat didn't burn, someone might find it downriver. It's a miracle it wasn't dislodged or destroyed when the shell hit."

And what of the other three men who had been aboard with them: The engineer from the fort, the officer, and the sailor? She asked Franklin if anyone else had been pulled out of the river.

His face darkened. "Only the man Fein identified as a Confederate deserter. Or what was left of him. Nobody else."

"I see."

"Was he a friend of yours?"

"I only met him at the fort. But in those few days . . . connections were made." Something ached deep in her belly. "He didn't deserve to die."

"I understand. And I'm sorry."

What vagaries life held—that her writing had emerged unscathed, while a man was cut in two, and several others went missing, presumed dead. Also saved had been that cursed Oriental box. She couldn't understand it.

"Are you ready?" Franklin asked.

Josephine took a moment to collect her wits; then she gathered up her pages. She verified the satchel was dry enough not to cause further damage before she put the papers inside. She took out the turtle comb and used it to rake out her hair and then pin it back from her face. She handed Franklin the pocket watch.

"I believe this is yours," she said. "Safe and sound, through fire and water."

CHAPTER 31

The Union sloop *Hartford* emerged from the early-morning mist as the sailors rowed Josephine and Franklin across to it. The mighty warship wallowed in the middle of the river like a sea monster that had come swimming up the river from the Gulf. It had three masts, plus a stack in the middle for the boiler when under steam power. Cannons bristled from her side. All around, lesser ships seemed to give homage with their posture.

A bell sounded on the deck of *Hartford*, and a voice shouted a challenge. The officer at the head of the launch answered with a watchword, and a rope came flying over to haul them in. Once on board, Josephine and Franklin were issued into the officers' mess, where Flag Officer Farragut was drinking coffee and going over reports with several of his officers. The men rose when she entered.

Farragut came over. "You must be Miss Breaux. I would be honored if I could shake your hand."

Surprised at the offer, Josephine took his hand, returning his firm grip with her own.

Farragut was an older man, perhaps in his early sixties, clean-shaven and with a high, bald forehead. Gray hair curled over his ears. His clothing looked freshly laundered, and his gold epaulets, cuffs, and the brass buttons of his double-breasted jacket all gleamed. In spite of his age, she sensed a man of determination and energy as he seemed to size her up in turn.

"I hope my dispatches have been helpful, sir."

"Indispensable." Farragut indicated an officer with a full, bushy beard who stood by his side. "This is Commander Porter, whose chowderpots have been raining down on you these past several days."

Porter had a gruff look about him, and the bags under his eyes spoke to the exhaustion of maintaining the continuous bombardment from his mortar schooners. On the way over, Franklin had told Josephine in a low voice that there was disagreement between the two officers as to the effectiveness of Porter's bombing, and whether they should continue to reduce the enemy position, or make an attempt to run the two forts. Porter wanted to keep bombing, while Farragut was not convinced the mortars were making any noticeable difference. To make matters more interesting, she knew that Porter was the younger adopted brother of Farragut, and an intensely ambitious man in his own right.

Josephine and Franklin took a seat at the end of the table, opposite Farragut, Porter, and three other officers, two of whom appeared to be captains of ships in the navy, and the remaining man Farragut's staff officer.

To her surprise, Farragut didn't immediately grill her about the condition of the forts, but instead had a servant bring her fresh coffee while he shared more information than he took.

"I know it appears as though we could keep this bombardment for ages," Farragut said, "but in truth, I've been forced to borrow powder, shot, even coal from General Butler's army, which will raise hell in Washington. Even so, we're running short. How fare the rebels?"

"General Lovell has begun to ration powder." Josephine nodded in Franklin's direction. "Thanks to the attack at the Marine Hospital, Lovell has never recovered his stores. But he has a good week left without resupply."

"That's longer than we can carry on," Farragut said with a glance at Porter, who was scowling from above his thick whiskers. "Yesterday, a ship of English military observers came downstream. Did you see them pass the forts?"

"I didn't see, but I heard they'd done so."

"They assured me the forts would never fall unless by ground attack."

"You'd be hard pressed to get artillery over the swamp," she said, "and a siege would allow the Confederates to send reinforcements."

"My thinking precisely. I asked the English fellow if the forts could be run with wooden warships. He said we might get through with a few, but the rest would be sent down to the mud. Those few that made it would be facing rebel ironclads. *Louisiana* alone could sink half our fleet. Or so they say. Then there's the ram. What do you think?"

If the flag officer had thought to soften Josephine up by bombarding her with respect, it had worked. She'd entered expecting her opinions to be dismissed because of her age and sex, but instead he spoke to her as if she were an equal. The hot coffee was beginning to wake her up, and she was exhilarated by the thought that she might contribute to Farragut's plans.

"I wouldn't worry about the ironclads," she said. "*Louisiana* has no working engines, and is nothing more than a floating battery at the moment, and not a very good one. They don't even dare send her below the barricade to attack the mortar boats."

"I worked on *Louisiana*," Franklin said after clearing his throat. "And I can tell you she looks more intimidating than she is. Yes, she can carry sixteen guns, but nobody at the yard understood how to mount them. Perhaps things have changed since December."

"Not significantly," Josephine said. "Of her sixteen guns, I'd say only ten or twelve will serve in a fight. The others have been mounted in the wrong carriages, and another is in the right carriage, but mismounted and useless."

"You sound quite certain," Farragut said, and for the first time she detected skepticism in his voice.

"That I am. The guns are manned by the Crescent Regiment, an artillery company with no experience with naval guns. *Louisiana* is yet another obstacle to run, but not so daunting when compared to the forts."

Farragut stroked his chin and seemed to give this some thought.

His adopted brother Porter lit a pipe. "What about Fort Jackson? The Englishman said it would never fall. Was he deceived about that as well?"

She remembered what Franklin had warned her in the crossing. She didn't want the head of the mortar fleet to feel put down in front of his comrades. Not by a twenty-year-old civilian, and a woman, to boot.

"Your fire has been completely demoralizing. The citadel has burned, as have most of the outbuildings, the moat bridge, and the docks. Bombs nearly penetrated the magazines on two separate occasions. There's barely an unburned scrap of bedding in the entire fort. You've dismounted a number of guns."

"Then it *is* effective," Porter said. He turned to the flag officer. "Another week and we'll turn it to rubble."

"And do you have a week of powder?" Farragut demanded.

"Not entirely, no. But if you could lend—"

"I have nothing to lend," the flag officer said. "You forget that I have been slugging it out with the fort. What powder remains is needed for the battle."

Porter grunted.

During this exchange, three more officers had come into the room. They took coffee, and now servants appeared with plates of eggs and biscuits for the men at the table, who ate as the conversation continued.

"Tell me about St. Philip," Farragut said to Josephine.

"Nearly unscathed, of course," she said. "They'll riddle you with enfilading fire as you pass. But it's the weaker of the two. Most of its guns are old smoothbores. If you can get past Jackson with the bulk of your fleet, I see no reason why St. Philip would give you trouble. That leaves the Confederate fleet."

"Yes, what about that?"

She laid out the boats as best she could, the ironclad and cottonclad side-wheel steamers, the converted revenue cutters, and even what she knew about the fire rafts and the small steamer launches. Anything that could carry guns and men, or do damage in any way. Several of the officers took notes.

Josephine took out her own notes from the satchel, but only so they'd know she wasn't simply making up the numbers. She already held the numbers in her head. "Leaving aside *Louisiana*, the enemy can put boats into the water holding no more than forty guns and roughly eighteen hundred men. In comparison, *Hartford* alone has, how many? Twenty-six guns? Twenty-eight if you count howitzers?"

There was dumbfounded surprise at this. At her side, Franklin was beaming.

"Thank God she's on our side," one of the ship captains muttered.

Josephine tried to be casual as she lifted her cup to take a sip. Inside, she was swelling with pride. But while she'd been pontificating, a servant had refilled her cup, and the coffee was scalding.

She sputtered and spit up coffee as she tried to keep from burning her mouth.

"Only human after all," Franklin said with a grin, and the men burst into laughter.

Josephine blushed and wanted to slink out of the room. There was no malice in the laughter, though, and soon she found herself smiling along with the rest of them.

Farragut was the first to turn serious again, and in seconds the group of men, now numbering a dozen with recent additions, quieted.

"What about the ram?" Farragut pressed.

"*Manassas* is up there," she said, "and may give you some headache. She caused plenty of trouble during the battle at Head of Passes."

"Ah, yes. Pope's Run, as they're calling it. We are better prepared this time. There will be no panic should the turtle show itself. But she concerns me. There will be moments when the entire battle will pivot. If she appears at the wrong time, all may be lost."

"The weakness of *Manassas*," Josephine said, "is that she is underpowered and poorly maneuverable. Coming with the current, she has one dangerous attack, and then she'll struggle to get back into the fight."

"Good," Farragut said. "Then all the pieces are together. Thank you for your service, Miss Breaux. I would not trade you for a dozen warships."

And with that, Farragut's staff officer led Josephine and Franklin out of the mess room so the ship captains could plan their attack. She was not happy to be dismissed, but had a hard time staying upset given how well she had been treated.

She and Franklin went out to the deck, where they had more time to share information about how they'd respectively spent the previous few months. Within a few minutes it became clear that

Franklin's ardor for her had been no passing fancy. He stood close to her on the deck, was overly solicitous of her comfort, and found excuses to touch her hand when it rested on the rail.

Josephine didn't exactly resist the overtures. Her fondness for him had deepened, and she had worried about him every day since seeing him off at the levee. She'd felt such relief at seeing him last night, such warmth when he reappeared holding her precious writing, that she knew that in another time, under other circumstances, it would take little effort at all to fall into his arms.

This was not that time, nor those circumstances.

So when the coffee began to wear off a couple of hours later, she let the yawns come out, and didn't resist when he offered to find her a stateroom so she could sleep.

In spite of the welcome she'd received, her dismissal from Flag Officer Farragut's council of war proved a harbinger of the dearth of good information following the initial meeting. The federal sailors were more closedmouthed than their Confederate counterparts, any of whom would have shared everything from the menu of his worm-infested supper to the number of kegs of powder in the magazine. In contrast, each Union man knew little, and was willing to share less.

Even so, over the next two days her persistence yielded information about the size of the fleet, the simmering rivalry between Porter of the mortar fleet and his older brother, the flag officer. She heard about General Butler, waiting downstream with his troops. A political general more than a fighting man, he was less expected to seize New Orleans than to hold it once it had been conquered.

Josephine wrote everything down, from numbers of guns, men, and ships, to personal observations about powder-streaked sailors, their fears of combat and of a hostile reception in New Orleans. She spoke to an idealistic young Rhode Islander with a face so pretty he might have been a girl, whose father was a Unitarian minister and a fierce abolitionist. She talked to a German with broken English who seemed hard pressed to say who they were fighting or why, and an Irishman who had only been in the country three weeks before he joined in order to buy passage for a wife and two children who remained in Ulster. Some sailors were hardened old sea salts, while others were so green that they'd been relieved to get onto the river simply to escape the crippling seasickness suffered on the open ocean.

As for what she intended to do with this information, she'd started to contemplate writing a war memoir. Yes, it was hubris to imagine that a twenty year-old would have cogent thoughts about what was developing into the most deadly and terrible military struggle since the Napoleonic Wars, but it was a story she had to write.

Though it had seemed certain that Farragut would attempt to storm past the forts right away, the mortar bombardment picked up again by late morning and continued throughout the day and into the night. Finally, on the evening of the twenty-third, two men came to Josephine's cabin, where she'd fallen asleep on her writing desk over an open book of naval strategy. The lamp had burned out. When the two men led her onto the deck, she found sailors setting out buckets of water for dousing flames, and casting handfuls of sand across the deck to keep it from becoming slick with blood when the fighting started. Other sailors slouched against the squat, ugly-looking mortars, drinking coffee from tin cups and gnawing on hardtack. Carpenters worked sawing patches to plug holes from enemy shot. All this work was done by light of hooded lanterns, to hide the scope of Union actions on this moonless night.

Josephine took one glance at the preparations and then spotted servants and other civilians loading into a small launch. She backed away from the two men who'd led her up.

"Oh, no. If you think I'm going ashore now, of all times . . ."

"No, miss," one of the men said. "Flag Officer Farragut wishes to speak with you." The man pointed, and she saw Farragut with Franklin and his adjutants.

When she arrived, Farragut was muttering oaths about the captain of *Pensacola*, who was supposed to fall into position in the vanguard but claimed trouble hauling up anchor. Farragut looked up as she approached.

"You look as exhausted as the rest of us, Miss Breaux," he said. "Someone get this woman some coffee."

"Then you're not sending me ashore?"

"Good Lord, no. Unless you want to, of course."

"You'd have to drag me away." Her words sounded brave, but her heart was dancing like a flatboat crew to a double-time jig.

Farragut gestured at Franklin. "Mr. Gray predicted as much. Promise me you'll keep your heads down, the both of you."

A light flashed over from *Pensacola*.

"Damn you, Morris," Farragut grumbled. "Get your anchor up and get in line or the devil take you."

He stomped off, followed by his staff officers.

Left alone, the two Pinkerton agents made their way to the railing. Moments later, the long black shadow of *Pensacola* began to move at last. Together with six other ships, and the smaller *Cayuga* guiding, Captain Morris's vanguard fleet began to ease slowly upriver. As soon as they had passed, *Hartford*'s boilers built a head of steam and led the second fleet up the river after them.

"Is it always like this?" Franklin whispered.

"Like what?"

"The tension. My God, I can't take it."

"You're about to see the elephant."

Her voice sounded hollow, lost in the mist that swirled up from the river to envelop the sides of the boat. The calm she heard in it belied the clenching and unclenching in her stomach, the racing pace of her heartbeat.

"When the arsenal blew up, I had no time to think, I just acted," he said. "But now . . . I wish I'd put to shore. Damn it all, I'm a coward."

Josephine reached out in the darkness and squeezed his hand. "You're not a coward. There isn't one person on this ship who isn't terrified, Farragut included."

He fell silent, and she didn't know if she'd made him feel better or worse. His hand was trembling in hers, but she wasn't convinced that she wasn't the one shaking, and making him shake in turn.

For several minutes they slid silently upriver, not a light visible, only dark shapes, each one following the lead of the ship ahead. For one brief, desperate moment she thought that Farragut's plan was to sneak by the forts undetected. Inside, the men of the forts might be too exhausted to notice, the watchmen all fallen into slumber. It might work!

And then the gates of hell opened before them.

CHAPTER 32

The bummers of Porter's mortar fleet opened up first. It was more of the same bombardment that had punished Fort Jackson for the past week, but now the firepower was directed at the water battery below. It lay uncovered, with no bombproofs, but boasted earthen breastworks and moats, and had six downward-facing guns that would have the first shot at the approaching fleet.

Mortars exploded over the water battery or landed directly within to illuminate the works like lightning in a storm cloud. For several minutes, the water battery absorbed this punishment. Then the guns responded. Lights flashed at *Cayuga* and *Pensacola* in the van. The warships bellowed a response. In an instant, the entire formation of Union steamers lay illuminated in the river in a garish tableau.

Within minutes, the head of the formation was beneath the guns of Fort Jackson, whose guns roared again and again. Upriver, St.

Philip let loose with her own devastating, enfilading fire. Shells tore through the masts and rigging. The ships returned their own punishing fire, but it looked as though they would soon be overwhelmed.

Smoke enveloped the van now, and Josephine could no longer see the forts or any of the other ships, only the continual flashes of light, behind, ahead, off port, and overhead. The boom and shake and fury of war was overwhelming. Between explosions, bells rang on the ship, warning of fire, ordering changes of course, giving directions to other ships in the fleet. How any man could think over the chaos was beyond her.

A shell slammed into the mainmast. Josephine and Franklin covered their heads as splinters came raining down. The ship leaned to starboard, and she thought they must be taking on water, but it was only a hard turn toward the right bank.

A flash of light burst over *Hartford*, together with a ripping explosion. Josephine was flat on her belly before she realized she was throwing herself down. Franklin was with her, asking if she was hurt. More explosions, as if the magazines had gone off. The ship felt like it was tearing itself to pieces beneath her, and she expected to feel the water sucking her down again. Belatedly, she realized these new roars were only *Hartford*'s guns answering fire.

Josephine rose shakily, and she and Franklin went over to help Farragut to his feet. The older man seemed more defiant than shaken, and glared toward Fort Jackson from where the shot had come. But shortly after, they had passed mostly beyond Jackson and were taking fire from St. Philip instead. Fortunately, the second fort was poorly positioned to hit them, and most of the shots went flying harmlessly overhead.

A fire raft came roaring down the channel, and the helmsman swung hard to starboard to get out of the way. But then the smoke cleared and they realized they were too close to the shore. Before the helmsman could correct, the keel drove into the mud, and the ship shuddered. They'd run aground trying to avoid the raft. Now right beneath St. Philip's water battery, Josephine was close enough to hear the Confederates screaming orders through the smoke. Meanwhile, the fire raft, which had supposedly floated harmlessly downriver, began to cut upstream toward them. How was that possible?

When the smoke cleared, Josephine saw with horror that a Confederate tug had hooked it and was bringing it in alongside *Hartford*. The men of *Hartford* fired with rifles and deck guns, but were unable to drive away the tug before it had pushed the fire raft alongside. Flames shot skyward, and a wave of heat rolled over the deck. Within moments, *Hartford*'s entire portside was a bonfire, engulfed to the mizzen tops.

Men were crying for orders whether or not they should abandon ship, and Franklin grabbed Josephine as if to haul her to the opposite side, where they could leap into the muddy shallows and make their way to shore to surrender. The Confederate guns kept up a steady pounding. A blast of grapeshot crashed through the rigging overhead.

But Farragut's men held firm. Two lieutenants raced along the deck, organizing a bucket brigade, and sailors manned the pumps. A man climbed into the rigging with a hose. Farragut paced the deck, shouting encouragement. Josephine and Franklin joined the bucket brigade.

But none of the effort would help if they couldn't rid themselves of the fire raft. Three men raced up to the portside with twenty-pound shells, which they dropped overboard into the fire raft. The shells exploded as they hit the fire, one after another, and shortly the raft was sinking in the river.

Even as the fight against the fire continued, *Hartford* reversed her engines and broke free of the bank. The water battery continued to attack, but now *Hartford* was able to respond with a broadside, and shortly they were past it and continuing upriver. They fired more broadsides at St. Philip as they passed, and then they were into the open river above, where they emerged into another fight.

More fire rafts drifted downstream. Union ships were turned about, some having been confused by the darkness, the smoke, and the bends in the river. The enemy steamers were lined up against them, blasting away.

Louisiana still lurked on the opposite side of the river, and let loose a barrage as one of the Union sloops passed. It returned fire, but the shells bounced harmlessly off its plating. Unfortunately for *Louisiana*, she couldn't seem to hit anything in turn.

"Those guns," Franklin muttered. "I knew they would be useless."

But seeing the monster lurking there on the riverbank, she could only imagine what damage it could have done steaming up and down the river with full power and well-mounted guns. And if *Louisiana* had been joined by her sister ship *Mississippi*, still presumably under construction in New Orleans, the Union expedition would have been doomed.

"The ram!" someone screamed.

It was *Manassas*, the low-slung turtle with its huffing stack, bearing down on them. Now that Josephine was on the receiving end, the ram didn't look so harmless. Not like a cucumber at all, but a black metal spear point. For several seconds the impact looked inevitable, a slow-motion blow backed by thousands of pounds of force and momentum that would cut *Hartford* in two. But *Manassas's* poor maneuverability was the decider, and *Hartford* slipped by unscathed. She fired a broadside at the ram in passing. A few shells bounced off *Manassas's* back, and the rest plopped harmlessly into the water.

Hartford now found itself in the middle of a ferocious battle between Farragut's sloops and the mosquito fleet upriver, which was mounting a spirited and desperate struggle to keep the Union forces bottled up in range of the forts. If kept from breaking free, the wooden warships would inevitably be sunk or driven off by the guns at their rear.

Two more fire rafts came floating down the river. *Hartford* maneuvered between them and continued upstream to join *Pensacola*, which was blasting away at two Confederate ships. *Hartford* swung wide and released her own broadside. For several minutes, the four ships fired back and forth, with another of Farragut's sloops joining. The smaller, weaker Confederate ships couldn't sustain the fight and were soon fleeing the battle upstream, pursued by a federal gunboat.

Meanwhile, so many Union ships were piling up in the river that they were struggling to keep from shooting at each other. A burning Confederate ship drifted downstream, while other crippled ships of the mosquito fleet had run against the bank to be scuttled.

Dawn had arrived at last. Downriver, the gunfire from the last division of Farragut's fleet and the two Confederate forts continued unabated. Within twenty minutes the last few Union stragglers arrived. The bulk of the fleet was safely above the forts, and the enemy had been destroyed or driven from the river.

While the fleet organized itself for emergency repairs and to tend the wounded, Farragut called up the band, who came onto the charred, blood-streaked deck of *Hartford* and played "The Star-Spangled Banner." A great cheer came up from the exhausted, powder-stained crew, which quickly spread from boat to boat.

Josephine fell asleep on deck in the shadow of *Hartford*'s side-wheel. Exhausted men slept all around her. She woke when the sun cut through her shady spot, and found Franklin squatting nearby, holding her satchel. He handed it over.

"There are carpenters working in your room. I thought I'd retrieve your possessions."

"Thank you," she said. A quick glance inside showed everything in place, including the Colonel's Oriental box. "What time is it?"

"Afternoon. We'll be heading upstream shortly. Word has it there's fighting at Quarantine. Farragut will want to seize its battery before we continue on to New Orleans."

She rubbed at her temples to ease the headache settling in. By now, New Orleans would know that the fleet had passed the forts. She imagined that General Lovell would be organizing the militia, but apart from that, she couldn't decide if the people would be defiant or panicked.

"There's one other thing," Franklin began hesitantly. "A prisoner. He heard you were on board and wants to speak with you."

"Is it Fein?" she asked, feeling suddenly nervous.

She hadn't seen him since they'd been rescued from the wreckage of the rowboat. By now he'd no doubt heard of her perfidy, and she was afraid to face him. He had always treated her fairly, yet she had lied to him repeatedly, had taken advantage of his trust to smuggle Franklin out of New Orleans.

"No. It's an officer from Fort Jackson, captured when he led a group of men attempting to free one of the enemy boats that had run aground. An old friend of yours. Major Dunbar."

Josephine chewed on her lip. Her first inclination was to refuse. What could Dunbar do, other than accuse her of treachery? To spit in her face and promise that she would forever be seen as a villain and symbol of Northern aggression?

But that was the coward's way. Even angry, he might still give up information about the condition of the forts, the attitude of the remaining defenders. Would they surrender? Fight on until food and powder ran out?

"I know it's a lot to ask," Franklin said. "I told Flag Officer Farragut, and he said—"

"No," she interrupted, "you don't need to say anything more. I'll go see the major."

They had lodged Dunbar in a small cabin not far from the flag officer's own berth. There was only a single guard posted, who inclined his head when Josephine entered. She shut the door behind her to keep the guard on the outside.

The major was lying on his bed, his hands behind his head, staring up at the wood beams of the ceiling. His face was heavily stubbled, his hair a wild mop, and his shirt was splattered with mud, but somehow he maintained his dignified appearance.

Dunbar looked up with a dejected expression, but as soon as he met her gaze, he sprang to his feet. "Miss Breaux!" He hastily fastened the top two buttons of his shirt and grabbed for his gray jacket.

"Please don't trouble yourself," she said. "Look at me—I'm worse."

"You're as beautiful as ever."

"You're a bad liar, Major. I've been into the river and through two battles. My clothes are torn and my hair is an egret's nest." She rubbed her hands together nervously. "Have they been treating you well?"

"Well enough. They separated me from my men and confiscated my pistol and sword, but I have not been abused in any way. How about yourself?"

"I've been treated well," she said. "But I'm not a prisoner."

"That's a mercy. Given your reputation, I'd worried that you'd be hard put upon, lady or no."

He seemed genuinely relieved, and she flinched from her duty. He didn't understand; he still thought she was a Confederate patriot. It would be an easy task to make him talk. All she had to do was sit next to him on his bed, lay her hand over his, and ask direct questions. He'd tell her everything about the fort and what he'd heard about defenses upriver at Quarantine and New Orleans. She couldn't do it.

"Well, I suppose I should leave. I wish you the best, Major."

"Wait! If you're not a prisoner, does that mean you're free to come and go?"

"Yes, of course."

"This is a lucky stroke. That they would leave us alone . . . What a bit of fortune at our darkest hour! I need you to pass a message to General Lovell."

"Major . . ."

"You won't be in any danger. If you're caught, blame me, say I pressed until you couldn't say no. Farragut is a gentleman. He was born in Tennessee and his wife is from Virginia. He knows we aren't monsters. He's only doing his duty, and his duty doesn't include hanging a young lady caught with compromising military intelligence." Dunbar reached into the pocket of his jacket and removed a folded piece of paper. "I have critical information about Butler's troops. I wrote it down this morning, scarcely daring to hope that it would find its way to General Lovell."

"Major Dunbar, please don't tell me any more." She held out her hands as he pushed the note at her. "No, I won't take it."

She knew she should take Dunbar's letter and hand it over to either Franklin or Farragut, but what difference would it make at this late hour? General Butler had fifteen thousand troops downriver, ready to assault the forts if they couldn't be made to surrender without further violence. And once the forts fell, what then? Lovell might have a few thousand militia in New Orleans, but that

included such units of dubious worth as the riverboat gamblers of
the Blackleg Cavalry. And as she had so carefully described in her
dispatches, the federal fleet could easily puncture the levee and
flood the city, rendering helpless any defense.

Her work done, Josephine desperately wanted to avoid this final
betrayal.

"Please remember," she said gently in response to his befuddled
frown. "I have experience passing behind enemy lines. I don't only
work for the newspaper, I work for the government. What information I collect, I pass along to my superiors. Think about that for
a moment."

"Like you did in Virginia," he stumbled on. "At Manassas. If
you'd do that for General Beauregard, why can't you do it for me?
All I'm asking is that you carry this information to Lovell. If you
can get this to him before the Yankees arrive . . . Can't you do that
for me? Josephine, for the love of God."

"You still don't understand," she said sadly. "I can't do that for
you because I'm not your ally. I never have been. I don't want you
to win."

His face fell slack. She could see his final, desperate hope drain-
ing away. "What?"

"Major, I'm sorry. I work for the other side."

CHAPTER 33

Fighting continued on the river as the fleet steamed toward New Orleans. There was a brief skirmish at Quarantine before Farragut sent marines ashore to seize the guns. Then, when they approached the city on the morning of the twenty-fifth, they had to dodge more fire rafts sent downstream in a desperate attempt to drive them off. A few small batteries at the city fired a handful of volleys before they were silenced by the big guns of the fleet.

Josephine and Franklin stood on the deck of *Hartford* as they pulled up to the levee. Rain poured from the sky, as if the city were weeping, but it didn't cut the fires roaring along the wharfs. A mob was burning and looting the warehouses, tossing flaming bales of cotton into the river. They smashed barrels of rum and molasses and threw them in. Boats of all kinds—barges, launches, tugs, flatboats—burned, either sinking or joining the vast quantity of debris floating down the river. Anything that could potentially aid the Union forces was dumped into the Mississippi.

From upriver floated a huge, flaming object that she couldn't identify at first, so much smoke was roiling from it into the sky. She supposed it was another fire raft. But as it drew nearer, she saw that it was the burning hulk of a massive ironclad vessel.

"*Mississippi*," Franklin said. "I suppose they never did finish her."

A note of melancholy had entered his voice. Franklin had worked for months at the yards building the two boats that had been meant to change the course of the war. He must have been curious to know how *Louisiana* and *Mississippi* would fare had they been completed and properly armed. But perhaps it was more, a sense of betrayal to those he'd worked beside, not unlike how Josephine felt about Solomon Fein and Major Dunbar.

By early afternoon, most of Farragut's fleet lay anchored in the river facing New Orleans. Word came that Lovell had fled New Orleans with the militia, and there would be no opposition. With this news, Farragut sent a small company of men ashore under flag of truce.

Cleaned up and ready to report on the capture of the city, Josephine went ashore with them, together with Franklin. A mob was gathering, some of them singing Confederate hymns or waving rebel battle flags, while others jeered and hurled bottles and other rubbish at the men in blue. For a moment it seemed as though there would be violence, but then the band on one of the ships struck up "The Star-Spangled Banner." The crowd fell silent. A few handkerchiefs came out. The song was an anthem for all Americans, the North and South alike.

Josephine was scanning the crowd with a newspaper reporter's eye when her gaze fell on a woman with wet, dripping hair and streaked makeup. The woman stared back with a morose expression. That expression was unlike the anger and sorrow in most of the crowd, deeper somehow, more intense.

A jolt of recognition. The woman was Francesca Díaz.

Josephine hadn't recognized her at first glance because of the haggard expression, the reddish hair made dull and sodden by the rain, with an inch of gray showing at the roots. And the utter defeat in Francesca's expression. It was as if she were battered down, had personally suffered great ruin.

You did it. You ruined her.

It was an accusation born of the self-pitying note Francesca had sent in February, the one that had left Josephine baffled. And it was hardly fair. Francesca had threatened her with exposure and destruction, not the other way around.

Francesca leaned against a cane. Not the elegant, ivory-topped cane from that day in Congo Square, when she'd walked in the company of the Colonel, but a hickory walking stick, scuffed and splitting at the end. Not an affectation, then, but to help support her weight, the more elegant stick apparently having been sold in response to her reduced situation. That limp Josephine had first spotted at the Cajun fisherman's shack must be a real and permanent injury, not a twisted ankle, not gout.

And suddenly Josephine understood. Francesca had taken lame during her dancing days, fallen, perhaps, broken a bone. Reduced in her ability to earn a living, she had fastened herself to her old friend's partner, had perhaps married him during one of the riverboat gambler's flush periods, when it seemed that he might provide for her in return for what remained of her youth and beauty.

Had Francesca's attempts to blackmail Josephine been a similar act of desperation? Had there been no real malice behind it?

Josephine shook her head to clear it, confused and unsettled. The Colonel, Josephine, even the whole confounded war: Did she understand any of it?

The moment the federal band stopped playing "The Star-Spangled Banner," the tumult started up again, and when Josephine looked back, she had lost Francesca in the crowd. In spite of the pouring rain, people kept rushing in to join the mob. By the time two Union soldiers set off under flag of truce, they were surrounded by cursing, spitting civilians, some of them waving pistols in their faces. They disappeared into the crowd, and Josephine couldn't see how they'd reach the mayor's office alive. And then the fleet would shell the city in revenge.

But shortly the men returned to the flag officer with a short note from the mayor, which was later shown to Josephine.

> *Come and take the city; we are powerless.*
> *As to the hoisting of any flag than the flag of*
> *our own adoption and allegiance, let me say to you,*
> *sir, that the man lives not in our midst whose hand*
> *and heart would not be palsied at the mere thought*
> *of such an act.*

The implication was obvious. Take the city if you think you can. Raise the Stars and Stripes. Come in with a few marines, risk the mob.

The Confederates still hoped to hold the city, hoped that a counterattack would come downriver or across Lake Pontchartrain. And with General Butler's bluecoats still bottled up below the forts, there was a real question as to how the occupation could be managed.

Farragut kept the bulk of the fleet anchored off the levee while he took *Hartford* and several other sloops upriver to destroy batteries and shell a few small fortifications. They returned to New Orleans towing a number of captured vessels. The flag officer told Josephine that he wanted to let the fire-eaters in the city tire of their wrath, but upon their return, they found New Orleans as hostile as ever.

In another obvious attempt to buy time, the mayor sent his private secretary and the chief of police out to *Hartford* to haggle with Farragut, who was clearly losing his patience. He sent another demand for complete surrender.

For two days the mob had maintained an angry, cursing vigil on the levee, and there were dozens of pistols and shotguns in evidence. If fighting should start, Farragut warned that he would open a broadside from *Hartford* and every other ship at his command until the city burned to the ground, and this seemed to keep the hotheads in check.

On April 28, word came that Fort Jackson and Fort St. Philip had surrendered to Porter's mortar fleet and General Butler's troops. After Porter resumed shelling, the defenders of Jackson, low on food and fuel, their morale at the muddy bottom of the Mississippi, had mutinied against their officers. Once Jackson surrendered, St. Philip also abandoned the struggle.

And this news took what remained of the fighting spirit from the people of New Orleans. The mob began to melt away, and Farragut felt secure enough to send in a company of 250 marines to seize key buildings until General Butler could arrive with his large occupying force.

On the evening of May 1, Josephine and Franklin stood in Jackson Square, opposite the Cabildo and the cathedral, while the Thirtieth Massachusetts Infantry came down from the levee. Marching with a jaunty step behind the regimental band, which played "Yankee Doodle" with flair and confidence, the troops passed through the square and up the streets of the French Quarter.

Some in the crowd booed, other cheered, and all seemed to settle in for the great change that had swept over the city. New Orleans had fallen.

Josephine opened the Oriental box on the desk. Inside she put the two photographs, the first with a beautiful woman and an angular, bony girl of eight on the deck of *Crescent Queen*. In the second, she was older and standing with the man who would be her father.

The Colonel. What had become of him? Was he still in the city with Francesca? She wasn't sure if she wanted to know, but the not knowing was almost worse. Like her mother, who had drowned on the river but had never been recovered. It left the imagination to fester, to postulate scenarios by which a woman who must be dead had somehow survived. Or, in this case, to imagine how an old gambler, unreliable as rainfall on the plains of Nebraska, might have changed his ways. Might have become a father.

No.

She put them away. Then she tucked in her banknotes and what silver she'd managed to get from the worthless greybacks Fein had paid her at the *Crescent*. She put the lacquered box into her carpetbag and snapped the latch shut.

When she came downstairs with her bag and her spare dress draped over one arm, Nellie was standing stiff and cold in the front room. Josephine had kept out two dollars in silver, which she attempted to hand over.

Nellie shook her head.

"I stayed in the room; I ate your food."

"Treacherously, yes. You did."

"Please take what I owe you."

"I won't take it."

Nellie Gill's husband was a prisoner in a Union camp after the fall of Fort Henry. She had few resources. Her larder was nearly empty. What little money she had was in greybacks and Confederate war bonds, both nearly worthless in the city since its fall.

Josephine made for the front door. She left the coins on the entry table as she passed. Nellie made a hiss behind her. As Josephine went down the stairs toward the cab waiting out front, she expected Nellie to open the door and throw the money after her. This she did not do.

Franklin jumped out to grab Josephine's bag. She held her dress and petticoats on her lap as she climbed up.

"I suppose leaving the city would be for the best," she told Franklin. "Every time I'm recognized I'm abused. Such invective as would make the Cyprians of Gallatin blush."

He reached into his jacket pocket and removed a folded telegraph fixed with a military seal. "Ready for your orders?"

"No, not yet. Part of me wants to stay, the other part wants to get as far away as possible. But I have one more thing troubling me before I face that. Do you need to go back to General Butler's headquarters? I can drop you at the end of Toulouse to catch another cab."

"I'm too anxious to hear your news," he said with a smile. "Let's get on with this other business."

The driver looked back through the window from his perch up front. "Where to, miss?"

"Do you know the *Crescent*? Good. Take me there."

Every voice fell silent as she entered. The men operating the press eased up on the pedals, and it clacked to a halt with a groan of the gears. Some men glared at her, others looked away. One man, a fellow named Weitzel, who she'd always taken for a fire-eater, gave her a curt, conspiratorial nod. A secret Unionist, then. Harold Keller, the fool who couldn't write a laundry list without factual errors, sneered.

Fein rose from a table where he'd been editing something. He pushed his new eyeglasses to the bridge of his nose and stared at her.

"Well," he said at last. "Didn't expect to see you again."

"I don't like to run off without explanation."

"No need for explanation. You presumably have your reasons."

"Or without doing what I said I'd do."

Josephine had brought in a sheaf of papers. She handed the topmost to Fein, a folded letter, stained by river water, but otherwise intact.

"The young soldier's letter to his mother?" he asked.

She nodded.

"And what does it say? The usual regrets of a condemned man, etcetera?"

"I couldn't say. I haven't read it."

Fein raised an eyebrow. "A bit of private correspondence chanced to fall into your hands, and you didn't read it? That beggars the imagination."

Josephine couldn't help but wince. Of course she had been tempted. Of *course*. She didn't even know the young man's name and had been itching to at least open it and read the signature. But if she had done so, nothing would have stopped her from perusing the rest of the letter as well. And she had never forgotten, nor forgiven her own culpability in the boy's death. If she had sent him to the infirmary with a stern word, he would no doubt be alive today. Instead, she had encouraged him to desert, and he'd been caught.

Fein must have seen the pain in her eyes, because now he tucked the letter away without further comment. "What else do you have?"

"Stories." She handed over the sheaf of papers. "You'll find it all, an accurate story of what happened before, during, and after the battle. Some smaller pieces of interest. Anything I can share, I did share. Change the byline—I know you can't use my name.

He didn't look down at the papers. "You're a damn fine writer, Josephine. I hope this isn't the end of it for the *Crescent*."

"You would keep me?" she asked. "After everything that has happened?"

"I'm a practical man. We move and shift with the times. And you know my stance on political matters. But . . ." He ran his fingers through his hair as he glanced around the room at the other employees of the *Crescent.*

"But . . . ?"

"Things are hot at the moment. We have readers to think about, copies to move. You understand."

"Of course. I don't think I'm staying, anyway. Most likely, they're sending me away."

"After the war, though. If you need a job, don't waste your efforts anywhere else. Come home. All will be forgiven someday; you know how these things go. Memories fade, time heals wounds."

She suspected that the collective memory of New Orleans was longer than that, but perhaps he was right. The side that won would bend the narrative. If that was the Union, the city would remember itself as an international port, a reluctant participant in the foolhardy bloodshed that had plagued the rest of the nation.

"Maybe I will," she said. "Thank you all the same for the offer." She turned toward the door. "Oh, if you must put someone else's name on my story, make sure it's not the *wrong* name."

Neither of them had to look at Harold Keller to know who she meant.

Franklin was waiting in the cab. He placed the telegram on Josephine's lap as they set off again. She waited until the cab had almost reached Jackson Square before she broke the seal. Her stomach twisted in anticipation. She knew only that it came straight from Allan Pinkerton, and that he'd supposedly consulted with the secretary of war. She half expected to be thanked and told her services were no longer needed.

Franklin, on the other hand, was now attached to General Butler's occupying force, and he would have plenty of work in the city, which was seething with intrigue. Less than three weeks into the federal occupation and Butler had earned the title of the most unpopular Yankee south of the Mason–Dixon. A few days earlier, he'd issued a widely loathed edict directed toward the women of the city for their continued insults of Union soldiers. From henceforth, declared General Order Number 28, women behaving uncivilly would be treated as if they were prostitutes, arrested, charged, and fined five dollars for plying their illegal business. Among the out-raged were the actual prostitutes of the city, who had been tearing down official postings with the general's likeness and pasting them to the inside of their chamber pots.

"Well?" Franklin said. "Are you going to read it or not?"

Josephine opened the telegram.

With commendation for meritorious service, you are hereby ordered to return to Washington with the outgoing steamer Newport. *Upon arrival, you will be given honors at the Executive Mansion before receiving new orders.*

E. J. Allen

The telegram had come from Pinkerton himself. She now knew that E. J. Allen was his nom de guerre.

She handed it to Franklin, who whistled. "Honors at the Executive Mansion. No doubt from the president himself." A teasing element entered his voice. "Maybe he'll offer you a position in his cabinet. No doubt you suggested it in your last dispatch."

"And why not? I'm sure I could do better than some of those old fools."

"You have done well," he said, and this time he sounded sincere. "You deserve honors and recognition."

It was everything she'd hoped for, yet somehow she felt deflated. A heroine in Washington, but a monster in her homeland.

"I suppose they'll send me to Richmond next," she said.

"You'll have to disguise yourself." And now it was Franklin's turn to sound disappointed. She knew why. "They'll tar and feather you if they catch you."

"It's not as though the rebs are distributing my likeness on wanted posters."

"I wouldn't be so sure about that."

The cab continued through the square and up toward the Paris Hotel. It was where she had begun her adventure in the city almost nine months earlier, when she'd first dined with Francesca without knowing that she'd been recognized. Now Josephine was back at the hotel for her final two days in the city.

"And thus ends our glorious adventure together," Franklin said when the cab clattered to a stop on the slick cobblestones.

"*Newport* doesn't leave until Tuesday." She hesitated. "You could join me for supper tonight at the hotel, if you'd like. The food is good enough, so long as you avoid the haddock."

"I'm going upstream with Farragut this afternoon. There's action brewing at Baton Rouge. I might not be back for a week."

"And you're needed?"

"Apparently I'm indispensable for the expedition."

"How cocky!" Josephine raised an eyebrow. "If you were a woman, I might even accuse you of being a petticoat general."

He laughed, but his expression quickly turned serious again. "I don't see it, myself, but the flag officer insists that I will be needed. So I must obey orders."

She opened the door. "Well, then. I suppose this *is* good-bye for now."

Two porters came trotting down from the hotel. One man took her carpetbag, and the other her dresses.

Franklin climbed down after her and told the cab driver to wait. He took Josephine's hands. "You don't have to go."

"Should I stow away in your steamer trunk?"

"Please, can we be serious for a moment?"

"I am being serious," Josephine said. "You said you have your orders. Well, so do I. You saw them. What can I do about it?" The words sounded cavalier as they came out, but she didn't say them without a twinge of regret.

"I know it would be difficult, given your reputation down here, but if you resigned your position with the Pinkertons . . ."

"Resigned?"

"It wouldn't come as a surprise in Washington. You're a young woman, after all. The most beautiful woman I've ever seen."

"Please, now you're being ridiculous."

"The point is, everybody knows what to expect in those cases. If you were to get married, for example—"

"No, don't say any more," she interrupted. She still held his hands. "There are men fighting and dying to preserve the Union. Why shouldn't a woman sacrifice to save her country? Why shouldn't she have that duty—no, not duty, that *privilege*? I took an oath of loyalty to the Union that day when you tried to row me across the Potomac. I meant every word."

He looked pained. "What about loyalty to your heart? Does that have a place in your plans?"

"I . . . I don't know, Franklin."

"That night on the levee, when you spurned me as you sent me downriver—no, don't interrupt. I *was* spurned. That was your right, even though I could see in your eyes that you felt something. I told myself that it was your tender care after the explosion at the hospital that had addled my brains. Once I was away from you for a stretch I'd regain my wits. But I never did. I only loved you more."

Josephine didn't speak right away, and he made to withdraw his hands. She didn't let him. Not yet.

"Franklin, listen to me. I am not . . . indifferent. But the time isn't right. We're halfway through the second year of the war already. Surely, this can't last much longer. It might be over by summer."

"You don't know that. It might be years."

"Maybe, but you're twenty-five, and I'm not yet twenty-one. We have a lifetime ahead of us." She nodded, growing more confident. "Soon enough, the war will be over. Then, if you're still interested—"

"Of course I will be."

"If you're still interested," she repeated, "then I would be pleased to consider your offer under more tranquil circumstances."

Her heart was thumping as she said this. Even this small gesture felt like tearing open her rib cage and exposing her heart to fire. He couldn't know what this would cost her.

Franklin was silent for several seconds. Then he nodded. "I shall write you often, if you promise you won't laugh at the poor quality of my writing."

"The only writing I'll laugh at is the kind with sappy poetry. That would be more than I could bear." Josephine smiled. "I'll answer every letter with one of my own."

He cleared his throat. "I should report to *Hartford*. May I . . ."

"Yes?"

"May I kiss you before I go?"

Josephine's face flushed. "You may."

Later that afternoon, standing on the levee, watching ships from Farragut's fleet pull anchor and huff upstream, she thought she could feel the press of Franklin's lips against hers. She'd expected it to feel pleasant, but she hadn't expected the warm feeling that had flooded through her.

She'd spent so long with her heart closed that it was difficult imagining opening it again. When she opened her heart, people disappeared. They might appear months or years later, but only to hurt again. An urgent voice insisted that this time might be different. That this time she was being offered something genuine, she only had to accept it.

And what about the Colonel? What about his offer?

It's not too late. We can start over. I'll be your father if you let me.

Had he meant it? She thought he did. He was sincere enough, but was he capable? That was the question.

A patrol of bluecoats strolled by, tipping their hats gratefully when Josephine offered a friendly greeting. From behind came the tinny sound of a trumpet playing at Jackson Square. It was Sunday afternoon, with the sun dropping slowly toward the marshes west of the city. Sunset came later this time of year, and it wouldn't be dark for two more hours.

As soon as the war ended, she told herself. As soon as she had done her duty. She would do two things. First, she would search out the Colonel. She would make him an offer, but on her terms, not his. If he would accept those terms, she would be open herself, in turn, to some kind of relationship. Something that looked like family. She would even speak to Francesca, to listen, her mind open and her heart softened.

When that was settled, she would speak openly with Franklin. Again, on her own terms. She would continue to write for publication; nothing would stop her from that pursuit. Could Franklin take a woman who was only partially domesticated? She could be strong willed, and her confidence sometimes crossed the line to arrogance. Could he accept that?

Josephine made her way down from the levee, suddenly knowing how she would spend her last Sunday afternoon in New Orleans. A few miles away, in Congo Square, the slaves would be dancing hard with anticipation of the closing of the square at nightfall. She wondered if she would find the dancing today just a little more frenzied, the banging of the beef bones on the cask more vigorous, in anticipation that they would soon be set free by the victorious blue-clad army from the North. She intended to find out.

The rest of the city also waited in anticipation, its gas lamps flickering, the vines and tree roots of the subtropical river port always trying to pull the city down. In the Irish Channel and on Gallatin, the riverboat men would be drinking, gambling, and whoring. In the Garden District, the society women would be scheming for the return of their men in gray, even as they gossiped about money and fashion and status.

New Orleans would continue on when Josephine had left. The Mississippi would continue its slow, muddy roll to the sea, carrying the water and debris of half a continent. Upriver, the battles would continue, with or without her. But this wasn't the end for her. When the time came, she would return.

ABOUT THE AUTHOR

Michael Wallace was born in California and raised in a small religious community in Utah, eventually heading east to live in Rhode Island and Vermont. In addition to working as a literary agent and innkeeper, he previously worked as a software engineer for a Department of Defense contractor, programming simulators for nuclear submarines. He is the author of more than twenty novels, including the *Wall Street Journal* bestselling series The Righteous, set in a polygamist enclave in the desert.